FROM THE PAGES OF
THE HOUSE OF MIRTH

Selden paused in surprise. In the afternoon rush of the Grand Central Station his eyes had been refreshed by the sight of Miss Lily Bart. (page 5)

Why must a girl pay so dearly for her least escape from routine? (page 19)

She had been bored all the afternoon by Percy Gryce—the mere thought seemed to waken an echo of his droning voice—but she could not ignore him on the morrow, she must follow up her success, must submit to more boredom, must be ready with fresh compliances and adaptabilities, and all on the bare chance that he might ultimately decide to do her the honour of boring her for life. (page 30)

Society is a revolving body which is apt to be judged according to its place in each man's heaven; and at present it was turning its illuminated face to Lily. (page 56)

She was always scrupulous about keeping up appearances to herself. Her personal fastidiousness had a moral equivalent, and when she made a tour of inspection in her own mind there were certain closed doors she did not open. (page 91)

She had, to a shade, the exact manner between victory and defeat: every insinuation was shed without an effort by the bright indifference of her manner. But she was beginning to feel the strain of the attitude; the reaction was more rapid, and she lapsed to a deeper self-disgust. (pages 108–109)

Old habits, old restraints, the hand of inherited order, plucked back the bewildered mind which passion had jolted from its ruts. (page 162)

"Can you imagine looking into your glass some morning and seeing a disfigurement—some hideous change that has come to you while you slept? Well, I seem to myself like that—I can't bear to see myself in my own thoughts—I hate ugliness." (page 181)

She had suffered for the very faithfulness with which she had carried out her part of the tacit compact, but the part was not a handsome one at best, and she saw it now in all the ugliness of failure. (page 249)

That was all he knew—all he could hope to unravel of the story. The mute lips on the pillow refused him more than this—unless indeed they had told him the rest in the kiss they had left upon his forehead. Yes, he could now read into that farewell all that his heart craved to find there; he could even draw from it courage not to accuse himself for having failed to reach the height of his opportunity. (page 359)

THE HOUSE OF MIRTH

EDITH WHARTON

With an Introduction and
Notes by Jeffrey Meyers

George Stade
Consulting Editorial Director

BARNES & NOBLE CLASSICS
NEW YORK

♪♭

BARNES & NOBLE CLASSICS
NEW YORK

The House of Mirth was first published in 1905.

Introduction, Notes, and For Further Reading
Copyright © 2003 by Jeffrey Meyers.

Note on Edith Wharton, The World of Edith Wharton and *The House of Mirth*, Inspired by *The House of Mirth*, and Comments & Questions Copyright © 2003 by Fine Creative Media, Inc.

The House of Mirth
ISBN 1-59308-104-9
LC Control Number 2003106735

Produced by:
Fine Creative Media, Inc.
322 Eighth Avenue
New York, NY 10001

President & Publisher: Michael J. Fine
Consulting Editorial Director: George Stade
Editor: Jeffrey Broesche
Editorial Research: Jason Baker
Vice-President Production: Stan Last
Senior Production Manager: Mark A. Jordan
Production Editor: Kerriebeth Mello

Printed in the United States of America
QB
3 5 7 9 10 8 6 4 2

EDITH WHARTON

Edith Newbold Jones was born January 24, 1862, into such wealth and privilege that her family inspired the phrase "keeping up with the Joneses." The youngest of three children, Edith spent her early years touring Europe with her parents and, upon the family's return to the United States, enjoyed a privileged childhood in New York and Newport, Rhode Island. Edith's creativity and talent soon became obvious: By the age of eighteen she had written a novella, *Fast and Loose* (as well as witty reviews of it) and published poetry in the *Atlantic Monthly*.

After a failed engagement, Edith married a wealthy sportsman, Edward Wharton. Despite similar backgrounds and a shared taste for travel, the marriage was not a success. Many of Wharton's novels chronicle unhappy marriages, in which the demands of love and vocation often conflict with the expectations of society. Wharton's first major novel, *The House of Mirth*, published in 1905, enjoyed considerable literary success. *Ethan Frome* appeared six years later, solidifying Wharton's reputation as an important novelist. Often in the company of her close friend Henry James, Wharton mingled with some of the most famous writers and artists of the day, including F. Scott Fitzgerald, André Gide, Sinclair Lewis, Jean Cocteau, and Jack London.

In 1913 Edith divorced Edward. She lived mostly in France for the remainder of her life. When World War I broke out, she organized hostels for refugees, worked as a fund-raiser, and wrote for American publications from battlefield frontlines. She was awarded the French Legion of Honor for her courage and distinguished work.

The Age of Innocence, a novel about New York in the 1870s, earned Wharton the Pulitzer Prize for fiction in 1921—the first time the award had been bestowed on a woman. Wharton traveled throughout Europe to encourage young authors. She also continued to write, lying in her bed every morning, as she had always done, dropping each newly penned page on the floor to be collected and arranged when she was finished. Wharton suffered a stroke and died on August 11, 1937. She is buried in the American Cemetery in Versailles, France.

TABLE OF CONTENTS

THE WORLD OF EDITH WHARTON
AND *THE HOUSE OF MIRTH*

1862   Edith Newbold Jones is born January 24 in New York City, the last of three children. Her parents are wealthy and socially well-connected.

1866   The Jones family leaves for Europe, where they will live for the next six years.

1870   In Germany, Edith falls ill with typhoid fever and for a time hovers between life and death. When she recovers, the family moves to Florence. Edith begins writing stories, which she recites to her family.

1872   The Joneses return to America, where they live in New York City and Newport, Rhode Island.

1877   Edith finishes a novella, *Fast and Loose*, which will be published a century later, in 1977. Henry James's novel *The American* appears.

1878   Edith's mother pays to publish a collection of Edith's poems, *Verses*.

1879   Edith is presented to society in New York City.

1880   A wealthy young man, Henry Leyden Stevens, proposes to Wharton. The *Atlantic Monthly* magazine publishes five of Wharton's poems.

1881   Henry James's novel *Portrait of a Lady* appears.

1882   Edith's father dies in the south of France. Edith and her mother return to the United States to find that Henry Stevens's mother disapproves of the engagement. It is broken off, and the Jones women return to France.

1883   While summering in Bar Harbor, Maine, Edith agrees to marry Edward Wharton, an independently wealthy sportsman from Massachusetts.

1885   Edith and Edward wed and over the next several years divide their time between Europe, New York, and Newport.

1889   Wharton's poems appear in *Scribner's Magazine* and the *Atlantic Monthly*.

1891   Wharton's first published story, "Mrs. Manstey's View," appears in *Scribner's Magazine*.

1897   *The Decoration of Houses* appears; a nonfiction work on interior design written by Wharton and architect Ogden Codman, Jr.

1898   Henry James's *The Turn of the Screw* is published.

1901   The Whartons begin to build The Mount, their summer home near Lenox, Massachusetts. Edith's mother dies in Paris.

1905   *The House of Mirth* is published. The novel quickly becomes one of the best-selling books of the year; its popularity solidifies Wharton's reputation as a major novelist. Wharton and Henry James develop a close friendship. George Bernard Shaw's play *Major Barbara* is performed in London.

1908   Wharton publishes *A Motor-Flight through France*, in which she recounts her travels with Edward and Henry James. She meets Morton Fullerton, an American journalist living in London who is a friend of Henry James, and the two begin a passionate though short-lived love affair.

1911   Wharton's *Ethan Frome* is published; it was inspired by the New England life the author witnessed near her home in Lenox.

1912   Wharton begins a friendship with art historian Bernard Berenson.

1913   Edith and Edward divorce. Wharton moves to France, where she will spend most of the rest of her life. Willa Cather's *O Pioneers!* is published.

1914   Wharton travels to Tunisia and Algiers, then undertakes relief efforts during World War I. She finds homes for hundreds of Belgian orphans and raises money for refugees.

1916   Henry James dies. Wharton receives the French Legion of Honor award for her war relief activities.

1917   T. S. Eliot's book of poetry *Prufrock and Other Observations* appears.

1920   *The Age of Innocence*, a novel about New York society, is published to great success.

1921   Wharton becomes the first woman to be awarded the Pulitzer Prize for fiction, which she receives for *The Age of Innocence*. Eugene O'Neill's play *Anna Christie* opens in New York City.

1922   T. S. Eliot's *The Waste Land* is published.

1923   Yale University awards Wharton an honorary doctorate. Edna St. Vincent Millay receives the Pulitzer Prize for poetry.

1924   Wharton publishes a collection of novellas and short stories as *Old New York*.

1925   Sinclair Lewis publishes *Arrowsmith*, which he dedicates to Wharton. Fitzgerald's *The Great Gatsby* is published. Gertrude Stein publishes *The Making of Americans*.

1926   Ernest Hemingway publishes *The Sun Also Rises*.

1928   Edward Wharton dies. Poet Carl Sandburg's *Good Morning, America* is published.

1930   Wharton is elected to the American Academy of Arts and Letters. She continues to write, although her health is failing. Robert Frost's *Collected Poems* is published.

1934   Wharton publishes "Roman Fever" in *Liberty* magazine for the then-astronomical sum of $3,000; one of her best-known short stories, it is based on her travels in Italy.

1937   After a severe stroke, Edith Wharton dies on August 11. She is buried in Versailles, France.

INTRODUCTION

I

At a London dinner party in 1908, the young Somerset Maugham found Edith Wharton, then aged forty-six, impressive and condescending: "She was a smallish woman, with fine eyes, regular features and a pale clear skin drawn rather tightly over the bones of her face. She was dressed with the sober magnificence suitable to a woman of birth, of wealth and of letters." When he asked if she ever read thrillers, she disdainfully replied: "No." "Never has a monosyllable contained more frigid displeasure, more shocked disapproval nor more wounded surprise. . . . Her manner was that of a woman to whom a man has made proposals offensive to her modesty, but which her good breeding tells her it will be more dignified to ignore than to make a scene about."[1]

Wharton's encounters with the young and socially insecure Scott Fitzgerald also revealed her forbidding, imperious character. When they met in Charles Scribner's office in 1920, just after Fitzgerald's first novel was published, he impulsively threw himself at her feet and exclaimed: "Could I let the author of *Ethan Frome* pass through New York without paying my respects?" Five years later, after complimenting him on *The Great Gatsby*, she invited him to tea at her house outside Paris. Swaying against the mantelpiece after a few drinks, Fitzgerald tried to enliven the dull party by telling a couple of "rather rough stories." When Wharton, not nearly as strait-laced as she seemed to be, encouraged him to proceed, he became entangled in a tale about a young couple, perhaps based on himself and his wife Zelda, who spent a night in a French whorehouse. Listening attentively, his hostess icily commented that the story "lacked data"—the kind of precise description he felt unable to provide. She made no effort to put her nervous guest at ease, deliberately led him into a situation which he was not quite drunk enough to ignore or brazen out, and seemed to enjoy his discomfort.[2]

Edith Wharton, a very grande dame indeed, was born in New York City in 1862, during the American Civil War, with the unpoetic name of Edith Jones. Her wealthy and privileged family, her biographer wrote, "reached back to the early eighteenth century, to Ebenezer Stevens, a gallant artillery commander and a fellow officer of the Marquis de Lafayette during the Revolutionary War, and to William and Frederick Rhinelander, who built a flourishing business in sugar and shipbuilding in the 1780s."[3]

From the ages of four through ten, Edith traveled and lived with her family in England, France, Spain, Italy, and Germany. She was educated by governesses in the language and literature of each country. In 1870 Edith had a near-fatal attack of typhoid fever that weakened her hold on life. Two years later the family returned to America and to their homes in New York and Newport, Rhode Island. The old conservative New York families were indifferent, even hostile, to culture. In a telling anecdote in her autobiography, she recalled composing a novel when she was eleven that began, "Oh, how do you do, Mrs. Brown? . . . If only I had known you were going to call, I should have tidied up the drawing room," to which her mother, discouraging her attempt to write, frostily replied: "Drawing rooms are always tidy."[4]

Edith was rather plain, with thin lips and a long, underslung chin. A late, unexpected child, she was twelve to sixteen years younger than her brothers and suspected she was the illegitimate offspring of their English tutor. This uncertainty about her parentage contributed to her haughty but defensive demeanor. The American writer Iris Origo called her "elegant, formidable, as hard and dry as porcelain."[5] The art historian Kenneth Clark agreed, but also stressed her more positive qualities: "She was, on many counts, a formidable person, extremely intelligent, immensely well read in four languages, witty, self-disciplined."[6] But Wharton lived in two worlds and couldn't quite bring them together. In her autobiography she wrote that her intelligence frightened her fashionable friends as much as her elegance dismayed her intellectual companions.

In 1877 and 1878, the teenaged Edith finished her first novella and published her first book of poems, and made her debut in society. In 1882 her father died and left her $20,000 (now worth about $240,000). She also became engaged, and then broke the engagement when her fiancé's mother opposed the match. In *The House of Mirth* two of Lily's minor suitors have obstructive mothers. Dillworth's mother was afraid Lily would have the family jewels reset and redecorate the always tidy drawing room. Percy Gryce, a grown-up mama's boy, had solemnly promised his mother that he'd never go out in the rain without his overshoes.

In 1885 Edith married Edward Wharton, a handsome and appealing Harvard graduate with a modest income, twelve years her senior. Mainly interested in hunting and fishing, he did not share her intellectual interests, and it's hard to imagine her sleeping out in the woods. Their sex life was unsatisfactory and, after a time, nonexistent. They lived in Italy and in a cottage on her mother's Newport estate. After Edith inherited $120,000 from a cousin, the Whartons returned to New York in 1889 and bought houses there and in Newport. In 1894 and 1895 the tensions and conflicts in Wharton's life became unbearable and she suffered a protracted nervous breakdown.

In 1901 Wharton inherited another $90,000 on the death of her mother, bought a 100-acre property in Lenox, Massachusetts, in the Berkshires, and began to build her grand estate, The Mount. Henry James—a longtime correspondent, frequent visitor, and major influence on her work—called it "a French château mirrored in a Massachusetts pond." The critic Edmund Wilson visited The Mount, after Wharton's death, in the 1940s. He described its "white façade with rather small windows . . . and a little gray cupola with a weather vane—all in imitation of a French château. . . . Stable-garage . . . and gatehouse to match: winding drives, rolling lawn with terraces, views of the hills and the little lake . . . rich grassy tree-grown country, so luxuriously upholstered, richly lined."[7] Wharton, who shared the auto-eroticism of Mr. Toad in *The Wind in the Willows*, bought her first car as early as 1904. She motored extensively, sometimes with Henry James perched in the back seat, and wrote travel books on Italy, France, and Morocco.

In 1905 Wharton dined with President Theodore Roosevelt in the White House, and in October published her first important book, *The House of Mirth.* Though her heroine Lily Bart dies instead of marrying Lawrence Selden in a conventionally happy conclusion, the novel sold an astonishing 140,000 copies by the end of the year. Readers were riveted by the beautiful, charming, and sacrificial Lily as well as by the satiric but authoritative portrayal of American high society, seen for the first time from the inside. Attempting to capitalize on its success, Wharton wrote a stage version of the novel. It opened in 1906, was condemned as "dreadful" by the *New York Times,* and promptly closed. A French translation, *Chez les heureux du monde,* appeared in 1907.

The publication of the novel made Wharton famous and even richer than she already was. In 1908 she began a three-year affair with the Paris-based bisexual American journalist Morton Fullerton and experienced for the first time in her life real sexual passion. Rapturously describing their bed after an encounter in the decidedly unromantic Charing Cross Hotel, on the Strand in London, she exclaimed in Whitmanesque lines:

> perchance it has also thrilled
> With the pressure of bodies ecstatic, bodies like ours,
> Seeking each other's souls in the depths of unfathomed caresses.[8]

Though she had not met Fullerton when she created the character of Lawrence Selden, they were remarkably similar. Wharton, like Lily Bart, seems to have been drawn to the type of man who "was curiously insubstantial on the human side; he seems to have had almost no impulse to engage another person to the full depths of the other's being."[9]

In 1909, during Edith's affair with Fullerton, Teddy Wharton embezzled a substantial amount of her money, and bought a Boston apartment for his mistress. Increasingly abusive, often violent, and wildly manic depressive, he was finally placed in a mental institution in 1912. Henry James, in a fine phrase, called Teddy "cerebrally compromised." The following year Edith divorced Teddy and returned to Europe. In *The House of Mirth* Edith gives two minor villains—the old lecher Ned Van Alstyne and Bertha Dorset's lover Ned Silverton—her husband's name.

In 1912 Edith began her close friendship with the influential art historian Bernard Berenson. When the Great War broke out in France, she devoted herself to relief work for French and Belgian refugees, provided medical supplies, and took care of more than 600 war orphans. She was the first woman to be awarded the Légion d'honneur. After the war she had splendid houses with magnificent gardens, outside Paris and in Hyères on the French Riviera, and employed nineteen servants of various nationalities to run them. But she was less fortunate with men. After her unhappy marriage and ultimately unsatisfactory love affair, she formed a lifelong friendship with the Paris-based American lawyer Walter Berry. According to Edmund Wilson, Berry had syphilis, which explains why they never married or had sexual relations.[10] Edith Wharton died near Paris, at the age of seventy-five, in 1937.

James and Wharton saw the merits of, though they didn't much like, each other's work. In 1902, when they began to correspond, the Master wrote Wharton's sister-in-law and close friend: "I take to her very kindly as regards her diabolical little cleverness, the quantity of intention and intelligence in her style, and her sharp eye for an interesting *kind* of subject."[11] When *The House of Mirth* was published, he gratifyingly told her that "the book remains one that does you great honour . . . it is indeed throughout *extremely* well written, and in places quite 'consummately.' "[12] Reading *A Backward Glance* in 1934, Virginia Woolf agreed about her intelligence and style: "There's a shell of a distinguished mind; I like the way she places colour in her sentences."[13] Wharton's finest novels are, in addition to *The House of Mirth, Ethan Frome* (1911), *The Custom of the Country* (1913), and *The Age of Innocence* (1920), for which she won the Pulitzer Prize. These works influenced two generations of American authors who followed the tradition of the novel of manners: Sinclair Lewis, John Marquand, Scott Fitzgerald, James Gould Cozzens, John O'Hara, and Louis Auchincloss, and, in her portrayal of sensitive women who fail to marry, the English novelist Anita Brookner.

II

The House of Mirth, conventional in form but still very readable and perceptive about the social roles of modern women, appeared almost a century ago, in 1905. That year, Japan's defeat of Russia led to the first Russian Revolution, the formation of workers' Soviets, and the mutiny on the battleship *Potemkin*. In 1905 Einstein proposed his First Theory of Relativity and Freud published his *Three Contributions to the Theory of Sex*. There were also new currents of modernism in art, music, and literature. John Singer Sargent painted *The Marlborough Family*, Henri Rousseau *The Hungry Lion*, and Henri Matisse *La Joie de vivre*. Franz Léhar composed *The Merry Widow*, Claude Debussy *La Mer*, and Richard Strauss *Salome*. G. B. Shaw brought out *Major Barbara*, H. G. Wells *Kipps*, and E. M. Forster *Where Angels Fear to Tread*. There was considerable unrest in the United States as well as in Russia, and as the historian John Higham noted, "It was a time of mass strikes, widening social chasms, unstable prices, and a degree of economic hardship unfamiliar in earlier American history."[14]

Edith Wharton was intimately acquainted with the ruling class, with people who had money and property, wealth and power. As Louis Auchincloss observed: "She knew their history and their origins, their prejudices and ideals, the source of their money and how they spent their summers."[15] She seemed to hate the society she belonged to, and described it with pervasive irony and sharp wit. Her philistine and hypocritical characters are spoiled and selfish, idle and self-indulgent, hedonistic and materialistic; their social hierarchy, through which Lily Bart makes her tragic descent, is as rigid as the Army or the Church. In a society rife with financial scandal and sexual intrigue, anything is allowed as long as the transgressors are wealthy and maintain a respectable façade. The "vulture" Carry Fisher, who's twice been divorced and receives money from Gus Trenor, has powerful protectors and is invited everywhere. The fierce and vindictive Bertha Dorset has flagrantly indiscreet affairs with Selden and Silverton but, ironically protected by her victim Lily Bart, manages to maintain both her reputation and her marriage.

In her revealing introduction to the 1936 reprint of *The House of Mirth*, Wharton explained her choice of subject and suggested her major theme: "When I wrote *The House of Mirth* I held, without knowing it, two trumps in my hand. One was the fact that New York society in the nineties was a field as yet un-exploited by a novelist who had grown up in that little hot-house of traditions and conventions; and the other, that as yet these traditions and conventions were unassailed, and tacitly regarded as unassailable." She admitted that she "wrote about totally insignificant people, and 'dated' them by an elaborate stage-setting of manners, furniture and costume." Such people, she said, "always rest on an underpinning of wasted human possibilities," and their sadly vulnerable victim was "the tame and blameless Lily Bart." Ironically listing Lily's misdemeanors, Wharton described her as "a young girl of their world who rouged, smoked, ran into debt, borrowed money, gambled and—crowning horror!—went home with a bachelor friend to take tea in his flat!"[16]

Wharton's caustic novel, piercing the secure stockade of convention, alarmed and disturbed the rulers of New York. In a letter of November 11, 1905, a month after the book appeared, Wharton defended her work. She said that the American upper classes lacked the sense of social responsibility, the noblesse oblige still maintained by their aristocratic counterparts in Europe: "I must protest, & emphatically, against the suggestion that I have 'stripped' New York society. New York society is still amply clad, & the little corner of its garment that I lifted was meant to show only that little atrophied organ—the group of idle & dull people . . . [whose] sudden possession of money has come without inherited obligations, or any traditional sense of solidarity between the classes."[17]

Lily's quest for mirth, or amusement, is both innocent and foolish. When she returns to town after her ill-fated excursion to the Trenors' country house, her preoccupations, "for the moment, had the happy effect of banishing troublesome thoughts" (p. 144). In a similar way, John Milton's famous "L'Allegro" (1631) opens with the banishment of "loathed Melancholy" and the invocation of "heart-easing Mirth," whose pleasures it then celebrates:

> Mirth, admit me of thy crew
> To live with her and live with thee,
> In unreprovéd pleasures free. . . .

> These delights if thou canst give,
> Mirth, with thee I mean to live.

But Ecclesiastes 7:4, the biblical text that supplies the title of the novel—"the heart of the wise is in the house of mourning; but the heart of fools is in the house of mirth"—opposes Milton's evocation of happiness and gloomily asserts that the wise realize that life is tragic; the foolish, like Lily, do not. Oliver Goldsmith's tender, bittersweet song in *The Vicar of Wakefield* (1766) also expresses the universal characters and themes of Wharton's novel—a foolish beauty and treacherous men, profound melancholy and irremediable guilt:

> When lovely woman stoops to folly,
> And finds too late that men betray,
> What charm can soothe her melancholy?
> What art can wash her guilt away?

In her review of Howard Sturgis's *Belchamber*, published a few months before *The House of Mirth*, Wharton expressed the theme of her own novel—lost illusions and destructive melancholy: "A handful of vulgar people, bent only on spending and enjoying, may seem a negligible factor in the social development of the race; but they become an engine of destruction through the illusions they kill and the generous ardor they turn to despair."[18] This is very close to her thematic statement in *The House of Mirth* when the disillusioned Lily realizes "for the first time that a woman's dignity may cost more to keep up than her carriage; and that the maintenance of a moral attribute should be dependent on dollars and cents, made the world appear a more sordid place than she had conceived it" (p. 187). Wharton stated this theme for the third time in her last major novel, *The Age of Innocence* (1920), when she condemned people "who dreaded scandal more than disease, who placed decency above courage, and who considered that nothing was more ill-bred than 'scenes,' except the behavior of those who give rise to them."[19]

Wharton indicates the dominant themes of the novel through another literary work, Jean de la Bruyère's *Caractères*

(1688), which Lily examines on her first visit to Selden's apartment and sees again at the end of the book. It is the only book in Selden's extensive library that Wharton specifically mentions. La Bruyère's ironic and pessimistic observations on the French nobility, especially in the section "On Women," suggest the way that Selden, and the rest of New York society, observe Lily's conduct and interpret her character:

> *There's a certain woman who annihilates or buries her husband to such a point that he is never mentioned in society; is he still alive? Is he dead? Nobody knows. In his own family he serves only as an example of timid silence and perfect submissiveness.*

Lily's stern, grasping mother has annihilated her husband in precisely this way. In childhood Lily seldom saw her father during the day; and after he could no longer earn money, he became extinct to his wife and almost undistinguishable to his daughter.

> *There comes a time when the richest of girls must take a husband; if she lets slip early opportunities, she must repent at leisure.*

Lily was taught to consider a conventional rich marriage the sole end of her existence. Having rejected numerous suitors during her ten years on the marriage market, she's extremely vulnerable to the malicious attacks of her enemies.

> *Women consult their glass to see whether they are far enough removed from their natural selves.*

Lily often looks in the mirror and ponders the dual nature of her real and artificial self.

> *One's age is written on one's face.*

As time passes, Lily is troubled by the lines and creases in her lovely face, signs of encroaching age.

> *A man of no judgement and of a licentious imagination lacks nothing to make many women worship him but fine features and a handsome figure.*

This exactly defines the good-looking but shallow Selden. He lacks judgment and imagines that the innocent Lily is guilty of sexual immorality, but is loved by Bertha Dorset, Gerty Farish, and Lily herself.

> *Most women . . . follow their hearts, and depend for their morals on the men they love.*

Lily behaves spontaneously, impulsively, even self-destructively, and depends on Selden for moral guidance.

> *A woman conceals from a man all the passion that she feels for him, while he, on his side, simulates a passion for her which he does not feel.*

After Lily appears in the *tableaux vivants* and kisses Selden for the first and only time, she insists on true feeling rather than false speech, and tells him: "Ah, love me, love me—but don't tell me so!" (p. 152)

> *Few amorous intrigues can be kept secret.*

Indeed, all the people in her circle know the intimate details of Lily's life, and all misinterpret her behavior.

> *Certain women have sought to hide their conduct under a veil of modesty . . . and have it said of them: "You'd have taken her for a vestal virgin."*

Lily remains a virgin, but her lack of caution leads men to misjudge her character.

> *The countless ways by which women arouse strong passions in men give rise to an aversion and antipathy in their own sex.*

Lily's beauty arouses jealousy and vengeance, not only in Bertha, but also in Grace Stepney and even Gerty Farish.

> *A woman's untarnished and well-founded reputation . . . should remain untouched by her intimacy with women of a different sort.*[20]

For this reason, Selden warns Lily, who's compromised herself by covering up Bertha's adultery with Silverton and assisting in Norma Hatch's vulgar schemes, to leave Bertha's yacht and Norma's hotel.

III

The names of the characters in *The House of Mirth*, chosen with great care and wit, have subtly negative connotations. The wealthy but undesirable Percy Gryce suggests "grease" and "price." The blackmailing charwoman Mrs. Haffen does not, as her name suggests in German, provide a haven or refuge. The name of the milliner's harsh forewoman, Miss Haines, means "hatred" in French. Rosedale, the name of the grasping Jewish financier, is an anglicization of Rosenthal (in German, *Tal* means valley or "dale"), an attempt to cover up his German origins. The treacherous Grace Stepney's surname is that of a slum area in the East End of London. The poet Ned Silverton (silver tongue) seductively reads Paul Verlaine when seducing Bertha. The rich, pleasure-loving Gormers suggest "gourmand." Norma Hatch blatantly hatches plots to buy her way into society. The odious, social climbing Wellington Bry combines the name of the ambitious Iron Duke with bryony, a climbing plant with an acrid juice. Caroline, the first name of Carry Fisher, is the feminine version of Charles (Latin: Carolus), which Lily associates with the pleasure loving court of King Charles II. The twice-divorced Carry, a "fisher of men" whose alimony is paid by other women's husbands and who lures Lily into dangerous liaisons with destructive women, ironically recalls Christ's words in Matthew 4:19: "Follow me, and I will make you fishers of men." Gus Trenor, owner of the magnificent Bellomont estate, recalls the fabulously wealthy German-born financier August Belmont (1816-1890), who was the agent in America of the great banking family, the Rothschilds. The name of Lily's cruel aunt Julia *Penis*ton is as audacious, if taken in the crudest sexual sense, as that of Henry James's leaking Mrs. Condrip, sister of Kate Croy, in *The Wings of the Dove*;[21] both can be seen to suggest sexual undercurrents in apparently respectable society.

Lily Bart's surname means "beard" in German; and in English "to beard" means "to defy" and "to oppose boldly." Though Lily defies social conventions, her first name is the Virgin Mary's symbol of purity and innocence, and she retains these qualities throughout the novel. In the Sermon on the Mount in Matthew 6:28–29, Christ says: "Consider the lilies of the field, how they grow; they toil not, neither do they spin . . . [but] Solomon in all his glory was not arrayed like one of these." Lily, a delicate beauty, is not meant to toil. She'd begged her father to have the florist send a bunch of lilies-of-the-valley every day; and when she's forced to join the "underworld of toilers" at the milliner's, she cannot bear the work.

The lily, one of Wharton's childhood names, was particularly associated with beauty, and with the Pre-Raphaelite and Aesthetic movements in the decades before her novel was published. In 1886 John Singer Sargent, who portrayed several members of Wharton's social circle, painted one of his major works, *Carnation, Lily, Lily, Rose* (in the Tate Gallery, London), which shows two white-gowned little girls holding Chinese lanterns in a flower-filled garden. In the first act of Gilbert and Sullivan's *Patience* (1881), the feminine lily is ironically associated with a precious young man like Selden, who walks "down Piccadilly with a poppy or a lily in [his] medieval hand" and whose "vegetable love" would be far too tame for Lily Bart.

The structure of the novel, which began to be serialized in *Scribner's Magazine* before it was completed, is as skillful as its delineation of character. Wharton confessed to her editor that "the whole thing strikes me as so loosely built, with so many dangling threads, & *cul-de-sacs*, & long dusty stretches."[22] The novel sometimes seems trivial when portraying snobbery and social climbing, relies too heavily on chance encounters and sudden turns of plot, and subjects the heroine to a deterministic fate that's heavily weighted against her. But the themes evoked in the opening chapters are brilliantly resolved in the conclusion. The novel takes place over two years: Book One portrays Lily's slow rise in society and the false accusations against her; Book Two shows her rapid descent and unjust conviction.

The first chapter opens as Selden, in the first of many accidental meetings, runs into Lily waiting between trains in Grand Central Station. Instead of taking tea at Sherry's as he properly suggests, they walk for a bit and wind up on his street. On the way he carefully observes her as if she were a particularly fine piece of exterior decoration. Luxuriating in the pleasure of her proximity, he admires "the modelling of her little ear, the crisp upward wave of her hair . . . and the thick planting of her straight black lashes" (p. 7). Though aware that her behavior has always aroused speculation, she's tempted by the risk of entering his apartment, and he's delighted by the spontaneity of her consent. When she contrasts her luxurious way of life to the dingy existence of Selden's cousin Gerty Farish, Lily seems to him like a victim manacled to her fate.

Lily, whose vocation is marriage, is very fond of Selden but doesn't want to marry him because he hasn't got enough money—though he's sufficiently wealthy to sail suddenly down to Havana or across to Europe for important legal cases. She also presciently admits that her best friends, despite generous invitations, don't really care what happens to her. Taking a cigarette to smoke and several others to keep in reserve, she mentions losing Dillworth, a prospective husband, and questions Selden about the fine points of Americana, which she'll use to entice Percy Gryce. As she studies herself in the mirror, Selden anticipates the woodland setting of the *tableau vivant*, emphasizes her sexy figure, and compares her to a dryad. He notices "the long slope of her slender sides, which gave a kind of wild-wood grace to her outline—as though she were a captured dryad subdued to the conventions of the drawing-room" (p. 16). He also reflects in her duality of sylvan freedom and urban artifice.

This apparently trivial meeting with Selden establishes Lily's heedless nature and determines her future. On her way out, she passes a charwoman scrubbing the stairs on her hands and knees, and has another chance encounter, this time with Simon Rosedale, "a plump rosy man of the blond Jewish type, with smart London clothes fitting him like upholstery" (p. 17). In the first of many lies, she tells Rosedale that she's been to her dressmaker, though as the owner of the building he knows there are no dressmakers on the premises. Several motifs in this chapter reverberate throughout the novel: dinginess, which Lily abhors but which overwhelms her at the end; mirrors and the duality of her nature; transparent lies (for she's basically honest and a poor liar); apparent but not real rescues: first by Selden in the train station, then by a "rescuing vehicle" that enables her to escape from Rosedale; and a dark fate that pursues her to the end.

In the opening of the second chapter Lily uneasily asks herself: "Why must a girl pay so dearly for her least escape from routine?" (p. 19). Lily frequently refers to herself as "a girl," and by doing so suggests her childhood innocence, her undeveloped moral awareness, and her lack of responsibility for her own behavior. Playing high-stakes bridge at Bellomont, Lily loses $300—a very considerable sum, about $3,600 in today's money—and though she can't afford it, later gives the same amount to Gerty's charity. As she wonders whether it's her fault or her destiny, a poignant flashback describes her family background. Her hardworking but weak, pathetic father "filled an intermediate space between the butler and the man who came to wind the clocks" (p. 34). She seldom saw him during the day, and when he joined his family for summer weekends "he was even more effaced and silent than in winter" (p. 34). Lily's childhood house, like the house in D. H. Lawrence's "The Rocking-Horse Winner" (1926), seemed "to be haunted by the unspoken phrase: There must be more money! There must be more money!"[23] Mrs. Bart would reproach her husband by asking if he expected her to "live like a pig" (p. 35). In a climactic moment, Mr. Bart tells his daughter to order twelve *hundred* lilies—and then confesses that he's ruined. Mrs. Bart, lacking sympathy for her husband's desperate plight, is furious about what he's done to them. Lily is merely relieved when he dies.

Lily's father was either absent or remote; her mother felt only contempt for him. Both taught her to worship wealth and trained her solely for marriage—though she has no real desire to get married. Like Wharton herself, Lily has never had a mother's love. When the novel opens, Lily, an orphan with no mother to protect her, must look after herself. On Bertha's yacht in Monte Carlo, Lord Hubert tells Selden that Lily has an aunt in New York, but that New York is a long way off. By then, though Lily doesn't yet know it, her Aunt Julia Peniston has died, disinherited her, and left her with no place to live. After Gus Trenor's assault, she seeks refuge with Gerty and sleeps like a baby in a mother's arms. Just before Lily dies, she imagines herself (for the first and only time) as a mother and with a baby sleeping in *her* arms.

Lily's nemesis Bertha Dorset makes a dramatic and domineering entrance on the train to Bellomont: "a pretty woman, who entered the train accompanied by a maid, a bull-terrier, and a footman struggling under a load of bags and dressing-cases. 'Oh, Lily—are you going to Bellomont? Then you can't let me have your seat, I suppose? But I *must* have a seat in this carriage—porter, you must find me a place at once. Can't someone be put somewhere else? I want to be with my friends'" (p. 27). Bertha interrupts Lily's courtship of the excessively rich and exceedingly shy Percy Gryce. Once at Bellomont and jealous of Selden's romantic interest in her friend, Bertha detaches Gryce from Lily, who loses him to another woman.

Lily obtains a potentially lethal hold over Bertha when Mrs. Haffen, the charwoman in Selden's building, sells her the incriminating love letters that Bertha has written to Selden in the course of their affair. The normally cautious and fastidious Selden quite uncharacteristically (a minor flaw in the plot) had torn them up and thrown them into the wastebasket. The innocent "girl" is disillusioned and shocked by this evidence of their sexual passion, later echoed in the illicit relations between Bertha and Silverton, Carry Fisher and Gus Trenor, Nettie and the unnamed gentleman who seduced her.

The young Edith Wharton had been as innocent as Lily. Her mother, who insisted on approving all the novels Wharton read before she married, never explained the nature of sexual relations, which remained a mystery to Wharton until well after her wedding. Wharton's astonishing pornographic passage—describing incestuous relations and found among her papers after her death—explicitly reveals the sexual feelings that lie beneath the surface of the novel but cannot be expressed. In the "Beatrice Palmato" fragment, the father caresses his daughter's sexual parts:

> As his hand stole higher she felt the secret bud of her body swelling, yearning, quivering hotly to burst into bloom. Ah, here was his subtle fore-finger pressing it, forcing its tight petals softly apart, and laying on their sensitive edges a circular touch so soft and yet so fiery that already lightnings of heat shot from that palpitating centre all over her surrendered body.[24]

The most crucial scene in *The House of Mirth* and the one that comes closest to overt sexuality is Lily's *tableau vivant* during the party at Wellington Bry's palatial residence. The mansion, well designed for a theatrical display, blurs—like the performance itself—the distinction between appearance and reality: "so rapidly-evoked was the whole *mise-en-scène* that one had to touch the marble columns to learn they were not of cardboard, to seat one's self in one of the damask-and-gold armchairs to be sure it was not painted against the wall" (p. 145).

Lily's sensational appearance as Mrs. Lloyd (1776) was the fin-de-siècle equivalent of modeling a bikini in a modern fashion show. In Sir Joshua Reynolds's painting of the same name, the tall beauty is portrayed in profile, standing and leaning slightly forward, her left hand resting on a stone plinth and right hand carving her husband's name on a tree. Her brown hair is piled high on her head; she wears a classical gown with a sash and low neckline, decorated by a pin, and blue sandals on her crossed feet. Though not quite dressed for a ramble in the woods, her body is as willowy as the increasingly slender trees in the background. A shaft of light—focusing on her belly, genitals, and thighs—seems to foreshadow the children she will bear. Carving a lover's name on a tree was once a familiar poetic conceit. In *As You Like It* (act 3, scene 2), for example, Shakespeare wrote: "Run, run, Orlando, carve on every tree / The fair, the chaste, and unexpressive she." Since the first "L" in "Lloyd" is rather faint, it looks as if Mrs. Lloyd is beginning to carve the word "LOVE"—the "unspoken word" in the last sentence of *The House of Mirth*.

Wharton offers a rapturous description of Lily posing as Mrs. Lloyd: "Her pale draperies, and the background of foliage against which she stood, served only to relieve the long dryad-like curves that swept upward from her poised foot to her lifted arm. The noble buoyancy of her attitude, its suggestion of soaring grace, revealed the touch of poetry in her beauty that Selden always felt in her presence" (pp. 148–149). Lily's appearance, which shows her as she appears to be rather than she really is, has seismic effects on all the men. It provokes Ned Van Alstyne's crude remarks about her voluptuous figure, Trenor's assault, George Dorset's proposal, and (as word gets around) Rosedale's offer of marriage. Later on, Lily rejects a tableau-like role as model at the milliner's and perversely tries to earn her keep by sewing hats.

The spectacular setting and theatrical performance at the Brys' was based on an actual event that took place a few years before *The House of Mirth* was published and was attended by August Belmont, a model for Gus Trenor. In *The Robber Barons*, Matthew Josephson wrote that

> A costume ball given by Bradley Martin, a New York aristocrat, in 1897, reached the very climax of lavish expenditure and "dazed the entire Western world." "The interior of the Waldorf-Astoria Hotel was transformed into a replica of Versailles, and rare tapestries, beautiful flowers and countless lights made an effective background for the wonderful gowns and their wearers." One lady, impersonating Mary Stuart, wore a gold-embroidered gown, trimmed with pearls and precious stones. "The suit of gold-inlaid armor worn by Mr. Belmont was valued at ten thousand dollars."[25]

Belmont's gold armor reappears in the novel in a story from Roman history that Rosedale tells Lily. The virgin daughter of Tarpeius, the commander of the citadel, betrayed the Romans for a bribe and was crushed to death under the golden shields of the invading Sabines. Lily, too, accepts a bribe—Trenor's "gains" on the stock market—and will also be crushed by her false friends.

Gus Trenor, no doubt fantasizing about Lily's luscious body, feels he has a sexual as well as financial claim on her and intends to collect his debt. Short of funds after her gambling losses and trying to keep up with the rich instead of being supported by them, Lily asked Trenor to invest $1,000 of her own money. He eventually gives her $10,000, which she naively thinks her money has earned; it is actually *his* money, and he uses it to keep her in his power. Lily now owes him $9,000 (though he paid no interest on her original $1,000), and she rightly fears that Gus will, like Bertha and Grace Stepney, spread ugly rumors about her.

When Lily accepts the invitation of Judy Trenor, Gus's wife and her "best friend," to visit her New York townhouse, Gus first says Judy is upstairs with a headache, then admits that she's not in the house, nor even in town, and that he'd intercepted Judy's message canceling her appointment with Lily. Desperate to escape, Lily tries to remain calm as Gus—fat, red, and sweating as always—blocks her exit. He insists that she must pay her debt with sex rather than with money. As she continues to defy him, his will collapses and a remnant of chivalrous feeling reasserts itself. Punning on the sexual meaning of the last word in the sentence, Wharton explains that "Old habits, old restraints, the hand of inherited order, plucked back the bewildered mind which passion had jolted from its ruts" (p. 162).

Lily manages to escape from Gus, but is still pursued by the same inexorable Furies that tormented Orestes in Aeschylus' Greek tragedy. "The Furies might sometimes sleep," she thinks, "but they were there, always there in the dark corners. . . . She was alone in a place of darkness and pollution" (p. 163). She is seen leaving Gus's house late at night by Selden and Van Alstyne, just as she'd been seen by Rosedale leaving Selden's flat. Knowing that Lily owes Gus money and that Judy is out of town, the two men draw the obvious conclusion and believe she's just given Gus the long-sought sexual payoff. Completely disenchanted, Selden loses all interest in marrying her and escapes on a boat to Havana.

IV

After Selden disappears, Lily, to escape from Trenor, accepts Bertha's invitation to join her on a Mediterranean cruise. The scene shifts, at the beginning of Book Two, to Monte Carlo. Lily soon realizes that Bertha has invited her in order to distract her husband's attention from her current affair with Ned Silverton. During the water festival in Nice, Bertha disappears with Silverton in a closed carriage, leaving Lily and George Dorset alone in the train station and on the yacht. When Dorset discovers that Bertha missed the last train to Monte Carlo, spent the night with Silverton, and did not come aboard until seven the next morning, he pours out his wretched soul to Lily and threatens to get a divorce. To mask her infidelity and win back her malleable husband, Bertha blames Lily for being "so conspicuously on his hands . . . in such a scandalous place after midnight" (p. 227). Then, after the Brys give another lavish dinner party, Bertha publicly dismisses Lily by announcing: "Miss Bart is not going back to the yacht" (p. 238). No one defends Lily after her cruel dismissal, though both Dorset and Carry Fisher later apologize for their cowardly behavior. Bertha has no moral scruples; Lily has far too many. Bertha is a Fury and avenger, yet Lily has committed no crime. Wharton makes her heroine the ironic embodiment of Aeschylus' great theme: suffering teaches wisdom.

Lily returns to New York to find that Grace Stepney has told her aunt that Lily lost money gambling and that Gus Trenor has paid her bills, poisoning the severe and disapproving Julia Peniston against her. Horrified by Lily's behavior, Julia disinherits her and leaves $400,000 to Grace. Lily's legacy, though only a fraction of Grace's inheritance, would still be a sizable sum—if she didn't owe most of it to Gus. When Lily tries to borrow money from Grace, as she previously tried to borrow from Julia, Grace gives the same sanctimonious refusal as her aunt.

Carry told Lily that George Dorset would be eager to marry her after he divorced Bertha. George is completely uncultured: he describes the opera as "caterwauling" and is "as difficult to amuse as a savage." But he reveals the sensitive and vulnerable side of his character when he tells Lily that she can set him free if she will provide evidence of Bertha's infidelity. Yet Lily refuses to take revenge against her enemy and rehabilitate herself in society.

Lily's refusal to help Dorset means she can only save herself by marrying Simon Rosedale. At the beginning of the novel

Rosedale is described with all the repulsive anti-Semitic clichés of Wharton's class and time. He "had his race's accuracy in the appraisal of values" (p. 19) and all the "business astuteness which characterizes his race" (p. 20). He's "fat and shiny, and has a shoppy manner!" (p. 90), and pushy and insensitive, he's compared to a bluebottle fly that bangs itself against the window panes of fashionable drawing rooms. Wharton twice calls him "the little Jew"—the very phrase Virginia Woolf used to describe her devoted husband, Leonard.

During the Edwardian era, when *The House of Mirth* was published, Jews had an ambiguous place in English and American society, which despised and accepted them. Benjamin Disraeli had been prime minister in Victoria's reign and Rufus Isaacs became Lord Chief Justice in 1913. King Edward VII was philo-Semitic at a time when the German Kaiser demeaned Jews and the Russian Czar persecuted them in pogroms. Czar Nicholas II was astonished to find the Jewish railroad tycoon and horse breeder, Baron Hirsch, among the guests at Edward's estate at Sandringham. The Rothschilds and Sassoons, and the South African Randlords, with great fortunes from diamonds and gold, played a prominent part in English society. They also paved the way for the social acceptance of the leading Jewish financiers in America.

In the course of the novel Rosedale rises as Lily descends. He becomes increasingly sympathetic and cares much more than Selden does about her desperate situation. Rosedale's proposal to Lily—"I've got the money . . . and what I want is the woman— and I mean to have her too" (p. 193)—provides a crude commercial contrast to Lily's lyrical moments with Selden at Bellomont and after her tableau. But when she next meets Rosedale, the increasingly desperate Lily—who's squandered her chances with Dillworth and the Italian prince as well as with Gryce, Selden, and Dorset—is moved by his tender concern and interrupts his impassioned declaration by prematurely announcing: "I *do* believe what you say, Mr. Rosedale . . . and I am ready to marry you whenever you wish" (p. 277). Rosedale then frankly explains that though he loves her as much as ever, she's no longer in a position to help him enter society. He's not willing to marry her unless, with his backing, she uses the letters to regain her friendship with Bertha and get back into the society that has excluded her. She refuses Rosedale's advice to blackmail Bertha, just as she'd refused Dorset's. At their last meeting Rosedale, unlike Selden, shows true compassion for her degradation and exclaims: "If you'd only let me, I'd set you up over them all—I'd put you where you could wipe your feet on 'em!" (p. 328).

Lily's marriage to Gryce, Dorset, or Rosedale would have been, like Edith's to Teddy Wharton, essentially meaningless. She loves only Selden. But she refuses to marry him, for financial reasons, when he's willing to marry her; and he refuses to marry her, for moral reasons, when she's willing to marry him. When he finally realizes her true worth, it's too late. During their six meetings—in his apartment, at Bellomont, at the Brys' tableaux, in Monte Carlo, in Norma Hatch's hotel room, and again in his apartment on the day of her death—Selden has fine manners but no heart. A cold and fatally vacillating prig, he avoids true intimacy and cannot respond to her passionate feelings. He likes the idea of Lily more than Lily herself. Though he often comes to the "rescue," he never really rescues her. He assumes the role of moral advisor while having an affair with another man's wife, and he expresses emotions in his letters to Bertha that he cannot reveal to Lily.

Though the novel has two redemptive declassé, or working-class, women, Gerty Farish and Nettie Struthers, all the men are portrayed negatively. Selden (like Lily's father) is well meaning but ineffectual; Gryce a milksop and a bore; Trenor a liar and swindler, a betrayer and would-be rapist; Silverton a phony; Dorset a crude and pathetic cuckold; Rosedale a pushy manipulator. In *The House of Mirth*, as Irving Howe observed, "human beings seem always to prove inadequate, always to fail each other, always to be victims of an innate disharmony between love and response, need and capacity."[26]

Lily Bart, a camp follower in the army of pleasure, is both a victim and heroine, who despises the society she's trying to enter. She's respectable but doesn't maintain a respectable facade; compromises herself but cannot save herself; and never quite realizes the enormity of her situation. Both extremely conventional and dangerously impulsive, she's foolish about her rashness and opportunities, finances and obligations, loyalty and sacrifices. With no parents or money to protect her, smoking and gambling, borrowing money and associating with dubious companions, she's fatally compromised when seen leaving Selden's apartment and Trenor's townhouse, and again when she is forced to remain alone at night with Dorset.

Lily descends from the strict, puritanical Penniston-Gryce-Van Osburgh circle, and the more lenient Trenors and Dorsets, who allow ladies to smoke and gamble, to the conspicuously consuming Wellington Brys and the pleasure-loving Gormers, to the flashy upstart Norma Hatch. In the course of her descent Lily works as a social secretary for Judy Trenor, supplementary hostess and scapegoat for Bertha Dorset, social manager for Norma Hatch, and incompetent seamstress for the milliner. Finally, she joins the ranks of the unemployed. The reader winces at her series of social humiliations: she's assaulted by Gus, brutally dismissed by Bertha, cut by the Trenors at the restaurant, betrayed by Grace and disinherited by Julia, rebuffed by Rosedale, fired by the milliner, abandoned by Selden, and bad-mouthed by everyone.

Wharton emphasizes throughout that Lily is alone in the world. When Selden joins Lily at Bellomont—and she lies to, abandons, and loses Gryce—Selden thinks, after seeing her that morning in a moment of intimate disarray, "*That is how she looks when she is alone!*" (p. 77). The thought of her in solitude excites him and finally provokes him to propose to her in a characteristically half-hearted fashion. He has the rare ability, she later notes, to draw out her real self, which "was so little accustomed to go alone!" (p. 104). In the final chapter, when he rushes, too late, to her room in the boarding house and discovers her dead, Gerty leaves the room and Selden stands "alone with the motionless sleeper on the bed" (p. 356).

Insufficiently calculating and with no instinct for self-preservation, Lily is prevented by moral scruples from saving herself. All her choices would have been preferable to the pathetic but noble death she finally chose. She could have married any of her suitors, used the incriminating letters against Bertha, borrowed money from Rosedale, learned to live modestly like Gerty, become a milliner's model, repudiated her extortionate debt to Trenor and kept her inheritance. But blackmailing

Bertha would have betrayed Selden and made her complicit with the repulsive Mrs. Haffen. Secretly burning the letters (as Selden failed to do) was Lily's way of proving her love for him and achieving a spiritual victory by returning good for evil. But Selden never knows about her sacrifice and, in the final irony, she gives up her life for an unworthy man. Torn between her faults and her destiny, Lily dies for a scruple in a tragedy that seems both avoidable and inevitable.

V

The weakest, most sentimental part of the novel, Lily's late encounter with Nettie Struther, is also ironic. Some of the money she received from Gus and donated to Gerty's charity has saved Nettie but helped ruin Lily. After being seduced, Nettie is rescued by a man who forgives and marries her; Lily remains chaste but is doomed when she fails to marry a protector. If Nettie's baby grows up like her benefactor Lily and like her namesake Marie Antoinette, then she is also doomed.

Wharton's description of Lily's suicidal overdose of chloral, just after she leaves the protection of Nettie's kitchen, draws on two of the greatest narcotic passages in English literature. Her longing to achieve oblivion, "to perpetuate, the momentary exaltation of her spirit . . . [and] end on this tragic yet sweet vision" (p. 350), recalls the rapturous longing for intoxicated extinction in John Keats's "Ode to a Nightingale":

> My heart aches, and a drowsy numbness pains
> My sense, as though of hemlock I had drunk,
> Or emptied some dull opiate to the drains
> One minute past, and Lethe-wards had sunk. . . .
> I have been half in love with easeful Death,
> Called him soft names in many a muséd rhyme,
> To take into the air my quiet breath;
> Now more than ever seems it rich to die,
> To cease upon the midnight with no pain.

Keat's third line—"emptied some dull opiate to the drains"—is closely echoed in the last sentence of the novel, "draining their last moment to its lees."

The other model for Lily's death scene was *Romeo and Juliet*. In act 4, scene 1, Friar Laurence describes, like the druggist telling Lily about the potential danger of chloral, the effect the drug will have on Juliet:

> Take thou this vial, being then in bed,
> And this distilled liquor drink thou off;
> When presently through all thy veins shall run
> A cold and drowsy humor, for no pulse
> Shall keep his native progress, but surcease:
> No warmth, no breath, shall testify thou livest;
> The roses in thy lips and cheeks shall fade
> To paly ashes, thy eyes' windows fall,
> Like death when he shuts up the day of life.

In act 5, scene 3, when Romeo discovers Juliet, apparently dead in the tomb, she seems more beautiful than ever:

> For here lies Juliet, and her beauty makes
> This vault a feasting presence full of light. . . .
>   Beauty's ensign yet
> Is crimson in thy lips and in thy cheeks,
> And death's pale flag is not advancéd there.

In the final chapter Selden, in a Poe-like scene with ghoulish overtones, confronts Lily's corpse. Like Romeo, he discovers a *tableau mort* rather than a living woman. Still trying to distinguish between the real and artificial Lily, "He stood looking down on the sleeping face which seemed to be like a delicate impalpable mask over the living lineaments he had known. He felt that the real Lily was still there, close to him, yet invisible and inaccessible; and the tenuity of the barrier between them mocked him with a sense of helplessness" (p. 356). When he finds the check that she'd made out to Trenor and left on her table, and that freed her from an intolerable obligation, Selden finally realizes, from factual rather than circumstantial evidence, that Lily has sacrificed herself to save him from an ugly scandal. Romeo kills himself when he discovers Juliet; Selden merely feels penitential.

Lily is granted a more easeful death than other fallen women who commit suicide in nineteenth-century novels, and is spared Emma Bovary's prussic acid, Anna Karenina's fall under a train, and Maggie's death (in Stephen Crane's novella) by drowning. Lily, a tragic heroine, *had* to die rather than survive and marry Selden. As Wharton explained in *A Backward Glance*, "a frivolous society can acquire dramatic significance only through what its frivolity destroys."[27] Only Lily's death could lead her as well as Selden to that "sharpening of the moral vision which makes all human suffering so near and insistent" (p. 167).[28]

———————————

Jeffrey Meyers, a Fellow of the Royal Society of Literature, has published forty-three books, including biographies of Ernest Hemingway, Edmund Wilson, Robert Frost, D. H. Lawrence, Joseph Conrad, and George Orwell. His life of Somerset Maugham will be published by Knopf in February 2004.

Notes to Introduction

1. Somerset Maugham, *The Vagrant Mood* (1952; London: Mandarin, 1988), pp. 197, 199. In *Edith Wharton: A Biography* (New York: Harper and Row, 1975), p. 521, R. W. B. Lewis mistakenly writes that Wharton never met Maugham.

2. Jeffrey Meyers, *Scott Fitzgerald: A Biography* (New York: HarperCollins, 1994), pp. 156–157.

3. Edith Wharton, *Letters*, edited by R. W. B. Lewis and Nancy Lewis (New York: Scribner's, 1988), p. 5.

4. Edith Wharton, *A Backward Glance* (1934. Reprint: New York: Scribner's, 1964), p. 73.

5. Quoted in Louis Auchincloss, *Edith Wharton: A Woman in Her Time* (New York: Viking Press, 1971), p. 142.

6. Kenneth Clark, *Another Part of the Wood: A Self-Portrait* (1974. Reprint: New York: Ballantine, 1976), p. 206.

7. Edmund Wilson, *The Forties*, edited with an introduction by Leon Edel (New York: Farrar, Straus and Giroux, 1983), p. 209.

8. Quoted in Henry James and Edith Wharton, *Letters, 1900–1915*, edited by Lyall Powers (New York: Scribner's, 1990), p. 16.

9. Lewis and Lewis, Introduction to Edith Wharton, *Letters*, p. 17.

10. Edmund Wilson, *The Twenties*, edited and with an introduction by Leon Edel (New York: Farrar, Straus and Giroux, 1975), p. 76.

11. Henry James, *Letters: Volume IV, 1895–1916*, edited by Leon Edel (Cambridge, Mass.: Harvard University Press, 1984), p. 237.

12. James, *Letters: Volume IV*, p. 373.

13. Virginia Woolf, *Letters: Volume Five, 1932–1935*, edited by Nigel Nicolson and Joanne Trautmann (New York: Harcourt Brace Jovanovich, 1979), p. 305.

14. John Higham, *Send These to Me: Immigrants in Urban America* (Baltimore: Johns Hopkins University Press, 1984), p. 129.

15. Louis Auchincloss, "Edith Wharton and Her New Yorks," *Reflections of a Jacobite* (Boston: Houghton Mifflin, 1961), pp. 13-14.

16. Edith Wharton, Introduction to *The House of Mirth* (1936), in *Uncollected Critical Writings*, edited and with an introduction by

Frederick Wegener (Princeton, NJ: Princeton University Press, 1996), pp. 265–266, 268–269.

17. Wharton, *Letters*, pp. 96–97, 99.

18. Edith Wharton, "Mr. Sturgis' *Belchamber*," *Bookman*, 21 (May 1905), 309–310.

19. Edith Wharton, *The Age of Innocence* (New York: Scribner's, 1920), p. 335.

20. Jean de la Bruyère, "On Women," *Characters*, translated by Jean Stewart (London: Penguin, 1970), pp. 55–68.

21. In the psychoanalytical *A Feast of Words: The Triumph of Edith Wharton* (New York: Oxford University Press, 1977), p. 117, Cynthia Griffin Wolff makes a Freudian slip and refers to her as "Mrs. Penniston." Many of Wharton's critics, thinking of Dreiser's *Sister Carrie* (written in 1905, but not published until 1912), misspell Carry Fisher's first name.

22. Wharton, *Letters*, p. 94.

23. D. H. Lawrence, "The Rocking-Horse Winner" (1926), *Complete Short Stories* (New York: Viking, 1961), vol. 3, p. 791.

24. Quoted in Lewis, *Edith Wharton*, p. 548.

25. Matthew Josephson, *The Robber Barons* (1934. Reprint: New York: Harcourt, Brace and World, 1962), p. 339.

26. Irving Howe, "The Achievement of Edith Wharton," *Edith Wharton: A Collection of Critical Essays*, edited by Irving Howe (Englewood Cliffs, NJ: Prentice-Hall, 1962), p. 15.

27. Wharton, *Backward Glance*, p. 207.

28. The film adaptation of *The House of Mirth*, which appeared in 2000, provides another way of interpreting the novel and a chance to see how popular actors of today portray the characters. Gillian Anderson, who plays Lily, is too noble and dignified; Laura Linney, who plays Bertha, seems too nice for the role; Eric Stoltz lacks the irresistible sex appeal of Selden; Anthony LaPaglia is insufficiently vile and villainous as Rosedale; Dan Aykroyd is unconvincing as the repulsive tycoon Gus Trenor. Written and directed by Terence Davies, the film is slavishly truthful to the novel, though it drops the Gerty-Nettie working-girl subplot. It is static and stagy, languid, mannered, and artificial, and depends too heavily on lavish costumes, heavy furniture, and stilted diction. The film fails to realize the dramatic potential of the most brilliant scenes in the novel: Selden's

proposal, Haffen's blackmail, the *tableaux vivants*, Trenor's near rape, Bertha's dismissal of Lily, the reading of Aunt Julia's will, Dorset's pathetic plea for help, Rosedale's crude proposition, the last meeting with Selden, his discovery of Lily's dead body, and his tragic failure to understand the meaning of her sacrifice.

THE HOUSE OF MIRTH[*]

*From the Bible, Ecclesiastes 7:4: "The heart of the wise is in the house of mourning; but the heart of fools is in the house of mirth" (King James Version; henceforth, KJV).

BOOK ONE

I

SELDEN PAUSED IN SURPRISE. In the afternoon rush of the Grand Central Station his eyes had been refreshed by the sight of Miss Lily Bart.

It was a Monday in early September, and he was returning to his work from a hurried dip into the country; but what was Miss Bart doing in town at that season? If she had appeared to be catching a train, he might have inferred that he had come on her in the act of transition between one and another of the country-houses which disputed her presence after the close of the Newport* season; but her desultory air perplexed him. She stood apart from the crowd, letting it drift by her to the platform or the street, and wearing an air of irresolution which might, as he surmised, be the mask of a very definite purpose. It struck him at once that she was waiting for some one, but he hardly knew why the idea arrested him. There was nothing new about Lily Bart, yet he could never see her without a faint movement of interest: it was characteristic of her that she always roused speculation, that her simplest acts seemed the result of far-reaching intentions.

An impulse of curiosity made him turn out of his direct line to the door, and stroll past her. He knew that if she did not wish to be seen she would contrive to elude him; and it amused him to think of putting her skill to the test.

"Mr. Selden—what good luck!"

She came forward smiling, eager almost, in her resolve to intercept him. One or two persons, in brushing past them, lin-

*Fashionable resort on the coast of Rhode Island, noted for its many sumptuous mansions.

gered to look; for Miss Bart was a figure to arrest even the sub-
urban traveller rushing to his last train.

Selden had never seen her more radiant. Her vivid head, relieved against the dull tints of the crowd, made her more conspicuous than in a ball-room, and under her dark hat and veil
she regained the girlish smoothness, the purity of tint, that she
was beginning to lose after eleven years of late hours and indefatigable dancing. Was it really eleven years, Selden found
himself wondering, and had she indeed reached the nine-and-
twentieth birthday with which her rivals credited her?

"What luck!" she repeated. "How nice of you to come to my
rescue!"

He responded joyfully that to do so was his mission in life,
and asked what form the rescue was to take.

"Oh, almost any—even to sitting on a bench and talking to
me. One sits out a cotillion—why not sit out a train? It isn't a bit
hotter here than in Mrs. Van Osburgh's conservatory—and
some of the women are not a bit uglier."

She broke off, laughing, to explain that she had come up to
town from Tuxedo, on her way to the Gus Trenors' at Bellomont, and had missed the three-fifteen train to Rhinebeck.*

"And there isn't another till half-past five." She consulted the
little jewelled watch among her laces. "Just two hours to wait.
And I don't know what to do with myself. My maid came up this
morning to do some shopping for me, and was to go on to Bellomont at one o'clock, and my aunt's house is closed, and I don't
know a soul in town." She glanced plaintively about the station.
"It *is* hotter than Mrs. Van Osburgh's, after all. If you can spare
the time, do take me somewhere for a breath of air."

He declared himself entirely at her disposal: the adventure
struck him as diverting. As a spectator, he had always enjoyed
Lily Bart; and his course lay so far out of her orbit that it amused

---

*The references are to country retreats for wealthy New Yorkers.
Rhinebeck is a town on the Hudson River, and Tuxedo Park is north
of the city in Orange County. Bellomont, the Trenors's country house,
is possibly named for Belmont in William Shakespeare's *The Merchant of Venice*; it is Portia's house, where her suitors are tested.

him to be drawn for a moment into the sudden intimacy which her proposal implied.

"Shall we go over to Sherry's* for a cup of tea?"

She smiled assentingly, and then made a slight grimace.

"So many people come up to town on a Monday—one is sure to meet a lot of bores. I'm as old as the hills, of course, and it ought not to make any difference; but if *I'm* old enough, you're not," she objected gaily. "I'm dying for tea—but isn't there a quieter place?"

He answered her smile, which rested on him vividly. Her discretions interested him almost as much as her imprudences: he was so sure that both were part of the same carefully-elaborated plan. In judging Miss Bart, he had always made use of the "argument from design."†

"The resources of New York are rather meagre," he said; "but I'll find a hansom first, and then we'll invent something."

He led her through the throng of returning holiday-makers, past shallow-faced girls in preposterous hats, and flat-chested women struggling with paper bundles and palm-leaf fans. Was it possible that she belonged to the same race? The dinginess, the crudity of this average section of womanhood made him feel how highly specialized she was.

A rapid shower had cooled the air, and clouds still hung refreshingly over the moist street.

"How delicious! Let us walk a little," she said as they emerged from the station.

They turned into Madison Avenue and began to stroll northward. As she moved beside him, with her long light step, Selden was conscious of taking a luxurious pleasure in her nearness: in the modelling of her little ear, the crisp upward wave of her hair—was it ever so slightly brightened by art?—and the thick planting of her straight black lashes. Everything about her was at once vigorous and exquisite, at once strong and fine. He had a confused sense that she must have cost a great deal to make, that a great many dull and ugly people must, in some

---

*Fashionable Fifth Avenue restaurant.
†In theology, finding proofs of God's existence in the natural world.

mysterious way, have been sacrificed to produce her. He was aware that the qualities distinguishing her from the herd of her sex were chiefly external: as though a fine glaze of beauty and fastidiousness had been applied to vulgar clay. Yet the analogy left him unsatisfied, for a coarse texture will not take a high finish; and was it not possible that the material was fine, but that circumstance had fashioned it into a futile shape?

As he reached this point in his speculations the sun came out, and her lifted parasol cut off his enjoyment. A moment or two later she paused with a sigh.

"Oh, dear, I'm so hot and thirsty—and what a hideous place New York is!" She looked despairingly up and down the dreary thoroughfare. "Other cities put on their best clothes in summer, but New York seems to sit in its shirt-sleeves." Her eyes wandered down one of the side-streets. "Some one has had the humanity to plant a few trees over there. Let us go into the shade."

"I am glad my street meets with your approval," said Selden as they turned the corner.

"Your street? Do you live here?"

She glanced with interest along the new brick and limestone house-fronts, fantastically varied in obedience to the American craving for novelty, but fresh and inviting with their awnings and flower-boxes.

"Ah, yes—to be sure: The Benedick.* What a nice-looking building! I don't think I've ever seen it before." She looked across at the flat-house with its marble porch and pseudo-Georgian façade. "Which are your windows? Those with the awnings down?"

"On the top floor—yes."

"And that nice little balcony is yours? How cool it looks up there!"

He paused a moment. "Come up and see," he suggested. "I can give you a cup of tea in no time—and you won't meet any bores."

---

*Apartment house for bachelors, named after the lively bachelor Benedick in William Shakespeare's *Much Ado About Nothing*. Selden, though tempted by Lily, remains a bachelor.

Her colour deepened—she still had the art of blushing at the right time—but she took the suggestion as lightly as it was made.

"Why not? It's too tempting—I'll take the risk," she declared.

"Oh, I'm not dangerous," he said in the same key. In truth, he had never liked her as well as at that moment. He knew she had accepted without afterthought: he could never be a factor in her calculations, and there was a surprise, a refreshment almost, in the spontaneity of her consent.

On the threshold he paused a moment, feeling for his latch-key.

"There's no one here; but I have a servant who is supposed to come in the mornings, and it's just possible he may have put out the tea-things and provided some cake."

He ushered her into a slip of a hall hung with old prints. She noticed the letters and notes heaped on the table among his gloves and sticks; then she found herself in a small library, dark but cheerful, with its walls of books, a pleasantly faded Turkey rug, a littered desk, and, as he had foretold, a tea-tray on a low table near the window. A breeze had sprung up, swaying inward the muslin curtains, and bringing a fresh scent of mignonette* and petunias from the flower-box on the balcony.

Lily sank with a sigh into one of the shabby leather chairs.

"How delicious to have a place like this all to one's self! What a miserable thing it is to be a woman." She leaned back in a luxury of discontent.

Selden was rummaging in a cupboard for the cake.

"Even women," he said, "have been known to enjoy the privileges of a flat."

"Oh, governesses—or widows. But not girls—not poor, miserable, marriageable girls!"

"I even know a girl who lives in a flat."

She sat up in surprise. "You do?"

"I do," he assured her emerging from the cupboard with the sought-for cake.

---

*Common garden plant with fragrant greenish-white flowers (French).

"Oh, I know—you mean Gerty Farish." She smiled a little unkindly. "But I said *marriageable*—and besides, she has a horrid little place, and no maid, and such queer things to eat. Her cook does the washing and the food tastes of soap. I should hate that, you know."

"You shouldn't dine with her on wash-days," said Selden, cutting the cake.

They both laughed, and he knelt by the table to light the lamp under the kettle, while she measured out the tea into a little tea-pot of green glaze. As he watched her hand, polished as a bit of old ivory, with its slender pink nails, and the sapphire bracelet slipping over her wrist, he was struck with the irony of suggesting to her such a life as his cousin Gertrude Farish had chosen. She was so evidently the victim of the civilization which had produced her, that the links of her bracelet seemed like manacles chaining her to her fate.

She seemed to read his thought. "It was horrid of me to say that of Gerty," she said with charming compunction. "I forgot she was your cousin. But we're so different, you know: she likes being good, and I like being happy. And besides, she is free and I am not. If I were, I daresay I could manage to be happy even in her flat. It must be pure bliss to arrange the furniture just as one likes, and give all the horrors to the ash-man. If I could only do over my aunt's drawing-room I know I should be a better woman."

"Is it so very bad?" he asked sympathetically.

She smiled at him across the tea-pot which she was holding up to be filled.

"That shows how seldom you come there. Why don't you come oftener?"

"When I do come, it's not to look at Mrs. Peniston's furniture."

"Nonsense," she said. "You don't come at all—and yet we get on so well when we meet."

"Perhaps that's the reason," he answered promptly. "I'm afraid I haven't any cream, you know—shall you mind a slice of lemon instead?"

"I shall like it better." She waited while he cut the lemon and dropped a thin disk into her cup. "But that is not the reason," she insisted.

"The reason for what?"

"For your never coming." She leaned forward with a shade of perplexity in her charming eyes. "I wish I knew—I wish I could make you out. Of course I know there are men who don't like me—one can tell that at a glance. And there are others who are afraid of me: they think I want to marry them." She smiled up at him frankly. "But I don't think you dislike me—and you can't possibly think I want to marry you."

"No—I absolve you of that," he agreed.

"Well, then——?"

He had carried his cup to the fireplace, and stood leaning against the chimney-piece and looking down on her with an air of indolent amusement. The provocation in her eyes increased his amusement—he had not supposed she would waste her powder on such small game; but perhaps she was only keeping her hand in; or perhaps a girl of her type had no conversation but of the personal kind. At any rate, she was amazingly pretty, and he had asked her to tea and must live up to his obligations.

"Well, then," he said with a plunge, "perhaps *that's* the reason."

"What?"

"The fact that you don't want to marry me. Perhaps I don't regard it as such a strong inducement to go and see you." He felt a slight shiver down his spine as he ventured this, but her laugh reassured him.

"Dear Mr. Selden, that wasn't worthy of you. It's stupid of you to make love to me, and it isn't like you to be stupid." She leaned back, sipping her tea with an air so enchantingly judicial that, if they had been in her aunt's drawing-room, he might almost have tried to disprove her deduction.

"Don't you see," she continued, "that there are men enough to say pleasant things to me, and that what I want is a friend who won't be afraid to say disagreeable ones when I need them? Sometimes I have fancied you might be that friend—I don't know why, except that you are neither a prig nor a bounder, and that I shouldn't have to pretend with you or be on my guard against you." Her voice had dropped to a note of seriousness, and she sat gazing up at him with the troubled gravity of a child.

"You don't know how much I need such a friend," she said. "My aunt is full of copy-book axioms, but they were all meant to apply to conduct in the early fifties. I always feel that to live up to them would include wearing book-muslin with gigot sleeves.* And the other women—my best friends—well, they use me or abuse me; but they don't care a straw what happens to me. I've been about too long—people are getting tired of me; they are beginning to say I ought to marry."

There was a moment's pause, during which Selden meditated one or two replies calculated to add a momentary zest to the situation; but he rejected them in favour of the simple question: "Well, why don't you?"

She coloured and laughed. "Ah, I see you *are* a friend after all, and that is one of the disagreeable things I was asking for."

"It wasn't meant to be disagreeable," he returned amicably. "Isn't marriage your vocation? Isn't it what you're all brought up for?"

She sighed. "I suppose so. What else is there?"

"Exactly. And so why not take the plunge and have it over?"

She shrugged her shoulders. "You speak as if I ought to marry the first man who came along."

"I didn't mean to imply that you are as hard put to it as that. But there must be some one with the requisite qualifications."

She shook her head wearily. "I threw away one or two good chances when I first came out—I suppose every girl does; and you know I am horribly poor—and very expensive. I must have a great deal of money."

Selden had turned to reach for a cigarette-box on the mantel-piece.

"What's become of Dillworth?" he asked.

"Oh, his mother was frightened—she was afraid I should

---

*Book-muslin is a light cotton fabric; gigot sleeves are puffed at the shoulder and narrowed at the wrist.

have all the family jewels reset. And she wanted me to promise that I wouldn't do over the drawing-room."

"The very thing you are marrying for!"

"Exactly. So she packed him off to India."

"Hard luck—but you can do better than Dillworth."

He offered the box, and she took out three or four cigarettes, putting one between her lips and slipping the others into a little gold case attached to her long pearl chain.

"Have I time? Just a whiff, then." She leaned forward, holding the tip of her cigarette to his. As she did so, he noted, with a purely impersonal enjoyment, how evenly the black lashes were set in her smooth white lids, and how the purplish shade beneath them melted into the pure pallor of the cheek.

She began to saunter about the room, examining the book-shelves between the puffs of her cigarette-smoke. Some of the volumes had the ripe tints of good tooling and old morocco,* and her eyes lingered on them caressingly, not with the appreciation of the expert, but with the pleasure in agreeable tones and textures that was one of her inmost susceptibilities. Suddenly her expression changed from desultory enjoyment to active conjecture, and she turned to Selden with a question.

"You collect, don't you—you know about first editions and things?"

"As much as a man may who has no money to spend. Now and then I pick up something in the rubbish heap; and I go and look on at the big sales."

She had again addressed herself to the shelves, but her eyes now swept them inattentively, and he saw that she was preoccupied with a new idea.

"And Americana—do you collect Americana?"

Selden stared and laughed.

"No, that's rather out of my line. I'm not really a collector, you see; I simply like to have good editions of the books I am fond of."

---

*Tooling is a reference to ornamental designs in leather; fine book-bindings are made of goatskin from Morocco.

She made a slight grimace. "And Americana are horribly dull, I suppose?"

"I should fancy so—except to the historian. But your real collector values a thing for its rarity. I don't suppose the buyers of Americana sit up reading them all night—old Jefferson Gryce certainly didn't."

She was listening with keen attention. "And yet they fetch fabulous prices, don't they? It seems so odd to want to pay a lot for an ugly badly-printed book that one is never going to read! And I suppose most of the owners of Americana are not historians either?"

"No; very few of the historians can afford to buy them. They have to use those in the public libraries or in private collections. It seems to be the mere rarity that attracts the average collector."

He had seated himself on an arm of the chair near which she was standing, and she continued to question him, asking which were the rarest volumes, whether the Jefferson Gryce collection was really considered the finest in the world, and what was the largest price ever fetched by a single volume.

It was so pleasant to sit there looking up at her, as she lifted now one book and then another from the shelves, fluttering the pages between her fingers, while her drooping profile was outlined against the warm background of old bindings, that he talked on without pausing to wonder at her sudden interest in so unsuggestive a subject. But he could never be long with her without trying to find a reason for what she was doing, and as she replaced his first edition of La Bruyère* and turned away from the bookcases, he began to ask himself what she had been driving at. Her next question was not of a nature to enlighten him. She paused before him with a smile which seemed at once designed to admit him to her familiarity, and to remind him of the restrictions it imposed.

"Don't you ever mind," she asked suddenly, "not being rich enough to buy all the books you want?"

---

*Jean de la Bruyère (1645–1696), French author of *Caractères* (1688), which makes pessimistic and ironic observations on character and conduct.

He followed her glance about the room, with its worn furniture and shabby walls.

"Don't I just? Do you take me for a saint on a pillar?"

"And having to work—do you mind that?"

"Oh, the work itself is not so bad—I'm rather fond of the law."

"No; but the being tied down: the routine—don't you ever want to get away, to see new places and people?"

"Horribly—especially when I see all my friends rushing to the steamer."

She drew a sympathetic breath. "But do you mind enough—to marry to get out of it?"

Selden broke into a laugh. "God forbid!" he declared.

She rose with a sigh, tossing her cigarette into the grate.

"Ah, there's the difference—a girl must, a man may if he chooses." She surveyed him critically. "Your coat's a little shabby—but who cares? It doesn't keep people from asking you to dine. If I were shabby no one would have me: a woman is asked out as much for her clothes as for herself. The clothes are the background, the frame, if you like: they don't make success, but they are a part of it. Who wants a dingy woman? We are expected to be pretty and well-dressed till we drop—and if we can't keep it up alone, we have to go into partnership."

Selden glanced at her with amusement: it was impossible, even with her lovely eyes imploring him, to take a sentimental view of her case.

"Ah, well, there must be plenty of capital on the lookout for such an investment. Perhaps you'll meet your fate to-night at the Trenors'."

She returned his look interrogatively.

"I thought you might be going there—oh, not in that capacity! But there are to be a lot of your set—Gwen Van Osburgh, the Wetheralls, Lady Cressida Raith—and the George Dorsets."

She paused a moment before the last name, and shot a query through her lashes; but he remained imperturbable.

"Mrs. Trenor asked me; but I can't get away till the end of the week; and those big parties bore me."

"Ah, so they do me," she exclaimed.

"Then why go?"

"It's part of the business—you forget! And besides, if I didn't, I should be playing bézique with my aunt at Richfield Springs."*

"That's almost as bad as marrying Dillworth," he agreed, and they both laughed for pure pleasure in their sudden intimacy.

She glanced at the clock.

"Dear me! I must be off. It's after five."

She paused before the mantelpiece, studying herself in the mirror while she adjusted her veil. The attitude revealed the long slope of her slender sides, which gave a kind of wild-wood grace to her outline—as though she were a captured dryad† subdued to the conventions of the drawing-room; and Selden reflected that it was the same streak of sylvan freedom in her nature that lent such savour to her artificiality.

He followed her across the room to the entrance-hall; but on the threshold she held out her hand with a gesture of leave-taking.

"It's been delightful; and now you will have to return my visit."

"But don't you want me to see you to the station?"

"No, good-bye here, please."

She let her hand lie in his a moment, smiling up at him adorably.

"Good-bye, then—and good luck at Bellomont!" he said, opening the door for her.

On the landing she paused to look about her. There were a thousand chances to one against her meeting anybody, but one could never tell, and she always paid for her rare indiscretions by a violent reaction of prudence. There was no one in sight, however, but a char-woman who was scrubbing the stairs. Her own stout person and its surrounding implements took up so much room that Lily, to pass her, had to gather up her skirts and brush against the wall. As she did so, the woman paused in her work and looked up curiously, resting her clenched red fists on the wet

---

*Bézique is a game resembling pinochle, played with sixty-four cards. Richfield Springs is a health resort with sulfur springs in central New York.

†Wood nymph in classical mythology.

cloth she had just drawn from her pail. She had a broad sallow face, slightly pitted with small-pox, and thin straw-coloured hair through which her scalp shone unpleasantly.

"I beg your pardon," said Lily, intending by her politeness to convey a criticism of the other's manner.

The woman, without answering, pushed her pail aside, and continued to stare as Miss Bart swept by with a murmur of silken linings. Lily felt herself flushing under the look. What did the creature suppose? Could one never do the simplest, the most harmless thing, without subjecting one's self to some odious conjecture? Half way down the next flight, she smiled to think that a char-woman's stare should so perturb her. The poor thing was probably dazzled by such an unwonted apparition. But *were* such apparitions unwonted on Selden's stairs? Miss Bart was not familiar with the moral code of bachelors' flat-houses, and her colour rose again as it occurred to her that the woman's persistent gaze implied a groping among past associations. But she put aside the thought with a smile at her own fears, and hastened downward, wondering if she should find a cab short of Fifth Avenue.

Under the Georgian porch she paused again, scanning the street for a hansom.* None was in sight, but as she reached the sidewalk she ran against a small glossy-looking man with a gardenia in his coat, who raised his hat with a surprised exclamation.

"Miss Bart? Well—of all people! This *is* luck," he declared; and she caught a twinkle of amused curiosity between his screwed-up lids.

"Oh, Mr. Rosedale—how are you?" she said, perceiving that the irrepressible annoyance on her face was reflected in the sudden intimacy of his smile.

Mr. Rosedale stood scanning her with interest and approval. He was a plump rosy man of the blond Jewish type, with smart London clothes fitting him like upholstery, and small sidelong eyes which gave him the air of appraising people as if they were

---

*Two-wheeled, horse-drawn closed carriage for two passengers.

bric-a-brac. He glanced up interrogatively at the porch of the Benedick.

"Been up to town for a little shopping, I suppose?" he said, in a tone which had the familiarity of a touch.

Miss Bart shrank from it slightly, and then flung herself into precipitate explanations.

"Yes—I came up to see my dress-maker. I am just on my way to catch the train to the Trenors'."

"Ah—your dress-maker; just so," he said blandly: "I didn't know there were any dress-makers in the Benedick."

"The Benedick?" She looked gently puzzled. "Is that the name of this building?"

"Yes, that's the name: I believe it's an old word for bachelor, isn't it? I happen to own the building—that's the way I know." His smile deepened as he added with increasing assurance: "But you must let me take you to the station. The Trenors are at Bellomont, of course? You've barely time to catch the five-forty. The dress-maker kept you waiting, I suppose."

Lily stiffened under the pleasantry.

"Oh, thanks," she stammered; and at that moment her eye caught a hansom drifting down Madison Avenue, and she hailed it with a desperate gesture.

"You're very kind; but I couldn't think of troubling you," she said, extending her hand to Mr. Rosedale; and heedless of his protestations, she sprang into the rescuing vehicle, and called out a breathless order to the driver.

2

IN THE HANSOM SHE leaned back with a sigh.

Why must a girl pay so dearly for her least escape from routine? Why could one never do a natural thing without having to screen it behind a structure of artifice? She had yielded to a passing impulse in going to Lawrence Selden's rooms, and it was so seldom that she could allow herself the luxury of an impulse! This one, at any rate, was going to cost her rather more than she could afford. She was vexed to see that, in spite of so many years of vigilance, she had blundered twice within five minutes. That stupid story about her dress-maker was bad enough—it would have been so simple to tell Rosedale that she had been taking tea with Selden! The mere statement of the fact would have rendered it innocuous. But, after having let herself be surprised in a falsehood, it was doubly stupid to snub the witness of her discomfiture. If she had had the presence of mind to let Rosedale drive her to the station, the concession might have purchased his silence. He had his race's accuracy in the appraisal of values, and to be seen walking down the platform at the crowded afternoon hour in the company of Miss Lily Bart would have been money in his pocket, as he might himself have phrased it. He knew, of course, that there would be a large house-party at Bellomont, and the possibility of being taken for one of Mrs. Trenor's guests was doubtless included in his calculations. Mr. Rosedale was still at a stage in his social ascent when it was of importance to produce such impressions.

The provoking part was that Lily knew all this—knew how easy it would have been to silence him on the spot, and how difficult it might be to do so afterward. Mr. Simon Rosedale was a man who made it his business to know everything about every one, whose idea of showing himself to be at home in society was to display an inconvenient familiarity with the habits of those with whom he wished to be thought intimate. Lily was sure that within twenty-four hours the story of her visiting her dress-maker at the Benedick would be in active circulation among Mr. Rosedale's acquaintances. The worst of it was that she had always snubbed and ignored him. On his first appearance—when her improvident cousin, Jack Stepney, had obtained for him (in return for favours too easily guessed) a card to one of the vast impersonal Van Osburgh "crushes"*—Rosedale, with that mixture of artistic sensibility and business astuteness which characterizes his race, had instantly gravitated toward Miss Bart. She understood his motives, for her own course was guided by as nice calculations. Training and experience had taught her to be hospitable to newcomers, since the most unpromising might be useful later on, and there were plenty of available *oubliettes*† to swallow them if they were not. But some intuitive repugnance, getting the better of years of social discipline, had made her push Mr. Rosedale into his *oubliette* without a trial. He had left behind only the ripple of amusement which his speedy despatch had caused among her friends; and though later (to shift the metaphor) he reappeared lower down the stream, it was only in fleeting glimpses, with long submergences between.

Hitherto Lily had been undisturbed by scruples. In her little set Mr. Rosedale had been pronounced "impossible," and Jack Stepney roundly snubbed for his attempt to pay his debts in dinner invitations. Even Mrs. Trenor, whose taste for variety had led her into some hazardous experiments, resisted Jack's attempts to disguise Mr. Rosedale as a novelty, and declared that he was the same little Jew who had been served up and rejected at the social board a dozen times within her memory; and while Judy Trenor was obdurate there was small chance of Mr. Rosedale's penetrating beyond the outer limbo of the Van Osburgh crushes. Jack gave up the contest with a laughing "You'll see," and, sticking manfully to his guns, showed himself with Rosedale at the fashionable restaurants, in company with the personally vivid if socially obscure ladies who are available for such purposes. But

---

*Crowded social events.
†Secret dungeon with a trap door in its ceiling (French).

the attempt had hitherto been vain, and as Rosedale undoubt-
edly paid for the dinners, the laugh remained with his debtor.

Mr. Rosedale, it will be seen, was thus far not a factor to be
feared—unless one put one's self in his power. And this was precisely what Miss Bart had done. Her clumsy fib had let him see
that she had something to conceal; and she was sure he had a score
to settle with her. Something in his smile told her he had not forgotten. She turned from the thought with a little shiver, but it hung
on her all the way to the station, and dogged her down the platform with the persistency of Mr. Rosedale himself.

She had just time to take her seat before the train started; but
having arranged herself in her corner with the instinctive feeling
for effect which never forsook her, she glanced about in the hope
of seeing some other member of the Trenors' party. She wanted
to get away from herself, and conversation was the only means
of escape that she knew.

Her search was rewarded by the discovery of a very blond
young man with a soft reddish beard, who, at the other end of the
carriage, appeared to be dissembling himself behind an unfolded
newspaper. Lily's eye brightened, and a faint smile relaxed the
drawn lines of her mouth. She had known that Mr. Percy Gryce
was to be at Bellomont, but she had not counted on the luck of
having him to herself in the train; and the fact banished all per-
turbing thoughts of Mr. Rosedale. Perhaps, after all, the day was
to end more favourably than it had begun.

She began to cut the pages of a novel,* tranquilly studying
her prey through downcast lashes while she organized a method
of attack. Something in his attitude of conscious absorption told
her that he was aware of her presence: no one had ever been
quite so engrossed in an evening paper! She guessed that he was
too shy to come up to her, and that she would have to devise
some means of approach which should not appear to be an advance on her part. It amused her to think that any one as rich as
Mr. Percy Gryce should be shy; but she was gifted with treasures
of indulgence for such idiosyncrasies, and besides, his timidity

---

*At one time, book pages were folded together and had to be slit with
a knife.

might serve her purpose better than too much assurance. She had the art of giving self-confidence to the embarrassed, but she was not equally sure of being able to embarrass the self-confident.

She waited till the train had emerged from the tunnel and was racing between the ragged edges of the northern suburbs. Then, as it lowered its speed near Yonkers, she rose from her seat and drifted slowly down the carriage. As she passed Mr. Gryce, the train gave a lurch, and he was aware of a slender hand gripping the back of his chair. He rose with a start, his ingenuous face looking as though it had been dipped in crimson: even the reddish tint in his beard seemed to deepen.

The train swayed again, almost flinging Miss Bart into his arms. She steadied herself with a laugh and drew back; but he was enveloped in the scent of her dress, and his shoulder had felt her fugitive touch.

"Oh, Mr. Gryce, is it you? I'm so sorry—I was trying to find the porter and get some tea."

She held out her hand as the train resumed its level rush, and they stood exchanging a few words in the aisle. Yes—he was going to Bellomont. He had heard she was to be of the party—he blushed again as he admitted it. And was he to be there for a whole week? How delightful!

But at this point one or two belated passengers from the last station forced their way into the carriage, and Lily had to retreat to her seat.

"The chair next to mine is empty—do take it," she said over her shoulder; and Mr. Gryce, with considerable embarrassment, succeeded in effecting an exchange which enabled him to transport himself and his bags to her side.

"Ah—and here is the porter, and perhaps we can have some tea."

She signalled to that official, and in a moment, with the ease that seemed to attend the fulfilment of all her wishes, a little table had been set up between the seats, and she had helped Mr. Gryce to bestow his encumbering properties beneath it.

When the tea came he watched her in silent fascination while her hands flitted above the tray, looking miraculously fine and slender in contrast to the coarse china and lumpy bread. It seemed wonderful to him that any one should perform with such careless ease the difficult task of making tea in public in a lurching train. He would never have dared to order it for himself, lest he should attract the notice of his fellow-passengers; but, secure in the shelter of her conspicuousness, he sipped the inky draught with a delicious sense of exhilaration.

Lily, with the flavour of Selden's caravan tea* on her lips, had no great fancy to drown it in the railway brew which seemed such nectar to her companion; but, rightly judging that one of the charms of tea is the fact of drinking it together, she proceeded to give the last touch to Mr. Gryce's enjoyment by smiling at him across her lifted cup.

"Is it quite right—I haven't made it too strong?" she asked solicitously; and he replied with conviction that he had never tasted better tea.

"I daresay it is true," she reflected; and her imagination was fired by the thought that Mr. Gryce, who might have sounded the depths of the most complex self-indulgence, was perhaps actually taking his first journey alone with a pretty woman.

It struck her as providential that she should be the instrument of his initiation. Some girls would not have known how to manage him. They would have over-emphasized the novelty of the adventure, trying to make him feel in it the zest of an escapade. But Lily's methods were more delicate. She remembered that her cousin Jack Stepney had once defined Mr. Gryce as the young man who had promised his mother never to go out in the rain without his overshoes; and acting on this hint, she resolved to impart a gently domestic air to the scene, in the hope that her companion, instead of feeling that he was doing something reckless or unusual, would merely be led to dwell on the advantage of always having a companion to make one's tea in the train.

But in spite of her efforts, conversation flagged after the tray had been removed, and she was driven to take a fresh measurement of Mr. Gryce's limitations. It was not, after all, opportunity but imagination that he lacked: he had a mental palate which would never learn to distinguish between railway tea and nectar.

---

*Blend of black China teas.

There was, however, one topic she could rely on: one spring that she had only to touch to set his simple machinery in motion. She had refrained from touching it because it was a last resource, and she had relied on other arts to stimulate other sensations; but as a settled look of dulness began to creep over his candid features, she saw that extreme measures were necessary.

"And how," she said, leaning forward, "are you getting on with your Americana?"

His eye became a degree less opaque: it was as though an incipient film had been removed from it, and she felt the pride of a skilful operator.

"I've got a few new things," he said, suffused with pleasure, but lowering his voice as though he feared his fellow-passengers might be in league to despoil him.

She returned a sympathetic enquiry, and gradually he was drawn on to talk of his latest purchases. It was the one subject which enabled him to forget himself, or allowed him, rather, to remember himself without constraint, because he was at home in it, and could assert a superiority that there were few to dispute. Hardly any of his acquaintances cared for Americana, or knew anything about them; and the consciousness of this ignorance threw Mr. Gryce's knowledge into agreeable relief. The only difficulty was to introduce the topic and to keep it to the front; most people showed no desire to have their ignorance dispelled, and Mr. Gryce was like a merchant whose warehouses are crammed with an unmarketable commodity.

But Miss Bart, it appeared, really did want to know about Americana; and moreover, she was already sufficiently informed to make the task of farther instruction as easy as it was agreeable. She questioned him intelligently, she heard him submissively; and, prepared for the look of lassitude which usually crept over his listeners' faces, he grew eloquent under her receptive gaze. The "points" she had had the presence of mind to glean from Selden, in anticipation of this very contingency, were serving her to such good purpose that she began to think her visit to him had been the luckiest incident of the day. She had once more shown her talent for profiting by the unexpected, and dangerous theories as to the advisability of yielding to impulse were germinating under the surface of smiling attention which she continued to present to her companion.

Mr. Gryce's sensations, if less definite, were equally agreeable. He felt his confused titillation with which the lower organisms welcome the gratification of their needs, and all his senses floundered in a vague well-being, through which Miss Bart's personality was dimly but pleasantly perceptible.

Mr. Gryce's interest in Americana had not originated with himself: it was impossible to think of him as evolving any taste of his own. An uncle had left him a collection already noted among bibliophiles; the existence of the collection was the only fact that had ever shed glory on the name of Gryce, and the nephew took as much pride in his inheritance as though it had been his own work. Indeed, he gradually came to regard it as such, and to feel a sense of personal complacency when he chanced on any reference to the Gryce Americana. Anxious as he was to avoid personal notice, he took, in the printed mention of his name, a pleasure so exquisite and excessive that it seemed a compensation for his shrinking from publicity.

To enjoy the sensation as often as possible, he subscribed to all the reviews dealing with book-collecting in general, and American history in particular, and as allusions to his library abounded in the pages of these journals, which formed his only reading, he came to regard himself as figuring prominently in the public eye, and to enjoy the thought of the interest which would be excited if the persons he met in the street, or sat among in travelling, were suddenly to be told that he was the possessor of the Gryce Americana.

Most timidities have such secret compensations, and Miss Bart was discerning enough to know that the inner vanity is generally in proportion to the outer self-deprecation. With a more confident person she would not have dared to dwell so long on one topic, or to show such exaggerated interest in it; but she had rightly guessed that Mr. Gryce's egoism was a thirsty soil, requiring constant nurture from without. Miss Bart had the gift of following an undercurrent of thought while she appeared to be sailing on the surface of conversation; and in this case her mental excursion took the form of a rapid survey of Mr. Percy Gryce's future as combined with her own. The Gryces were from

Albany, and but lately introduced to the metropolis, where the
mother and son had come, after old Jefferson Gryce's death, to
take possession of his house in Madison Avenue—an appalling
house, all brown stone without and black walnut within, with
the Gryce library in a fire-proof annex that looked like a mau-
soleum. Lily, however, knew all about them: young Mr. Gryce's
arrival had fluttered the maternal breasts of New York, and when
a girl has no mother to palpitate for her she must needs be on
the alert for herself. Lily, therefore, had not only contrived to put
herself in the young man's way, but had made the acquaintance
of Mrs. Gryce, a monumental woman with the voice of a pulpit
orator and a mind preoccupied with the iniquities of her servants, who came sometimes to sit with Mrs. Peniston and learn
from that lady how she managed to prevent the kitchen-maid's
smuggling groceries out of the house. Mrs. Gryce had a kind of
impersonal benevolence: cases of individual need she regarded
with suspicion, but she subscribed to Institutions when their annual reports showed an impressive surplus. Her domestic duties
were manifold, for they extended from furtive inspections of the
servants' bedrooms to unannounced descents to the cellar; but
she had never allowed herself many pleasures. Once, however,
she had had a special edition of the Sarum Rule* printed in
rubric and presented to every clergyman in the diocese; and the
gilt album in which their letters of thanks were pasted formed
the chief ornament of her drawing-room table.

Percy had been brought up in the principles which so excellent a woman was sure to inculcate. Every form of prudence and
suspicion had been grafted on a nature originally reluctant and
cautious, with the result that it would have seemed hardly needful for Mrs. Gryce to extract his promise about the over-shoes,
so little likely was he to hazard himself abroad in the rain. After
attaining his majority, and coming into the fortune which the
late Mr. Gryce had made out of a patent device for excluding

---

*The reference is to "Sarum Use," the order of divine service used in
the English diocese of Salisbury (which traces its roots to the nearby
Iron Age settlement of Old Sarum) from the Middle Ages to the Re-
formation.

fresh air from hotels, the young man continued to live with his mother in Albany; but on Jefferson Gryce's death, when another large property passed into her son's hands, Mrs. Gryce thought that what she called his "interests" demanded his presence in New York. She accordingly installed herself in the Madison Avenue house, and Percy, whose sense of duty was not inferior to his mother's, spent all his week days in the handsome Broad St reet office where a batch of pale men on small salaries had grown grey in the management of the Gryce estate, and where he was initiated with becoming reverence into every detail of the art of accumulation.

As far as Lily could learn, this had hitherto been Mr. Gryce's only occupation, and she might have been pardoned for thinking it not too hard a task to interest a young man who had been kept on such low diet. At any rate, she felt herself so completely in command of the situation that she yielded to a sense of security in which all fear of Mr. Rosedale, and of the difficulties on which that fear was contingent, vanished beyond the edge of thought.

The stopping of the train at Garrisons would not have distracted her from these thoughts, had she not caught a sudden look of distress in her companion's eye. His seat faced toward the door, and she guessed that he had been perturbed by the approach of an acquaintance; a fact confirmed by the turning of heads and general sense of commotion which her own entrance into a railway-carriage was apt to produce.

She knew the symptoms at once, and was not surprised to be hailed by the high notes of a pretty woman, who entered the train accompanied by a maid, a bull-terrier, and a footman staggering under a load of bags and dressing-cases.

"Oh, Lily—are you going to Bellomont? Then you can't let me have your seat, I suppose? But I *must* have a seat in this carriage—porter, you must find me a place at once. Can't some one be put somewhere else? I want to be with my friends. Oh, how do you do, Mr. Gryce? Do please make him understand that I must have a seat next to you and Lily."

Mrs. George Dorset, regardless of the mild efforts of a traveller with a carpet-bag, who was doing his best to make room for her by getting out of the train, stood in the middle of the aisle,

diffusing about her that general sense of exasperation which a
pretty woman on her travels not infrequently creates.

She was smaller and thinner than Lily Bart, with a restless
pliability of pose, as if she could have been crumpled up and run
through a ring, like the sinuous draperies she affected. Her small
pale face seemed the mere setting of a pair of dark exaggerated
eyes, of which the visionary gaze contrasted curiously with her
self-assertive tone and gestures; so that, as one of her friends observed, she was like a disembodied spirit who took up a great
deal of room.

Having finally discovered that the seat adjoining Miss Bart's
was at her disposal, she possessed herself of it with a farther dis-
placement of her surroundings, explaining meanwhile that she
had come across from Mount Kisco* in her motor-car that
morning, and had been kicking her heels for an hour at Garrisons, without even the alleviation of a cigarette, her brute of a
husband having neglected to replenish her case before they
parted that morning.

"And at this hour of the day I don't suppose you've a single
one left, have you, Lily?" she plaintively concluded.

Miss Bart caught the startled glance of Mr. Percy Gryce,
whose own lips were never defiled by tobacco.

"What an absurd question, Bertha!" she exclaimed, blushing
at the thought of the store she had laid in at Lawrence Selden's.

"Why, don't you smoke? Since when have you given it up?
What—you never— And you don't either, Mr. Gryce? Ah, of
course—how stupid of me—I understand."

And Mrs. Dorset leaned back against her travelling cushions
with a smile which made Lily wish there had been no vacant seat
beside her own.

---

*Once fashionable suburb of New York City, in Westchester County.

3

BRIDGE AT BELLOMONT USUALLY lasted till the small hours; and when Lily went to bed that night she had played too long for her own good.

Feeling no desire for the self-communion which awaited her in her room, she lingered on the broad stairway, looking down into the hall below, where the last card-players were grouped about the tray of tall glasses and silver-collared decanters* which the butler had just placed on a low table near the fire.

The hall was arcaded, with a gallery supported on columns of pale yellow marble. Tall clumps of flowering plants were grouped against a background of dark foliage in the angles of the walls. On the crimson carpet a deer-hound and two or three spaniels dozed luxuriously before the fire, and the light from the great central lantern overhead shed a brightness on the women's hair and struck sparks from their jewels as they moved.

There were moments when such scenes delighted Lily, when they gratified her sense of beauty and her craving for the external finish of life; there were others when they gave a sharper edge to the meagreness of her own opportunities. This was one of the moments when the sense of contrast was uppermost, and she turned away impatiently as Mrs. George Dorset, glittering in serpentine spangles, drew Percy Gryce in her wake to a confidential nook beneath the gallery.

It was not that Miss Bart was afraid of losing her newly-acquired hold over Mr. Gryce. Mrs. Dorset might startle or dazzle him, but she had neither the skill nor the patience to effect his

---

*Cut-glass decanters containing whiskey, wine, and liqueurs, identified with silver-chained labels.

capture. She was too self-engrossed to penetrate the recesses of his shyness, and besides, why should she care to give herself the trouble? At most it might amuse her to make sport of his simplicity for an evening—after that he would be merely a burden to her, and knowing this, she was far too experienced to encourage him. But the mere thought of that other woman, who could take a man up and toss him aside as she willed, without having to regard him as a possible factor in her plans, filled Lily Bart with envy. She had been bored all the afternoon by Percy Gryce—the mere thought seemed to waken an echo of his droning voice—but she could not ignore him on the morrow, she must follow up her success, must submit to more boredom, must be ready with fresh compliances and adaptabilities, and all on the bare chance that he might ultimately decide to do her the honour of boring her for life.

It was a hateful fate—but how escape from it? What choice had she? To be herself, or a Gerty Farish. As she entered her bedroom, with its softly-shaded lights, her lace dressing-gown lying across the silken bedspread, her little embroidered slippers before the fire, a vase of carnations filling the air with perfume, and the last novels and magazines lying uncut on a table beside the reading-lamp, she had a vision of Miss Farish's cramped flat, with its cheap conveniences and hideous wall-papers. No; she was not made for mean and shabby surroundings, for the squalid compromises of poverty. Her whole being dilated in an atmosphere of luxury; it was the background she required, the only climate she could breathe in. But the luxury of others was not what she wanted. A few years ago it had sufficed her: she had taken her daily meed of pleasures without caring who provided it. Now she was beginning to chafe at the obligations it imposed, to feel herself a mere pensioner on the splendour which had once seemed to belong to her. There were even moments when she was conscious of having to pay her way.

For a long time she had refused to play bridge. She knew she could not afford it, and she was afraid of acquiring so expensive a taste. She had seen the danger exemplified in more than one of her associates—in young Ned Silverton, for instance, the charming fair boy now seated in abject rapture at the elbow of Mrs. Fisher, a striking divorcée with eyes and gowns as emphatic as the head-lines of her "case."* Lily could remember when young Silverton had stumbled into their circle, with the air of a strayed Arcadian† who has published charming sonnets in his college journal. Since then he had developed a taste for Mrs. Fisher and bridge, and the latter at least had involved him in expenses from which he had been more than once rescued by harassed maiden sisters, who treasured the sonnets, and went without sugar in their tea to keep their darling afloat. Ned's case was familiar to Lily: she had seen his charming eyes—which had a good deal more poetry in them than the sonnets—change from surprise to amusement, and from amusement to anxiety, as he passed under the spell of the terrible god of chance; and she was afraid of discovering the same symptoms in her own case.

For in the last year she had found that her hostesses expected her to take a place at the card-table. It was one of the taxes she had to pay for their prolonged hospitality, and for the dresses and trinkets which occasionally replenished her insufficient wardrobe. And since she had played regularly the passion had grown on her. Once or twice of late she had won a large sum, and instead of keeping it against future losses, had spent it in dress or jewelry; and the desire to atone for this imprudence, combined with the increasing exhilaration of the game, drove her to risk higher stakes at each fresh venture. She tried to excuse herself on the plea that, in the Trenor set, if one played at all one must either play high or be set down as priggish or stingy; but she knew that the gambling passion was upon her, and that in her present surroundings there was small hope of resisting it.

Tonight the luck had been persistently bad, and the little gold purse which hung among her trinkets was almost empty when she returned to her room. She unlocked the wardrobe, and taking out her jewel-case, looked under the tray for the roll of bills from which she had replenished the purse before going down to dinner. Only twenty dollars were left: the discovery was so startling that

---

*Her divorce case.

†Referring to a mountainous region in ancient Greece, symbolic of pastoral innocence.

for a moment she fancied she must have been robbed. Then she took paper and pencil, and seating herself at the writing-table, tried to reckon up what she had spent during the day. Her head was throbbing with fatigue, and she had to go over the figures again and again; but at last it became clear to her that she had lost three hundred dollars at cards. She took out her cheque-book to see if her balance was larger than she remembered, but found she had erred in the other direction. Then she returned to her calculations; but figure as she would, she could not conjure back the vanished three hundred dollars. It was the sum she had set aside to pacify her dress-maker—unless she should decide to use it as a sop to the jeweller. At any rate, she had so many uses for it that its very insufficiency had caused her to play high in the hope of doubling it. But of course she had lost—she who needed every penny, while Bertha Dorset, whose husband showered money on her, must have pocketed at least five hundred, and Judy Trenor, who could have afforded to lose a thousand a night, had left the table clutching such a heap of bills that she had been unable to shake hands with her guests when they bade her good night.

A world in which such things could be seemed a miserable place to Lily Bart; but then she had never been able to understand the laws of a universe which was so ready to leave her out of its calculations.

She began to undress without ringing for her maid, whom she had sent to bed. She had been long enough in bondage to other people's pleasure to be considerate of those who depended on hers, and in her bitter moods it sometimes struck her that she and her maid were in the same position, except that the latter received her wages more regularly.

As she sat before the mirror brushing her hair, her face looked hollow and pale, and she was frightened by two little lines near her mouth, faint flaws in the smooth curve of the cheek.

"Oh, I must stop worrying!" she exclaimed. "Unless it's the electric light—" she reflected, springing up from her seat and lighting the candles on the dressing-table.

She turned out the wall-lights, and peered at herself between the candle-flames. The white oval of her face swam out waveringly from a background of shadows, the uncertain light blurring it like a haze; but the two lines about the mouth remained.

Lily rose and undressed in haste.

"It is only because I am tired and have such odious things to think about," she kept repeating; and it seemed an added injustice that petty cares should leave a trace on the beauty which was her only defence against them.

But the odious things were there, and remained with her. She returned wearily to the thought of Percy Gryce, as a wayfarer picks up a heavy load and toils on after a brief rest. She was almost sure she had "landed" him: a few days' work and she would win her reward. But the reward itself seemed unpalatable just then: she could get no zest from the thought of victory. It would be a rest from worry, no more—and how little that would have seemed to her a few years earlier! Her ambitions had shrunk gradually in the desiccating air of failure. But why had she failed? Was it her own fault or that of destiny?

She remembered how her mother, after they had lost their money, used to say to her with a kind of fierce vindictiveness: "But you'll get it all back—you'll get it all back, with your face." . . . The remembrance roused a whole train of association, and she lay in the darkness reconstructing the past out of which her present had grown.

A house in which no one ever dined at home unless there was "company"; a door-bell perpetually ringing; a hall-table showered with square envelopes which were opened in haste, and oblong envelopes* which were allowed to gather dust in the depths of a bronze jar; a series of French and English maids giving warning amid a chaos of hurriedly-ransacked wardrobes and dress-closets; an equally changing dynasty of nurses and footmen; quarrels in the pantry, the kitchen and the drawing-room; precipitate trips to Europe, and returns with gorged trunks and days of interminable unpacking; semi-annual discussions as to where the summer should be spent, grey interludes of economy

---

*Social invitations traditionally came in square envelopes; bills came in oblong envelopes.

and brilliant reactions of expense—such was the setting of Lily
Bart's first memories.

Ruling the turbulent element called home was the vigorous
and determined figure of a mother still young enough to dance
her ball-dresses to rags, while the hazy outline of a neutral-
tinted father filled an intermediate space between the butler and
the man who came to wind the clocks. Even to the eyes of in-
fancy, Mrs. Hudson Bart had appeared young; but Lily could not
recall the time when her father had not been bald and slightly
stooping, with streaks of grey in his hair, and a tired walk. It was
a shock to her to learn afterward that he was but two years older
than her mother.

Lily seldom saw her father by daylight. All day he was "down
town"; and in winter it was long after nightfall when she heard his
fagged step on the stairs and his hand on the school-room door.
He would kiss her in silence, and ask one or two questions of the
nurse or the governess; then Mrs. Bart's maid would come to remind him that he was dining out, and he would hurry away with
a nod to Lily. In summer, when he joined them for a Sunday at
Newport or Southampton,* he was even more effaced and silent
than in winter. It seemed to tire him to rest, and he would sit for
hours staring at the sea-line from a quiet corner of the verandah,
while the clatter of his wife's existence went on unheeded a few
feet off. Generally, however, Mrs. Bart and Lily went to Europe
for the summer, and before the steamer was half way over Mr.
Bart had dipped below the horizon. Sometimes his daughter
heard him denounced for having neglected to forward Mrs. Bart's
remittances; but for the most part he was never mentioned or
thought of till his patient stooping figure presented itself on the
New York dock as a buffer between the magnitude of his wife's
luggage and the restrictions of the American custom-house.

In this desultory yet agitated fashion life went on through
Lily's teens: a zig-zag broken course down which the family craft
glided on a rapid current of amusement, tugged at by the under-
flow of a perpetual need—the need of more money. Lily could
not recall the time when there had been money enough, and in

---

*Southampton is a fashionable resort on Long Island.

some vague way her father seemed always to blame for the defi-
ciency. It could certainly not be the fault of Mrs. Bart, who was
spoken of by her friends as a "wonderful manager." Mrs. Bart
was famous for the unlimited effect she produced on limited
means; and to the lady and her acquaintances there was something heroic in living as though one were much richer than one's
bankbook denoted.

Lily was naturally proud of her mother's aptitude in this line:
she had been brought up in the faith that, whatever it cost, one
must have a good cook, and be what Mrs. Bart called "decently
dressed." Mrs. Bart's worst reproach to her husband was to ask
him if he expected her to "live like a pig"; and his replying in the
negative was always regarded as a justification for cabling to Paris
for an extra dress or two, and telephoning to the jeweller that he
might, after all, send home the turquoise bracelet which Mrs.
Bart had looked at that morning.

Lily knew people who "lived like pigs," and their appearance
and surroundings justified her mother's repugnance to that form
of existence. They were mostly cousins, who inhabited dingy
houses with engravings from Cole's *Voyage of Life** on the drawing-room walls, and slatternly parlour-maids who said "I'll go
and see" to visitors calling at an hour when all right-minded persons are conventionally if not actually out. The disgusting part
of it was that many of these cousins were rich, so that Lily im-
bibed the idea that if people lived like pigs it was from choice,
and through the lack of any proper standard of conduct. This
gave her a sense of reflected superiority, and she did not need
Mrs. Bart's comments on the family frumps and misers to foster
her naturally lively taste for splendour.

Lily was nineteen when circumstances caused her to revise
her view of the universe.

The previous year she had made a dazzling début fringed by
a heavy thunder-cloud of bills. The light of the début still lingered on the horizon, but the cloud had thickened; and suddenly
it broke. The suddenness added to the horror; and there were

---

*Thomas Cole (1801–1848), leading artist of the Hudson River
school, painted the allegorical *The Voyage of Life* (1840).

still times when Lily relived with painful vividness every detail
of the day on which the blow fell. She and her mother had been
seated at the luncheon-table, over the *chaufroix** and cold salmon
of the previous night's dinner: it was one of Mrs. Bart's few
economies to consume in private the expensive remnants of her
hospitality. Lily was feeling the pleasant languor which is youth's
penalty for dancing till dawn; but her mother, in spite of a few
lines about the mouth, and under the yellow waves on her temples, was as alert, determined and high in colour as if she had
risen from an untroubled sleep.

In the centre of the table, between the melting *marrons glacés*†
and candied cherries, a pyramid of American Beauties‡ lifted
their vigorous stems; they held their heads as high as Mrs. Bart,
but their rose-colour had turned to a dissipated purple, and
Lily's sense of fitness was disturbed by their reappearance on the
luncheon-table.

"I really think, mother," she said reproachfully, "we might afford a few fresh flowers for luncheon. Just some jonquils or
lilies-of-the-valley——"

Mrs. Bart stared. Her own fastidiousness had its eye fixed on
the world, and she did not care how the luncheon-table looked
when there was no one present at it but the family. But she
smiled at her daughter's innocence.

"Lilies-of-the-valley," she said calmly, "cost two dollars a
dozen at this season."

Lily was not impressed. She knew very little of the value of
money.

"It would not take more than six dozen to fill that bowl," she
argued.

"Six dozen what?" asked her father's voice in the doorway.

The two women looked up in surprise; though it was a Saturday, the sight of Mr. Bart at luncheon was an unwonted one.
But neither his wife nor his daughter was sufficiently interested
to ask an explanation.

---

*Cooked jellied chicken, served cold (French).
†Candied chestnuts (French).
‡American variety of rose, with large crimson blossoms.

Mr. Bart dropped into a chair, and sat gazing absently at the fragment of jellied salmon which the butler had placed before him.

"I was only saying," Lily began, "that I hate to see faded flowers at luncheon; and mother says a bunch of lilies-of-the-valley would not cost more than twelve dollars. Mayn't I tell the florist to send a few every day?"

She leaned confidently toward her father: he seldom refused her anything, and Mrs. Bart had taught her to plead with him when her own entreaties failed.

Mr. Bart sat motionless, his gaze still fixed on the salmon, and his lower jaw dropped; he looked even paler than usual, and his thin hair lay in untidy streaks on his forehead. Suddenly he looked at his daughter and laughed. The laugh was so strange that Lily coloured under it: she disliked being ridiculed, and her father seemed to see something ridiculous in the request. Perhaps he thought it foolish that she should trouble him about such a trifle.

"Twelve dollars—twelve dollars a day for flowers? Oh, certainly, my dear—give him an order for twelve hundred." He continued to laugh.

Mrs. Bart gave him a quick glance.

"You needn't wait, Poleworth—I will ring for you," she said to the butler.

The butler withdrew with an air of silent disapproval, leaving the remains of the *chaufroix* on the sideboard.

"What is the matter, Hudson? Are you ill?" said Mrs. Bart severely.

She had no tolerance for scenes which were not of her own making, and it was odious to her that her husband should make a show of himself before the servants.

"Are you ill?" he repeated.

"Ill?—No, I'm ruined," he said.

Lily made a frightened sound, and Mrs. Bart rose to her feet.

"Ruined—?" she cried; but controlling herself instantly, she turned a calm face to Lily.

"Shut the pantry door," she said.

Lily obeyed, and when she turned back into the room her father was sitting with both elbows on the table, the plate of salmon between them, and his head bowed on his hands.

Mrs. Bart stood over him with a white face which made her hair unnaturally yellow. She looked at Lily as the latter approached: her look was terrible, but her voice was modulated to a ghastly cheerfulness.

"Your father is not well—he doesn't know what he is saying. It is nothing—but you had better go upstairs; and don't talk to the servants," she added.

Lily obeyed; she always obeyed when her mother spoke in that voice. She had not been deceived by Mrs. Bart's words: she knew at once that they were ruined. In the dark hours which followed, that awful fact overshadowed even her father's slow and difficult dying. To his wife he no longer counted: he had become extinct when he ceased to fulfil his purpose, and she sat at his side with the provisional air of a traveller who waits for a belated train to start. Lily's feelings were softer: she pitied him in a frightened ineffectual way. But the fact that he was for the most part unconscious, and that his attention, when she stole into the room, drifted away from her after a moment, made him even more of a stranger than in the nursery days when he had never come home till after dark. She seemed always to have seen him through a blur—first of sleepiness, then of distance and indifference—and now the fog had thickened till he was almost indistinguishable. If she could have performed any little services for him, or have exchanged with him a few of those affecting words which an extensive perusal of fiction had led her to connect with such occasions, the filial instinct might have stirred in her; but her pity, finding no active expression, remained in a state of spectatorship, overshadowed by her mother's grim unflagging resentment. Every look and act of Mrs. Bart's seemed to say: "You are sorry for him now—but you will feel differently when you see what he has done to us."

It was a relief to Lily when her father died.

Then a long winter set in. There was a little money left, but to Mrs. Bart it seemed worse than nothing—the mere mockery of what she was entitled to. What was the use of living if one had to live like a pig? She sank into a kind of furious apathy, a state of inert anger against fate. Her faculty for "managing" deserted her, or she no longer took sufficient pride in it to exert it. It was well enough to "manage" when by so doing one could keep one's own carriage; but when one's best contrivance did not conceal the fact that one had to go on foot, the effort was no longer worth making.

Lily and her mother wandered from place to place, now paying long visits to relations whose house-keeping Mrs. Bart criticized, and who deplored the fact that she let Lily breakfast in bed when the girl had no prospects before her, and now vegetating in cheap continental refuges, where Mrs. Bart held herself fiercely aloof from the frugal tea-tables of her companions in misfortune. She was especially careful to avoid her old friends and the scenes of her former successes. To be poor seemed to her such a confession of failure that it amounted to disgrace; and she detected a note of condescension in the friendliest advances.

Only one thought consoled her, and that was the contemplation of Lily's beauty. She studied it with a kind of passion, as though it were some weapon she had slowly fashioned for her vengeance. It was the last asset in their fortunes, the nucleus around which their life was to be rebuilt. She watched it jealously, as though it were her own property and Lily its mere custodian; and she tried to instil into the latter a sense of the responsibility that such a charge involved. She followed in imagination the career of other beauties, pointing out to her daughter what might be achieved through such a gift, and dwelling on the awful warning of those who, in spite of it, had failed to get what they wanted: to Mrs. Bart, only stupidity could explain the lamentable dénouement of some of her examples. She was not above the inconsistency of charging fate, rather than herself, with her own misfortunes; but she inveighed so acrimoniously against love-matches that Lily would have fancied her own marriage had been of that nature, had not Mrs. Bart frequently assured her that she had been "talked into it"—by whom, she never made clear.

Lily was duly impressed by the magnitude of her opportunities. The dinginess of her present life threw into enchanting relief the existence to which she felt herself entitled. To a less illuminated intelligence Mrs. Bart's counsels might have been dangerous, but Lily understood that beauty is only the raw ma-

terial of conquest, and that to convert it into success other arts
are required. She knew that to betray any sense of superiority
was a subtler form of the stupidity her mother denounced, and
it did not take her long to learn that a beauty needs more tact
than the possessor of an average set of features.

Her ambitions were not as crude as Mrs. Bart's. It had been
among that lady's grievances that her husband—in the early
days, before he was too tired—had wasted his evenings in what
she vaguely described as "reading poetry"; and among the effects
packed off to auction after his death were a score or two of dingy
volumes which had struggled for existence among the boots and
medicine bottles of his dressing-room shelves. There was in Lily
a vein of sentiment, perhaps transmitted from this source, which
gave an idealizing touch to her most prosaic purposes. She liked
to think of her beauty as a power for good, as giving her the opportunity to attain a position where she should make her influence felt in the vague diffusion of refinement and good taste.
She was fond of pictures and flowers, and of sentimental fiction,
and she could not help thinking that the possession of such
tastes ennobled her desire for worldly advantages. She would not
indeed have cared to marry a man who was merely rich: she was
secretly ashamed of her mother's crude passion for money. Lily's
preference would have been for an English nobleman with po-
litical ambitions and vast estates; or, for second choice, an Italian prince with a castle in the Apennines* and an hereditary
office in the Vatican. Lost causes had a romantic charm for her,
and she liked to picture herself as standing aloof from the vulgar
press of the Quirinal,† and sacrificing her pleasure to the claims
of an immemorial tradition. . . .

How long ago and how far off it all seemed! Those ambitions
were hardly more futile and childish than the earlier ones which
had centred about the possession of a French jointed doll with
real hair. Was it only ten years since she had wavered in imagi-

---

*Lily would know this romantic image from late-eighteenth-century
English Gothic novels, which often featured castles in this mountain
range in central Italy.
†Hill in Rome with palaces and tourist attractions.

nation between the English earl and the Italian prince? Relentlessly her mind travelled on over the dreary interval. . . .

After two years of hungry roaming Mrs. Bart had died—died of a deep disgust. She had hated dinginess, and it was her fate to be dingy. Her visions of a brilliant marriage for Lily had faded after the first year.

"People can't marry you if they don't see you—and how can they see you in these holes where we're stuck?" That was the burden of her lament; and her last adjuration to her daughter was to escape from dinginess if she could.

"Don't let it creep up on you and drag you down. Fight your way out of it somehow—you 're young and can do it," she insisted.

She had died during one of their brief visits to New York, and there Lily at once became the centre of a family council composed of the wealthy relatives whom she had been taught to despise for living like pigs. It may be that they had an inkling of the sentiments in which she had been brought up, for none of them manifested a very lively desire for her company; indeed, the question threatened to remain unsolved till Mrs. Peniston with a sigh announced: "I'll try her for a year."

Every one was surprised, but one and all concealed their surprise, lest Mrs. Peniston should be alarmed by it into reconsidering her decision.

Mrs. Peniston was Mr. Bart's widowed sister, and if she was by no means the richest of the family group, its other members nevertheless abounded in reasons why she was clearly destined by Providence to assume the charge of Lily. In the first place she was alone, and it would be charming for her to have a young companion. Then she sometimes travelled, and Lily's familiarity with foreign customs—deplored as a misfortune by her more conservative relatives—would at least enable her to act as a kind of courier. But as a matter of fact Mrs. Peniston had not been affected by these considerations. She had taken the girl simply because no one else would have her, and because she had the kind of moral *mauvaise honte** which makes the public display of self-

---

*False shame (French).

ishness difficult, though it does not interfere with its private indulgence. It would have been impossible for Mrs. Peniston to be
heroic on a desert island, but with the eyes of her little world
upon her she took a certain pleasure in her act.

She reaped the reward to which disinterestedness is entitled,
and found an agreeable companion in her niece. She had expected to find Lily headstrong, critical and "foreign"—for even
Mrs. Peniston, though she occasionally went abroad, had the
family dread of foreignness—but the girl showed a pliancy,
which, to a more penetrating mind than her aunt's, might have
been less reassuring than the open selfishness of youth. Misfortune had made Lily supple instead of hardening her, and a pli-
able substance is less easy to break than a stiff one.

Mrs. Peniston, however, did not suffer from her niece's
adaptability. Lily had no intention of taking advantage of her
aunt's good nature. She was in truth grateful for the refuge offered her: Mrs. Peniston's opulent interior was at least not externally dingy. But dinginess is a quality which assumes all manner
of disguises; and Lily soon found that it was as latent in the expensive routine of her aunt's life as in the makeshift existence of
a continental pension.

Mrs. Peniston was one of the episodical persons who form
the padding of life. It was impossible to believe that she had herself ever been a focus of activities. The most vivid thing about
her was the fact that her grandmother had been a Van Alstyne.
This connection with the well-fed and industrious stock of early
New York revealed itself in the glacial neatness of Mrs. Peniston's drawing-room and in the excellence of her cuisine. She belonged to the class of old New Yorkers who have always lived
well, dressed expensively, and done little else; and to these inherited obligations Mrs. Peniston faithfully conformed. She had
always been a looker-on at life, and her mind resembled one of
those little mirrors which her Dutch ancestors were accustomed
to affix to their upper windows, so that from the depths of an
impenetrable domesticity they might see what was happening in
the street.

Mrs. Peniston was the owner of a country-place in New Jer-
sey, but she had never lived there since her husband's death—a
remote event, which appeared to dwell in her memory chiefly as

a dividing point in the personal reminiscences that formed the staple of her conversation. She was a woman who remembered dates with intensity, and could tell at a moment's notice whether the drawing-room curtains had been renewed before or after Mr. Peniston's last illness.

Mrs. Peniston thought the country lonely and trees damp, and cherished a vague fear of meeting a bull. To guard against such contingencies she frequented the more populous watering-places, where she installed herself impersonally in a hired house and looked on at life through the matting screen of her verandah. In the care of such a guardian, it soon became clear to Lily that she was to enjoy only the material advantages of good food and expensive clothing; and, though far from underrating these, she would gladly have exchanged them for what Mrs. Bart had taught her to regard as opportunities. She sighed to think what her mother's fierce energies would have accomplished, had they been coupled with Mrs. Peniston's resources. Lily had abundant energy of her own, but it was restricted by the necessity of adapting herself to her aunt's habits. She saw that at all costs she must keep Mrs. Peniston's favour till, as Mrs. Bart would have phrased it, she could stand on her own legs. Lily had no mind for the vagabond life of the poor relation, and to adapt herself to Mrs. Peniston she had, to some degree, to assume that lady's passive attitude. She had fancied at first that it would be easy to draw her aunt into the whirl of her own activities, but there was a static force in Mrs. Peniston against which her niece's efforts spent themselves in vain. To attempt to bring her into active relation with life was like tugging at a piece of furniture which has been screwed to the floor. She did not, indeed, expect Lily to remain equally immovable: she had all the American guardian's indulgence for the volatility of youth. She had indulgence also for certain other habits of her niece's. It seemed to her natural that Lily should spend all her money on dress, and she supplemented the girl's scanty income by occasional "handsome presents" meant to be applied to the same purpose. Lily, who was intensely practical, would have preferred a fixed allowance; but Mrs. Peniston liked the periodical recurrence of gratitude evoked by unexpected cheques, and was perhaps shrewd enough to perceive that such a method of giving kept alive in her niece a salutary sense of dependence.

Beyond this, Mrs. Peniston had not felt called upon to do anything for her charge: she had simply stood aside and let her take the field. Lily had taken it, at first with the confidence of assured possessorship, then with gradually narrowing demands, till now she found herself actually struggling for a foothold on the broad space which had once seemed her own for the asking. How it happened she did not yet know. Sometimes she thought it was because Mrs. Peniston had been too passive, and again she feared it was because she herself had not been passive enough. Had she shown an undue eagerness for victory? Had she lacked patience, pliancy and dissimulation? Whether she charged herself with these faults or absolved herself from them, made no difference in the sum-total of her failure. Younger and plainer girls had been married off by dozens, and she was nine-and-twenty, and still Miss Bart.

She was beginning to have fits of angry rebellion against fate, when she longed to drop out of the race and make an independent life for herself. But what manner of life would it be? She had barely enough money to pay her dress-makers' bills and her gambling debts; and none of the desultory interests which she dignified with the name of tastes was pronounced enough to enable her to live contentedly in obscurity. Ah, no—she was too intelligent not to be honest with herself. She knew that she hated dinginess as much as her mother had hated it, and to her last breath she meant to fight against it, dragging herself up again and again above its flood till she gained the bright pinnacles of success which presented such a slippery surface to her clutch.

4

THE NEXT MORNING IN her breakfast tray, Miss Bart found a note from her hostess.

"Dearest Lily," it ran, "if it is not too much of a bore to be down by ten, will you come to my sitting-room to help me with some tiresome things?"

Lily tossed aside the note and subsided on her pillows with a sigh. It *was* a bore to be down by ten—an hour regarded at Bellomont as vaguely synchronous with sunrise—and she knew too well the nature of the tiresome things in question. Miss Pragg, the secretary, had been called away, and there would be notes and dinner-cards to write, lost addresses to hunt up, and other social drudgery to perform. It was understood that Miss Bart should fill the gap in such emergencies, and she usually recognized the obligation without a murmur.

Today, however, it renewed the sense of servitude which the previous night's review of her cheque-book had produced. Everything in her surroundings ministered to feelings of ease and amenity. The windows stood open to the sparkling freshness of the September morning, and between the yellow boughs she caught a perspective of hedges and parterres leading by degrees of lessening formality to the free undulations of the park. Her maid had kindled a little fire on the hearth, and it contended cheerfully with the sunlight which slanted across the moss-green carpet and caressed the curved sides of an old marquetry desk. Near the bed stood a table holding her breakfast tray, with its harmonious porcelain and silver, a handful of violets in a slender glass, and the morning paper folded beneath her letters. There was nothing new to Lily in these tokens of a studied luxury; but, though they formed a part of her atmosphere, she never lost her sensitiveness to their charm. Mere display left her with a sense of superior distinction; but she felt an affinity to all the subtler manifestations of wealth.

Mrs. Trenor's summons, however, suddenly recalled her state of dependence, and she rose and dressed in a mood of irritability that she was usually too prudent to indulge. She knew that such emotions leave lines on the face as well as in the character, and she had meant to take warning by the little creases which her midnight survey had revealed.

The matter-of-course tone of Mrs. Trenor's greeting deepened her irritation. If one did drag one's self out of bed at such an hour, and come down fresh and radiant to the monotony of note-writing, some special recognition of the sacrifice seemed fitting. But Mrs. Trenor's tone showed no consciousness of the fact.

"Oh, Lily, that's nice of you," she merely sighed across the chaos of letters, bills and other domestic documents which gave an incongruously commercial touch to the slender elegance of her writing-table.

"There are such lots of horrors this morning," she added, clearing a space in the centre of the confusion and rising to yield her seat to Miss Bart.

Mrs. Trenor was a tall fair woman, whose height just saved her from redundancy. Her rosy blondness had survived some forty years of futile activity without showing much trace of ill-usage except in a diminished play of feature. It was difficult to define her beyond saying that she seemed to exist only as a hostess, not so much from any exaggerated instinct of hospitality as because she could not sustain life except in a crowd. The collective nature of her interests exempted her from the ordinary rivalries of her sex, and she knew no more personal emotion than that of hatred for the woman who presumed to give bigger dinners or have more amusing house-parties than herself. As her social talents, backed by Mr. Trenor's bank-account, almost always assured her ultimate triumph in such competitions, success had developed in her an unscrupulous good nature toward the rest of her sex, and in Miss Bart's utilitarian classification of her friends, Mrs. Trenor ranked as the woman who was least likely to "go back" on her.

"It was simply inhuman of Pragg to go off now," Mrs. Trenor

declared, as her friend seated herself at the desk. "She says her sister is going to have a baby—as if that were anything to having a house-party! I'm sure I shall get most horribly mixed up and there will be some awful rows. When I was down at Tuxedo I asked a lot of people for next week, and I've mislaid the list and can't remember who is coming. And this week is going to be a horrid failure too—and Gwen Van Osburgh will go back and tell her mother how bored people were. I didn't mean to ask the Wetheralls—that was a blunder of Gus's. They disapprove of Carry Fisher, you know. As if one could help having Carry Fisher! It *was* foolish of her to get that second divorce—Carry always overdoes things—but she said the only way to get a penny out of Fisher was to divorce him and make him pay alimony. And poor Carry has to consider every dollar. It's really absurd of Alice Wetherall to make such a fuss about meeting her, when one thinks of what society is coming to. Some one said the other day that there was a divorce and a case of appendicitis in every family one knows. Besides, Carry is the only person who can keep Gus in a good humour when we have bores in the house. Have you noticed that *all* the husbands like her? All, I mean, except her own. It's rather clever of her to have made a specialty of devoting herself to dull people—the field is such a large one, and she has it practically to herself. She finds compensations, no doubt—I know she borrows money of Gus—but then I'd *pay* her to keep him in a good humour, so I can't complain, after all."

Mrs. Trenor paused to enjoy the spectacle of Miss Bart's efforts to unravel her tangled correspondence.

"But it isn't only the Wetheralls and Carry," she resumed, with a fresh note of lament. "The truth is, I'm awfully disappointed in Lady Cressida Raith."

"Disappointed? Hadn't you known her before?"

"Mercy, no—never saw her till yesterday. Lady Skiddaw sent her over with letters to the Van Osburghs, and I heard that Maria Van Osburgh was asking a big party to meet her this week, so I thought it would be fun to get her away, and Jack Stepney, who knew her in India, managed it for me. Maria was furious, and actually had the impudence to make Gwen invite herself here, so that they shouldn't be *quite* out of it—if I'd

known to what Lady Cressida was like, they could have had her
and welcome! But I thought any friend of the Skiddaws' was
sure to be amusing. You remember what fun Lady Skiddaw was?
There were times when I simply had to send the girls out of the
room. Besides, Lady Cressida is the Duchess of Beltshire's sister, and I naturally supposed she was the same sort; but you
never can tell in those English families. They are so big that
there's room for all kinds, and it turns out that Lady Cressida is
the moral one—married a clergyman and does missionary work
in the East End.* Think of my taking such a lot of trouble about
a clergyman's wife, who wears Indian jewelry and botanizes! She
made Gus take her all through the glass-houses yesterday, and
bothered him to death by asking him the names of the plants.
Fancy treating Gus as if he were the gardener!"

Mrs. Trenor brought this out in a *crescendo* of indignation.

"Oh, well, perhaps Lady Cressida will reconcile the Wetheralls to meeting Carry Fisher," said Miss Bart pacifically.

"I'm sure I hope so! But she is boring all the men horribly,
and if she takes to distributing tracts, as I hear she does, it will
be too depressing. The worst of it is that she would have been so
useful at the right time. You know we have to have the Bishop
once a year, and she would have given just the right tone to
things. I always have horrid luck about the Bishop's visits,"
added Mrs. Trenor, whose present misery was being fed by a
rapidly rising tide of reminiscence; "last year, when he came,
Gus forgot all about his being here, and brought home the Ned
Wintons and the Farleys—five divorces and six sets of children
between them!"

"When is Lady Cressida going?" Lily enquired.

Mrs. Trenor cast up her eyes in despair. "My dear, if one only
knew! I was in such a hurry to get her away from Maria that I
actually forgot to name a date, and Gus says she told some one
she meant to stop here all winter."

"To stop here? In this house?"

"Don't be silly—in America. But if no one else asks her—you
know they *never* go to hotels."

---

*District of London once known for its slums.

"Perhaps Gus only said it to frighten you."

"No—I heard her tell Bertha Dorset that she had six months to put in while her husband was taking the cure in the Engadine.* You should have seen Bertha look vacant! But it's no joke, you know—if she stays here all the autumn she'll spoil everything, and Maria Van Osburgh will simply exult."

At this affecting vision Mrs. Trenor's voice trembled with self-pity.

"Oh, Judy—as if any one were ever bored at Bellomont!" Miss Bart tactfully protested. "You know perfectly well that, if Mrs. Van Osburgh were to get all the right people and leave you with all the wrong ones, you'd manage to make things go off, and she wouldn't."

Such an assurance would usually have restored Mrs. Trenor's complacency; but on this occasion it did not chase the cloud from her brow.

"It isn't only Lady Cressida," she lamented. "Everything has gone wrong this week. I can see that Bertha Dorset is furious with me."

"Furious with you? Why?"

"Because I told her that Lawrence Selden was coming; but he wouldn't, after all, and she's quite unreasonable enough to think it's my fault."

Miss Bart put down her pen and sat absently gazing at the note she had begun.

"I thought that was all over," she said.

"So it is, on his side. And of course Bertha hasn't been idle since. But I fancy she's out of a job just at present—and some one gave me a hint that I had better ask Lawrence. Well, I *did* ask him—but I couldn't make him come; and now I suppose she'll take it out of me by being perfectly nasty to every one else."

"Oh, she may take it out of *him* by being perfectly charming—to some one else."

Mrs. Trenor shook her head dolefully. "She knows he wouldn't mind. And who else is there? Alice Wetherall won't let

---

*Valley in eastern Switzerland with many popular resorts.

Lucius out of her sight. Ned Silverton can't take his eyes off Carry Fisher—poor boy! Gus is bored by Bertha, Jack Stepney knows her too well—and—well, to be sure, there's Percy Gryce!"

She sat up smiling at the thought.

Miss Bart's countenance did not reflect the smile.

"Oh, she and Mr. Gryce would not be likely to hit it off."

"You mean that she'd shock him and he'd bore her? Well, that's not such a bad beginning, you know. But I hope she won't take it into her head to be nice to him, for I asked him here on purpose for you."

Lily laughed. *"Merci du compliment!"** I should certainly have no show against Bertha?"

"Do you think I am uncomplimentary? I'm not really, you know. Every one knows you're a thousand times handsomer and cleverer than Bertha; but then you're not nasty. And for always getting what she wants in the long run, commend me to a nasty woman."

Miss Bart stared in affected reproval. "I thought you were so fond of Bertha."

"Oh, I am—it's much safer to be fond of dangerous people. But she *is* dangerous—and if I ever saw her up to mischief it's now. I can tell by poor George's manner. That man is a perfect barometer—he always knows when Bertha is going to——"

"To fall?" Miss Bart suggested.

"Don't be shocking! You know he believes in her still. And of course I don't say there's any real harm in Bertha. Only she delights in making people miserable, and especially poor George."

"Well, he seems cut out for the part—I don't wonder she likes more cheerful companionship."

"Oh, George is not as dismal as you think. If Bertha didn't worry him he would be quite different. Or if she'd leave him alone, and let him arrange his life as he pleases. But she doesn't dare lose her hold of him on account of the money, and so when *he* isn't jealous she pretends to be."

Miss Bart went on writing in silence, and her hostess sat following her train of thought with frowning intensity.

---

*Thanks for the compliment (French).

"Do you know," she exclaimed after a long pause, "I believe I'll call up Lawrence on the telephone and tell him he simply *must* come?"

"Oh, don't," said Lily, with a quick suffusion of colour. The blush surprised her almost as much as it did her hostess, who, though not commonly observant of facial changes, sat staring at her with puzzled eyes.

"Good gracious, Lily, how handsome you are!—— Why? Do you dislike him so much?"

"Not at all; I like him. But if you are actuated by the benevolent intention of protecting me from Bertha—I don't think I need your protection."

Mrs. Trenor sat up with an exclamation. "Lily!—— *Percy!* Do you mean to say you've actually done it?"

Miss Bart smiled. "I only mean to say that Mr. Gryce and I are getting to be very good friends."

"H'm—I see." Mrs. Trenor fixed a rapt eye upon her. "You know they say he has eight hundred thousand a year—and spends nothing, except on some rubbishy old books. And his mother has heart-disease and will leave him a lot more. *Oh, Lily, do go slowly,*" her friend adjured her.

Miss Bart continued to smile without annoyance. "I shouldn't, for instance," she remarked, "be in any haste to tell him that he had a lot of rubbishy old books."

"No, of course not; I know you're wonderful about getting up people's subjects. But he's horribly shy, and easily shocked, and—and——"

"Why don't you say it, Judy? I have the reputation of being on the hunt for a rich husband?"

"Oh, I don't mean that; he wouldn't believe it of you—at first," said Mrs. Trenor, with candid shrewdness. "But you know things are rather lively here at times—I must give Jack and Gus a hint—and if he thought you were what his mother would call fast—oh, well, you know what I mean. Don't wear your scarlet *crêpe-de-chine** for dinner, and don't smoke if you can help it, Lily dear!"

---

*Soft, thin silk with slightly ruffled surface.

Lily pushed aside her finished work with a dry smile. "You're very kind, Judy: I'll lock up my cigarettes and wear that last year's dress you sent me this morning. And if you are really interested in my career, perhaps you'll be kind enough not to ask me to play bridge again this evening."

"Bridge? Does he mind bridge, too? Oh, Lily, what an awful life you'll lead! But of course I won't—why didn't you give me a hint last night? There's nothing I wouldn't do, you poor duck, to see you happy!"

And Mrs. Trenor, glowing with her sex's eagerness to smooth the course of true love, enveloped Lily in a long embrace.

"You're quite sure," she added solicitously, as the latter extricated herself, "that you wouldn't like me to telephone for Lawrence Selden?"

"Quite sure," said Lily.

The next three days demonstrated to her own complete satisfaction Miss Bart's ability to manage her affairs without extraneous aid.

As she sat, on the Saturday afternoon, on the terrace at Bellomont, she smiled at Mrs. Trenor's fear that she might go too fast. If such a warning had ever been needful, the years had taught her a salutary lesson, and she flattered herself that she now knew how to adapt her pace to the object of pursuit. In the case of Mr. Gryce she had found it well to flutter ahead, losing herself elusively and luring him on from depth to depth of unconscious intimacy. The surrounding atmosphere was propitious to this scheme of courtship. Mrs. Trenor, true to her word, had shown no signs of expecting Lily at the bridge-table, and had even hinted to the other card-players that they were to betray no surprise at her unwonted defection. In consequence of this hint, Lily found herself the centre of that feminine solicitude which envelops a young woman in the mating season. A solitude was tacitly created for her in the crowded existence of Bellomont, and her friends could not have shown a greater readiness for self-effacement had her wooing been adorned with all the attributes of romance. In Lily's set this conduct implied a sympathetic comprehension of her motives, and Mr. Gryce rose in her esteem as she saw the consideration he inspired.

The terrace at Bellomont on a September afternoon was a spot propitious to sentimental musings, and as Miss Bart stood leaning against the balustrade above the sunken garden, at a little distance from the animated group about the tea-table, she might have been lost in the mazes of an inarticulate happiness. In reality, her thoughts were finding definite utterance in the tranquil recapitulation of the blessings in store for her. From where she stood she could see them embodied in the form of Mr. Gryce, who, in a light overcoat and muffler, sat somewhat nervously on the edge of his chair, while Carry Fisher, with all the energy of eye and gesture with which nature and art had combined to endow her, pressed on him the duty of taking part in the task of municipal reform.

Mrs. Fisher's latest hobby was municipal reform. It had been preceded by an equal zeal for socialism, which had in turn replaced an energetic advocacy of Christian Science. Mrs. Fisher was small, fiery and dramatic; and her hands and eyes were admirable instruments in the service of whatever cause she happened to espouse. She had, however, the fault common to enthusiasts of ignoring any slackness of response on the part of her hearers, and Lily was amused by her unconsciousness of the resistance displayed in every angle of Mr. Gryce's attitude. Lily herself knew that his mind was divided between the dread of catching cold if he remained out of doors too long at that hour, and the fear that, if he retreated to the house, Mrs. Fisher might follow him up with a paper to be signed. Mr. Gryce had a constitutional dislike to what he called "committing himself," and tenderly as he cherished his health, he evidently concluded that it was safer to stay out of reach of pen and ink till chance released him from Mrs. Fisher's toils. Meanwhile he cast agonized glances in the direction of Miss Bart, whose only response was to sink into an attitude of more graceful abstraction. She had learned the value of contrast in throwing her charms into relief, and was fully aware of the extent to which Mrs. Fisher's volubility was enhancing her own repose.

She was roused from her musings by the approach of her cousin Jack Stepney who, at Gwen Van Osburgh's side, was returning across the garden from the tennis court.

The couple in question were engaged in the same kind of romance in which Lily figured, and the latter felt a certain annoyance in contemplating what seemed to her a caricature of her own situation. Miss Van Osburgh was a large girl with flat surfaces and no high lights. Jack Stepney had once said of her that she was as reliable as roast mutton. His own taste was in the line of less solid and more highly-seasoned diet; but hunger makes any fare palatable, and there had been times when Mr. Stepney had been reduced to a crust.

Lily considered with interest the expression of their faces: the girl's turned toward her companion's like an empty plate held up to be filled, while the man lounging at her side already betrayed the encroaching boredom which would presently crack the thin veneer of his smile.

"How impatient men are!" Lily reflected. "All Jack has to do to get everything he wants is to keep quiet and let that girl marry him; whereas I have to calculate and contrive, and retreat and advance, as if I were going through an intricate dance, when one misstep would throw me hopelessly out of time."

As they drew nearer she was whimsically struck by a kind of family likeness between Miss Van Osburgh and Percy Gryce. There was no resemblance of feature. Gryce was handsome in a didactic way—he looked like a clever pupil's drawing from a plaster-cast—while Gwen's countenance had no more modeling than a face painted on a toy balloon. But the deeper affinity was unmistakable: the two had the same prejudices and ideals, and the same quality of making other standards non-existent by ignoring them. This attribute was common to most of Lily's set: as they had a force of negation which eliminated everything beyond their own range of perception. Gryce and Miss Van Osburgh were, in short, made for each other by every law of moral and physical correspondence— "Yet they wouldn't look at each other," Lily mused, "they never do. Each of them wants a creature of a different race, of Jack's race and mine, with all sorts of intuitions, sensations and perceptions that they don't even guess the existence of. And they always get what they want."

She stood talking with her cousin and Miss Van Osburgh, till a slight cloud on the latter's brow advised her that even cousinly amenities were subject to suspicion, and Miss Bart, mindful of the necessity of not exciting enmities at this crucial point of her career, dropped aside while the happy couple proceeded toward the tea-table.

Seating herself on the upper step of the terrace, Lily leaned her head against the honeysuckles wreathing the balustrade. The fragrance of the late blossoms seemed an emanation of the tranquil scene, a landscape tutored to the last degree of rural elegance. In the foreground glowed the warm tints of the gardens. Beyond the lawn, with its pyramidal pale-gold maples and velvety firs, sloped pastures dotted with cattle; and through a long glade the river widened like a lake under the silver light of September. Lily did not want to join the circle about the tea-table. They represented the future she had chosen, and she was content with it, but in no haste to anticipate its joys. The certainty that she could marry Percy Gryce when she pleased had lifted a heavy load from her mind, and her money troubles were too recent for their removal not to leave a sense of relief which a less discerning intelligence might have taken for happiness. Her vulgar cares were at an end. She would be able to arrange her life as she pleased, to soar into that empyrean* of security where creditors cannot penetrate. She would have smarter gowns than Judy Trenor, and far, far more jewels than Bertha Dorset. She would be free forever from the shifts, the expedients, the humiliations of the relatively poor. Instead of having to flatter, she would be flattered; instead of being grateful, she would receive thanks. There were old scores she could pay off as well as old benefits she could return. And she had no doubts as to the extent of her power. She knew that Mr. Gryce was of the small chary type most inaccessible to impulses and emotions. He had the kind of character in which prudence is a vice, and good advice the most dangerous nourishment. But Lily had known the species before: she was aware that such a guarded nature must find one huge outlet of egoism, and she determined to be to him what his Americana had hitherto been: the one possession in which he took sufficient pride to spend money on it. She knew that this generosity to self is one of the forms of meanness, and she re-

---

*In ancient and medieval cosmology, term for the highest heaven; often used in reference to the ultimate paradise.

solved so to identify herself with her husband's vanity that to gratify her wishes would be to him the most exquisite form of self-indulgence. The system might at first necessitate a resort to some of the very shifts and expedients from which she intended it should free her; but she felt sure that in a short time she would be able to play the game in her own way. How should she have distrusted her powers? Her beauty itself was not the mere ephemeral possession it might have been in the hands of inexperience: her skill in enhancing it, the care she took of it, the use she made of it, seemed to give it a kind of permanence. She felt she could trust it to carry her through to the end.

And the end, on the whole, was worth while. Life was not the mockery she had thought it three days ago. There was room for her, after all, in this crowded selfish world of pleasure whence, so short a time since, her poverty had seemed to exclude her. These people whom she had ridiculed and yet envied were glad to make a place for her in the charmed circle about which all her desires revolved. They were not as brutal and self-engrossed as she had fancied—or rather, since it would no longer be necessary to flatter and humour them, that side of their nature became less conspicuous. Society is a revolving body which is apt to be judged according to its place in each man's heaven; and at present it was turning its illuminated face to Lily.

In the rosy glow it diffused her companions seemed full of amiable qualities. She liked their elegance; their lightness, their lack of emphasis: even the self-assurance which at times was so like obtuseness now seemed the natural sign of social ascendency. They were lords of the only world she cared for, and they were ready to admit her to their ranks and let her lord it with them. Already she felt within her a stealing allegiance to their standards, an acceptance of their limitations, a disbelief in the things they did not believe in, a contemptuous pity for the people who were not able to live as they lived.

The early sunset was slanting across the park. Through the boughs of the long avenue beyond the gardens she caught the flash of wheels, and divined that more visitors were approaching. There was a movement behind her, a scattering of steps and voices: it was evident that the party about the tea-table was breaking up. Presently she heard a tread behind her on the terrace. She supposed that Mr. Gryce had at last found means to escape from his predicament, and she smiled at the significance of his coming to join her instead of beating an instant retreat to the fire-side.

She turned to give him the welcome which such gallantry deserved; but her greeting wavered into a blush of wonder, for the man who had approached her was Lawrence Selden.

"You see I came after all," he said; but, before she had time to answer, Mrs. Dorset, breaking away from a lifeless colloquy with her host, had stepped between them with a little gesture of appropriation.

5

THE OBSERVANCE OF SUNDAY at Bellomont was chiefly marked by the punctual appearance of the smart omnibus destined to convey the household to the little church at the gates. Whether any one got into the omnibus or not was a matter of secondary importance, since by standing there it not only bore witness to the orthodox intentions of the family, but made Mrs. Trenor feel, when she finally heard it drive away, that she had somehow vicariously made use of it.

It was Mrs. Trenor's theory that her daughters actually did go to church every Sunday; but their French governess's convictions calling her to the rival fane,* and the fatigues of the week keeping their mother in her room till luncheon, there was seldom any one present to verify the fact. Now and then, in a spasmodic burst of virtue—when the house had been too uproarious over night—Gus Trenor forced his genial bulk into a tight frock-coat and routed his daughters from their slumbers; but habitually, as Lily explained to Mr. Gryce, this parental duty was forgotten till the church bells were ringing across the park, and the omnibus had driven away empty.

Lily had hinted to Mr. Gryce that this neglect of religious observances was repugnant to her early traditions, and that during her visits to Bellomont she regularly accompanied Muriel and Hilda to church. This tallied with the assurance, also confidentially imparted, that, never having played bridge before, she had been "dragged into it" on the night of her arrival, and had lost an appalling amount of money in consequence of her ignorance of the game and of the rules of betting. Mr. Gryce was un-

*Archaic word for church; the French governess went to the rival Catholic Church.

doubtedly enjoying Bellomont. He liked the ease and glitter of the life, and the lustre conferred on him by being a member of this group of rich and conspicuous people. But he thought it a very materialistic society; there were times when he was frightened by the talk of the men and the looks of the ladies, and he was glad to find that Miss Bart, for all her ease and self-possession, was not at home in so ambiguous an atmosphere. For this reason he had been especially pleased to learn that she would, as usual, attend the young Trenors to church on Sunday morning; and as he paced the gravel sweep before the door, his light overcoat on his arm and his prayer-book in one carefully-gloved hand, he reflected agreeably on the strength of character which kept her true to her early training in surroundings so subversive to religious principles.

For a long time Mr. Gryce and the omnibus had the gravel sweep to themselves; but, far from regretting this deplorable indifference on the part of the other guests, he found himself nourishing the hope that Miss Bart might be unaccompanied. The precious minutes were flying, however; the big chestnuts* pawed the ground and flecked their impatient sides with foam; the coachman seemed to be slowly petrifying on the box, and the groom on the doorstep; and still the lady did not come. Suddenly, however, there was a sound of voices and a rustle of skirts in the doorway, and Mr. Gryce, restoring his watch to his pocket, turned with a nervous start; but it was only to find himself handing Mrs. Wetherall into the carriage.

The Wetheralls always went to church. They belonged to the vast group of human automata who go through life without neglecting to perform a single one of the gestures executed by the surrounding puppets. It is true that the Bellomont puppets did not go to church; but others equally important did—and Mr. and Mrs. Wetherall's circle was so large that God was included in their visiting-list. They appeared, therefore, punctual and resigned, with the air of people bound for a dull "At Home,"† and after them Hilda and Muriel straggled, yawning and pinning

---

*Reddish-brown horses.

†Period of the day when social callers were received.

each other's veils and ribbons as they came. They had promised Lily to go to church with her, they declared, and Lily was such a dear old duck that they didn't mind doing it to please her, though they couldn't fancy what had put the idea in her head, and though for their own part they would much rather have played lawn tennis with Jack and Gwen, if she hadn't told them she was coming. The Misses Trenor were followed by Lady Cressida Raith, a weather-beaten person in Liberty silk* and ethnological trinkets, who, on seeing the omnibus, expressed her surprise that they were not to walk across the park; but at Mrs. Wetherall's horrified protest that the church was a mile away, her ladyship, after a glance at the height of the other's heels, acquiesced in the necessity of driving, and poor Mr. Gryce found himself rolling off between four ladies for whose spiritual welfare be felt not the least concern.

It might have afforded him some consolation could he have known that Miss Bart had really meant to go to church. She had even risen earlier than usual in the execution of her purpose. She had no idea that the sight of her in a grey gown of devotional cut, with her famous lashes drooped above a prayer-book, would put the finishing touch to Mr. Gryce's subjugation, and render inevitable a certain incident which she had resolved should form a part of the walk they were to take together after luncheon. Her intentions in short had never been more definite; but poor Lily, for all the hard glaze of her exterior, was inwardly as malleable as wax. Her faculty for adapting herself, for entering into other people's feelings, if it served her now and then in small contingencies, hampered her in the decisive moments of life. She was like a water-plant in the flux of the tides, and today the whole current of her mood was carrying her toward Lawrence Selden. Why had he come? Was it to see herself or Bertha Dorset? It was the last question which, at that moment, should have engaged her. She might better have contented herself with thinking that he had simply responded to the despairing summons of his hostess, anxious to interpose him between herself and the ill-

---

*Fabric from a fashionable store in London.

humour of Mrs. Dorset. But Lily had not rested till she learned from Mrs. Trenor that Selden had come of his own accord.

"He didn't even wire me—he just happened to find the trap at the station. Perhaps it's not over with Bertha after all," Mrs. Trenor musingly concluded, and went away to arrange her dinner-cards accordingly.

Perhaps it was not, Lily reflected; but it should be soon, unless she had lost her cunning. If Selden had come at Mrs. Dorset's call, it was at her own that he would stay. So much the previous evening had told her. Mrs. Trenor, true to her simple principle of making her married friends happy, had placed Selden and Mrs. Dorset next to each other at dinner; but, in obedience to the time-honoured traditions of the match-maker, she had separated Lily and Mr. Gryce, sending in the former with George Dorset, while Mr. Gryce was coupled with Gwen Van Osburgh.

George Dorset's talk did not interfere with the range of his neighbour's thoughts. He was a mournful dyspeptic, intent on finding out the deleterious ingredients of every dish and diverted from this care only by the sound of his wife's voice. On this occasion, however, Mrs. Dorset took no part in the general conversation. She sat talking in low murmurs with Selden, and turning a contemptuous and denuded shoulder toward her host, who, far from resenting his exclusion, plunged into the excesses of the *menu* with the joyous irresponsibility of a free man. To Mr. Dorset, however, his wife's attitude was a subject of such evident concern that, when he was not scraping the sauce from his fish, or scooping the moist bread-crumbs from the interior of his roll, he sat straining his thin neck for a glimpse of her between the lights.

Mrs. Trenor, as it chanced, had placed the husband and wife on opposite sides of the table, and Lily was therefore able to observe Mrs. Dorset also, and by carrying her glance a few feet farther, to set up a rapid comparison between Lawrence Selden and Mr. Gryce. It was that comparison which was her undoing. Why else had she suddenly grown interested in Selden? She had known him for eight years or more: ever since her return to America he had formed a part of her background. She had always been glad to sit next to him at dinner, had found him more

agreeable than most men, and had vaguely wished that he possessed the other qualities needful to fix her attention; but till
now she had been too busy with her own affairs to regard him as
more than one of the pleasant accessories of life. Miss Bart was
a keen reader of her own heart, and she saw that her sudden pre-
occupation with Selden was due to the fact that his presence
shed a new light on her surroundings. Not that he was notably
brilliant or exceptional; in his own profession he was surpassed
by more than one man who had bored Lily through many a
weary dinner. It was rather that he had preserved a certain social
detachment, a happy air of viewing the show objectively, of having points of contact outside the great gilt cage in which they
were all huddled for the mob to gape at. How alluring the world
outside the cage appeared to Lily, as she heard its door clang on
her! In reality, as she knew, the door never clanged: it stood always open; but most of the captives were like flies in a bottle,
and having once flown in, could never regain their freedom. It
was Selden's distinction that he had never forgotten the way out.

That was the secret of his way of readjusting her vision. Lily,
turning her eyes from him, found herself scanning her little
world through his retina: it was as though the pink lamps had
been shut off and the dusty daylight let in. She looked down the
long table, studying its occupants one by one, from Gus Trenor,
with his heavy carnivorous head sunk between his shoulders, as
he preyed on a jellied plover,* to his wife, at the opposite end of
the long bank of orchids, suggestive, with her glaring good-
looks, of a jeweller's window lit by electricity. And between the
two, what a long stretch of vacuity! How dreary and trivial these
people were! Lily reviewed them with a scornful impatience:
Carry Fisher, with her shoulders, her eyes, her divorces, her general air of embodying a "spicy paragraph"; young Silverton, who
had meant to live on proof-reading and write an epic, and who
now lived on his friends and had become critical of truffles;
Alice Wetherall, an animated visiting-list, whose most fervid
convictions turned on the wording of invitations and the en-
graving of dinner-cards; Wetherall, with his perpetual nervous

---

*Small, edible shore bird.

nod of acquiescence, his air of agreeing with people before he knew what they were saying; Jack Stepney, with his confident smile and anxious eyes, half way between the sheriff and an heiress; Gwen Van Osburgh, with all the guileless confidence of a young girl who has always been told that there is no one richer than her father.

Lily smiled at her classification of her friends. How different they had seemed to her a few hours ago! Then they had symbolized what she was gaining, now they stood for what she was giving up. That very afternoon they had seemed full of brilliant qualities; now she saw that they were merely dull in a loud way. Under the glitter of their opportunities she saw the poverty of their achievement. It was not that she wanted them to be more disinterested; but she would have liked them to be more picturesque. And she had a shamed recollection of the way in which, a few hours since, she had felt the centripetal force of their standards. She closed her eyes an instant, and the vacuous routine of the life she had chosen stretched before her like a long white road without dip or turning: it was true she was to roll over it in a carriage instead of trudging it on foot, but sometimes the pedestrian enjoys the diversion of a short cut which is denied to those on wheels.

She was roused by a chuckle which Mr. Dorset seemed to eject from the depths of his lean throat.

"I say, do look at her," he exclaimed, turning to Miss Bart with lugubrious merriment—"I beg your pardon, but do just look at my wife making a fool of that poor devil over there! One would really suppose she was gone on him—and it's all the other way round, I assure you."

Thus adjured, Lily turned her eyes on the spectacle which was affording Mr. Dorset such legitimate mirth. It certainly appeared, as he said, that Mrs. Dorset was the more active participant in the scene: her neighbour seemed to receive her advances with a temperate zest which did not distract him from his dinner. The sight restored Lily's good humour, and knowing the peculiar disguise which Mr. Dorset's marital fears assumed, she asked gaily: "Aren't you horribly jealous of her?"

Dorset greeted the sally with delight. "Oh, abominably—you've just hit it—keeps me awake at night. The doctors tell me that's what has knocked my digestion out—being so infernally jealous of her.—I can't eat a mouthful of this stuff, you know," he added suddenly, pushing back his plate with a clouded countenance; and Lily, unfailingly adaptable, accorded her radiant attention to his prolonged denunciation of other people's cooks, with a supplementary tirade on the toxic qualities of melted butter.

It was not often that he found so ready an ear; and, being a man as well as a dyspeptic, it may be that as he poured his grievances into it he was not insensible to its rosy symmetry. At any rate he engaged Lily so long that the sweets were being handed when she caught a phrase on her other side, where Miss Corby, the comic woman of the company, was bantering Jack Stepney on his approaching engagement. Miss Corby's rôle was jocularity: she always entered the conversation with a hand-spring.

"And of course you'll have Sim Rosedale as best man!" Lily heard her fling out as the climax of her prognostications; and Stepney responded, as if struck: "Jove, that's an idea. What a thumping present I'd get out of him!"

Sim Rosedale! The name, made more odious by its diminutive, obtruded itself on Lily's thoughts like a leer. It stood for one of the many hated possibilities hovering on the edge of life. If she did not marry Percy Gryce, the day might come when she would have to be civil to such men as Rosedale. *If she did not marry him?* But she meant to marry him—she was sure of him and sure of herself. She drew back with a shiver from the pleasant paths in which her thoughts had been straying, and set her feet once more in the middle of the long white road. . . . When she went upstairs that night she found that the late post had brought her a fresh batch of bills. Mrs. Peniston, who was a conscientious woman, had forwarded them all to Bellomont.

Miss Bart, accordingly, rose the next morning with the most earnest conviction that it was her duty to go to church. She tore herself betimes from the lingering enjoyment of her breakfast-tray, rang to have her grey gown laid out, and despatched her maid to borrow a prayer-book from Mrs. Trenor.

But her course was too purely reasonable not to contain the germs of rebellion. No sooner were her preparations made than they roused a smothered sense of resistance. A small spark was enough to kindle Lily's imagination, and the sight of the grey dress and the borrowed prayer-book flashed a long light down the years. She would have to go to church with Percy Gryce every Sunday. They would have a front pew in the most expensive church in New York, and his name would figure handsomely in the list of parish charities. In a few years, when he grew stouter, he would be made a warden. Once in the winter the rector would come to dine, and her husband would beg her to go over the list and see that no *divorcées* were included, except those who had showed signs of penitence by being re-married to the very wealthy. There was nothing especially arduous in this round of religious obligations; but it stood for a fraction of that great bulk of boredom which loomed across her path. And who could consent to be bored on such a morning? Lily had slept well, and her bath had filled her with a pleasant glow, which was becomingly reflected in the clear curve of her cheek. No lines were visible this morning, or else the glass was at a happier angle.

And the day was the accomplice of her mood: it was a day for impulse and truancy. The light air seemed full of powdered gold; below the dewy bloom of the lawns the woodlands blushed and smouldered, and the hills across the river swam in molten blue. Every drop of blood in Lily's veins invited her to happiness.

The sound of wheels roused her from these musings, and leaning behind her shutters she saw the omnibus take up its freight. She was too late, then—but the fact did not alarm her. A glimpse of Mr. Gryce's crestfallen face even suggested that she had done wisely in absenting herself, since the disappointment he so candidly betrayed would surely whet his appetite for the afternoon walk. That walk she did not mean to miss; one glance at the bills on her writing-table was enough to recall its necessity. But meanwhile she had the morning to herself, and could muse pleasantly on the disposal of its hours. She was familiar enough with the habits of Bellomont to know that she was likely to have a free field till luncheon. She had seen the Wetheralls, the Trenor girls and Lady Cressida packed safely into the omnibus; Judy Trenor was sure to be having her hair shampooed; Carry Fisher had doubtless carried off her host for a drive, Ned

Silverton was probably smoking the cigarette of young despair in his bedroom; and Kate Corby was certain to be playing tennis with Jack Stepney and Miss Van Osburgh. Of the ladies, this left only Mrs. Dorset unaccounted for, and Mrs. Dorset never came down till luncheon: her doctors, she averred, had forbidden her to expose herself to the crude air of the morning.

To the remaining members of the party Lily gave no special thought; wherever they were, they were not likely to interfere with her plans. These, for the moment, took the shape of assuming a dress somewhat more rustic and summerlike in style than the garment she had first selected, and rustling downstairs, sunshade in hand, with the disengaged air of a lady in quest of exercise. The great hall was empty but for the knot of dogs by the fire, who, taking in at a glance the out-door aspect of Miss Bart, were upon her at once with lavish offers of companionship. She put aside the ramping paws which conveyed these offers, and assuring the joyous volunteers that she might presently have a use for their company, sauntered on through the empty drawing-room to the library at the end of the house. The library was almost the only surviving portion of the old manor-house of Bellomont: a long spacious room, revealing the traditions of the mother-country in its classically-cased doors, the Dutch tiles of the chimney, and the elaborate hobgrate* with its shining brass urns. A few family portraits of lantern-jawed gentlemen in tie-wigs,† and ladies with large head-dresses and small bodies, hung between the shelves lined with pleasantly shabby books: books mostly contemporaneous with the ancestors in question, and to which the subsequent Trenors had made no perceptible additions. The library at Bellomont was in fact never used for reading, though it had a certain popularity as a smoking-room or a quiet retreat for flirtation. It had occurred to Lily, however, that it might on this occasion have been resorted to by the only member of the party in the least likely to put it to its original use. She advanced noiselessly over the dense old rug scattered with easy-chairs, and before she reached the middle of the room

---

*A shelf in a fireplace, used to warm food.
†Wigs tied in the back with ribbons.

she saw that she had not been mistaken. Lawrence Selden was in fact seated at its farther end; but though a book lay on his knee, his attention was not engaged with it, but directed to a lady whose lace-clad figure, as she leaned back in an adjoining chair, detached itself with exaggerated slimness against the dusky leather of the upholstery.

Lily paused as she caught sight of the group; for a moment she seemed about to withdraw, but thinking better of this, she announced her approach by a slight shake of her skirts which made the couple raise their heads, Mrs. Dorset with a look of frank displeasure, and Selden with his usual quiet smile. The sight of his composure had a disturbing effect on Lily; but to be disturbed was in her case to make a more brilliant effort at self-possession.

"Dear me, am I late?" she asked, putting a hand in his as he advanced to greet her.

"Late for what?" enquired Mrs. Dorset tartly. "Not for luncheon, certainly—but perhaps you had an earlier engagement?"

"Yes, I had," said Lily confidingly.

"Really? Perhaps I am in the way, then? But Mr. Selden is entirely at your disposal." Mrs. Dorset was pale with temper, and her antagonist felt a certain pleasure in prolonging her distress.

"Oh, dear, no—do stay," she said good-humouredly. "I don't in the least want to drive you away."

"You're awfully good, dear, but I never interfere with Mr. Selden's engagements."

The remark was uttered with a little air of proprietorship not lost on its object, who concealed a faint blush of annoyance by stooping to pick up the book he had dropped at Lily's approach. The latter's eyes widened charmingly and she broke into a light laugh.

"But I have no engagement with Mr. Selden! My engagement was to go to church; and I'm afraid the omnibus has started without me. *Has* it started, do you know?"

She turned to Selden, who replied that he had heard it drive away some time since.

"Ah, then I shall have to walk; I promised Hilda and Muriel to go to church with them. It's too late to walk there, you say? Well, I shall have the credit of trying, at any rate—and the ad-

vantage of escaping part of the service. I'm not so sorry for myself, after all!"

And with a bright nod to the couple on whom she had in-
truded, Miss Bart strolled through the glass doors and carried
her rustling grace down the long perspective of the garden walk.

She was taking her way churchward, but at no very quick
pace; a fact not lost on one of her observers, who stood in the
doorway looking after her with an air of puzzled amusement.
The truth is that she was conscious of a somewhat keen shock
of disappointment. All her plans for the day had been built on
the assumption that it was to see her that Selden had come to
Bellomont. She had expected, when she came downstairs, to
find him on the watch for her; and she had found him, instead,
in a situation which might well denote that he had been on the
watch for another lady. Was it possible, after all, that he had
come for Bertha Dorset? The latter had acted on the assumption
to the extent of appearing at an hour when she never showed
herself to ordinary mortals, and Lily, for the moment, saw no
way of putting her in the wrong. It did not occur to her that
Selden might have been actuated merely by the desire to spend
a Sunday out of town: women never learn to dispense with the
sentimental motive in their judgments of men. But Lily was not
easily disconcerted; competition put her on her mettle, and she
reflected that Selden's coming, if it did not declare him to be still
in Mrs. Dorset's toils, showed him to be so completely free from
them that he was not afraid of her proximity.

These thoughts so engaged her that she fell into a gait hardly
likely to carry her to church before the sermon, and at length,
having passed from the gardens to the wood-path beyond, so far
forgot her intention as to sink into a rustic seat at a bend of the
walk. The spot was charming, and Lily was not insensible to the
charm, or to the fact that her presence enhanced it; but she was
not accustomed to taste the joys of solitude except in company,
and the combination of a handsome girl and a romantic scene
struck her as too good to be wasted. No one, however, appeared
to profit by the opportunity; and after a half hour of fruitless
waiting she rose and wandered on. She felt a stealing sense of fatigue as she walked; the sparkle had died out of her, and the taste
of life was stale on her lips. She hardly knew what she had been

seeking, or why the failure to find it had so blotted the light from her sky: she was only aware of a vague sense of failure, of an inner isolation deeper than the loneliness about her.

Her footsteps flagged, and she stood gazing listlessly ahead, digging the ferny edge of the path with the tip of her sun-shade. As she did so a step sounded behind her, and she saw Selden at her side.

"How fast you walk!" he remarked. "I thought I should never catch up with you."

She answered gaily: "You must be quite breathless! I've been sitting under that tree for an hour."

"Waiting for me, I hope?" he rejoined; and she said with a vague laugh:

"Well—waiting to see if you would come."

"I seize the distinction, but I don't mind it, since doing the one involved doing the other. But weren't you sure that I should come?"

"If I waited long enough—but you see I had only a limited time to give to the experiment"

"Why limited? Limited by luncheon?"

"No; by my other engagement."

"Your engagement to go to church with Muriel and Hilda?"

"No; but to come home from church with another person."

"Ah, I see; I might have known you were fully provided with alternatives. And is the other person coming home this way?"

Lily laughed again. "That's just what I don't know; and to find out, it is my business to get to church before the service is over."

"Exactly; and it is my business to prevent your doing so; in which case the other person, piqued by your absence, will form the desperate resolve of driving back in the omnibus."

Lily received this with fresh appreciation; his nonsense was like the bubbling of her inner mood. "Is that what you would do in such an emergency?" she enquired.

Selden looked at her with solemnity. "I am here to prove to you," he cried, "what I am capable of doing in an emergency!"

"Walking a mile in an hour—you must own that the omnibus would be quicker!"

"Ah—but will he find you in the end? That's the only test of success."

They looked at each other with the same luxury of enjoyment that they had felt in exchanging absurdities over his tea-table; but suddenly Lily's face changed, and she said: "Well, if it is, he has succeeded."

Selden, following her glance, perceived a party of people advancing toward them from the farther bend of the path. Lady Cressida had evidently insisted on walking home, and the rest of the church-goers had thought it their duty to accompany her. Lily's companion looked rapidly from one to the other of the two men of the party; Wetherall walking respectfully at Lady Cressida's side with his little sidelong look of nervous attention, and Percy Gryce bringing up the rear with Mrs. Wetherall and the Trenors.

"Ah—now I see why you were getting up your Americana!" Selden exclaimed with a note of the freest admiration; but the blush with which the sally was received checked whatever amplifications he had meant to give it.

That Lily Bart should object to being bantered about her suitors, or even about her means of attracting them, was so new to Selden that he had a momentary flash of surprise, which lit up a number of possibilities; but she rose gallantly to the defence of her confusion, by saying, as its object approached: "That was why I was waiting for you—to thank you for having given me so many points!"

"Ah, you can hardly do justice to the subject in such a short time," said Selden, as the Trenor girls caught sight of Miss Bart; and while she signalled a response to their boisterous greeting, he added quickly: "Won't you devote your afternoon to it? You know I must be off tomorrow morning. We'll take a walk, and you can thank me at your leisure."

6

THE AFTERNOON WAS PERFECT. A deeper stillness possessed the air, and the glitter of the American autumn was tempered by a haze which diffused the brightness without dulling it.

In the woody hollows of the park there was already a faint chill; but as the ground rose the air grew lighter, and ascending the long slopes beyond the high-road, Lily and her companion reached a zone of lingering summer. The path wound across a meadow with scattered trees; then it dipped into a lane plumed with asters and purpling sprays of bramble, whence, through the light quiver of ash-leaves, the country unrolled itself in pastoral distances.

Higher up, the lane showed thickening tufts of fern and of the creeping glossy verdure of shaded slopes; trees began to over-hang it, and the shade deepened to the checkered dusk of a beech-grove. The boles of the trees stood well apart, with only a light feathering of undergrowth; the path wound along the edge of the wood, now and then looking out on a sunlit pasture or on an orchard spangled with fruit.

Lily had no real intimacy with nature, but she had a passion for the appropriate and could be keenly sensitive to a scene which was the fitting background of her own sensations. The landscape outspread below her seemed an enlargement of her present mood, and she found something of herself in its calm-ness, its breadth, its long free reaches. On the nearer slopes the sugar-maples wavered like pyres of light; lower down was a massing of grey orchards, and here and there the lingering green of an oak-grove. Two or three red farm-houses dozed under the apple-trees, and the white wooden spire of a village church showed beyond the shoulder of the hill; while far below, in a haze of dust, the high-road ran between the fields.

"Let us sit here," Selden suggested, as they reached an open ledge of rock above which the beeches rose steeply between mossy boulders.

Lily dropped down on the rock, glowing with her long climb. She sat quiet, her lips parted by the stress of the ascent, her eyes wandering peacefully over the broken ranges of the landscape. Selden stretched himself on the grass at her feet, tilting his hat against the level sun-rays, and clasping his hands behind his head, which rested against the side of the rock. He had no wish to make her talk; her quick-breathing silence seemed a part of the general hush and harmony of things. In his own mind there was only a lazy sense of pleasure, veiling the sharp edges of sensation as the September haze veiled the scene at their feet. But Lily, though her attitude was as calm as his, was throbbing inwardly with a rush of thoughts. There were in her at the moment two beings, one drawing deep breaths of freedom and exhilaration, the other gasping for air in a little black prison-house of fears. But gradually the captive's gasps grew fainter, or the other paid less heed to them: the horizon expanded, the air grew stronger, and the free spirit quivered for flight.

She could not herself have explained the sense of buoyancy which seemed to lift and swing her above the sun-suffused world at her feet. Was it love, she wondered, or a mere fortuitous combination of happy thoughts and sensations? How much of it was owing to the spell of the perfect afternoon, the scent of the fading woods, the thought of the dulness she had fled from? Lily had no definite experience by which to test the quality of her feelings. She had several times been in love with fortunes or careers, but only once with a man. That was years ago, when she first came out, and had been smitten with a romantic passion for a young gentleman named Herbert Melson, who had blue eyes and a little wave in his hair. Mr. Melson, who was possessed of no other negotiable securities, had hastened to employ these in capturing the eldest Miss Van Osburgh: since then he had grown stout and wheezy, and was given to telling anecdotes about his children. If Lily recalled this early emotion it was not to compare it with that which now possessed her; the only point of comparison was the sense of lightness, of emancipation, which she remembered feeling, in the whirl of a waltz or the seclusion of a conservatory, during the brief course of her youthful romance. She had not known again till today that lightness, that glow of freedom; but now it was something more than a blind groping of the blood. The peculiar charm of her feeling for Selden was that she understood it; she could put her finger on every link of the chain that was drawing them together. Though his popularity was of the quiet kind, felt rather than actively expressed among his friends, she had never mistaken his inconspicuousness for obscurity. His reputed cultivation was generally regarded as a slight obstacle to easy intercourse, but Lily, who prided herself on her broad-mind recognition of literature, and always carried an Omar Khayyam* in her travelling-bag, was attracted by this attribute, which she felt would have had its distinction in an older society. It was, moreover, one of his gifts to look his part; to have a height which lifted his head above the crowd, and the keenly-modelled dark features which, in a land of amorphous types, gave him the air of belonging to a more specialized race, of carrying the impress of a concentrated past. Expansive persons found him a little dry, and very young girls thought him sarcastic; but this air of friendly aloofness, as far removed as possible from any assertion of personal advantage, was the quality which piqued Lily's interest. Everything about him accorded with the fastidious element in her taste, even to the light irony with which he surveyed what seemed to her most sacred. She admired him most of all, perhaps, for being able to convey as distinct a sense of superiority as the richest man she had ever met.

It was the unconscious prolongation of this thought which led her to say presently, with a laugh: "I have broken two engagements for you today. How many have you broken for me?"

"None," said Selden calmly. "My only engagement at Bellomont was with you."

She glanced down at him, faintly smiling.

"Did you really come to Bellomont to see me?"

"Of course I did."

Her look deepened meditatively. "Why?" she murmured,

---

*Eleventh- to twelfth-century Persian poet whose *Rubáiyát* was translated into English by Edward FitzGerald in 1859.

with an accent which took all tinge of coquetry from the question.

"Because you're such a wonderful spectacle: I always like to see what you are doing."

"How do you know what I should be doing if you were not here?"

Selden smiled. "I don't flatter myself that my coming has deflected your course of action by a hair's breadth."

"That's absurd—since, if you were not here, I could obviously not be taking a walk with you."

"No, but your taking a walk with me is only another way of making use of your material. You are an artist and I happen to be the bit of colour you are using today. It's a part of your cleverness to be able to produce premeditated effects extemporaneously."

Lily smiled also: his words were too acute not to strike her sense of humour. It was true that she meant to use the accident of his presence as part of a very definite effect; or that, at least, was the secret pretext she had found for breaking her promise to walk with Mr. Gryce. She had sometimes been accused of being too eager—even Judy Trenor had warned her to go slowly. Well, she would not be too eager in this case; she would give her suitor a longer taste of suspense. Where duty and inclination jumped together, it was not in Lily's nature to hold them asunder. She had excused herself from the walk on the plea of a headache: the horrid headache which, in the morning, had prevented her venturing to church. Her appearance at luncheon justified the excuse. She looked languid, full of a suffering sweetness; she carried a scent-bottle in her hand. Mr. Gryce was new to such manifestations; he wondered rather nervously if she were delicate, having far-reaching fears about the future of his progeny. But sympathy won the day, and he besought her not to expose herself: he always connected the outer air with ideas of exposure.

Lily had received his sympathy with languid gratitude, urging him, since she should be such poor company, to join the rest of the party who, after luncheon, were starting in automobiles on a visit to the Van Osburghs at Peekskill.* Mr. Gryce was

---

*Once-fashionable suburb of New York City.

touched by her disinterestedness, and, to escape from the threatened vacuity of the afternoon, had taken her advice and departed mournfully, in a dust-hood and goggles:* as the motor-car plunged down the avenue she smiled at his resemblance to a baffled beetle.

Selden had watched her manœuvres with lazy amusement. She had made no reply to his suggestion that they should spend the afternoon together, but as her plan unfolded itself he felt fairly confident of being included in it. The house was empty when at length he heard her step on the stair and strolled out of the billiard-room to join her. She had on a hat and walking-dress, and the dogs were bounding at her feet.

"I thought, after all, the air might do me good," she explained; and he agreed that so simple a remedy was worth trying.

The excursionists would be gone at least four hours; Lily and Selden had the whole afternoon before them, and the sense of leisure and safety gave the last touch of lightness to her spirit. With so much time to talk, and no definite object to be led up to, she could taste the rare joys of mental vagrancy.

She felt so free from ulterior motives that she took up his charge with a touch of resentment.

"I don't know," she said, "why you are always accusing me of premeditation."

"I thought you confessed to it: you told me the other day that you had to follow a certain line—and if one does a thing at all it is a merit to do it thoroughly."

"If you mean that a girl who has no one to think for her is obliged to think for herself, I am quite willing to accept the imputation. But you must find me a dismal kind of person if you suppose that I never yield to an impulse."

"Ah, but I don't suppose that: haven't I told you that your genius lies in converting impulses into intentions?"

"My genius?" she echoed with a sudden note of weariness. "Is there any final test of genius but success? And I certainly haven't succeeded."

---

*To protect clothes and eyes when driving in an open car.

Selden pushed his hat back and took a side-glance at her. "Success—what is success? I shall be interested to have your definition."

"Success?" She hesitated. "Why, to get as much as one can out of life, I suppose. It's a relative quality, after all. Isn't that your idea of it?"

"My idea of it? God forbid!" He sat up with sudden energy, resting his elbows on his knees and staring out upon the mellow fields. "My idea of success," he said, "is personal freedom."

"Freedom? Freedom from worries?"

"From everything—from money, from poverty, from ease and anxiety, from all the material accidents. To keep a kind of republic of the spirit—that's what I call success."

She leaned forward with a responsive flash. "I know—I know—it's strange; but that's just what I've been feeling today."

He met her eyes with the latent sweetness of his. "Is the feeling so rare with you?" he said.

She blushed a little under his gaze. "You think me horribly sordid, don't you? But perhaps it's rather that I never had any choice. There was no one, I mean, to tell me about the republic of the spirit."

"There never is—it's a country one has to find the way to one's self."

"But I should never have found my way there if you hadn't told me."

"Ah, there are sign-posts—but one has to know how to read them."

"Well, I have known, I have known!" she cried with a glow of eagerness. "Whenever I see you, I find myself spelling out a letter of the sign—and yesterday—last evening at dinner—I suddenly saw a little way into your republic."

Selden was still looking at her, but with a changed eye. Hitherto he had found, in her presence and her talk, the æsthetic amusement which a reflective man is apt to seek in desultory intercourse with pretty women. His attitude had been one of admiring spectatorship, and he would have been almost sorry to detect in her any emotional weakness which should interfere with the fulfilment of her aims. But now the hint of this weakness had become the most interesting thing about her. He had come on her that morning in a moment of disarray; her face had been pale and altered, and the diminution of her beauty had lent her a poignant charm. *That is how she looks when she is alone!* had been his first thought; and the second was to note in her the change which his coming produced. It was the danger-point of their intercourse that he could not doubt the spontaneity of her liking. From whatever angle he viewed their dawning intimacy, he could not see it as part of her scheme of life; and to be the unforeseen element in a career so accurately planned was stimulating even to a man who had renounced sentimental experiments.

"Well," he said, "did it make you want to see more? Are you going to become one of us?"

He had drawn out his cigarettes as he spoke, and she reached her hand toward the case.

"Oh, do give me one—I haven't smoked for days!"

"Why such unnatural abstinence? Everybody smokes at Bellomont."

"Yes—but it is not considered becoming in a *jeune fille à marier;** and at the present moment I am a *jeune fille à marier.*"

"Ah, then I'm afraid we can't let you into the republic."

"Why not? Is it a celibate order?"

"Not in the least, though I'm bound to say there are not many married people in it. But you will marry some one very rich, and it's as hard for rich people to get into as the kingdom of heaven."†

"That's unjust, I think, because, as I understand it, one of the conditions of citizenship is not to think too much about money, and the only way not to think about money is to have a great deal of it."

"You might as well say that the only way not to think about air is to have enough to breathe. That is true enough in a sense; but your lungs are thinking about the air, if you are not. And so it is with your rich people—they may not be thinking of money,

---

*Marriageable young lady (French).
†Reference to the Bible, Matthew 19:24: "It is easier for a camel to go through the eye of a needle, than for a rich man to enter into the kingdom of God" (KJV).

but they're breathing it all the while; take them into another element and see how they squirm and gasp!"

Lily sat gazing absently through the blue rings of her cigarette-smoke.

"It seems to me," she said at length, "that you spend a good deal of your time in the element you disapprove of."

Selden received this thrust without discomposure. "Yes; but I have tried to remain amphibious: it's all right as long as one's lungs can work in another air. The real alchemy consists in being able to turn gold back again into something else; and that's the secret that most of your friends have lost."

Lily mused. "Don't you think," she rejoined after a moment, "that the people who find fault with society are too apt to regard it as an end and not a means, just as the people who despise money speak as if its only use were to be kept in bags and gloated over? Isn't it fairer to look at them both as opportunities, which may be used either stupidly or intelligently, according to the capacity of the user?"

"That is certainly the sane view; but the queer thing about society is that the people who regard it as an end are those who are in it, and not the critics on the fence. It's just the other way with most shows—the audience may be under the illusion, but the actors know that real life is on the other side of the footlights. The people who take society as an escape from work are putting it to its proper use; but when it becomes the thing worked for it distorts all the relations of life." Selden raised himself on his elbow. "Good heavens!" he went on, "I don't underrate the decorative side of life. It seems to me the sense of splendour has justified itself by what it has produced. The worst of it is that so much human nature is used up in the process. If we're all the raw stuff of the cosmic effects, one would rather be the fire that tempers a sword than the fish that dyes a purple cloak. And a society like ours wastes such good material in producing its little patch of purple! Look at a boy like Ned Silverton—he's really too good to be used to refurbish anybody's social shabbiness. There's a lad just setting out to discover the universe. Isn't it a pity he should end by finding it in Mrs. Fisher's drawing-room?"

"Ned is a dear boy, and I hope he will keep his illusions long enough to write some nice poetry about them; but do you think it is only in society that he is likely to lose them?"

Selden answered her with a shrug. "Why do we call all our generous ideas illusions, and the mean ones truths? Isn't it a sufficient condemnation of society to find one's self accepting such phraseology? I very nearly acquired the jargon at Silverton's age, and I know how names can alter the colour of beliefs."

She had never heard him speak with such energy of affirmation. His habitual touch was that of the eclectic, who lightly turns over and compares; and she was moved by this sudden glimpse into the laboratory where his faiths were formed.

"Ah, you are as bad as the other sectarians," she exclaimed; "why do you call your republic a republic? It is a close corporation, and you create arbitrary objections in order to keep people out."

"It is not *my* republic; if it were, I should have a *coup d'état* and seat you on the throne."

"Whereas, in reality, you think I can never even get my foot across the threshold? Oh, I understand what you mean. You despise my ambitions—you think them unworthy of me!"

Selden smiled, but not ironically. "Well, isn't that a tribute? I think them quite worthy of most of the people who live by them."

She had turned to gaze on him gravely. "But isn't it possible that, if I had the opportunities of these people, I might make a better use of them? Money stands for all kinds of things—its purchasing quality isn't limited to diamonds and motor-cars."

"Not in the least: you might expiate your enjoyment of them by founding a hospital."

"But if you think they are what I should really enjoy, you must think my ambitions are good enough for me."

Selden met this appeal with a laugh. "Ah, my dear Miss Bart, I am not divine Providence, to guarantee your enjoying the things you are trying to get!"

"Then the best you can say for me is, that after struggling to get them I probably shan't like them?" She drew a deep breath. "What a miserable future you foresee for me!"

"Well—have you never foreseen it for yourself?"

The slow colour rose to her cheek, not a blush of excitement but drawn from the deep wells of feeling; it was as if the effort of her spirit had produced it.

"Often and often," she said. "But it looks so much darker when you show it to me!"

He made no answer to this exclamation, and for a while they sat silent, while something throbbed between them in the wide quiet of the air. But suddenly she turned on him with a kind of vehemence.

"Why do you do this to me?" she cried. "Why do you make the things I have chosen seem hateful to me, if you have nothing to give me instead?"

The words roused Selden from the musing fit into which he had fallen. He himself did not know why he had led their talk along such lines; it was the last use he would have imagined himself making of an afternoon's solitude with Miss Bart. But it was one of those moments when neither seemed to speak deliberately, when an indwelling voice in each called to the other across unsounded depths of feeling.

"No, I have nothing to give you instead," he said, sitting up and turning so that he faced her. "If I had, it should be yours, you know."

She received this abrupt declaration in a way even stranger than the manner of its making: she dropped her face on her hands and he saw that for a moment she wept.

It was for a moment only, however; for when he leaned nearer and drew down her hands with a gesture less passionate than grave, she turned on him a face softened but not disfigured by emotion, and he said to himself, somewhat cruelly, that even her weeping was an art.

The reflection steadied his voice as he asked, between pity and irony: "Isn't it natural that I should try to belittle all the things I can't offer you?"

Her face brightened at this, but she drew her hand away, not with a gesture of coquetry, but as though renouncing something to which she had no claim.

"But you belittle *me*, don't you," she returned gently, "in being so sure they are the only things I care for?"

Selden felt an inner start; but it was only the last quiver of his egoism. Almost at once he answered quite simply: "But you do care for them, don't you? And no wishing of mine can alter that."

He had so completely ceased to consider how far this might carry him, that he had a distinct sense of disappointment when she turned on him a face sparkling with derision.

"Ah," she cried, "for all your fine phrases you're really as great a coward as I am, for you wouldn't have made one of them if you hadn't been so sure of my answer."

The shock of this retort had the effect of crystallizing Selden's wavering intentions.

"I am not so sure of your answer," he said quietly. "And I do you the justice to believe that you are not either."

It was her turn to look at him with surprise; and after a moment—"Do you want to marry me?" she asked.

He broke into a laugh. "No, I don't want to—but perhaps I should if you did!"

"That's what I told you—you're so sure of me that you can amuse yourself with experiments." She drew back the hand he had regained, and sat looking down on him sadly.

"I am not making experiments," he returned. "Or if I am, it is not on you but on myself. I don't know what effect they are going to have on me—but if marrying you is one of them, I will take the risk."

She smiled faintly. "It would be a great risk, certainly—I have never concealed from you how great."

"Ah, it's you who are the coward!" he exclaimed.

She had risen, and he stood facing her with his eyes on hers. The soft isolation of the falling day enveloped them: they seemed lifted into a finer air. All the exquisite influences of the hour trembled in their veins, and drew them to each other as the loosened leaves were drawn to the earth.

"It's you who are the coward," he repeated, catching her hands in his.

She leaned on him for a moment, as if with a drop of tired wings: he felt as though her heart were beating rather with the stress of a long flight than the thrill of new distances. Then, drawing back with a little smile of warning—"I shall look hideous in dowdy clothes; but I can trim my own hats," she declared.

They stood silent for a while after this, smiling at each other like adventurous children who have climbed to a forbidden height from which they discover a new world. The actual world at their feet was veiling itself in dimness, and across the valley a clear moon rose in the denser blue.

Suddenly they heard a remote sound, like the hum of a giant insect, and following the high-road, which wound whiter through the surrounding twilight, a black object rushed across their vision.

Lily started from her attitude of absorption; her smile faded and she began to move toward the lane.

"I had no idea it was so late. We shall not be back till after dark," she said, almost impatiently.

Selden was looking at her with surprise: it took him a moment to regain his usual view of her; then he said, with an uncontrollable note of dryness: "That was not one of our party; the motor was going the other way."

"I know—I know—" She paused, and he saw her redden through the twilight. "But I told them I was not well—that I should not go out. Let us go down!" she murmured.

Selden continued to look at her; then he drew his cigarette-case from his pocket and slowly lit a cigarette. It seemed to him necessary, at that moment, to proclaim, by some habitual gesture of this sort, his recovered hold on the actual: he had an almost puerile wish to let his companion see that, their flight over, he had landed on his feet.

She waited while the spark flickered under his curved palm; then he held out the cigarettes to her.

She took one with an unsteady hand, and putting it to her lips, leaned forward to draw her light from his. In the indistinctness the little red gleam lit up the lower part of her face, and he saw her mouth tremble into a smile

"Were you serious?" she asked, with an odd thrill of gaiety which she might have caught up, in haste, from a heap of stock inflections, without having time to select the just note.

Selden's voice was under better control. "Why not?" he returned. "You see I took no risks in being so." And as she continued to stand before him, a little pale under the retort, he added quickly: "Let us go down."

7

It spoke much for the depth of Mrs. Trenor's friendship that her voice, in admonishing Miss Bart, took the same note of personal despair as if she had been lamenting the collapse of a house-party.

"All I can say is, Lily, that I can't make you out!" She leaned back, sighing, in the morning abandon of lace and muslin, turning an indifferent shoulder to the heaped-up importunities of her desk, while she considered, with the eye of a physician who has given up the case, the erect exterior of the patient confronting her.

"If you hadn't told me you were going in for him seriously—but I'm sure you made that plain enough from the beginning! Why else did you ask me to let you off bridge, and to keep away Carry and Kate Corby? I don't suppose you did it because he amused you; we could none of us imagine your putting up with him for a moment unless you meant to marry him. And I'm sure everybody played fair! They all wanted to help it along. Even Bertha kept her hands off—I will say that—till Lawrence came down and you dragged him away from her. After that she had a right to retaliate—why on earth did you interfere with her? You've known Lawrence Selden for years—why did you behave as if you had just discovered him? If you had a grudge against Bertha it was a stupid time to show it—you could have paid her back just as well after you were married! I told you Bertha was dangerous. She was in an odious mood when she came here, but Lawrence's turning up put her in a good humour, and if you'd only let her think he came for *her* it would have never occurred to her to play this trick. Oh, Lily, you'll never do anything if you're not serious!"

Miss Bart accepted this exhortation in a spirit of the purest impartiality. Why should she have been angry? It was the voice of her own conscience which spoke to her through Mrs. Trenor's reproachful accents. But even to her own conscience she must trump up a semblance of defence.

"I only took a day off—I thought he meant to stay on all this week, and I knew Mr. Selden was leaving this morning."

Mrs. Trenor brushed aside the plea with a gesture which laid bare its weakness.

"He did mean to stay—that's the worst of it. It shows that he's run away from you; that Bertha's done her work and poisoned him thoroughly."

Lily gave a slight laugh. "Oh, if he's running I'll overtake him!"

Her friend threw out an arresting hand. "Whatever you do, Lily, do nothing!"

Miss Bart received the warning with a smile. "I don't mean, literally, to take the next train. There are ways—" But she did not go on to specify them.

Mrs. Trenor sharply corrected the tense. "There *were* ways—plenty of them! I didn't suppose you needed to have them pointed out. But don't deceive yourself—he's thoroughly frightened. He has run straight home to his mother, and she'll protect him!"

"Oh, to the death," Lily agreed, dimpling at the vision.

"How you can *laugh*—" her friend rebuked her; and she dropped back to a soberer perception of things with the question: "What was it Bertha really told him?"

"Don't ask me—horrors! She seemed to have raked up everything. Oh, you know what I mean—of course there isn't anything, *really;* but I suppose she brought in Prince Varigliano—and Lord Hubert—and there was some story of your having borrowed money of old Ned Van Alstyne: did you ever?"

"He is my father's cousin," Miss Bart interposed.

"Well, of course she left *that* out. It seems Ned told Carry Fisher; and she told Bertha, naturally. They're all alike, you know: they hold their tongues for years, and you think you're safe, but when their opportunity comes they remember everything."

Lily had grown pale: her voice had a harsh note in it. "It was some money I lost at bridge at the Van Osburghs'. I repaid it, of course."

"Ah, well, they wouldn't remember that; besides, it was the idea of the gambling debt that frightened Percy. Oh, Bertha knew her man—she knew just what to tell him!"

In this strain Mrs. Trenor continued for nearly an hour to admonish her friend. Miss Bart listened with admirable equanimity. Her naturally good temper had been disciplined by years of enforced compliance, since she had almost always had to attain her ends by the circuitous path of other people's; and, being naturally inclined to face unpleasant facts as soon as they presented themselves, she was not sorry to hear an impartial statement of what her folly was likely to cost, the more so as her own thoughts were still insisting on the other side of the case. Presented in the light of Mrs. Trenor's vigorous comments, the reckoning was certainly a formidable one, and Lily, as she listened, found herself gradually reverting to her friend's view of the situation. Mrs. Trenor's words were moreover emphasized for her hearer by anxieties which she herself could scarcely guess. Affluence, unless stimulated by a keen imagination, forms but the vaguest notion of the practical strain of poverty. Judy knew it must be "horrid" for poor Lily to have to stop to consider whether she could afford real lace on her petticoats, and not to have a motor-car and a steam-yacht at her orders; but the daily friction of unpaid bills, the daily nibble of small temptations to expenditure, were trials as far out of her experience as the domestic problems of the char-woman. Mrs. Trenor's unconsciousness of the real stress of the situation had the effect of making it more galling to Lily. While her friend reproached her for missing the opportunity to eclipse her rivals, she was once more battling in imagination with the mounting tide of indebtedness from which she had so nearly escaped. What wind of folly had driven her out again on those dark seas?

If anything was needed to put the last touch to her self-abasement it was the sense of the way her old life was opening its ruts again to receive her. Yesterday her fancy had fluttered free pinions above a choice of occupations; now she had to drop to the level of the familiar routine, in which moments of seeming brilliancy and freedom alternated with long hours of subjection.

She laid a deprecating hand on her friend's. "Dear Judy! I'm sorry to have been such a bore, and you are very good to me. But you must have some letters for me to answer—let me at least be useful."

She settled herself at the desk, and Mrs. Trenor accepted her resumption of the morning's task with a sigh which implied that, after all, she had proved herself unfit for higher uses.

The luncheon table showed a depleted circle. All the men but Jack Stepney and Dorset had returned to town (it seemed to Lily a last touch of irony that Selden and Percy Gryce should have gone in the same train), and Lady Cressida and the attendant Wetheralls had been despatched by motor to lunch at a distant country-house. At such moments of diminished interest it was usual for Mrs. Dorset to keep her room till the afternoon; but on this occasion she drifted in when luncheon was half over, hollow-eyed and drooping, but with an edge of malice under her indifference.

She raised her eyebrows as she looked about the table. "How few of us are left! I do so enjoy the quiet—don't you, Lily? I wish the men would always stop away—it's really much nicer without them. Oh, you don't count, George: one doesn't have to talk to one's husband. But I thought Mr. Gryce was to stay for the rest of the week?" she added enquiringly. "Didn't he intend to, Judy? He's such a nice boy—I wonder what drove him away? He is rather shy, and I'm afraid we may have shocked him: he has been brought up in such an old-fashioned way. Do you know, Lily, he told me he had never seen a girl play cards for money till he saw you doing it the other night? And he lives on the interest of his income, and always has a lot left over to invest!"

Mrs. Fisher leaned forward eagerly. "I do believe it is some one's duty to educate that young man. It is shocking that he has never been made to realize his duties as a citizen. Every wealthy man should be compelled to study the laws of his country."

Mrs. Dorset glanced at her quietly. "I think he *has* studied the divorce laws. He told me he had promised the Bishop to sign some kind of a petition against divorce."

Mrs. Fisher reddened under her powder, and Stepney said

with a laughing glance at Miss Bart: "I suppose he is thinking of marriage, and wants to tinker up the old ship before he goes aboard."

His betrothed looked shocked at the metaphor, and George Dorset exclaimed with a sardonic growl: "Poor devil! It isn't the ship that will do for him, it's the crew."

"Or the stowaways," said Miss Corby brightly. "If I contemplated a voyage with him I should try to start with a friend in the hold."

Miss Van Osburgh's vague feeling of pique was struggling for appropriate expression. "I'm sure I don't see why you laugh at him; I think he's very nice," she exclaimed; "and, at any rate, a girl who married him would always have enough to be comfortable."

She looked puzzled at the redoubled laughter which hailed her words, but it might have consoled her to know how deeply they had sunk into the breast of one of her hearers.

Comfortable! At that moment the word was more eloquent to Lily Bart than any other in the language. She could not even pause to smile over the heiress's view of a colossal fortune as a mere shelter against want: her mind was filled with the vision of what that shelter might have been to her. Mrs. Dorset's pin-pricks did not smart, for her own irony cut deeper: no one could hurt her as much as she was hurting herself, for no one else—not even Judy Trenor—knew the full magnitude of her folly.

She was roused from these unprofitable considerations by a whispered request from her hostess, who drew her apart as they left the luncheon-table.

"Lily, dear, if you've nothing special to do, may I tell Carry Fisher that you intend to drive to the station and fetch Gus? He will be back at four, and I know she has it in her mind to meet him. Of course I'm very glad to have him amused, but I happen to know that she has bled him rather severely since she's been here, and she is so keen about going to fetch him that I fancy she must have got a lot more bills this morning. It seems to me," Mrs. Trenor feelingly concluded, "that most of her alimony is paid by other women's husbands!"

Miss Bart, on her way to the station, had leisure to muse over her friend's words, and their peculiar application to herself. Why should she have to suffer for having once, for a few hours, borrowed money of an elderly cousin, when a woman like Carry Fisher could make a living unrebuked from the good-nature of her men friends and the tolerance of their wives? It all turned on the tiresome distinction between what a married woman might, and a girl might not, do. Of course it was shocking for a married woman to borrow money—and Lily was expertly aware of the implication involved—but still, it was the mere *malum prohibitum** which the world decries but condones, and which, though it may be punished by private vengeance, does not provoke the collective disapprobation of society. To Miss Bart, in short, no such opportunities were possible. She could of course borrow from her women friends—a hundred here or there, at the utmost—but they were more ready to give a gown or a trinket, and looked a little askance when she hinted her preference for a cheque. Women are not generous lenders, and those among whom her lot was cast were either in the same case as herself, or else too far removed from it to understand its necessities. The result of her meditations was the decision to join her aunt at Richfield. She could not remain at Bellomont without playing bridge, and being involved in other expenses; and to continue her usual series of autumn visits would merely prolong the same difficulties. She had reached a point where abrupt retrenchment was necessary, and the only cheap life was a dull life. She would start the next morning for Richfield.

At the station she thought Gus Trenor seemed surprised, and not wholly unrelieved, to see her. She yielded up the reins of the light runabout† in which she had driven over, and as he climbed heavily to her side, crushing her into a scant third of the seat, he said: "Halloo! It isn't often you honour me. You must have been uncommonly hard up for something to do."

The afternoon was warm, and propinquity made her more than usually conscious that he was red and massive, and that beads of moisture had caused the dust of the train to adhere unpleasantly to the broad expanse of cheek and neck which he

---

*Prohibited evil; unlawful act (Latin).
†Light carriage with an open top.

turned to her; but she was aware also, from the look in his small dull eyes, that the contact with her freshness and slenderness was as agreeable to him as the sight of a cooling beverage.

The perception of this fact helped her to answer gaily: "It's not often I have the chance. There are too many ladies to dispute the privilege with me."

"The privilege of driving me home? Well, I'm glad you won the race, anyhow. But I know what really happened—my wife sent you. Now didn't she?"

He had the dull man's unexpected flashes of astuteness, and Lily could not help joining in the laugh with which he had pounced on the truth.

"You see, Judy thinks I'm the safest person for you to be with; and she's quite right," she rejoined.

"Oh, is she, though? If she is, it's because you wouldn't waste your time on an old hulk like me. We married men have to put up with what we can get: all the prizes are for the clever chaps who've kept a free foot. Let me light a cigar, will you? I've had a beastly day of it."

He drew up in the shade of the village street, and passed the reins to her while he held a match to his cigar. The little flame under his hand cast a deeper crimson on his puffing face, and Lily averted her eyes with a momentary feeling of repugnance. And yet some women thought him handsome!

As she handed back the reins, she said sympathetically: "Did you have such a lot of tiresome things to do?"

"I should say so—rather!" Trenor, who was seldom listened to, either by his wife or her friends, settled down into the rare enjoyment of a confidential talk. "You don't know how a fellow has to hustle to keep this kind of thing going." He waved his whip in the direction of the Bellomont acres, which lay outspread before them in opulent undulations. "Judy has no idea of what she spends—not that there isn't plenty to keep the thing going," he interrupted himself, "but a man has got to keep his eyes open and pick up all the tips he can. My father and mother used to live like fighting-cocks on their income, and put by a good bit of it too—luckily for me—but at the pace we go now, I don't know where I should be if it weren't for taking a flyer now and then. The women all think—I mean Judy thinks—I've nothing to do but to go down town once a month and cut off coupons,* but the truth is it takes a devilish lot of hard work to keep the machinery running. Not that I ought to complain today, though," he went on after a moment, "for I did a very neat stroke of business, thanks to Stepney's friend Rosedale: by the way, Miss Lily, I wish you'd try to persuade Judy to be decently civil to that chap. He's going to be rich enough to buy us all out one of these days, and if she'd only ask him to dine now and then I could get almost anything out of him. The man is mad to know the people who don't want to know him, and when a fellow's in that state there is nothing he won't do for the first woman who takes him up."

Lily hesitated a moment. The first part of her companion's discourse had started an interesting train of thought, which was rudely interrupted by the mention of Mr. Rosedale's name. She uttered a faint protest.

"But you know Jack did try to take him about, and he was impossible."

"Oh, hang it—because he's fat and shiny, and has a shoppy manner! Well, all I can say is that the people who are clever enough to be civil to him now will make a mighty good thing of it. A few years from now he'll be in it whether we want him or not, and then he won't be giving away a half-a-million tip for a dinner."

Lily's mind had reverted from the intrusive personality of Mr. Rosedale to the train of thought set in motion by Trenor's first words. This vast mysterious Wall Street world of "tips" and "deals"—might she not find in it the means of escape from her dreary predicament? She had often heard of women making money in this way through their friends: she had no more notion than most of her sex of the exact nature of the transaction, and its vagueness seemed to diminish its indelicacy. She could not, indeed, imagine herself, in any extremity, stooping to extract a "tip" from Mr. Rosedale; but at her side was a man in possession of that precious commodity, and who, as the husband of her

---

*Bond owners received interest by redeeming the coupons that were attached.

dearest friend, stood to her in a relation of almost fraternal intimacy.

In her inmost heart Lily knew it was not by appealing to the fraternal instinct that she was likely to move Gus Trenor; but this way of explaining the situation helped to drape its crudity, and she was always scrupulous about keeping up appearances to herself. Her personal fastidiousness had a moral equivalent, and when she made a tour of inspection in her own mind there were certain closed doors she did not open.

As they reached the gates of Bellomont she turned to Trenor with a smile.

"The afternoon is so perfect—don't you want to drive me a little farther? I've been rather out of spirits all day, and it's so restful to be away from people, with some one who won't mind if I'm a little dull."

She looked so plaintively lovely as she proffered the request, so trustfully sure of his sympathy and understanding, that Trenor felt himself wishing that his wife could see how other women treated him—not battered wire-pullers like Mrs. Fisher, but a girl that most men would have given their boots to get such a look from.

"Out of spirits? Why on earth should you ever be out of spirits? Is your last box of Doucet* dresses a failure, or did Judy rook you out of everything at bridge last night?"

Lily shook her head with a sigh. "I have had to give up Doucet; and bridge too—I can't afford it. In fact I can't afford any of the things my friends do, and I am afraid Judy often thinks me a bore because I don't play cards any longer, and because I am not as smartly dressed as the other women. But you will think me a bore too if I talk to you about my worries, and I only mention them because I want you to do me a favour—the very greatest of favours."

Her eyes sought his once more, and she smiled inwardly at the tinge of apprehension that she read in them.

"Why, of course—if it's anything I can manage——" He

---

*Fashionable French couturier and art collector Jacques Doucet (1853–1929).

broke off, and she guessed that his enjoyment was disturbed by the remembrance of Mrs. Fisher's methods.

"The greatest of favours," she rejoined gently. "The fact is, Judy is angry with me, and I want you to make my peace."

"Angry with you? Oh, come, nonsense——" his relief broke through in a laugh. "Why, you know she's devoted to you."

"She is the best friend I have, and that is why I mind having to vex her. But I daresay you know what she has wanted me to do. She has set her heart—poor dear—on my marrying—marrying a great deal of money."

She paused with a slight falter of embarrassment, and Trenor, turning abruptly, fixed on her a look of growing intelligence.

"A great deal of money? Oh, by Jove—you don't mean Gryce? What—you do? Oh, no, of course I won't mention it—you can trust me to keep my mouth shut—but Gryce—good Lord, *Gryce!* Did Judy really think you could bring yourself to marry that portentous little ass? But you couldn't, eh? And so you gave him the sack, and that's the reason why he lit out by the first train this morning?" He leaned back, spreading himself farther across the seat, as if dilated by the joyful sense of his own discernment. "How on earth could Judy think you would do such a thing? *I* could have told her you'd never put up with such a little milksop!"

Lily sighed more deeply. "I sometimes think," she murmured, "that men understand a woman's motives better than other women do."

"Some men—I'm certain of it! I could have *told* Judy," he repeated, exulting in the implied superiority over his wife.

"I thought you would understand; that's why I wanted to speak to you," Miss Bart rejoined. "I *can't* make that kind of marriage; it's impossible. But neither can I go on living as all the women in my set do. I am almost entirely dependent on my aunt, and though she is very kind to me she makes me no regular allowance, and lately I've lost money at cards, and I don't dare tell her about it. I have paid my card debts, of course, but there is hardly anything left for my other expenses, and if I go on with my present life I shall be in horrible difficulties. I have a tiny income of my own, but I'm afraid it's badly invested, for it seems to bring in less every year, and I am so ignorant of money matters that I don't know if my aunt's agent, who looks after it, is a good adviser." She paused a moment, and added in a lighter tone: "I didn't mean to bore you with all this, but I want your help in making Judy understand that I can't, at present, go on living as one must live among you all. I am going away tomorrow to join my aunt at Richfield, and I shall stay there for the rest of the autumn, and dismiss my maid and learn how to mend my own clothes."

At this picture of loveliness in distress, the pathos of which was heightened by the light touch with which it was drawn, a murmur of indignant sympathy broke from Trenor. Twenty-four hours earlier, if his wife had consulted him on the subject of Miss Bart's future, he would have said that a girl with extravagant tastes and no money had better marry the first rich man she could get; but with the subject of discussion at his side, turning to him for sympathy, making him feel that he understood her better than her dearest friends, and confirming the assurance by the appeal of her exquisite nearness, he was ready to swear that such a marriage was a desecration, and that, as a man of honour, he was bound to do all he could to protect her from the results of her disinterestedness. This impulse was reinforced by the reflection that if she had married Gryce she would have been surrounded by flattery and approval, whereas, having refused to sacrifice herself to expediency, she was left to bear the whole cost of her resistance. Hang it, if he could find a way out of such difficulties for a professional sponge like Carry Fisher, who was simply a mental habit corresponding to the physical titillations of the cigarette or the cock-tail, he could surely do as much for a girl who appealed to his highest sympathies, and who brought her troubles to him with the trustfulness of a child.

Trenor and Miss Bart prolonged their drive till long after sunset; and before it was over he had tried, with some show of success, to prove to her that, if she would only trust him, he could make a handsome sum of money for her without endangering the small amount she possessed. She was too genuinely ignorant of the manipulations of the stock-market to understand his technical explanations, or even perhaps to perceive that certain points in them were slurred; the haziness enveloping the transaction served as a veil for her embarrassment, and through the general blur her hopes dilated like lamps in a fog. She understood only that her modest investments were to be mysteriously multiplied without risk to herself; and the assurance that this miracle would take place within a short time, that there would be no tedious interval for suspense and reaction, relieved her of her lingering scruples.

Again she felt the lightening of her load, and with it the release of repressed activities. Her immediate worries conjured, it was easy to resolve that she would never again find herself in such straits, and as the need of economy and self-denial receded from her foreground she felt herself ready to meet any other demand which life might make. Even the immediate one of letting Trenor, as they drove homeward, lean a little nearer and rest his hand reassuringly on hers, cost her only a momentary shiver of reluctance. It was part of the game to make him feel that her appeal had been an uncalculated impulse, provoked by the liking he inspired; and the renewed sense of power in handling men, while it consoled her wounded vanity, helped also to obscure the thought of the claim at which his manner hinted. He was a coarse dull man who, under all his show of authority, was a mere supernumerary in the costly show for which his money paid: surely, to a clever girl, it would be easy to hold him by his vanity, and so keep the obligation on his side.

8

THE FIRST THOUSAND DOLLAR cheque which Lily received with a blotted scrawl from Gus Trenor strengthened her self-confidence in the exact degree to which it effaced her debts.

The transaction had justified itself by its results: she saw now how absurd it would have been to let any primitive scruple deprive her of this easy means of appeasing her creditors. Lily felt really virtuous as she dispensed the sum in sops to her tradesmen, and the fact that a fresh order accompanied each payment did not lessen her sense of disinterestedness. How many women, in her place, would have given the orders without making the payment!

She had found it reassuringly easy to keep Trenor in a good humour. To listen to his stories, to receive his confidences and laugh at his jokes, seemed for the moment all that was required of her, and the complacency with which her hostess regarded these attentions freed them of the least hint of ambiguity. Mrs. Trenor evidently assumed that Lily's growing intimacy with her husband was simply an indirect way of returning her own kindness.

"I'm so glad you and Gus have become such good friends," she said approvingly. "It's too delightful of you to be so nice to him, and put up with all his tiresome stories. I know what they are, because I had to listen to him when we were engaged—I'm sure he is telling the same ones still. And now I shan't always have to be asking Carry Fisher here to keep him in a good humour. She's a perfect vulture, you know; and she hasn't the least moral sense. She is always getting Gus to speculate for her, and I'm sure she never pays when she loses."

Miss Bart could shudder at this state of things without the embarrassment of a personal application. Her own position was surely quite different. There could be no question of her not paying when she lost, since Trenor had assured her that she was certain not to lose. In sending her the cheque he had explained that he had made five thousand for her out of Rosedale's "tip," and put four thousand back in the same venture, as there was the promise of another "big rise"; she understood therefore that he was now speculating with her own money, and that she consequently owed him no more than the gratitude which such a trifling service demanded. She vaguely supposed that, to raise the first sum, he had borrowed on her securities; but this was a point over which her curiosity did not linger. It was concentrated, for the moment, on the probable date of the next "big rise."

The news of this event was received by her some weeks later, on the occasion of Jack Stepney's marriage to Miss Van Osburgh. As a cousin of the bridegroom, Miss Bart had been asked to act as bridesmaid; but she had declined on the plea that, since she was much taller than the other attendant virgins, her presence might mar the symmetry of the group. The truth was, she had attended too many brides to the altar: when next seen there she meant to be the chief figure in the ceremony. She knew the pleasantries made at the expense of young girls who have been too long before the public, and she was resolved to avoid such assumptions of youthfulness as might lead people to think her older than she really was.

The Van Osburgh marriage was celebrated in the village church near the paternal estate on the Hudson. It was the "simple country wedding" to which guests are conveyed in special trains, and from which the hordes of the uninvited have to be fended off by the intervention of the police. While these sylvan rites were taking place, in a church packed with fashion and festooned with orchids, the representatives of the press were threading their way, note-book in hand, through the labyrinth of wedding presents, and the agent of a cinematograph syndicate was setting up his apparatus at the church door. It was the kind of scene in which Lily had often pictured herself as taking the principal part, and on this occasion the fact that she was once more merely a casual spectator, instead of the mystically veiled figure occupying the centre of attention, strengthened her resolve to assume the latter part before the year was over. The fact that her immediate anxieties were relieved did not blind her to a possibility of their recurrence; it merely gave her enough buoyancy to rise once more above her doubts and feel a renewed faith in her beauty, her power, and her general fitness to attract a brilliant destiny. It could not be that one conscious of such aptitudes for mastery and enjoyment was doomed to a perpetuity of failure; and her mistakes looked easily reparable in the light of her restored self-confidence.

A special appositeness was given to these reflections by the discovery, in a neighbouring pew, of the serious profile and neatly-trimmed beard of Mr. Percy Gryce. There was something almost bridal in his own aspect: his large white gardenia had a symbolic air that struck Lily as a good omen. After all, seen in an assemblage of his kind he was not ridiculous-looking: a friendly critic might have called his heaviness weighty, and he was at his best in the attitude of vacant passivity which brings out the oddities of the restless. She fancied he was the kind of man whose sentimental associations would be stirred by the conventional imagery of a wedding, and she pictured herself, in the seclusion of the Van Osburgh conservatories, playing skilfully upon sensibilities thus prepared for her touch. In fact, when she looked at the other women about her, and recalled the image she had brought away from her own glass, it did not seem as though any special skill would be needed to repair her blunder and bring him once more to her feet.

The sight of Selden's dark head, in a pew almost facing her, disturbed for a moment the balance of her complacency. The rise of her blood as their eyes met was succeeded by a contrary motion, a wave of resistance and withdrawal. She did not wish to see him again, not because she feared his influence, but because his presence always had the effect of cheapening her aspirations, of throwing her whole world out of focus. Besides, he was a living reminder of the worst mistake in her career, and the fact that he had been its cause did not soften her feelings toward him. She could still imagine an ideal state of existence in which, all else being superadded, intercourse with Selden might be the last touch of luxury; but in the world as it was, such a privilege was likely to cost more than it was worth.

"Lily, dear, I never saw you look so lovely! You look as if something delightful had just happened to you!"

The young lady who thus formulated her admiration of her brilliant friend did not, in her own person, suggest such happy possibilities. Miss Gertrude Farish, in fact, typified the mediocre and the ineffectual. If there were compensating qualities in her wide frank glance and the freshness of her smile, these were qualities which only the sympathetic observer would perceive before noticing that her eyes were of a workaday grey and her lips without haunting curves. Lily's own view of her wavered between pity for her limitations and impatience at her cheerful acceptance of them. To Miss Bart, as to her mother, acquiescence in dinginess was evidence of stupidity; and there were moments when, in the consciousness of her own power to look and to be so exactly what the occasion required, she almost felt that other girls were plain and inferior from choice. Certainly no one need have confessed such acquiescence in her lot as was revealed in the "useful" colour of Gerty Farish's gown and the subdued lines of her hat: it is almost as stupid to let your clothes betray that you know you are ugly as to have them proclaim that you think you are beautiful.

Of course, being fatally poor and dingy, it was wise of Gerty to have taken up philanthropy and symphony concerts; but there was something irritating in her assumption that existence yielded no higher pleasures, and that one might get as much interest and excitement out of life in a cramped flat as in the splendours of the Van Osburgh establishment. Today, however, her chirping enthusiasms did not irritate Lily. They seemed only to throw her own exceptionalness into becoming relief, and give a soaring vastness to her scheme of life.

"Do let us go and take a peep at the presents before every one else leaves the dining-room!" suggested Miss Farish, linking her arm in her friend's. It was characteristic of her to take a sentimental and unenvious interest in all the details of a wedding: she was the kind of person who always kept her handkerchief out during the service, and departed clutching a box of wedding-cake.

"Isn't everything beautifully done?" she pursued, as they entered the distant drawing-room assigned to the display of Miss Van Osburgh's bridal spoils. "I always say no one does things better than cousin Grace! Did you ever taste anything more delicious than that *mousse* of lobster with champagne sauce? I made up my mind weeks ago that I wouldn't miss this wedding, and just fancy how delightfully it all came about. When Lawrence Selden heard I was coming, he insisted on fetching me himself and driving me to the station, and when we go back this evening I am to dine with him at Sherry's. I really feel as excited as if I were getting married myself!"

Lily smiled: she knew that Selden had always been kind to his dull cousin, and she had sometimes wondered why he wasted so much time in such an unremunerative manner; but now the thought gave her a vague pleasure.

"Do you see him often?" she asked.

"Yes; he is very good about dropping in on Sundays. And now and then we do a play together; but lately I haven't seen much of him. He doesn't look well, and he seems nervous and unsettled. The dear fellow! I do wish he would marry some nice girl. I told him so today, but he said he didn't care for the really nice ones, and the other kind didn't care for him—but that was just his joke, of course. He could never marry a girl who *wasn't* nice. Oh, my dear, did you ever see such pearls?"

They had paused before the table on which the bride's jewels were displayed, and Lily's heart gave an envious throb as she caught the refraction of light from their surfaces—the milky gleam of perfectly matched pearls, the flash of rubies relieved against contrasting velvet, the intense blue rays of sapphires kindled into light by surrounding diamonds: all these precious tints enhanced and deepened by the varied art of their setting. The glow of the stones warmed Lily's veins like wine. More completely than any other expression of wealth they symbolized the life she longed to lead, the life of fastidious aloofness and refinement in which every detail should have the finish of a jewel, and the whole form a harmonious setting to her own jewel-like rareness.

"Oh, Lily, do look at this diamond pendant—it's as big as a dinner-plate! Who can have given it?" Miss Farish bent shortsightedly over the accompanying card. "*Mr. Simon Rosedale.* What, that horrid man? Oh, yes—I remember he's a friend of Jack's, and I suppose cousin Grace had to ask him here today;

but she must rather hate having to let Gwen accept such a present from him."

Lily smiled. She doubted Mrs. Van Osburgh's reluctance, but was aware of Miss Farish's habit of ascribing her own delicacies of feeling to the persons least likely to be encumbered by them.

"Well, if Gwen doesn't care to be seen wearing it she can always exchange it for something else," she remarked.

"Ah, here is something so much prettier," Miss Farish continued. "Do look at this exquisite white sapphire. I'm sure the person who chose it must have taken particular pains. What is the name? Percy Gryce? Ah, then I'm not surprised!" She smiled significantly as she replaced the card. "Of course you've heard that he's perfectly devoted to Evie Van Osburgh? Cousin Grace is so pleased about it—it's quite a romance! He met her first at the George Dorsets', only about six weeks ago, and it's just the nicest possible marriage for dear Evie. Oh, I don't mean the money—of course she has plenty of her own—but she's such a quiet stay-at-home kind of girl, and it seems he has just the same tastes; so they are exactly suited to each other."

Lily stood staring vacantly at the white sapphire on its velvet bed. Evie Van Osburgh and Percy Gryce? The names rang derisively through her brain. *Evie Van Osburgh?* The youngest, dumpiest, dullest of the four dull and dumpy daughters whom Mrs. Van Osburgh, with unsurpassed astuteness, had "placed" one by one in enviable niches of existence. Ah, lucky girls who grow up in the shelter of a mother's love—a mother who knows how to contrive opportunities without conceding favours, how to take advantage of propinquity without allowing appetite to be dulled by habit! The cleverest girl may miscalculate where her own interests are concerned, may yield too much at one moment and withdraw too far at the next: it takes a mother's unerring vigilance and foresight to land her daughters safely in the arms of wealth and suitability.

Lily's passing light-heartedness sank beneath a renewed sense of failure. Life was too stupid, too blundering! Why should Percy Gryce's millions be joined to another great fortune, why should this clumsy girl be put in possession of powers she would never know how to use?

She was roused from these speculations by a familiar touch

on her arm, and turning saw Gus Trenor beside her. She felt a thrill of vexation: what right had he to touch her? Luckily Gerty Farish had wandered off to the next table, and they were alone.

Trenor, looking stouter than ever in his tight frock-coat, and unbecomingly flushed by the bridal libations, gazed at her with undisguised approval.

"By Jove, Lily, you do look a stunner!" He had slipped insensibly into the use of her Christian name, and she had never found the right moment to correct him. Besides, in her set all the men and women called each other by their Christian names; it was only on Trenor's lips that the familiar address had an unpleasant significance.

"Well," he continued, still jovially impervious to her annoyance, "have you made up your mind which of these little trinkets you mean to duplicate at Tiffany's* tomorrow? I've got a cheque for you in my pocket that will go a long way in that line!"

Lily gave him a startled look: his voice was louder than usual, and the room was beginning to fill with people. But as her glance assured her that they were still beyond ear-shot a sense of pleasure replaced her apprehension.

"Another dividend?" she asked, smiling and drawing near him in the desire not to be overheard.

"Well, not exactly: I sold out on the rise and I've pulled off four thou' for you. Not so bad for a beginner, eh? I suppose you'll begin to think you're a pretty knowing speculator. And perhaps you won't think poor old Gus such an awful ass as some people do."

"I think you the kindest of friends; but I can't thank you properly now."

She let her eyes shine into his with a look that made up for the hand-clasp he would have claimed if they had been alone—and how glad she was that they were not! The news filled her with the glow produced by a sudden cessation of physical pain. The world was not so stupid and blundering after all: now and

---

*New York jewelry store founded by Charles Lewis Tiffany (1812–1902), father of renowned glassmaker and interior decorator Louis Comfort Tiffany (1848–1933).

then a stroke of luck came to the unluckiest. At the thought her spirits began to rise: it was characteristic of her that one trifling piece of good fortune should give wings to all her hopes. Instantly came the reflection that Percy Gryce was not irretrievably lost; and she smiled to think of the excitement of recapturing him from Evie Van Osburgh. What chance could such a simpleton have against her if she chose to exert herself? She glanced about, hoping to catch a glimpse of Gryce; but her eyes lit instead on the glossy countenance of Mr. Rosedale, who was slipping through the crowd with an air half obsequious, half obtrusive, as though, the moment his presence was recognized, it would swell to the dimensions of the room.

Not wishing to be the means of effecting this enlargement, Lily quickly transferred her glance to Trenor, to whom the expression of her gratitude seemed not to have brought the complete gratification she had meant it to give.

"Hang thanking me—I don't want to be thanked, but I *should* like the chance to say two words to you now and then," he grumbled. "I thought you were going to spend the whole autumn with us, and I've hardly laid eyes on you for the last month. Why can't you come back to Bellomont this evening? We're all alone, and Judy is as cross as two sticks. Do come and cheer a fellow up. If you say yes I'll run you over in the motor, and you can telephone your maid to bring your traps* from town by the next train."

Lily shook her head with a charming semblance of regret. "I wish I could—but it's quite impossible. My aunt has come back to town, and I must be with her for the next few days."

"Well, I've seen a good deal less of you since we've got to be such pals than I used to when you were Judy's friend," he continued with unconscious penetration.

"When I was Judy's friend? Am I not her friend still? Really, you say the most absurd things! If I were always at Bellomont you would tire of me much sooner than Judy—but come and see me at my aunt's the next afternoon you are in town; then we can have a nice quiet talk, and you can tell me how I had better invest my fortune."

---

*Personal effects.

It was true that, during the last three or four weeks, she had absented herself from Bellomont on the pretext of having other visits to pay; but she now began to feel that the reckoning she had thus contrived to evade had rolled up interest in the interval.

The prospect of the nice quiet talk did not appear as all-sufficing to Trenor as she had hoped, and his brows continued to lower as he said: "Oh, I don't know that I can promise you a fresh tip every day. But there's one thing you might do for me; and that is, just to be a little civil to Rosedale. Judy has promised to ask him to dine when we get to town, but I can't induce her to have him at Bellomont, and if you would let me bring him up now it would make a lot of difference. I don't believe two women have spoken to him this afternoon, and I can tell you he's a chap it pays to be decent to."

Miss Bart made an impatient movement, but suppressed the words which seemed about to accompany it. After all, this was an unexpectedly easy way of acquitting her debt; and had she not reasons of her own for wishing to be civil to Mr. Rosedale?

"Oh, bring him by all means," she said smiling; "perhaps I can get a tip out of him on my own account."

Trenor paused abruptly, and his eyes fixed themselves on hers with a look which made her change colour.

"I say, you know—you'll please remember he's a blooming bounder," he said; and with a slight laugh she turned toward the open window near which they had been standing.

The throng in the room had increased, and she felt a desire for space and fresh air. Both of these she found on the terrace, where only a few men were lingering over cigarettes and liqueur, while scattered couples strolled across the lawn to the autumn-tinted borders of the flower-garden.

As she emerged, a man moved toward her from the knot of smokers, and she found herself face to face with Selden. The stir of the pulses which his nearness always caused was increased by a slight sense of constraint. They had not met since their Sunday afternoon walk at Bellomont, and that episode was still so vivid to her that she could hardly believe him to be less conscious of it. But his greeting expressed no more than the satisfaction which every pretty woman expects to see reflected in masculine eyes; and the discovery, if distasteful to her vanity, was reassuring to her nerves. Between the relief of her escape from Trenor, and the vague apprehension of her meeting with Rosedale, it was pleasant to rest a moment on the sense of complete understanding which Lawrence Selden's manner always conveyed.

"This is luck," he said smiling. "I was wondering if I should be able to have a word with you before the special snatches us away. I came with Gerty Farish, and promised not to let her miss the train, but I am sure she is still extracting sentimental solace from the wedding presents. She appears to regard their number and value as evidence of the disinterested affection of the contracting parties."

There was not the least trace of embarrassment in his voice, and as he spoke, leaning slightly against the jamb of the window, and letting his eyes rest on her in the frank enjoyment of her grace, she felt with a faint chill of regret that he had gone back without an effort to the footing on which they had stood before their last talk together. Her vanity was stung by the sight of his unscathed smile. She longed to be to him something more than a piece of sentient prettiness, a passing diversion to his eye and brain; and the longing betrayed itself in her reply.

"Ah," she said, "I envy Gerty that power she has of dressing up with romance all our ugly and prosaic arrangements! I have never recovered my self-respect since you showed me how poor and unimportant my ambitions were."

The words were hardly spoken when she realized their infelicity. It seemed to her her fate to appear at her worst to Selden.

"I thought, on the contrary," he returned lightly, "that I had been the means of proving they were more important to you than anything else."

It was as if the eager current of her being had been checked by a sudden obstacle which drove it back upon itself. She looked at him helplessly, like a hurt or frightened child: this real self of hers, which he had the faculty of drawing out of the depths, was so little accustomed to go alone!

The appeal of her helplessness touched in him, as it always did, a latent chord of inclination. It would have meant nothing to him to discover that his nearness made her more brilliant, but this glimpse of a twilight mood to which he alone had the clue seemed once more to set him in a world apart with her.

"At least you can't think worse things of me than you say!" she exclaimed with a trembling laugh; but before he could answer, the flow of comprehension between them was abruptly stayed by the reappearance of Gus Trenor, who advanced with Mr. Rosedale in his wake.

"Hang it, Lily, I thought you'd given me the slip: Rosedale and I have been hunting all over for you!"

His voice had a note of conjugal familiarity: Miss Bart fancied she detected in Rosedale's eye a twinkling perception of the fact, and the idea turned her dislike of him to repugnance.

She returned his profound bow with a slight nod, made more disdainful by the sense of Selden's surprise that she should number Rosedale among her acquaintances. Trenor had turned away, and his companion continued to stand before Miss Bart, alert and expectant, his lips parted in a smile at whatever she might be about to say, and his very back conscious of the privilege of being seen with her.

It was the moment for tact; for the quick bridging over of gaps; but Selden still leaned against the window, a detached observer of the scene, and under the spell of his observation Lily felt herself powerless to exert her usual arts. The dread of Selden's suspecting that there was any need for her to propitiate such a man as Rosedale checked the trivial phrases of politeness. Rosedale still stood before her in an expectant attitude, and she continued to face him in silence, her glance just level with his polished baldness. The look put the finishing touch to what her silence implied.

He reddened slowly, shifting from one foot to the other, fingered the plump black pearl in his tie, and gave a nervous twist to his moustache; then, running his eye over her, he drew back, and said, with a side-glance at Selden: "Upon my soul, I never saw a more ripping get-up. Is that the last creation of the dressmaker you go to see at the Benedick? If so, I wonder all the other women don't go to her too!"

The words were projected sharply against Lily's silence, and she saw in a flash that her own act had given them their emphasis. In ordinary talk they might have passed unheeded; but following on her prolonged pause they acquired a special meaning. She felt, without looking, that Selden had immediately seized it, and would inevitably connect the allusion with her visit to himself. The consciousness increased her irritation against Rosedale, but also her feeling that now, if ever, was the moment to propitiate him, hateful as it was to do so in Selden's presence.

"How do you know the other women don't go to my dressmaker?" she returned. "You see I'm not afraid to give her address to my friends!"

Her glance and accent so plainly included Rosedale in this privileged circle that his small eyes puckered with gratification, and a knowing smile drew up his moustache.

"By Jove, you needn't be!" he declared. "You could give 'em the whole outfit and win at a canter!"

"Ah, that's nice of you; and it would be nicer still if you would carry me off to a quiet corner, and get me a glass of lemonade or some innocent drink before we all have to rush for the train."

She turned away as she spoke, letting him strut at her side through the gathering groups on the terrace, while every nerve in her throbbed with the consciousness of what Selden must have thought of the scene.

But under her angry sense of the perverseness of things, and the light surface of her talk with Rosedale, a third idea persisted: she did not mean to leave without an attempt to discover the truth about Percy Gryce. Chance, or perhaps his own resolve, had kept them apart since his hasty withdrawal from Bellomont; but Miss Bart was an expert in making the most of the unexpected, and the distasteful incidents of the last few minutes— the revelation to Selden of precisely that part of her life which she most wished him to ignore—increased her longing for shelter, for escape from such humiliating contingencies. Any definite situation would be more tolerable than this buffeting of chances, which kept her in an attitude of uneasy alertness toward every possibility of life.

Indoors there was a general sense of dispersal in the air, as of an audience gathering itself up for departure after the principal actors had left the stage; but among the remaining groups, Lily could discover neither Gryce nor the youngest Miss Van Osburgh. That both should be missing struck her with foreboding;

and she charmed Mr. Rosedale by proposing that they should make their way to the conservatories at the farther end of the house. There were just enough people left in the long suite of rooms to make their progress conspicuous, and Lily was aware of being followed by looks of amusement and interrogation, which glanced off as harmlessly from her indifference as from her companion's self-satisfaction. She cared very little at that moment about being seen with Rosedale: all her thoughts were centred on the object of her search. The latter, however, was not discoverable in the conservatories, and Lily, oppressed by a sudden conviction of failure, was casting about for a way to rid herself of her now superfluous companion, when they came upon Mrs. Van Osburgh, flushed and exhausted, but beaming with the consciousness of duty performed.

She glanced at them a moment with the benign but vacant eye of the tired hostess, to whom her guests have become mere whirling spots in a kaleidoscope of fatigue; then her attention became suddenly fixed, and she seized on Miss Bart with a confidential gesture.

"My dear Lily, I haven't had time for a word with you, and now I suppose you are just off. Have you seen Evie? She's been looking everywhere for you: she wanted to tell you her little secret; but I daresay you have guessed it already. The engagement is not to be announced till next week—but you are such a friend of Mr. Gryce's that they both wished you to be the first to know of their happiness."

9

IN MRS. PENISTON'S YOUTH, fashion had returned to town in October; therefore on the tenth day of the month the blinds of her Fifth Avenue residence were drawn up, and the eyes of the Dying Gladiator* in bronze who occupied the drawing-room window resumed their survey of that deserted thoroughfare.

The first two weeks after her return represented to Mrs. Peniston the domestic equivalent of a religious retreat. She "went through" the linen and blankets in the precise spirit of the penitent exploring the inner folds of conscience; she sought for moths as the stricken soul seeks for lurking infirmities. The topmost shelf of every closet was made to yield up its secret, cellar and coal-bin were probed to their darkest depths and, as a final stage in the lustral rites, the entire house was swathed in penitential white and deluged with expiatory soapsuds.

It was on this phase of the proceedings that Miss Bart entered on the afternoon of her return from the Van Osburgh wedding. The journey back to town had not been calculated to soothe her nerves. Though Evie Van Osburgh's engagement was still officially a secret, it was one of which the innumerable intimate friends of the family were already possessed; and the trainful of returning guests buzzed with allusions and anticipations. Lily was acutely aware of her own part in this drama of innuendo: she knew the exact quality of the amusement the situation evoked. The crude forms in which her friends took their pleasure included a loud enjoyment of such complications: the zest of surprising destiny in the act of playing a practical joke. Lily knew well enough how to bear herself in difficult situations. She had, to a shade, the exact manner between victory and defeat:

---

*Copy of a famous Greek statue of a wounded Gaul.

every insinuation was shed without an effort by the bright in-difference of her manner. But she was beginning to feel the strain of the attitude; the reaction was more rapid, and she lapsed to a deeper self-disgust.

As was always the case with her, this moral repulsion found a physical outlet in a quickened distaste for her surroundings. She revolted from the complacent ugliness of Mrs. Peniston's black walnut, from the slippery gloss of the vestibule tiles, and the mingled odour of sapolio* and furniture-polish that met her at the door.

The stairs were still carpetless, and on the way up to her room she was arrested on the landing by an encroaching tide of soapsuds. Gathering up her skirts, she drew aside with an impa-tient gesture; and as she did so she had the odd sensation of hav-ing already found herself in the same situation but in different surroundings. It seemed to her that she was again descending the staircase from Selden's rooms; and looking down to remon-strate with the dispenser of the soapy flood, she found herself met by a lifted stare which had once before confronted her under similar circumstances. It was the char-woman of the Benedick who, resting on crimson elbows, examined her with the same unflinching curiosity, the same apparent reluctance to let her pass. On this occasion, however, Miss Bart was on her own ground.

"Don't you see that I wish to go by? Please move your pail," she said sharply.

The woman at first seemed not to hear; then, without a word of excuse, she pushed back her pail and dragged a wet floor-cloth across the landing, keeping her eyes fixed on Lily while the latter swept by. It was insufferable that Mrs. Peniston should have such creatures about the house; and Lily entered her room resolved that the woman should be dismissed that evening.

Mrs. Peniston, however, was at the moment inaccessible to remonstrance: since early morning she had been shut up with her maid, going over her furs, a process which formed the cul-minating episode in the drama of household renovation. In the

---

*Oil-based cleaning soap.

evening also Lily found herself alone, for her aunt, who rarely dined out, had responded to the summons of a Van Alstyne cousin who was passing through town. The house, in its state of unnatural immaculateness and order, was as dreary as a tomb, and as Lily, turning from her brief repast between shrouded side-boards, wandered into the newly-uncovered glare of the drawing-room she felt as though she were buried alive in the stifling limits of Mrs. Peniston's existence.

She usually contrived to avoid being at home during the season of domestic renewal. On the present occasion, however, a variety of reasons had combined to bring her to town; and foremost among them was the fact that she had fewer invitations than usual for the autumn. She had so long been accustomed to pass from one country-house to another, till the close of the holidays brought her friends to town, that the unfilled gaps of time confronting her produced a sharp sense of waning popularity. It was as she had said to Selden—people were tired of her. They would welcome her in a new character, but as Miss Bart they knew her by heart. She knew herself by heart too, and was sick of the old story. There were moments when she longed blindly for anything different, anything strange, remote and untried; but the utmost reach of her imagination did not go beyond picturing her usual life in a new setting. She could not figure herself as anywhere but in a drawing-room, diffusing elegance as a flower sheds perfume.

Meanwhile, as October advanced she had to face the alternative of returning to the Trenors or joining her aunt in town. Even the desolating dulness of New York in October, and the soapy discomforts of Mrs. Peniston's interior, seemed preferable to what might await her at Bellomont; and with an air of heroic devotion she announced her intention of remaining with her aunt till the holidays.

Sacrifices of this nature are sometimes received with feelings as mixed as those which actuate them; and Mrs. Peniston remarked to her confidential maid that, if any of the family were to be with her at such a crisis (though for forty years she had been thought competent to see to the hanging of her own curtains), she would certainly have preferred Miss Grace to Miss Lily. Grace Stepney was an obscure cousin, of adaptable man-

ners and vicarious interests, who "ran in" to sit with Mrs. Peniston when Lily dined out too continuously; who played bézique,
picked up dropped stitches, read out the deaths from the *Times*,
and sincerely admired the purple satin drawing-room curtains,
the Dying Gladiator in the window, and the seven-by-five
painting of Niagara which represented the one artistic excess of
Mr. Peniston's temperate career.

Mrs. Peniston, under ordinary circumstances, was as much
bored by her excellent cousin as the recipient of such services
usually is by the person who performs them. She greatly preferred the brilliant and unreliable Lily, who did not know one
end of a crochet-needle from the other, and had frequently
wounded her susceptibilities by suggesting that the drawing-
room should be "done over." But when it came to hunting for
missing napkins, or helping to decide whether the backstairs
needed recarpeting, Grace's judgment was certainly sounder
than Lily's: not to mention the fact that the latter resented the
smell of bees-wax and brown soap, and behaved as though she
thought a house ought to keep clean of itself, without extraneous assistance.

Seated under the cheerless blaze of the drawing-room chandelier—Mrs. Peniston never lit the lamps unless there was "company"—Lily seemed to watch her own figure retreating down
vistas of neutral-tinted dulness to a middle age like Grace Stepney's. When she ceased to amuse Judy Trenor and her friends
she would have to fall back on amusing Mrs. Peniston;
whichever way she looked she saw only a future of servitude to
the whims of others, never the possibility of asserting her own
eager individuality.

A ring at the door-bell, sounding emphatically through the
empty house, roused her suddenly to the extent of her boredom.
It was as though all the weariness of the past months had cul-
minated in the vacuity of that interminable evening. If only the
ring meant a summons from the outer world—a token that she
was still remembered and wanted!

After some delay a parlour-maid presented herself with the
announcement that there was a person outside who was asking
to see Miss Bart; and on Lily's pressing for a more specific description, she added:

"It's Mrs. Haffen, Miss; she won't say what she wants."

Lily, to whom the name conveyed nothing, opened the door upon a woman in a battered bonnet, who stood firmly planted under the hall-light. The glare of the unshaded gas shone familiarly on her pock-marked face and the reddish baldness visible through thin strands of straw-coloured hair. Lily looked at the char-woman in surprise.

"Do you wish to see me?" she asked.

"I should like to say a word to you, Miss." The tone was neither aggressive nor conciliatory: it revealed nothing of the speaker's errand. Nevertheless, some precautionary instinct warned Lily to withdraw beyond earshot of the hovering parlour-maid.

She signed to Mrs. Haffen to follow her into the drawing-room, and closed the door when they had entered.

"What is it that you wish?" she enquired.

The char-woman, after the manner of her kind, stood with her arms folded in her shawl. Unwinding the latter, she produced a small parcel wrapped in dirty newspaper.

"I have something here that you might like to see, Miss Bart." She spoke the name with an unpleasant emphasis, as though her knowing it made a part of her reason for being there. To Lily the intonation sounded like a threat.

"You have found something belonging to me?" she asked, extending her hand.

Mrs. Haffen drew back. "Well, if it comes to that, I guess it's mine as much as anybody's," she returned.

Lily looked at her perplexedly. She was sure, now, that her visitor's manner conveyed a threat; but, expert as she was in certain directions, there was nothing in her experience to prepare her for the exact significance of the present scene. She felt, however, that it must be ended as promptly as possible.

"I don't understand; if this parcel is not mine, why have you asked for me?"

The woman was unabashed by the question. She was evidently prepared to answer it, but like all her class she had to go a long way back to make a beginning, and it was only after a pause that she replied: "My husband was janitor to the Benedick till the first of the month; since then he can't get nothing to do."

Lily remained silent and she continued: "It wasn't no fault of our own, neither: the agent had another man he wanted the place for, and we was put out, bag and baggage, just to suit his fancy. I had a long sickness last winter, and an operation that ate up all we'd put by; and it's hard for me and the children, Haffen being so long out of a job."

After all, then, she had come only to ask Miss Bart to find a place for her husband; or, more probably, to seek the young lady's intervention with Mrs. Peniston. Lily had such an air of always getting what she wanted that she was used to being appealed to as an intermediary, and, relieved of her vague apprehension, she took refuge in the conventional formula.

"I am sorry you have been in trouble," she said.

"Oh, that we have, Miss, and it's on'y just beginning. If on'y we'd'a got another situation—but the agent, he's dead against us. It ain't no fault of ours, neither, but——"

At this point Lily's impatience overcame her. "If you have anything to say to me——" she interposed.

The woman's resentment of the rebuff seemed to spur her lagging ideas.

"Yes, Miss; I'm coming to that," she said. She paused again, with her eyes on Lily, and then continued, in a tone of diffuse narrative: "When we was at the Benedick I had charge of some of the gentlemen's rooms; leastways, I swep' 'em out on Saturdays. Some of the gentlemen got the greatest sight of letters: I never saw the like of it. Their waste-paper baskets 'd be fairly brimming, and papers falling over on the floor. Maybe havin' so many is how they get so careless. Some of 'em is worse than others. Mr. Selden, Mr. Lawrence Selden, he was always one of the carefullest: burnt his letters in winter, and tore 'em in little bits in summer. But sometimes he'd have so many he'd just bunch 'em together, the way the others did, and tear the lot through once—like this."

While she spoke she had loosened the string from the parcel in her hand, and now she drew forth a letter which she laid on the table between Miss Bart and herself. As she had said, the letter was torn in two; but with a rapid gesture she laid the torn edges together and smoothed out the page.

A wave of indignation swept over Lily. She felt herself in the presence of something vile, as yet but dimly conjectured—the kind of vileness of which people whispered, but which she had never thought of as touching her own life. She drew back with a motion of disgust, but her withdrawal was checked by a sudden discovery: under the glare of Mrs. Peniston's chandelier she had recognized the hand-writing of the letter. It was a large disjointed hand, with a flourish of masculinity which but slightly disguised its rambling weakness, and the words, scrawled in heavy ink on pale-tinted note-paper, smote on Lily's ear as though she had heard them spoken.

At first she did not grasp the full import of the situation. She understood only that before her lay a letter written by Bertha Dorset, and addressed, presumably, to Lawrence Selden. There was no date, but the blackness of the ink proved the writing to be comparatively recent. The packet in Mrs. Haffen's hand doubtless contained more letters of the same kind—a dozen, Lily conjectured from its thickness. The letter before her was short, but its few words, which had leapt into her brain before she was conscious of reading them, told a long history—a history over which, for the last four years, the friends of the writer had smiled and shrugged, viewing it merely as one among the countless "good situations" of the mundane comedy. Now the other side presented itself to Lily, the volcanic nether side of the surface over which conjecture and innuendo glide so lightly till the first fissure turns their whisper to a shriek. Lily knew that there is nothing society resents so much as having given its protection to those who have not known how to profit by it: it is for having betrayed its connivance that the body social punishes the offender who is found out. And in this case there was no doubt of the issue. The code of Lily's world decreed that a woman's husband should be the only judge of her conduct: she was technically above suspicion while she had the shelter of his approval, or even of his indifference. But with a man of George Dorset's temper there could be no thought of condonation—the possessor of his wife's letters could overthrow with a touch the whole structure of her existence. And into what hands Bertha Dorset's secret had been delivered! For a moment the irony of the coincidence tinged Lily's disgust with a confused sense of triumph. But the disgust prevailed—all her instinctive resistances, of taste, of training, of blind inherited scruples, rose against the other feeling. Her strongest sense was one of personal contamination.

She moved away, as though to put as much distance as possible between herself and her visitor. "I know nothing of these letters," she said; "I have no idea why you have brought them here."

Mrs. Haffen faced her steadily. "I'll tell you why, Miss. I brought 'em to you to sell, because I ain't got no other way of raising money, and if we don't pay our rent by tomorrow night we'll be put out. I never done anythin' of the kind before, and if you'd speak to Mr. Selden or to Mr. Rosedale about getting Haffen taken on again at the Benedick—I seen you talking to Mr. Rosedale on the steps that day you come out of Mr. Selden's rooms——"

The blood rushed to Lily's forehead. She understood now—Mrs. Haffen supposed her to be the writer of the letters. In the first leap of her anger she was about to ring and order the woman out; but an obscure impulse restrained her. The mention of Selden's name had started a new train of thought. Bertha Dorset's letters were nothing to her—they might go where the current of chance carried them! But Selden was inextricably involved in their fate. Men do not, at worst, suffer much from such exposure; and in this instance the flash of divination which had carried the meaning of the letters to Lily's brain had revealed also that they were appeals—repeated and therefore probably unanswered—for the renewal of a tie which time had evidently relaxed. Nevertheless, the fact that the correspondence had been allowed to fall into strange hands would convict Selden of negligence in a matter where the world holds it least pardonable; and there were graver risks to consider where a man of Dorset's ticklish balance was concerned.

If she weighed all these things it was unconsciously: she was aware only of feeling that Selden would wish the letters rescued, and that therefore she must obtain possession of them. Beyond that her mind did not travel. She had, indeed, a quick vision of returning the packet to Bertha Dorset, and of the opportunities the restitution offered; but this thought lit up abysses from which she shrank back ashamed.

Meanwhile Mrs. Haffen, prompt to perceive her hesitation, had already opened the packet and ranged its contents on the table. All the letters had been pieced together with strips of thin paper. Some were in small fragments, the others merely torn in half. Though there were not many, thus spread out they nearly covered the table. Lily's glance fell on a word here and there— then she said in a low voice: "What do you wish me to pay you?"

Mrs. Haffen's face reddened with satisfaction. It was clear that the young lady was badly frightened, and Mrs. Haffen was the woman to make the most of such fears. Anticipating an easier victory than she had foreseen, she named an exorbitant sum.

But Miss Bart showed herself a less ready prey than might have been expected from her imprudent opening. She refused to pay the price named, and after a moment's hesitation, met it by a counter-offer of half the amount.

Mrs. Haffen immediately stiffened. Her hand travelled toward the outspread letters, and folding them slowly, she made as though to restore them to their wrapping.

"I guess they're worth more to you than to me, Miss, but the poor has got to live as well as the rich," she observed sententiously.

Lily was throbbing with fear, but the insinuation fortified her resistance.

"You are mistaken," she said indifferently. "I have offered all I am willing to give for the letters; but there may be other ways of getting them."

Mrs. Haffen raised a suspicious glance: she was too experienced not to know that the traffic she was engaged in had perils as great as its rewards, and she had a vision of the elaborate machinery of revenge which a word of this commanding young lady's might set in motion.

She applied the corner of her shawl to her eyes, and murmured through it that no good came of bearing too hard on the poor, but that for her part she had never been mixed up in such a business before, and that on her honour as a Christian all she and Haffen had thought of was that the letters mustn't go any farther.

Lily stood motionless, keeping between herself and the charwoman the greatest distance compatible with the need of speaking in low tones. The idea of bargaining for the letters was intolerable to her, but she knew that, if she appeared to weaken Mrs. Haffen would at once increase her original demand.

She could never afterward recall how long the duel lasted, or what was the decisive stroke which finally, after a lapse of time recorded in minutes by the clock, in hours by the precipitate beat of her pulses, put her in possession of the letters; she knew only that the door had finally closed, and that she stood alone with the packet in her hand.

She had no idea of reading the letters; even to unfold Mrs. Haffen's dirty newspaper would have seemed degrading. But what did she intend to do with its contents? The recipient of the letters had meant to destroy them, and it was her duty to carry out his intention. She had no right to keep them—to do so was to lessen whatever merit lay in having secured their possession. But how destroy them so effectually that there should be no second risk of their falling in such hands? Mrs. Peniston's icy drawing-room grate shone with a forbidding lustre: the fire, like the lamps, was never lit except when there was company.

Miss Bart was turning to carry the letters upstairs when she heard the opening of the outer door, and her aunt entered the drawing-room. Mrs. Peniston was a small plump woman, with a colourless skin lined with trivial wrinkles. Her grey hair was arranged with precision, and her clothes looked excessively new and yet slightly old-fashioned. They were always black and tightly fitting, with an expensive glitter: she was the kind of woman who wore jet at breakfast. Lily had never seen her when she was not cuirassed in shining black, with small tight boots, and an air of being packed and ready to start; yet she never started.

She looked about the drawing-room with an expression of minute scrutiny. "I saw a streak of light under one of the blinds as I drove up: it's extraordinary that I can never teach that woman to draw them down evenly."

Having corrected the irregularity, she seated herself on one of the glossy purple arm-chairs; Mrs. Peniston always sat on a chair, never in it. Then she turned her glance to Miss Bart.

"My dear, you look tired; I suppose it's the excitement of the wedding. Cornelia Van Alstyne was full of it: Molly was there, and Gerty Farish ran in for a minute to tell us about it. I think it was odd, their serving melons before the *consommé:* a wedding break-

fast should always begin with *consommé*. Molly didn't care for the
bridesmaids' dresses. She had it straight from Julia Melson that
they cost three hundred dollars apiece at Céleste's, but she says
they didn't look it. I'm glad you decided not to be a bridesmaid;
that shade of salmon-pink wouldn't have suited you."

Mrs. Peniston delighted in discussing the minutest details of
festivities in which she had not taken part. Nothing would have
induced her to undergo the exertion and fatigue of attending the
Van Osburgh wedding, but so great was her interest in the event
that, having heard two versions of it, she now prepared to extract
a third from her niece. Lily, however, had been deplorably careless in noting the particulars of the entertainment. She had
failed to observe the colour of Mrs. Van Osburgh's gown, and
could not even say whether the old Van Osburgh Sévres had
been used at the bride's table: Mrs. Peniston, in short, found that
she was of more service as a listener than as a narrator.

"Really, Lily, I don't see why you took the trouble to go to the
wedding, if you don't remember what happened or whom you
saw there. When I was a girl I used to keep the *menu* of every
dinner I went to, and write the names of the people on the back;
and I never threw away my cotillion favours till after your uncle's
death, when it seemed unsuitable to have so many coloured
things about the house. I had a whole closet-full, I remember;
and I can tell to this day what balls I got them at. Molly Van Alstyne reminds me of what I was at that age; it's wonderful how
she notices. She was able to tell her mother exactly how the
wedding-dress was cut, and we knew at once, from the fold in
the back, that it must have come from Paquin."[*]

Mrs. Peniston rose abruptly, and, advancing to the ormulu
clock surmounted by a helmeted Minerva, which throned on the
chimney-piece between two malachite vases,[†] passed her lace
handkerchief between the helmet and its visor.

---

[*]Well-known Parisian fashion house headed by designer Jeanne
Beckers (1869–1936).

[†]On the mantle are a clock made of ormulu, a gilded metal used to
imitate gold, and decorated with a statue of the Roman goddess of
wisdom and the arts, and vases made from malachite, a green mineral.

"I knew it—the parlour-maid never dusts there!" she exclaimed, triumphantly displaying a minute spot on the handkerchief; then, reseating herself, she went on: "Molly thought Mrs. Dorset the best-dressed woman at the wedding. I've no doubt her dress *did* cost more than any one else's, but I can't quite like the idea—a combination of sable and *point de Milan.** It seems she goes to a new man in Paris, who won't take an order till his client has spent a day with him at his villa at Neuilly. He says he must study his subject's home life—a most peculiar arrangement, I should say! But Mrs. Dorset told Molly about it herself: she said the villa was full of the most exquisite things and she was really sorry to leave. Molly said she never saw her looking better; she was in tremendous spirits, and said she had made a match between Evie Van Osburgh and Percy Gryce. She really seems to have a very good influence on young men. I hear she is interesting herself now in that silly Silverton boy, who has had his head turned by Carry Fisher, and has been gambling so dreadfully. Well, as I was saying, Evie is really engaged: Mrs. Dorset had her to stay with Percy Gryce, and managed it all, and Grace Van Osburgh is in the seventh heaven—she had almost despaired of marrying Evie."

Mrs. Peniston again paused, but this time her scrutiny addressed itself, not to the furniture, but to her niece.

"Cornelia Van Alstyne was so surprised: she had heard that you were to marry young Gryce. She saw the Wetheralls just after they had stopped with you at Bellomont, and Alice Wetherall was quite sure there was an engagement. She said that when Mr. Gryce left unexpectedly one morning, they all thought he had rushed to town for the ring."

Lily rose and moved toward the door.

"I believe I *am* tired: I think I will go to bed," she said; and Mrs. Peniston, suddenly distracted by the discovery that the easel sustaining the late Mr. Peniston's crayon-portrait was not exactly in line with the sofa in front of it, presented an absent-minded brow to her kiss.

In her own room Lily turned up the gas-jet and glanced to-

---

*Fine handmade lace from Italy (French).

ward the grate. It was as brilliantly polished as the one below, but here at least she could burn a few papers with less risk of incurring her aunt's disapproval. She made no immediate motion to do so, however, but dropping into a chair looked wearily about her. Her room was large and comfortably-furnished—it was the envy and admiration of poor Grace Stepney, who boarded; but, contrasted with the light tints and luxurious appointments of the guest-rooms where so many weeks of Lily's existence were spent, it seemed as dreary as a prison. The monumental wardrobe and bedstead of black walnut had migrated from Mr. Peniston's bedroom, and the magenta "flock" wallpaper,* of a pattern dear to the early 'sixties, was hung with large steel engravings of an anecdotic character. Lily had tried to mitigate this charmless background by a few frivolous touches, in the shape of a lace-decked toilet table and a little painted desk surmounted by photographs; but the futility of the attempt struck her as she looked about the room. What a contrast to the subtle elegance of the setting she had pictured for herself—an apartment which should surpass the complicated luxury of her friends' surroundings by the whole extent of that artistic sensibility which made her feel herself their superior; in which every tint and line should combine to enhance her beauty and give distinction to her leisure. Once more the haunting sense of physical ugliness was intensified by her mental depression, so that each piece of the offending furniture seemed to thrust forth its most aggressive angle.

Her aunt's words had told her nothing new; but they had revived the vision of Bertha Dorset, smiling, flattered, victorious, holding her up to ridicule by insinuations intelligible to every member of their little group. The thought of the ridicule struck deeper than any other sensation: Lily knew every turn of the allusive jargon which could flay its victims without the shedding of blood. Her cheek burned at the recollection, and she rose and caught up the letters. She no longer meant to destroy them: that intention had been effaced by the quick corrosion of Mrs. Peniston's words.

---

*Wallpaper embossed with patterns.

Instead, she approached her desk, and lighting a taper, tied and sealed the packet; then she opened the wardrobe, drew out a despatch-box, and deposited the letters within it. As she did so, it struck her with a flash of irony that she was indebted to Gus Trenor for the means of buying them.

THE AUTUMN DRAGGED ON monotonously. Miss Bart had received one or two notes from Judy Trenor, reproaching her for not returning to Bellomont; but she replied evasively, alleging the obligation to remain with her aunt. In truth, however, she was fast wearying of her solitary existence with Mrs. Peniston, and only the excitement of spending her newly-acquired money lightened the dulness of the days.

All her life Lily had seen money go out as quickly as it came in, and whatever theories she cultivated as to the prudence of setting aside a part of her gains, she had unhappily no saving vision of the risks of the opposite course. It was a keen satisfaction to feel that, for a few months at least, she would be independent of her friends' bounty, that she could show herself abroad without wondering whether some penetrating eye would detect in her dress the traces of Judy Trenor's refurbished splendour. The fact that the money freed her temporarily from all minor obligations obscured her sense of the greater one it represented, and having never before known what it was to command so large a sum, she lingered delectably over the amusement of spending it.

It was on one of these occasions that, leaving a shop where she had spent an hour of deliberation over a dressing-case of the most complicated elegance, she ran across Miss Farish, who had entered the same establishment with the modest object of having her watch repaired. Lily was feeling unusually virtuous. She had decided to defer the purchase of the dressing-case till she should receive the bill for her new opera-cloak, and the resolve made her feel much richer than when she had entered the shop. In this mood of self-approval she had a sympathetic eye for others, and she was struck by her friend's air of dejection.

Miss Farish, it appeared, had just left the committee-meeting of a struggling charity in which she was interested. The object of the association was to provide comfortable lodgings, with a reading-room and other modest distractions, where young women of the class employed in down town offices might find a home when out of work, or in need of rest, and the first year's financial report showed so deplorably small a balance that Miss Farish, who was convinced of the urgency of the work, felt proportionately discouraged by the small amount of interest it aroused. The other-regarding sentiments had not been cultivated in Lily, and she was often bored by the relation of her friend's philanthropic efforts, but today her quick dramatizing fancy seized on the contrast between her own situation and that represented by some of Gerty's "cases." These were young girls, like herself: some perhaps pretty, some not without a trace of her finer sensibilities. She pictured herself leading such a life as theirs—a life in which achievement seemed as squalid as failure—and the vision made her shudder sympathetically. The price of the dressing-case was still in her pocket; and drawing out her little gold purse she slipped a liberal fraction of the amount into Miss Farish's hand.

The satisfaction derived from this act was all that the most ardent moralist could have desired. Lily felt a new interest in herself as a person of charitable instincts: she had never before thought of doing good with the wealth she had so often dreamed of possessing, but now her horizon was enlarged by the vision of a prodigal philanthropy. Moreover, by some obscure process of logic, she felt that her momentary burst of generosity had justified all previous extravagances, and excused any in which she might subsequently indulge. Miss Farish's surprise and gratitude confirmed this feeling, and Lily parted from her with a sense of self-esteem which she naturally mistook for the fruits of altruism.

About this time she was farther cheered by an invitation to spend the Thanksgiving week at a camp in the Adirondacks.* The invitation was one which, a year earlier, would have provoked a less ready response, for the party, though organized by

---

*Mountain range in northeastern New York where the wealthy once built retreats known as "camps."

Mrs. Fisher, was ostensibly given by a lady of obscure origin and indomitable social ambitions, whose acquaintance Lily had hitherto avoided. Now, however, she was disposed to coincide with Mrs. Fisher's view, that it didn't matter who gave the party, as long as things were well done; and doing things well (under competent direction) was Mrs. Wellington Bry's strong point. The lady (whose consort was known as "Welly" Bry on the Stock Exchange and in sporting circles) had already sacrificed one husband, and sundry minor considerations, to her determination to get on; and, having obtained a hold on Carry Fisher, she was astute enough to perceive the wisdom of committing herself entirely to that lady's guidance. Everything, accordingly, was well done, for there was no limit to Mrs. Fisher's prodigality when she was not spending her own money, and as she remarked to her pupil, a good cook was the best introduction to society. If the company was not as select as the *cuisine*, the Welly Brys at least had the satisfaction of figuring for the first time in the society columns in company with one or two noticeable names; and foremost among these was of course Miss Bart's. The young lady was treated by her hosts with corresponding deference; and she was in the mood when such attentions are acceptable, whatever their source. Mrs. Bry's admiration was a mirror in which Lily's self-complacency recovered its lost outline. No insect hangs its nest on threads as frail as those which will sustain the weight of human vanity; and the sense of being of importance among the insignificant was enough to restore to Miss Bart the gratifying consciousness of power. If these people paid court to her it proved that she was still conspicuous in the world to which they aspired; and she was not above a certain enjoyment in dazzling them by her fineness, in developing their puzzled perception of her superiorities.

Perhaps, however, her enjoyment proceeded more than she was aware from the physical stimulus of the excursion, the challenge of crisp cold and hard exercise, the responsive thrill of her body to the influences of the winter woods. She returned to town in a glow of rejuvenation, conscious of a clearer colour in her cheeks, a fresh elasticity in her muscles. The future seemed full of a vague promise, and all her apprehensions were swept out of sight on the buoyant current of her mood.

A few days after her return to town she had the unpleasant surprise of a visit from Mr. Rosedale. He came late, at the confidential hour when the tea-table still lingers by the fire in friendly expectancy; and his manner showed a readiness to adapt itself to the intimacy of the occasion.

Lily, who had a vague sense of his being somehow connected with her lucky speculations, tried to give him the welcome he expected; but there was something in the quality of his geniality which chilled her own, and she was conscious of marking each step in their acquaintance by a fresh blunder.

Mr. Rosedale—making himself promptly at home in an adjoining easy-chair, and sipping his tea critically, with the comment: "You ought to go to my man for something really good"—appeared totally unconscious of the repugnance which kept her in frozen erectness behind the urn. It was perhaps her very manner of holding herself aloof that appealed to his collector's passion for the rare and unattainable. He gave, at any rate, no sign of resenting it and seemed prepared to supply in his own manner all the ease that was lacking in hers.

His object in calling was to ask her to go to the opera in his box on the opening night, and seeing her hesitate he said persuasively: "Mrs. Fisher is coming, and I've secured a tremendous admirer of yours, who'll never forgive me if you don't accept."

As Lily's silence left him with this allusion on his hands, he added with a confidential smile: "Gus Trenor has promised to come to town on purpose. I fancy he'd go a good deal farther for the pleasure of seeing you."

Miss Bart felt an inward motion of annoyance: it was distasteful enough to hear her name coupled with Trenor's, and on Rosedale's lips the allusion was peculiarly unpleasant.

"The Trenors are my best friends—I think we should all go a long way to see each other," she said, absorbing herself in the preparation of fresh tea.

Her visitor's smile grew increasingly intimate. "Well, I wasn't thinking of Mrs. Trenor at the moment—they say Gus doesn't always, you know." Then, dimly conscious that he had not struck the right note, he added, with a well-meant effort at diversion: "How's your luck been going in Wall Street, by the way? I hear Gus pulled off a nice little pile for you last month."

Lily put down the tea-caddy with an abrupt gesture. She felt that her hands were trembling, and clasped them on her knee to steady them; but her lip trembled too, and for a moment she was afraid the tremor might communicate itself to her voice. When she spoke, however, it was in a tone of perfect lightness.

"Ah, yes—I had a little bit of money to invest, and Mr. Trenor, who helps me about such matters, advised my putting it in stocks instead of a mortgage, as my aunt's agent wanted me to do; and as it happened, I made a lucky 'turn'—is that what you call it? For you make a great many yourself, I believe."

She was smiling back at him now, relaxing the tension of her attitude, and admitting him, by imperceptible gradations of his glance and manner, a step farther toward intimacy. The protective instinct always nerved her to successful dissimulation, and it was not the first time she had used her beauty to divert attention from an inconvenient topic.

When Mr. Rosedale took leave, he carried with him, not only her acceptance of his invitation, but a general sense of having comported himself in a way calculated to advance his cause. He had always believed he had a light touch and a knowing way with women, and the prompt manner in which Miss Bart (as he would have phrased it) had "come into line," confirmed his confidence in his powers of handling the skittish sex. Her way of glossing over the transaction with Trenor he regarded at once as a tribute to his own acuteness, and a confirmation of his suspicions. The girl was evidently nervous, and Mr. Rosedale, if he saw no other means of advancing his acquaintance with her, was not above taking advantage of her nervousness.

He left Lily to a passion of disgust and fear. It seemed incredible that Gus Trenor should have spoken of her to Rosedale. With all his faults, Trenor had the safeguard of his traditions, and was the less likely to overstep them because they were so purely instinctive. But Lily recalled with a pang that there were convivial moments when, as Judy had confided to her, Gus "talked foolishly": in one of these, no doubt, the fatal word had slipped from him. As for Rosedale, she did not, after the first shock, greatly care what conclusions he had drawn. Though usually adroit enough where her own interests were concerned, she made the mistake, not uncommon to persons in whom the social habits are instinctive, of supposing that the inability to acquire them quickly implies a general dulness. Because a blue-bottle bangs irrationally against a window-pane, the drawing-room naturalist may forget that under less artificial conditions it is capable of measuring distances and drawing conclusions with all the accuracy needful to its welfare; and the fact that Mr. Rosedale's drawing-room manner lacked perspective made Lily class him with Trenor and the other dull men she knew, and assume that a little flattery, and the occasional acceptance of his hospitality, would suffice to render him innocuous. However, there could be no doubt of the expediency of showing herself in his box on the opening night of the opera; and after all, since Judy Trenor had promised to take him up that winter, it was as well to reap the advantage of being first in the field.

For a day or two after Rosedale's visit, Lily's thoughts were dogged by the consciousness of Trenor's shadowy claim, and she wished she had a clearer notion of the exact nature of the transaction which seemed to have put her in his power; but her mind shrank from any unusual application, and she was always helplessly puzzled by figures. Moreover she had not seen Trenor since the day of the Van Osburgh wedding, and in his continued absence the trace of Rosedale's words was soon effaced by other impressions.

When the opening night of the opera came, her apprehensions had so completely vanished that the sight of Trenor's ruddy countenance in the back of Mr. Rosedale's box filled her with a sense of pleasant reassurance. Lily had not quite reconciled herself to the necessity of appearing as Rosedale's guest on so conspicuous an occasion, and it was a relief to find herself supported by any one of her own set—for Mrs. Fisher's social habits were too promiscuous for her presence to justify Miss Bart's.

To Lily, always inspirited by the prospect of showing her beauty in public, and conscious tonight of all the added enhancements of dress, the insistency of Trenor's gaze merged itself in the general stream of admiring looks of which she felt herself the centre. Ah, it was good to be young, to be radiant, to glow with the sense of slenderness, strength and elasticity, of well-poised lines and happy tints, to feel one's self lifted to a height apart by that incommunicable grace which is the bodily counterpart of genius!

All means seemed justifiable to attain such an end, or rather, by a happy shifting of lights with which practice had familiarized Miss Bart, the cause shrank to a pin-point in the general brightness of the effect. But brilliant young ladies, a little blinded by their own effulgence, are apt to forget that the modest satellite drowned in their light is still performing its own revolutions and generating heat at its own rate. If Lily's poetic enjoyment of the moment was undisturbed by the base thought that her gown and opera cloak had been indirectly paid for by Gus Trenor, the latter had not sufficient poetry in his composition to lose sight of these prosaic facts. He knew only that he had never seen Lily look smarter in her life, that there wasn't a woman in the house who showed off good clothes as she did, and that hitherto he, to whom she owed the opportunity of making this display, had reaped no return beyond that of gazing at her in company with several hundred other pairs of eyes.

It came to Lily therefore as a disagreeable surprise when, in the back of the box, where they found themselves alone between two acts, Trenor said, without preamble, and in a tone of sulky authority: "Look here, Lily, how is a fellow ever to see anything of you? I'm in town three or four days in the week, and you know a line to the club will always find me, but you don't seem to remember my existence nowadays unless you want to get a tip out of me."

The fact that the remark was in distinctly bad taste did not make it any easier to answer, for Lily was vividly aware that it was not the moment for that drawing up of her slim figure and surprised lifting of the brows by which she usually quelled incipient signs of familiarity.

"I'm very much flattered by your wanting to see me," she returned, essaying lightness instead, "but, unless you have mislaid my address, it would have been easy to find me any afternoon at my aunt's—in fact, I rather expected you to look me up there."

If she hoped to mollify him by this last concession the attempt was a failure, for he only replied, with the familiar lowering of the brows that made him look his dullest when he was angry: "Hang going to your aunt's, and wasting the afternoon listening to a lot of other chaps talking to you! You know I'm not the kind to sit in a crowd and jaw—I'd always rather clear out when that sort of circus is going on. But why can't we go off somewhere on a little lark together—a nice quiet little expedition like that drive at Bellomont, the day you met me at the station?"

He leaned unpleasantly close in order to convey this suggestion, and she fancied she caught a significant aroma which explained the dark flush on his face and the glistening dampness of his forehead.

The idea that any rash answer might provoke an unpleasant outburst tempered her disgust with caution, and she answered with a laugh: "I don't see how one can very well take country drives in town, but I am not always surrounded by an admiring throng, and if you will let me know what afternoon you are coming I will arrange things so that we can have a nice quiet talk."

"Hang talking! That's what you always say," returned Trenor, whose expletives lacked variety. "You put me off with that at the Van Osburgh wedding—but the plain English of it is that, now you've got what you wanted out of me, you'd rather have any other fellow about."

His voice had risen sharply with the last words, and Lily flushed with annoyance, but she kept command of the situation and laid a persuasive hand on his arm.

"Don't be foolish, Gus; I can't let you talk to me in that ridiculous way. If you really want to see me, why shouldn't we take a walk in the Park some afternoon? I agree with you that it's amusing to be rustic in town, and if you like I'll meet you there, and we'll go and feed the squirrels, and you shall take me out on the lake in the steam-gondola."*

She smiled as she spoke, letting her eyes rest on his in a way that took the edge from her banter and made him suddenly malleable to her will.

"All right, then: that's a go. Will you come tomorrow? Tomorrow at three o'clock, at the end of the Mall? I'll be there sharp, remember; you won't go back on me, Lily?"

---

*Steam-powered pleasure boat.

But to Miss Bart's relief the repetition of her promise was cut short by the opening of the box door to admit George Dorset.

Trenor sulkily yielded his place, and Lily turned a brilliant smile on the newcomer. She had not talked with Dorset since their visit at Bellomont, but something in his look and manner told her that he recalled the friendly footing on which they had last met. He was not a man to whom the expression of admiration came easily: his long sallow face and distrustful eyes seemed always barricaded against the expansive emotions. But, where her own influence was concerned, Lily's intuitions sent out thread-like feelers, and as she made room for him on the narrow sofa she was sure he found a dumb pleasure in being near her. Few women took the trouble to make themselves agreeable to Dorset, and Lily had been kind to him at Bellomont, and was now smiling on him with a divine renewal of kindness.

"Well, here we are, in for another six months of caterwauling," he began complainingly. "Not a shade of difference between this year and last, except that the women have got new clothes and the singers haven't got new voices. My wife's musical, you know—puts me through a course of this every winter. It isn't so bad—Italian nights—then she comes late, and there's time to digest. But when they give Wagner* we have to rush dinner, and I pay up for it. And the draughts are damnable—asphyxia in front and pleurisy in the back. There's Trenor leaving the box without drawing the curtain! With a hide like that draughts don't make any difference. Did you ever watch Trenor eat? If you did, you'd wonder why he's alive; I suppose he's leather inside too.—But I came to say that my wife wants you to come down to our place next Sunday. Do for heaven's sake say yes. She's got a lot of bores coming—intellectual ones, I mean; that's her new line, you know, and I'm not sure it ain't worse than the music. Some of 'em have long hair, and they start an argument with the soup, and don't notice when things are handed to them. The consequence is the dinner gets cold, and I have dyspepsia. That silly ass Silverton brings them to the house—he

---

*Richard Wagner (1813–1883), German composer of operas who enjoyed godlike popularity in the nineteenth century.

writes poetry, you know, and Bertha and he are getting tremendously thick. She could write better than any of 'em if she chose, and I don't blame her for wanting clever fellows about; all I say is: 'Don't let me see 'em eat!'"

The gist of this strange communication gave Lily a distinct thrill of pleasure. Under ordinary circumstances, there would have been nothing surprising in an invitation from Bertha Dorset; but since the Bellomont episode an unavowed hostility had kept the two women apart. Now, with a start of inner wonder, Lily felt that her thirst for retaliation had died out. *If you would forgive your enemy,* says the Malay* proverb, *first inflict a hurt on him;* and Lily was experiencing the truth of the apothegm. If she had destroyed Mrs. Dorset's letters, she might have continued to hate her; but the fact that they remained in her possession had fed her resentment to satiety.

She uttered a smiling acceptance, hailing in the renewal of the tie an escape from Trenor's importunities.

---

*Muslim people of the Malay peninsula in southeast Asia.

MEANWHILE THE HOLIDAYS HAD gone by and the season was beginning. Fifth Avenue had become a nightly torrent of carriages surging upward to the fashionable quarters about the Park, where illuminated windows and outspread awnings betokened the usual routine of hospitality. Other tributary currents crossed the main stream, bearing their freight to the theatres, restaurants or opera; and Mrs. Peniston, from the secluded watch-tower of her upper window, could tell to a nicety just when the chronic volume of sound was increased by the sudden influx setting toward a Van Osburgh ball, or when the multiplication of wheels meant merely that the opera was over, or that there was a big supper at Sherry's.

Mrs. Peniston followed the rise and culmination of the season as keenly as the most active sharer in its gaieties; and, as a looker-on, she enjoyed opportunities of comparison and generalization such as those who take part must proverbially forego. No one could have kept a more accurate record of social fluctuations, or have put a more unerring finger on the distinguishing features of each season: its dulness, its extravagance, its lack of balls or excess of divorces. She had a special memory for the vicissitudes of the "new people" who rose to the surface with each recurring tide, and were either submerged beneath its rush or landed triumphantly beyond the reach of envious breakers; and she was apt to display a remarkable retrospective insight into their ultimate fate, so that, when they had fulfilled their destiny, she was almost always able to say to Grace Stepney—the recipient of her prophecies—that she had known exactly what would happen.

This particular season Mrs. Peniston would have characterized as that in which everybody "felt poor" except the Welly Brys and Mr. Simon Rosedale. It had been a bad autumn in Wall

Street, where prices fell in accordance with that peculiar law
which proves railway stocks and bales of cotton to be more sensitive to the allotment of executive power than many estimable
citizens trained to all the advantages of self-government. Even
fortunes supposed to be independent of the market either betrayed a secret dependence on it, or suffered from a sympathetic
affection: fashion sulked in its country-houses, or came to town
incognito, general entertainments were discountenanced, and
informality and short dinners became the fashion.

But society, amused for a while at playing Cinderella, soon
wearied of the hearthside rôle, and welcomed the Fairy God-
mother in the shape of any magician powerful enough to turn
the shrunken pumpkin back again into the golden coach. The
mere fact of growing richer at a time when most people's investments are shrinking, is calculated to attract envious attention;
and according to Wall Street rumours, Welly Bry and Rosedale
had found the secret of performing this miracle.

Rosedale, in particular, was said to have doubled his fortune,
and there was talk of his buying the newly-finished house of one
of the victims of the crash, who, in the space of twelve short
months, had made the same number of millions, built a house in
Fifth Avenue, filled a picture-gallery with old masters, enter-
tained all New York in it, and been smuggled out of the country
between a trained nurse and a doctor, while his creditors
mounted guard over the old masters, and his guests explained to
each other that they had dined with him only because they
wanted to see the pictures. Mr. Rosedale meant to have a less
meteoric career. He knew he should have to go slowly, and the
instincts of his race fitted him to suffer rebuffs and put up with
delays. But he was prompt to perceive that the general dulness
of the season afforded him an unusual opportunity to shine, and
he set about with patient industry to form a background for his
growing glory. Mrs. Fisher was of immense service to him at this
period. She had set off so many newcomers on the social stage
that she was like one of those pieces of stock scenery which tell
the experienced spectator exactly what is going to take place. But
Mr. Rosedale wanted, in the long run, a more individual environment. He was sensitive to shades of difference which Miss
Bart would never have credited him with perceiving, because he

had no corresponding variations of manner; and it was becoming more and more clear to him that Miss Bart herself possessed precisely the complementary qualities needed to round off his social personality.

Such details did not fall within the range of Mrs. Peniston's vision. Like many minds of panoramic sweep, hers was apt to overlook the *minutiæ* of the foreground, and she was much more likely to know where Carry Fisher had found the Welly Brys' *chef* for them, than what was happening to her own niece. She was not, however, without purveyors of information ready to supplement her deficiencies. Grace Stepney's mind was like a kind of moral fly-paper, to which the buzzing items of gossip were drawn by a fatal attraction, and where they hung fast in the toils of an inexorable memory. Lily would have been surprised to know how many trivial facts concerning herself were lodged in Miss Stepney's head. She was quite aware that she was of interest to dingy people, but she assumed that there is only one form of dinginess, and that admiration for brilliancy is the natural expression of its inferior state. She knew that Gerty Farish admired her blindly, and therefore supposed that she inspired the same sentiments in Grace Stepney, whom she classified as a Gerty Farish without the saving traits of youth and enthusiasm.

In reality, the two differed from each other as much as they differed from the object of their mutual contemplation. Miss Farish's heart was a fountain of tender illusions, Miss Stepney's a precise register of facts as manifested in their relation to herself. She had sensibilities which, to Lily, would have seemed comic in a person with a freckled nose and red eye-lids, who lived in a boarding-house and admired Mrs. Peniston's drawing-room; but poor Grace's limitations gave them a more concentrated inner life, as poor soil starves certain plants into intenser efflorescence. She had in truth no abstract propensity to malice: she did not dislike Lily because the latter was brilliant and predominant, but because she thought that Lily disliked her. It is less mortifying to believe one's self unpopular than insignificant, and vanity prefers to assume that indifference is a latent form of unfriendliness. Even such scant civilities as Lily accorded to Mr. Rosedale would have made Miss Stepney her friend for life; but how could she foresee that such a friend was worth cultivating?

How, moreover, can a young woman who has never been ignored measure the pang which this injury inflicts? And, lastly, how could Lily, accustomed to choose between a pressure of engagements, guess that she had mortally offended Miss Stepney by causing her to be excluded from one of Mrs. Peniston's infrequent dinner-parties?

Mrs. Peniston disliked giving dinners, but she had a high sense of family obligation, and on the Jack Stepneys' return from their honeymoon she felt it incumbent upon her to light the drawing-room lamps and extract her best silver from the Safe Deposit vaults. Mrs. Peniston's rare entertainments were preceded by days of heart-rending vacillation as to every detail of the feast, from the seating of the guests to the pattern of the table-cloth, and in the course of one of these preliminary discussions she had imprudently suggested to her cousin Grace that, as the dinner was a family affair, she might be included in it. For a week the prospect had lighted up Miss Stepney's colourless existence; then she had been given to understand that it would be more convenient to have her another day. Miss Stepney knew exactly what had happened. Lily, to whom family reunions were occasions of unalloyed dulness, had persuaded her aunt that a dinner of "smart" people would be much more to the taste of the young couple, and Mrs. Peniston, who leaned helplessly on her niece in social matters, had been prevailed upon to pronounce Grace's exile. After all, Grace could come any other day; why should she mind being put off?

It was precisely because Miss Stepney could come any other day—and because she knew her relations were in the secret of her unoccupied evenings—that this incident loomed gigantically on her horizon. She was aware that she had Lily to thank for it; and dull resentment was turned to active animosity.

Mrs. Peniston, on whom she had looked in a day or two after the dinner, laid down her crochet-work and turned abruptly from her oblique survey of Fifth Avenue.

"Gus Trenor?—Lily and Gus Trenor?" she said, growing so suddenly pale that her visitor was almost alarmed.

"Oh, cousin Julia . . . of course I don't mean . . ."

"I don't know what you *do* mean," said Mrs. Peniston, with a frightened quiver in her small fretful voice. "Such things were never heard of in my day. And my own niece! I'm not sure I understand you. Do people say he's in love with her?"

Mrs. Peniston's horror was genuine. Though she boasted an unequalled familiarity with the secret chronicles of society, she had the innocence of the school-girl who regards wickedness as a part of "history," and to whom it never occurs that the scandals she reads of in lesson-hours may be repeating themselves in the next street. Mrs. Peniston had kept her imagination shrouded, like the drawing-room furniture. She knew, of course, that society was "very much changed," and that many women her mother would have thought "peculiar" were now in a position to be critical about their visiting-lists; she had discussed the perils of divorce with her rector, and had felt thankful at times that Lily was still unmarried; but the idea that any scandal could attach to a young girl's name, above all that it could be lightly coupled with that of a married man, was so new to her that she was as much aghast as if she had been accused of leaving her carpets down all summer, or of violating any of the other cardinal laws of house-keeping.

Miss Stepney, when her first fright had subsided, began to feel the superiority that greater breadth of mind confers. It was really pitiable to be as ignorant of the world as Mrs. Peniston!

She smiled at the latter's question: "People always say unpleasant things—and certainly they're a great deal together. A friend of mine met them the other afternoon in the Park—quite late, after the lamps were lit. It's a pity Lily makes herself so conspicuous."

"Conspicuous!" gasped Mrs. Peniston. She bent forward, lowering her voice to mitigate the horror. "What sort of things do they say? That he means to get a divorce and marry her?"

Grace Stepney laughed outright. "Dear me, no! He would hardly do that. It—it's a flirtation—nothing more."

"A flirtation? Between my niece and a married man? Do you mean to tell me that, with Lily's looks and advantages, she could find no better use for her time than to waste it on a fat stupid man almost old enough to be her father?" This argument had such a convincing ring that it gave Mrs. Peniston sufficient reassurance to pick up her work, while she waited for Grace Stepney to rally her scattered forces.

But Miss Stepney was on the spot in an instant. "That's the worst of it—people say she isn't wasting her time! Every one knows, as you say, that Lily is too handsome and—and charming—to devote herself to a man like Gus Trenor unless——"

"Unless?" echoed Mrs. Peniston.

Her visitor drew breath nervously. It was agreeable to shock Mrs. Peniston, but not to shock her to the verge of anger. Miss Stepney was not sufficiently familiar with the classic drama to have recalled in advance how bearers of bad tidings are proverbially received but she now had a rapid vision of forfeited dinners and a reduced wardrobe as the possible consequence of her disinterestedness. To the honour of her sex, however, hatred of Lily prevailed over more personal considerations. Mrs. Peniston had chosen the wrong moment to boast of her niece's charms.

"Unless," said Grace, leaning forward to speak with low-toned emphasis, "unless there are material advantages to be gained by making herself agreeable to him."

She felt that the moment was tremendous, and remembered suddenly that Mrs. Peniston's black brocade, with the cut jet fringe, would have been hers at the end of the season.

Mrs. Peniston put down her work again. Another aspect of the same idea had presented itself to her, and she felt that it was beneath her dignity to have her nerves racked by a dependent relative who wore her old clothes.

"If you take pleasure in annoying me by mysterious insinuations," she said coldly, "you might at least have chosen a more suitable time than just as I am recovering from the strain of giving a large dinner."

The mention of the dinner dispelled Miss Stepney's last scruples. "I don't know why I should be accused of taking pleasure in telling you about Lily. I was sure I shouldn't get any thanks for it," she returned with a flare of temper. "But I have some family feeling left, and as you are the only person who has any authority over Lily, I thought you ought to know what is being said of her."

"Well," said Mrs. Peniston, "what I complain of is that you haven't told me yet what *is* being said."

"I didn't suppose I should have to put it so plainly. People say that Gus Trenor pays her bills."

"Pays her bills—her bills?" Mrs. Peniston broke into a laugh. "I can't imagine where you can have picked up such rubbish. Lily has her own income—and I provide for her very handsomely——"

"Oh, we all know that," interposed Miss Stepney drily. "But Lily wears a great many smart gowns——"

"I like her to be well-dressed—it's only suitable!"

"Certainly; but then there are her gambling debts besides."

Miss Stepney, in the beginning, had not meant to bring up this point; but Mrs. Peniston had only her own incredulity to blame. She was like the stiff-necked unbelievers of Scripture, who must be annihilated to be convinced.

"Gambling debts? Lily?" Mrs. Peniston's voice shook with anger and bewilderment. She wondered whether Grace Stepney had gone out of her mind. "What do you mean by her gambling debts?"

"Simply that if one plays bridge for money in Lily's set one is liable to lose a great deal—and I don't suppose Lily always wins."

"Who told you that my niece played cards for money?"

"Mercy, cousin Julia, don't look at me as if I were trying to turn you against Lily! Everybody knows she is crazy about bridge. Mrs. Gryce told me herself that it was her gambling that frightened Percy Gryce—it seems he was really taken with her at first. But, of course, among Lily's friends, it's quite the custom for girls to play for money. In fact, people are inclined to excuse her on that account——"

"To excuse her for what?"

"For being hard up—and accepting attentions from men like Gus Trenor—and George Dorset——"

Mrs. Peniston gave another cry. "George Dorset? Is there any one else? I should like to know the worst, if you please."

"Don't put it in that way, cousin Julia. Lately Lily has been a good deal with the Dorsets, and he seems to admire her—but of course that's only natural. And I'm sure there is no truth in the horrid things people say; but she *has* been spending a great deal of money this winter. Evie Van Osburgh was at Céleste's* ordering her trousseau the other day—yes, the marriage takes place next month—and she told me that Céleste showed her the most exquisite things she was just sending home to Lily. And people say that Judy Trenor has quarrelled with her on account of Gus; but I'm sure I'm sorry I spoke, though I only meant it as a kindness."

Mrs. Peniston's genuine incredulity enabled her to dismiss Miss Stepney with a disdain which boded ill for that lady's prospect of succeeding to the black brocade; but minds impenetrable to reason have generally some crack through which suspicion filters, and her visitor's insinuations did not glide off as easily as she had expected. Mrs. Peniston disliked scenes, and her determination to avoid them had always led her to hold herself aloof from the details of Lily's life. In her youth, girls had not been supposed to require close supervision. They were generally assumed to be taken up with the legitimate business of courtship and marriage, and interference in such affairs on the part of their natural guardians was considered as unwarrantable as a spectator's suddenly joining in a game. There had of course been "fast" girls even in Mrs. Peniston's early experience; but their fastness, at worst, was understood to be a mere excess of animal spirits, against which there could be no graver charge than that of being "unladylike." The modern fastness appeared synonymous with immorality, and the mere idea of immorality was as offensive to Mrs. Peniston as a smell of cooking in the drawing-room: it was one of the conceptions her mind refused to admit.

She had no immediate intention of repeating to Lily what she had heard, or even of trying to ascertain its truth by means of discreet interrogation. To do so might be to provoke a scene; and a scene, in the shaken state of Mrs. Peniston's nerves, with the effects of her dinner not worn off, and her mind still tremulous with new impressions, was a risk she deemed it her duty to avoid. But there remained in her thoughts a settled deposit of resentment against her niece, all the denser because it was not to

---

*Expensive lingerie shop.

be cleared by explanation or discussion. It was horrible of a young girl to let herself be talked about; however unfounded the charges against her, she must be to blame for their having been made. Mrs. Peniston felt as if there had been a contagious illness in the house, and she was doomed to sit shivering among her contaminated furniture.

12

MISS BART HAD IN fact been treading a devious way, and none of her critics could have been more alive to the fact than herself; but she had a fatalistic sense of being drawn from one wrong turning to another, without ever perceiving the right road till it was too late to take it.

Lily, who considered herself above narrow prejudices, had not imagined that the fact of letting Gus Trenor make a little money for her would ever disturb her self-complacency. And the fact in itself still seemed harmless enough; only it was a fertile source of harmful complications. As she exhausted the amusement of spending the money these complications became more pressing, and Lily, whose mind could be severely logical in tracing the causes of her ill-luck to others, justified herself by the thought that she owed all her troubles to the enmity of Bertha Dorset. This enmity, however, had apparently expired in a renewal of friendliness between the two women. Lily's visit to the Dorsets had resulted, for both, in the discovery that they could be of use to each other; and the civilized instinct finds a subtler pleasure in making use of its antagonist than in confounding him. Mrs. Dorset was, in fact, engaged in a new sentimental experiment, of which Mrs. Fisher's late property, Ned Silverton, was the rosy victim; and at such moments, as Judy Trenor had once remarked, she felt a peculiar need of distracting her husband's attention. Dorset was as difficult to amuse as a savage; but even his self-engrossment was not proof against Lily's arts, or rather these were especially adapted to soothe an uneasy egoism. Her experience with Percy Gryce stood her in good stead in ministering to Dorset's humours, and if the incentive to please was less urgent, the difficulties of her situation were teaching her to make much of minor opportunities.

Intimacy with the Dorsets was not likely to lessen such diffi-

culties on the material side. Mrs. Dorset had none of Judy Trenor's
lavish impulses, and Dorset's admiration was not likely to express
itself in financial "tips," even had Lily cared to renew her experiences in that line. What she required, for the moment, of the
Dorsets' friendship, was simply its social sanction. She knew that
people were beginning to talk of her; but this fact did not alarm
her as it had alarmed Mrs. Peniston. In her set such gossip was not
unusual, and a handsome girl who flirted with a married man was
merely assumed to be pressing to the limit of her opportunities. It
was Trenor himself who frightened her. Their walk in the Park
had not been a success. Trenor had married young, and since his
marriage his intercourse with women had not taken the form of
the sentimental small-talk which doubles upon itself like the
paths in a maze. He was first puzzled and then irritated to find
himself always led back to the same starting-point, and Lily felt
that she was gradually losing control of the situation. Trenor was
in truth in an unmanageable mood. In spite of his understanding
with Rosedale he had been somewhat heavily "touched" by the fall
in stocks; his household expenses weighed on him, and he seemed
to be meeting, on all sides, a sullen opposition to his wishes, instead of the easy good luck he had hitherto encountered.

Mrs. Trenor was still at Bellomont, keeping the townhouse
open, and descending on it now and then for a taste of the
world, but preferring the recurrent excitement of week-end parties to the restrictions of a dull season. Since the holidays she
had not urged Lily to return to Bellomont, and the first time
they met in town Lily fancied there was a shade of coldness in
her manner. Was it merely the expression of her displeasure at
Miss Bart's neglect, or had disquieting rumours reached her?
The latter contingency seemed improbable, yet Lily was not
without a sense of uneasiness. If her roaming sympathies had
struck root anywhere, it was in her friendship with Judy Trenor.
She believed in the sincerity of her friend's affection, though it
sometimes showed itself in self-interested ways, and she shrank
with peculiar reluctance from any risk of estranging it. But, aside
from this, she was keenly conscious of the way in which such an
estrangement would react on herself. The fact that Gus Trenor
was Judy's husband was at times Lily's strongest reason for dis-

liking him, and for resenting the obligation under which he had placed her.

To set her doubts at rest, Miss Bart, soon after the New Year, "proposed" herself for a week-end at Bellomont. She had learned in advance that the presence of a large party would protect her from too great assiduity on Trenor's part, and his wife's telegraphic "come by all means" seemed to assure her of her usual welcome.

Judy received her amicably. The cares of a large party always prevailed over personal feelings, and Lily saw no change in her hostess's manner. Nevertheless, she was soon aware that the experiment of coming to Bellomont was destined not to be successful. The party was made up of what Mrs. Trenor called "poky people"—her generic name for persons who did not play bridge—and, it being her habit to group all such obstructionists in one class, she usually invited them together, regardless of their other characteristics. The result was apt to be an irreducible combination of persons having no other quality in common than their abstinence from bridge, and the antagonisms developed in a group lacking the one taste which might have amalgamated them, were in this case aggravated by bad weather, and by the ill-concealed boredom of their host and hostess. In such emergencies, Judy would usually have turned to Lily to fuse the discordant elements; and Miss Bart, assuming that such a service was expected of her, threw herself into it with her accustomed zeal. But at the outset she perceived a subtle resistance to her efforts. If Mrs. Trenor's manner toward her was unchanged, there was certainly a faint coldness in that of the other ladies. An occasional caustic allusion to "your friends the Wellington Brys," or to "the little Jew who has bought the Greiner house—some one told us you knew him, Miss Bart,"—showed Lily that she was in disfavour with that portion of society which, while contributing least to its amusement, has assumed the right to decide what forms that amusement shall take. The indication was a slight one, and a year ago Lily would have smiled at it, trusting to the charm of her personality to dispel any prejudice against her. But now she had grown more sensitive to criticism and less confident in her power of disarming it. She knew, moreover, that if the ladies at Bellomont permitted themselves to criticize her friends openly, it was a proof that they were not afraid of subjecting her to the same treatment behind her back. The nervous dread lest anything in Trenor's manner should seem to justify their disapproval made her seek every pretext for avoiding him, and she left Bellomont conscious of having failed in every purpose which had taken her there.

In town she returned to preoccupations which, for the moment, had the happy effect of banishing troublesome thoughts. The Welly Brys, after much debate, and anxious counsel with their newly acquired friends, had decided on the bold move of giving a general entertainment. To attack society collectively, when one's means of approach are limited to a few acquaintances, is like advancing into a strange country with an insufficient number of scouts; but such rash tactics have sometimes led to brilliant victories, and the Brys had determined to put their fate to the touch. Mrs. Fisher, to whom they had entrusted the conduct of the affair, had decided that *tableaux vivants** and expensive music were the two baits most likely to attract the desired prey, and after prolonged negotiations, and the kind of wire-pulling in which she was known to excel, she had induced a dozen fashionable women to exhibit themselves in a series of pictures which, by a farther miracle of persuasion, the distinguished portrait painter, Paul Morpeth, had been prevailed upon to organize.

Lily was in her element on such occasions. Under Morpeth's guidance her vivid plastic sense, hitherto nurtured on no higher food than dress-making and upholstery, found eager expression in the disposal of draperies, the study of attitudes, the shifting of lights and shadows. Her dramatic instinct was roused by the choice of subjects, and the gorgeous reproductions of historic dress stirred an imagination which only visual impressions could reach. But keenest of all was the exhilaration of displaying her own beauty under a new aspect: of showing that her loveliness was no more fixed quality, but an element shaping all emotions to fresh forms of grace.

---

*Literally, living pictures (French); silent, static performances in which costumed characters represent well-known works of art.

Mrs. Fisher's measures had been well-taken, and society, surprised in a dull moment, succumbed to the temptation of Mrs. Bry's hospitality. The protesting minority were forgotten in the throng which abjured and came; and the audience was almost as brilliant as the show.

Lawrence Selden was among those who had yielded to the proffered inducements. If he did not often act on the accepted social axiom that a man may go where he pleases, it was because he had long since learned that his pleasures were mainly to be found in a small group of the like-minded. But he enjoyed spectacular effects, and was not insensible to the part money plays in their production: all he asked was that the very rich should live up to their calling as stage-managers, and not spend their money in a dull way. This the Brys could certainly not be charged with doing. Their recently built house, whatever it might lack as a frame for domesticity, was almost as well-designed for the display of a festal assemblage as one of those airy pleasure-halls which the Italian architects improvised to set off the hospitality of princes. The air of improvisation was in fact strikingly present: so recent, so rapidly-evoked was the whole *mise-en-scène** that one had to touch the marble columns to learn they were not of cardboard, to seat one's self in one of the damask†-and-gold arm-chairs to be sure it was not painted against the wall.

Selden, who had put one of these seats to the test, found himself, from an angle of the ball-room, surveying the scene with frank enjoyment. The company, in obedience to the decorative instinct which calls for fine clothes in fine surroundings, had dressed rather with an eye to Mrs. Bry's background than to herself. The seated throng, filling the immense room without undue crowding, presented a surface of rich tissues and jewelled shoulders in harmony with the festooned and gilded walls, and the flushed splendours of the Venetian ceiling. At the farther end of the room a stage had been constructed behind a proscenium arch curtained with folds of old damask; but in the pause before the parting of the folds there was little thought of what

---

*Stage setting (French).
†Fabric woven with patterns, originally from Damascus, Syria.

they might reveal, for every woman who had accepted Mrs. Bry's invitation was engaged in trying to find out how many of her friends had done the same.

Gerty Farish, seated next to Selden, was lost in that indiscriminate and uncritical enjoyment so irritating to Miss Bart's finer perceptions. It may be that Selden's nearness had something to do with the quality of his cousin's pleasure; but Miss Farish was so little accustomed to refer her enjoyment of such scenes to her own share in them, that she was merely conscious of a deeper sense of contentment.

"Wasn't it dear of Lily to get me an invitation? Of course it would never have occurred to Carry Fisher to put me on the list, and I should have been so sorry to miss seeing it all—and especially Lily herself. Some one told me the ceiling was by Veronese*—you would know, of course, Lawrence. I suppose it's very beautiful, but his women are so dreadfully fat. Goddesses? Well, I can only say that if they'd been mortals and had to wear corsets, it would have been better for them. I think our women are much handsomer. And this room is wonderfully becoming—every one looks so well! Did you ever see such jewels? Do look at Mrs. George Dorset's pearls—I suppose the smallest of them would pay the rent of our Girls' Club for a year. Not that I ought to complain about the club; every one has been so wonderfully kind. Did I tell you that Lily had given us three hundred dollars? Wasn't it splendid of her? And then she collected a lot of money from her friends—Mrs. Bry gave us five hundred, and Mr. Rosedale a thousand. I wish Lily were not so nice to Mr. Rosedale, but she says it's no use being rude to him, because he doesn't see the difference. She really can't bear to hurt people's feelings—it makes me so angry when I hear her called cold and conceited! The girls at the club don't call her that. Do you know she has been there with me twice?—yes, Lily! And you should have seen their eyes! One of them said it was as good as a day in the country just to look at her. And she sat there, and laughed and talked with them—not a bit as if she were being *charitable*,

---

*Paolo Veronese (1528–1588), Venetian painter of massive pictures with rich costumes and sumptuous architectural frameworks.

you know, but as if she liked it as much as they did. They've been asking ever since when she's coming back; and she's promised me——oh!"

Miss Farish's confidences were cut short by the parting of the curtain on the first *tableau*—a group of nymphs dancing across flower-strewn sward in the rhythmic postures of Botticelli's *Spring*.* *Tableaux vivants* depend for their effect not only on the happy disposal of lights and the delusive interposition of layers of gauze, but on a corresponding adjustment of the mental vision. To unfurnished minds they remain, in spite of every enhancement of art, only a superior kind of wax-works; but to the responsive fancy they may give magic glimpses of the boundary world between fact and imagination. Selden's mind was of this order: he could yield to vision-making influences as completely as a child to the spell of a fairy-tale. Mrs. Bry's *tableaux* wanted none of the qualities which go to the producing of such illusions, and under Morpeth's organizing hand the pictures succeeded each other with the rhythmic march of some splendid frieze, in which the fugitive curves of living flesh and the wandering light of young eyes have been subdued to plastic harmony without losing the charm of life.

The scenes were taken from old pictures, and the participators had been cleverly fitted with characters suited to their types. No one, for instance, could have made a more typical Goya[†] than Carry Fisher, with her short dark-skinned face, the exaggerated glow of her eyes, the provocation of her frankly-painted smile. A brilliant Miss Smedden from Brooklyn showed to perfection the sumptuous curves of Titian's *Daughter*, lifting her gold salver laden with grapes above the harmonizing gold of rippled hair and rich brocade, and a young Mrs. Van Alstyne, who showed the frailer Dutch type, with high blue-veined forehead and pale eyes and lashes, made a characteristic Vandyck, in black satin, against a curtained archway. Then there were Kauffmann nymphs garlanding the altar of Love; a Veronese supper, all

---

*An allegorical painting by the Florentine artist Sandro Botticelli (1445–1510).
†Francisco José Goya (1746–1828), Spanish painter and etcher.

sheeny textures, pearl-woven heads and marble architecture; and a Watteau* group of lute-playing comedians, lounging by a fountain in a sunlit glade.

Each evanescent picture touched the vision-building faculty in Selden, leading him so far down the vistas of fancy that even Gerty Farish's running commentary—"Oh, how lovely Lulu Melson looks!" or: "That must be Kate Corby, to the right there, in purple"—did not break the spell of the illusion. Indeed, so skilfully had the personality of the actors been subdued to the scenes they figured in that even the least imaginative of the audience must have felt a thrill of contrast when the curtain suddenly parted on a picture which was simply and undisguisedly the portrait of Miss Bart.

Here there could be no mistaking the predominance of personality—the unanimous "Oh!" of the spectators was a tribute, not to the brush-work of Reynolds's "Mrs. Lloyd" but to the flesh and blood loveliness of Lily Bart. She had shown her artistic intelligence in selecting a type so like her own that she could embody the person represented without ceasing to be herself. It was as though she had stepped, not out of, but into, Reynolds's canvas, banishing the phantom of his dead beauty by the beams of her living grace. The impulse to show herself in a splendid setting—she had thought for a moment of representing Tiepolo's Cleopatra†—had yielded to the truer instinct of trusting to her unassisted beauty, and she had purposely chosen a picture without distracting accessories of dress or surroundings. Her pale draperies, and the background of foliage against which

---

*References in this paragraph include *Artist's Daughter*, by the Venetian colorist Titian (c.1488–1576); Anthony Van Dyck (1599–1641), Flemish-born portrait artist; Angelica Kauffmann (1740–1807), Swiss painter of neoclassical decorative scenes; the Venetian painter Veronese (1528–1588); and French painter Jean-Antoine Watteau (1684–1721).

†Mentioned in this paragraph are Joshua Reynolds (1723–1792), who painted a well-known portrait, *Mrs. Lloyd*, and Venetian artist Giovanni Battista Tiepolo (1696–1770), who decorated the Palazzo Labia with scenes from the life of Cleopatra.

she stood, served only to relieve the long dryad-like curves that swept upward from her poised foot to her lifted arm. The noble buoyancy of her attitude, its suggestion of soaring grace, revealed the touch of poetry in her beauty that Selden always felt in her presence, yet lost the sense of when he was not with her. Its expression was now so vivid that for the first time he seemed to see before him the real Lily Bart, divested of the trivialities of her little world, and catching for a moment a note of that eternal harmony of which her beauty was a part.

"Deuced bold thing to show herself in that get-up; but, gad, there isn't a break in the lines anywhere, and I suppose she wanted us to know it!"

These words, uttered by that experienced connoisseur, Mr. Ned Van Alstyne, whose scented white moustache had brushed Selden's shoulder whenever the parting of the curtains presented any exceptional opportunity for the study of the female outline, affected their hearer in an unexpected way. It was not the first time that Selden had heard Lily's beauty lightly remarked on, and hitherto the tone of the comments had imperceptibly coloured his view of her. But now it woke only a motion of indignant contempt. This was the world she lived in, these were the standards by which she was fated to be measured! Does one go to Caliban for a judgment on Miranda?*

In the long moment before the curtain fell, he had time to feel the whole tragedy of her life. It was as though her beauty, thus detached from all that cheapened and vulgarized it, had held out suppliant hands to him from the world in which he and she had once met for a moment, and where he felt an over-mastering longing to be with her again.

He was roused by the pressure of ecstatic fingers. "Wasn't she too beautiful, Lawrence? Don't you like her best in that simple dress? It makes her look like the real Lily—the Lily I know."

He met Gerty Farish's brimming gaze. "The Lily *we* know," he corrected; and his cousin, beaming at the implied under-

---

*It would be absurd to ask Caliban, Prospero's deformed slave in William Shakespeare's *The Tempest*, to judge the beauty of Prospero's daughter Miranda.

standing, exclaimed joyfully: "I'll tell her that! She always says you dislike her."

The performance over, Selden's first impulse was to seek Miss Bart. During the interlude of music which succeeded the *tableaux*, the actors had seated themselves here and there in the audience, diversifying its conventional appearance by the varied picturesqueness of their dress. Lily, however, was not among them, and her absence served to protract the effect she had produced on Selden: it would have broken the spell to see her too soon in the surroundings from which accident had so happily detached her. They had not met since the day of the Van Osburgh wedding, and on his side the avoidance had been intentional. Tonight, however, he knew that, sooner or later, he should find himself at her side; and though he let the dispersing crowd drift him whither it would, without making an immediate effort to reach her, his procrastination was not due to any lingering resistance, but to the desire to luxuriate a moment in the sense of complete surrender.

Lily had not an instant's doubt as to the meaning of the murmur greeting her appearance. No other *tableau* had been received with that precise note of approval: it had obviously been called forth by herself, and not by the picture she impersonated. She had feared at the last moment that she was risking too much in dispensing with the advantages of a more sumptuous setting, and the completeness of her triumph gave her an intoxicating sense of recovered power. Not caring to diminish the impression she had produced, she held herself aloof from the audience till the movement of dispersal before supper, and thus had a second opportunity of showing herself to advantage, as the throng poured slowly into the empty drawing-room where she was standing.

She was soon the centre of a group which increased and renewed itself as the circulation became general, and the individual comments on her success were a delightful prolongation of the collective applause. At such moments she lost something of her natural fastidiousness, and cared less for the quality of the admiration received than for its quantity. Differences of personality were merged in a warm atmosphere of praise, in which her beauty expanded like a flower in sunlight; and if Selden had approached a moment or two sooner he would have seen her turning on Ned Van Alstyne and George Dorset the look he had dreamed of capturing for himself.

Fortune willed, however, that the hurried approach of Mrs. Fisher, as whose aide-de-camp Van Alstyne was acting, should break up the group before Selden reached the threshold of the room. One or two of the men wandered off in search of their partners for supper, and the others, noticing Selden's approach, gave way to him in accordance with the tacit free-masonry of the ball-room. Lily was therefore standing alone when he reached her; and finding the expected look in her eye, he had the satisfaction of supposing he had kindled it. The look did indeed deepen as it rested on him, for even in that moment of self-intoxication Lily felt the quicker beat of life that his nearness always produced. She read, too, in his answering gaze the delicious confirmation of her triumph, and for the moment it seemed to her that it was for him only she cared to be beautiful.

Selden had given her his arm without speaking. She took it in silence, and they moved away, not toward the supper-room, but against the tide which was setting thither. The faces about her flowed by like the streaming images of sleep: she hardly noticed where Selden was leading her, till they passed through a glass doorway at the end of the long suite of rooms and stood suddenly in the fragrant hush of a garden. Gravel grated beneath their feet, and about them was the transparent dimness of a midsummer night. Hanging lights made emerald caverns in the depths of foliage, and whitened the spray of a fountain falling among lilies. The magic place was deserted: there was no sound but the plash of the water on the lily-pads, and a distant drift of music that might have been blown across a sleeping lake.

Selden and Lily stood still, accepting the unreality of the scene as a part of their own dream-like sensations. It would not have surprised them to feel a summer breeze on their faces, or to see the lights among the boughs reduplicated in the arch of a starry sky. The strange solitude about them was no stranger than the sweetness of being alone in it together.

At length Lily withdrew her hand, and moved away a step, so that her white-robed slimness was outlined against the dusk of the branches. Selden followed her, and still without speaking they seated themselves on a bench beside the fountain.

Suddenly she raised her eyes with the beseeching earnestness of a child. "You never speak to me—you think hard things of me," she murmured.

"I think of you at any rate, God knows!" he said.

"Then why do we never see each other? Why can't we be friends? You promised once to help me," she continued in the same tone, as though the words were drawn from her unwillingly.

"The only way I can help you is by loving you," Selden said in a low voice.

She made no reply, but her face turned to him with the soft motion of a flower. His own met it slowly, and their lips touched.

She drew back and rose from her seat. Selden rose too, and they stood facing each other. Suddenly she caught his hand and pressed it a moment against her cheek.

"Ah, love me, love me—but don't tell me so!" she sighed with her eyes in his; and before he could speak she had turned and slipped through the arch of boughs, disappearing in the brightness of the room beyond.

Selden stood where she had left him. He knew too well the transiency of exquisite moments to attempt to follow her; but presently he reëntered the house and made his way through the deserted rooms to the door. A few sumptuously-cloaked ladies were already gathered in the marble vestibule, and in the coatroom he found Van Alstyne and Gus Trenor.

The former, at Selden's approach, paused in the careful selection of a cigar from one of the silver boxes invitingly set out near the door.

"Hallo, Selden, going too? You're an Epicurean* like myself, I see: you don't want to see all those goddesses gobbling terrapin. Gad, what a show of good-looking women; but not one of 'em could touch that little cousin of mine. Talk of jewels—what's a woman want with jewels when she's got herself to show? The trouble is that all these fal-bals† they wear cover up their figures

---

*One who believes that the highest good is pleasure.

†Flounces that decorate a dress to cover up a woman's body.

when they've got 'em. I never knew till tonight what an outline Lily has."

"It's not her fault if everybody don't know it now," growled Trenor, flushed with the struggle of getting into his fur-lined coat. "Damned bad taste, I call it—no, no cigar for me. You can't tell what you're smoking in one of these new houses—likely as not the *chef* buys the cigars. Stay for supper? Not if I know it! When people crowd their rooms so that you can't get near any one you want to speak to, I'd as soon sup in the elevated at the rush hour. My wife was dead right to stay away: she says life's too short to spend it in breaking in new people."

13

LILY WOKE FROM HAPPY dreams to find two notes at her bed-side.

One was from Mrs. Trenor, who announced that she was coming to town that afternoon for a flying visit, and hoped Miss Bart would be able to dine with her. The other was from Selden. He wrote briefly that an important case called him to Albany, whence he would be unable to return till the evening, and asked Lily to let him know at what hour on the following day she would see him.

Lily, leaning back among her pillows, gazed musingly at his letter. The scene in the Brys' conservatory had been like a part of her dreams; she had not expected to wake to such evidence of its reality. Her first movement was one of annoyance: this unforeseen act of Selden's added another complication to life. It was so unlike him to yield to such an irrational impulse! Did he really mean to ask her to marry him? She had once shown him the impossibility of such a hope, and his subsequent behaviour seemed to prove that he had accepted the situation with a reasonableness somewhat mortifying to her vanity. It was all the more agreeable to find that this reasonableness was maintained only at the cost of not seeing her; but, though nothing in life was as sweet as the sense of her power over him, she saw the danger of allowing the episode of the previous night to have a sequel. Since she could not marry him, it would be kinder to him, as well as easier for herself, to write a line amicably evading his request to see her: he was not the man to mistake such a hint, and when next they met it would be on their usual friendly footing.

Lily sprang out of bed, and went straight to her desk. She wanted to write at once, while she could trust to the strength of her resolve. She was still languid from her brief sleep and the exhilaration of the evening, and the sight of Selden's writing brought back the culminating moment of her triumph: the moment when she had read in his eyes that no philosophy was proof against her power. It would be pleasant to have that sensation again . . . no one else could give it to her in its fulness; and she could not bear to mar her mood of luxurious retrospection by an act of definite refusal. She took up her pen and wrote hastily: *"Tomorrow at four"*; murmuring to herself, as she slipped the sheet into its envelope: "I can easily put him off when tomorrow comes."

Judy Trenor's summons was very welcome to Lily. It was the first time she had received a direct communication from Bellomont since the close of her last visit there, and she was still visited by the dread of having incurred Judy's displeasure. But this characteristic command seemed to reestablish their former relations; and Lily smiled at the thought that her friend had probably summoned her in order to hear about the Brys' entertainment. Mrs. Trenor had absented herself from the feast, perhaps for the reason so frankly enunciated by her husband, perhaps because, as Mrs. Fisher somewhat differently put it, she "couldn't bear new people when she hadn't discovered them herself." At any rate, though she remained haughtily at Bellomont, Lily suspected in her a devouring eagerness to hear of what she had missed, and to learn exactly in what measure Mrs. Wellington Bry had surpassed all previous competitors for social recognition. Lily was quite ready to gratify this curiosity, but it happened that she was dining out. She determined, however, to see Mrs. Trenor for a few moments, and ringing for her maid she despatched a telegram to say that she would be with her friend that evening at ten.

She was dining with Mrs. Fisher, who had gathered at an informal feast a few of the performers of the previous evening. There was to be plantation music in the studio after dinner—for Mrs. Fisher, despairing of the republic, had taken up modelling, and annexed to her small crowded house a spacious apartment, which, whatever its uses in her hours of plastic inspiration, served at other times for the exercise of an indefatigable hospitality. Lily was reluctant to leave, for the dinner was amusing, and she would have liked to lounge over a cigarette and hear a few songs; but she could not break her engagement with Judy, and shortly after ten she asked her hostess to ring for a hansom, and drove up Fifth Avenue to the Trenors'.

She waited long enough on the doorstep to wonder that Judy's presence in town was not signalized by a greater promptness in admitting her; and her surprise was increased when, instead of the expected footman, pushing his shoulders into a tardy coat, a shabby caretaking person in calico let her into the shrouded hall. Trenor, however, appeared at once on the threshold of the drawing-room, welcoming her with unusual volubility while he relieved her of her cloak and drew her into the room.

"Come along to the den; it's the only comfortable place in the house. Doesn't this room look as if it was waiting for the body to be brought down? Can't see why Judy keeps the house wrapped up in this awful slippery white stuff—it's enough to give a fellow pneumonia to walk through these rooms on a cold day. You look a little pinched yourself, by the way: it's rather a sharp night out. I noticed it walking up from the club. Come along, and I'll give you a nip of brandy, and you can toast yourself over the fire and try some of my new Egyptians—that little Turkish chap at the Embassy put me on to a brand that I want you to try, and if you like 'em I'll get out a lot for you: they don't have 'em here yet, but I'll cable."

He led her through the house to the large room at the back, where Mrs. Trenor usually sat, and where, even in her absence, there was an air of occupancy. Here, as usual, were flowers, newspapers, a littered writing-table, and a general aspect of lamp-lit familiarity, so that it was a surprise not to see Judy's energetic figure start up from the arm-chair near the fire.

It was apparently Trenor himself who had been occupying the seat in question, for it was overhung by a cloud of cigar smoke, and near it stood one of those intricate folding tables which British ingenuity has devised to facilitate the circulation of tobacco and spirits. The sight of such appliances in a drawing-room was not unusual in Lily's set, where smoking and drinking were unrestricted by considerations of time and place, and her first movement was to help herself to one of the cigarettes recommended by Trenor, while she checked his loquacity by asking, with a surprised glance: "Where's Judy?"

Trenor, a little heated by his unusual flow of words, and perhaps by prolonged propinquity with the decanters, was bending over the latter to decipher their silver labels.

"Here, now, Lily, just a drop of cognac in a little fizzy water—you do look pinched, you know: I swear the end of your nose is red. I'll take another glass to keep you company—Judy?—Why, you see, Judy's got a devil of a headache—quite knocked out with it, poor thing—she asked me to explain—make it all right, you know—Do come up to the fire, though; you look dead-beat, really. Now do let me make you comfortable, there's a good girl."

He had taken her hand, half-banteringly, and was drawing her toward a low seat by the hearth; but she stopped and freed herself quietly.

"Do you mean to say that Judy's not well enough to see me? Doesn't she want me to go upstairs?"

Trenor drained the glass he had filled for himself, and paused to set it down before he answered.

"Why, no—the fact is, she's not up to seeing anybody. It came on suddenly, you know, and she asked me to tell you how awfully sorry she was—if she'd known where you were dining she'd have sent you word."

"She did know where I was dining; I mentioned it in my telegram. But it doesn't matter, of course. I suppose if she's so poorly she won't go back to Bellomont in the morning, and I can come and see her then."

"Yes, exactly—that's capital. I'll tell her you'll pop in tomorrow morning. And now do sit down a minute, there's a dear, and let's have a nice quiet jaw together. You won't take a drop, just for sociability? Tell me what you think of that cigarette. Why, don't you like it? What are you chucking it away for?"

"I am chucking it away because I must go, if you'll have the goodness to call a cab for me," Lily returned with a smile.

She did not like Trenor's unusual excitability, with its too evident explanation, and the thought of being alone with him, with her friend out of reach upstairs, at the other end of the great empty house, did not conduce to a desire to prolong their *tête-à-tête*.

But Trenor, with a promptness which did not escape her, had moved between herself and the door.

"Why must you go, I should like to know? If Judy'd been here you'd have sat gossiping till all hours—and you can't even give me five minutes! It's always the same story. Last night I couldn't get near you—I went to that damned vulgar party just to see you, and there was everybody talking about you, and asking me if I'd ever seen anything so stunning, and when I tried to come up and say a word, you never took any notice, but just went on laughing and joking with a lot of asses who only wanted to be able to swagger about afterward, and look knowing when you were mentioned."

He paused, flushed by his diatribe, and fixing on her a look in which resentment was the ingredient she least disliked. But she had regained her presence of mind, and stood composedly in the middle of the room, while her slight smile seemed to put an ever increasing distance between herself and Trenor.

Across it she said: "Don't be absurd, Gus. It's past eleven, and I must really ask you to ring for a cab."

He remained immovable, with the lowering forehead she had grown to detest.

"And supposing I won't ring for one—what'll you do then?"

"I shall go upstairs to Judy if you force me to disturb her."

Trenor drew a step nearer and laid his hand on her arm. "Look here, Lily: won't you give me five minutes of your own accord?"

"Not tonight, Gus: you——"

"Very good, then: I'll take 'em. And as many more as I want." He had squared himself on the threshold, his hands thrust deep in his pockets. He nodded toward the chair on the hearth.

"Go and sit down there, please: I've got a word to say to you."

Lily's quick temper was getting the better of her fears. She drew herself up and moved toward the door.

"If you have anything to say to me, you must say it another time. I shall go up to Judy unless you call a cab for me at once."

He burst into a laugh. "Go upstairs and welcome, my dear; but you won't find Judy. She ain't there."

Lily cast a startled look upon him. "Do you mean that Judy is not in the house—not in town?" she exclaimed.

"That's just what I do mean," returned Trenor, his bluster sinking to sullenness under her look.

"Nonsense—I don't believe you. I am going upstairs," she said impatiently.

He drew unexpectedly aside, letting her reach the threshold unimpeded.

"Go up and welcome; but my wife is at Bellomont."

But Lily had a flash of reassurance. "If she hadn't come she would have sent me word——"

"She did; she telephoned me this afternoon to let you know."

"I received no message."

"I didn't send any."

The two measured each other for a moment, but Lily still saw her opponent through a blur of scorn that made all other considerations indistinct.

"I can't imagine your object in playing such a stupid trick on me; but if you have fully gratified your peculiar sense of humour I must again ask you to send for a cab."

It was the wrong note, and she knew it as she spoke. To be stung by irony it is not necessary to understand it, and the angry streaks on Trenor's face might have been raised by an actual lash.

"Look here, Lily, don't take that high and mighty tone with me." He had again moved toward the door, and in her instinctive shrinking from him she let him regain command of the threshold. "I *did* play a trick on you; I own up to it; but if you think I'm ashamed you're mistaken. Lord knows I've been patient enough—I've hung round and looked like an ass. And all the while you were letting a lot of other fellows make up to you . . . letting 'em make fun of me, I daresay . . . I'm not sharp, and can't dress my friends up to look funny, as you do . . . but I can tell when it's being done to me . . . I can tell fast enough when I'm made a fool of . . ."

"Ah, I shouldn't have thought that!" flashed from Lily; but her laugh dropped to silence under his look.

"No; you wouldn't have thought it; but you'll know better now. That's what you're here for tonight. I've been waiting for a quiet time to talk things over, and now I've got it I mean to make you hear me out."

His first rush of inarticulate resentment had been followed

by a steadiness and concentration of tone more disconcerting to Lily than the excitement preceding it. For a moment her presence of mind forsook her. She had more than once been in situations where a quick sword-play of wit had been needful to cover her retreat; but her frightened heart-throbs told her that here such skill would not avail.

To gain time she repeated: "I don't understand what you want."

Trenor had pushed a chair between herself and the door. He threw himself in it, and leaned back, looking up at her.

"I'll tell you what I want: I want to know just where you and I stand. Hang it, the man who pays for the dinner is generally allowed to have a seat at table."

She flamed with anger and abasement, and the sickening need of having to conciliate where she longed to humble.

"I don't know what you mean—but you must see, Gus, that I can't stay here talking to you at this hour——"

"Gad, you go to men's houses fast enough in broad daylight—strikes me you're not always so deuced careful of appearances."

The brutality of the thrust gave her the sense of dizziness that follows on a physical blow. Rosedale had spoken then—this was the way men talked of her— She felt suddenly weak and defenceless: there was a throb of self-pity in her throat. But all the while another self was sharpening her to vigilance, whispering the terrified warning that every word and gesture must be measured.

"If you have brought me here to say insulting things——" she began.

Trenor laughed. "Don't talk stage-rot. I don't want to insult you. But a man's got his feelings—and you've played with mine too long. I didn't begin this business—kept out of the way, and left the track clear for the other chaps, till you rummaged me out and set to work to make an ass of me—and an easy job you had of it, too. That's the trouble—it was too easy for you—you got reckless—thought you could turn me inside out, and chuck me in the gutter like an empty purse. But, by gad, that ain't playing fair: that's dodging the rules of the game. Of course I know now what you wanted—it wasn't my beautiful eyes you were after—

but I tell you what, Miss Lily, you've got to pay up for making me think so——"

He rose, squaring his shoulders aggressively, and stepped toward her with a reddening brow; but she held her footing, though every nerve tore at her to retreat as he advanced.

"Pay up?" she faltered. "Do you mean that I owe you money?"

He laughed again. "Oh, I'm not asking for payment in kind. But there's such a thing as fair play—and interest on one's money—and hang me if I've had as much as a look from you——"

"Your money? What have I to do with your money? You advised me how to invest mine . . . you must have seen I knew nothing of business . . . you told me it was all right——"

"It *was* all right—it is, Lily: you're welcome to all of it, and ten times more. I'm only asking for a word of thanks from you." He was closer still, with a hand that grew formidable; and the frightened self in her was dragging the other down.

"I *have* thanked you; I've shown I was grateful. What more have you done than any friend might do, or any one accept from a friend?"

Trenor caught her up with a sneer. "I don't doubt you've accepted as much before—and chucked the other chaps as you'd like to chuck me. I don't care how you settled your score with them—if you fooled 'em I'm that much to the good. Don't stare at me like that—I know I'm not talking the way a man is supposed to talk to a girl—but, hang it, if you don't like it you can stop me quick enough—you know I'm mad about you—damn the money, there's plenty more of it—if *that* bothers you . . . I was a brute, Lily—Lily!—just look at me——"

Over and over her the sea of humiliation broke—wave crashing on wave so close that the moral shame was one with the physical dread. It seemed to her that self-esteem would have made her invulnerable—that it was her own dishonour which put a fearful solitude about her.

His touch was a shock to her drowning consciousness. She drew back from him with a desperate assumption of scorn.

"I've told you I don't understand—but if I owe you money you shall be paid——"

Trenor's face darkened to rage: her recoil of abhorrence had called out the primitive man.

"Ah—you'll borrow from Selden or Rosedale—and take your chances of fooling them as you've fooled me! Unless—unless you've settled your other scores already—and I'm the only one left out in the cold!"

She stood silent, frozen to her place. The words—the words were worse than the touch! Her heart was beating all over her body—in her throat, her limbs, her helpless useless hands. Her eyes travelled despairingly about the room—they lit on the bell, and she remembered that help was in call. Yes, but scandal with it—a hideous mustering of tongues. No, she must fight her way out alone. It was enough that the servants knew her to be in the house with Trenor—there must be nothing to excite conjecture in her way of leaving it.

She raised her head, and achieved a last clear look at him.

"I am here alone with you," she said. "What more have you to say?"

To her surprise, Trenor answered the look with a speechless stare. With his last gust of words the flame had died out, leaving him chill and humbled. It was as though a cold air had dispersed the fumes of his libations, and the situation loomed before him black and naked as the ruins of a fire. Old habits, old restraints, the hand of inherited order, plucked back the bewildered mind which passion had jolted from its ruts. Trenor's eye had the haggard look of the sleep-walker waked on a deathly ledge.

"Go home! Go away from here"——he stammered, and turning his back on her walked toward the hearth.

The sharp release from her fears restored Lily to immediate lucidity. The collapse of Trenor's will left her in control, and she heard herself, in a voice that was her own yet outside herself, bidding him ring for the servant, bidding him give the order for a hansom, directing him to put her in it when it came. Whence the strength came to her she knew not; but an insistent voice warned her that she must leave the house openly, and nerved her, in the hall before the hovering care-taker, to exchange light words with Trenor, and charge him with the usual messages for Judy, while all the while she shook with inward loathing. On the doorstep, with the street before her, she felt a mad throb of liberation, intoxicating as the prisoner's first draught of free air; but the clearness of brain continued, and she noted the mute aspect of Fifth Avenue, guessed at the lateness of the hour, and even observed a man's figure—was there something half-familiar in its outline?—which, as she entered the hansom, turned from the opposite corner and vanished in the obscurity of the side street.

But with the turn of the wheels reaction came, and shuddering darkness closed on her. "I can't think—I can't think," she moaned, and leaned her head against the rattling side of the cab. She seemed a stranger to herself, or rather there were two selves in her, the one she had always known, and a new abhorrent being to which it found itself chained. She had once picked up, in a house where she was staying, a translation of the *Eumenides*, and her imagination had been seized by the high terror of the scene where Orestes, in the cave of the oracle, finds his implacable huntresses asleep, and snatches an hour's repose.[1] Yes, the Furies* might sometimes sleep, but they were there, always there in the dark corners, and now they were awake and the iron clang of their wings was in her brain . . . She opened her eyes and saw the streets passing—the familiar alien streets. All she looked on was the same and yet changed. There was a great gulf fixed between today and yesterday. Everything in the past seemed simple, natural, full of daylight—and she was alone in a place of darkness and pollution.—Alone! It was the loneliness that frightened her. Her eyes fell on an illuminated clock at a street corner, and she saw that the hands marked the half hour after eleven. Only half-past eleven—there were hours and hours left of the night! And she must spend them alone, shuddering sleepless on her bed. Her soft nature recoiled from this ordeal, which had none of the stimulus of conflict to goad her through it. Oh, the slow cold drip of the minutes on her head! She had a vision of herself lying on the black walnut bed—and the darkness would frighten her, and if she left the light burning the dreary details of the room would brand themselves forever on her brain. She had always hated her room at Mrs. Peniston's—

---

*In ancient Greek and Roman mythology, an avenging female deity.

its ugliness, its impersonality, the fact that nothing in it was really hers. To a torn heart uncomforted by human nearness a room may open almost human arms, and the being to whom no four walls mean more than any others, is, at such hours, expatriate everywhere.

Lily had no heart to lean on. Her relation with her aunt was as superficial as that of chance lodgers who pass on the stairs. But even had the two been in closer contact, it was impossible to think of Mrs. Peniston's mind as offering shelter or comprehension to such misery as Lily's. As the pain that can be told is but half a pain, so the pity that questions has little healing in its touch. What Lily craved was the darkness made by enfolding arms, the silence which is not solitude, but compassion holding its breath.

She started up and looked forth on the passing streets. Gerty!—they were nearing Gerty's corner. If only she could reach there before this labouring anguish burst from her breast to her lips—if only she could feel the hold of Gerty's arms while she shook in the ague-fit of fear that was coming upon her! She pushed up the door in the roof and called the address to the driver. It was not so late—Gerty might still be waking. And even if she were not, the sound of the bell would penetrate every recess of her tiny apartment, and rouse her to answer her friend's call.

14

GERTY FARISH, THE MORNING after the Wellington Brys' entertainment, woke from dreams as happy as Lily's. If they were less vivid in hue, more subdued to the half-tints of her personality and her experience, they were for that very reason better suited to her mental vision. Such flashes of joy as Lily moved in would have blinded Miss Farish, who was accustomed, in the way of happiness, to such scant light as shone through the cracks of other people's lives.

Now she was the centre of a little illumination of her own: a mild but unmistakable beam, compounded of Lawrence Selden's growing kindness to herself and the discovery that he extended his liking to Lily Bart. If these two factors seem incompatible to the student of feminine psychology, it must be remembered that Gerty had always been a parasite in the moral order, living on the crumbs of other tables, and content to look through the window at the banquet spread for her friends. Now that she was enjoying a little private feast of her own, it would have seemed incredibly selfish not to lay a plate for a friend; and there was no one with whom she would rather have shared her enjoyment than Miss Bart.

As to the nature of Selden's growing kindness, Gerty would no more have dared to define it than she would have tried to learn a butterfly's colours by knocking the dust from its wings. To seize on the wonder would be to brush off its bloom, and perhaps see it fade and stiffen in her hand: better the sense of beauty palpitating out of reach, while she held her breath and watched where it would alight. Yet Selden's manner at the Brys' had brought the flutter of wings so close that they seemed to be beating in her own heart. She had never seen him so alert, so responsive, so attentive to what she had to say. His habitual manner had an absent-minded kindliness which she accepted, and was grateful for, as the liveliest sentiment her presence was likely to inspire; but she was quick to feel in him a change implying that for once she could give pleasure as well as receive it.

And it was so delightful that this higher degree of sympathy should be reached through their interest in Lily Bart! Gerty's affection for her friend—a sentiment that had learned to keep itself alive on the scantiest diet—had grown to active adoration since Lily's restless curiosity had drawn her into the circle of Miss Farish's work. Lily's taste of beneficence had wakened in her a momentary appetite for well-doing. Her visit to the Girls' Club had first brought her in contact with the dramatic contrasts of life. She had always accepted with philosophic calm the fact that such existences as hers were pedestalled on foundations of obscure humanity. The dreary limbo of dinginess lay all around and beneath that little illuminated circle in which life reached its finest efflorescence, as the mud and sleet of a winter night enclose a hothouse filled with tropical flowers. All this was in the natural order of things, and the orchid basking in its artificially created atmosphere could round the delicate curves of its petals undisturbed by the ice on the panes.

But it is one thing to live comfortably with the abstract conception of poverty, another to be brought in contact with its human embodiments. Lily had never conceived of these victims of fate otherwise than in the mass. That the mass was composed of individual lives, innumerable separate centres of sensation, with her own eager reachings for pleasure, her own fierce revulsions from pain—that some of these bundles of feeling were clothed in shapes not so unlike her own, with eyes meant to look on gladness, and young lips shaped for love—this discovery gave Lily one of those sudden shocks of pity that sometimes decentralize a life. Lily's nature was incapable of such renewal: she could feel other demands only through her own, and no pain was long vivid which did not press on an answering nerve. But for the moment she was drawn out of herself by the interest of her direct relation with a world so unlike her own. She had supplemented her first gift by personal assistance to one or two of Miss Farish's most appealing subjects, and the admiration and interest her presence excited among the tired workers at the club ministered in a new form to her insatiable desire to please.

Gerty Farish was not a close enough reader of character to disentangle the mixed threads of which Lily's philanthropy was woven. She supposed her beautiful friend to be actuated by the same motive as herself—that sharpening of the moral vision which makes all human suffering so near and insistent that the other aspects of life fade into remoteness. Gerty lived by such simple formulas that she did not hesitate to class her friend's state with the emotional "change of heart" to which her dealings with the poor had accustomed her; and she rejoiced in the thought that she had been the humble instrument of this renewal. Now she had an answer to all criticisms of Lily's conduct: as she had said, she knew "the real Lily," and the discovery that Selden shared her knowledge raised her placid acceptance of life to a dazzled sense of its possibilities—a sense farther enlarged, in the course of the afternoon, by the receipt of a telegram from Selden asking if he might dine with her that evening.

While Gerty was lost in the happy bustle which this announcement produced in her small household, Selden was at one with her in thinking with intensity of Lily Bart. The case which had called him to Albany was not complicated enough to absorb all his attention, and he had the professional faculty of keeping a part of his mind free when its services were not needed. This part—which at the moment seemed dangerously like the whole—was filled to the brim with the sensations of the previous evening. Selden understood the symptoms: he recognized the fact that he was paying up, as there had always been a chance of his having to pay up, for the voluntary exclusions of his past. He had meant to keep free from permanent ties, not from any poverty of feeling, but because, in a different way, he was, as much as Lily, the victim of his environment. There had been a germ of truth in his declaration to Gerty Farish that he had never wanted to marry a "nice" girl: the adjective connoting, in his cousin's vocabulary, certain utilitarian qualities which are apt to preclude the luxury of charm. Now it had been Selden's fate to have a charming mother: her graceful portrait, all smiles and Cashmere, still emitted a faded scent of the undefinable quality. His father was the kind of man who delights in a charming woman: who quotes her, stimulates her, and keeps her perennially charming. Neither one of the couple cared for money, but

their disdain of it took the form of always spending a little more
than was prudent. If their house was shabby, it was exquisitely
kept; if there were good books on the shelves there were also
good dishes on the table. Selden senior had an eye for a picture,
his wife an understanding of old lace; and both were so conscious of restraint and discrimination in buying that they never
quite knew how it was that the bills mounted up.

Though many of Selden's friends would have called his parents poor, he had grown up in an atmosphere where restricted
means were felt only as a check on aimless profusion: where the
few possessions were so good that their rarity gave them a mer-
ited relief, and abstinence was combined with elegance in a way
exemplified by Mrs. Selden's knack of wearing her old velvet as
if it were new. A man has the advantage of being delivered early
from the home point of view, and before Selden left college he
had learned that there are as many different ways of going without money as of spending it. Unfortunately, he found no way as
agreeable as that practised at home; and his views of womankind
in especial were tinged by the remembrance of the one woman
who had given him his sense of "values." It was from her that he
inherited his detachment from the sumptuary side of life: the
stoic's* carelessness of material things, combined with the Epicurean's pleasure in them. Life shorn of either feeling appeared
to him a diminished thing; and nowhere was the blending of the
two ingredients so essential as in the character of a pretty
woman.

It had always seemed to Selden that experience offered a
great deal besides the sentimental adventure, yet he could vividly
conceive of a love which should broaden and deepen till it became the central fact of life. What he could not accept, in his
own case, was the makeshift alternative of a relation that should
be less than this: that should leave some portions of his nature
unsatisfied, while it put an undue strain on others. He would

---

*The reference is to members of the ancient Greek school of philos-
ophy founded by Zeno, who believed in submitting without com-
plaint to unavoidable necessity. Their beliefs were in direct opposition
to those of pleasure-loving Epicureans.

not, in other words, yield to the growth of an affection which might appeal to pity yet leave the understanding untouched: sympathy should no more delude him than a trick of the eyes, the grace of helplessness than a curve of the cheek.

But now—that little *but* passed like a sponge over all his vows. His reasoned-out resistances seemed for the moment so much less important than the question as to when Lily would receive his note! He yielded himself to the charm of trivial preoccupations, wondering at what hour her reply would be sent, with what words it would begin. As to its import he had no doubt—he was as sure of her surrender as of his own. And so he had leisure to muse on all its exquisite details, as a hard worker, on a holiday morning, might lie still and watch the beam of light travel gradually across his room. But if the new light dazzled, it did not blind him. He could still discern the outline of facts, though his own relation to them had changed. He was no less conscious than before of what was said of Lily Bart, but he could separate the woman he knew from the vulgar estimate of her. His mind turned to Gerty Farish's words, and the wisdom of the world seemed a groping thing beside the insight of innocence. *Blessed are the pure in heart, for they shall see God**—even the hidden god in their neighbour's breast! Selden was in the state of impassioned self-absorption that the first surrender to love produces. His craving was for the companionship of one whose point of view should justify his own, who should confirm, by deliberate observation, the truth to which his intuitions had leaped. He could not wait for the midday recess, but seized a moment's leisure in court to scribble his telegram to Gerty Farish.

Reaching town, he was driven direct to his club, where he hoped a note from Miss Bart might await him. But his box contained only a line of rapturous assent from Gerty, and he was turning away disappointed when he was hailed by a voice from the smoking room.

"Hallo, Lawrence! Dining here? Take a bite with me—I've ordered a canvas-back."†

---

*The reference is to the Bible, Matthew 5:8 (KJV).
†North American duck, named for the color of its feathers.

He discovered Trenor, in his day clothes, sitting, with a tall glass at his elbow, behind the folds of a sporting journal.

Selden thanked him, but pleaded an engagement.

"Hang it, I believe every man in town has an engagement tonight. I shall have the club to myself. You know how I'm living this winter, rattling round in that empty house. My wife meant to come to town today, but she's put it off again, and how is a fellow to dine alone in a room with the looking-glasses covered, and nothing but a bottle of Harvey sauce on the sideboard? I say, Lawrence, chuck your engagement and take pity on me—it gives me the blue devils to dine alone, and there's nobody but that canting ass Wetherall in the club."

"Sorry, Gus—I can't do it."

As Selden turned away, he noticed the dark flush on Trenor's face, the unpleasant moisture of his intensely white forehead, the way his jewelled rings were wedged in the creases of his fat red fingers. Certainly the beast was predominating—the beast at the bottom of the glass. And he had heard this man's name coupled with Lily's! Bah—the thought sickened him; all the way back to his rooms he was haunted by the sight of Trenor's fat creased hands——

On his table lay the note: Lily had sent it to his rooms. He knew what was in it before he broke the seal—a grey seal with *Beyond!* beneath a flying ship. Ah, he would take her beyond—beyond the ugliness, the pettiness, the attrition and corrosion of the soul——

Gerty's little sitting-room sparkled with welcome when Selden entered it. Its modest "effects," compact of enamel paint and ingenuity, spoke to him in the language just then sweetest to his ear. It is surprising how little narrow walls and a low ceiling matter, when the roof of the soul has suddenly been raised. Gerty sparkled too; or at least shone with a tempered radiance. He had never before noticed that she had "points"—really, some good fellow might do worse . . . Over the little dinner (and here, again, the effects were wonderful) he told her she ought to marry—he was in a mood to pair off the whole world. She had made the caramel custard with her own hands. It was sinful to keep such gifts to herself. He reflected with a throb of pride that trim her own hats—she had told him so the day of their walk at Bellomont.

He did not speak of Lily till after dinner. During the little repast he kept the talk on his hostess, who, fluttered at being the centre of observation, shone as rosy as the candle-shades she had manufactured for the occasion. Selden evinced an extraordinary interest in her household arrangements: complimented her on the ingenuity with which she had utilized every inch of her small quarters, asked how her servant managed about afternoons out, learned that one may improvise delicious dinners in a chafing-dish, and uttered thoughtful generalizations on the burden of a large establishment.

When they were in the sitting-room again, where they fitted as snugly as bits in a puzzle, and she had brewed the coffee, and poured it into her grandmother's egg-shell cups, his eye, as he leaned back, basking in the warm fragrance, lighted on a recent photograph of Miss Bart, and the desired transition was effected without an effort. The photograph was well enough—but to catch her as she had looked last night! Gerty agreed with him—never had she been so radiant. But could photography capture that light? There had been a new look in her face—something different; yes, Selden agreed there had been something different. The coffee was so exquisite that he asked for a second cup: such a contrast to the watery stuff at the club! Ah, your poor bachelor with his impersonal club fare, alternating with the equally impersonal *cuisine* of the dinner-party! A man who lived in lodgings missed the best part of life—he pictured the flavourless solitude of Trenor's repast, and felt a moment's compassion for the man . . . But to return to Lily—and again and again he returned, questioning, conjecturing, leading Gerty on, draining her inmost thoughts of their stored tenderness for her friend.

At first she poured herself out unstintingly, happy in this perfect communion of their sympathies. His understanding of Lily helped to confirm her own belief in her friend. They dwelt together on the fact that Lily had had no chance. Gerty instanced her generous impulses—her restlessness and discontent. The fact that her life had never satisfied her proved that she was made for better things. She might have married more than once—the conventional rich marriage which she had been taught to consider the sole end of existence—but when the opportunity came she had always shrunk from it. Percy Gryce, for instance, had been in love with her—every one at Bellomont had supposed them to be engaged, and her dismissal of him was thought inexplicable. This view of the Gryce incident chimed too well with Selden's mood not to be instantly adopted by him, with a flash of retrospective contempt for what had once seemed the obvious solution. If rejection there had been—and he wondered now that he had ever doubted it!—then he held the key to the secret, and the hillsides of Bellomont were lit up, not with sunset, but with dawn. It was he who had wavered and disowned the face of opportunity—and the joy now warming his breast might have been a familiar inmate if he had captured it in its first flight.

It was at this point, perhaps, that a joy just trying its wings in Gerty's heart dropped to earth and lay still. She sat facing Selden, repeating mechanically: "No, she has never been understood——" and all the while she herself seemed to be sitting in the centre of a great glare of comprehension. The little confidential room, where a moment ago their thoughts had touched elbows like their chairs, grew to unfriendly vastness, separating her from Selden by all the length of her new vision of the future—and that future stretched out interminably, with her lonely figure toiling down it, a mere speck on the solitude.

"She is herself with a few people only; and you are one of them," she heard Selden saying. And again: "Be good to her, Gerty, won't you?" and: "She has it in her to become whatever she is believed to be—you'll help her by believing the best of her?"

The words beat on Gerty's brain like the sound of a language which has seemed familiar at a distance, but on approaching is found to be unintelligible. He had come to talk to her of Lily—that was all! There had been a third at the feast she had spread for him, and that third had taken her own place. She tried to follow what he was saying, to cling to her own part in the talk—but it was all as meaningless as the boom of waves in a drowning head, and she felt, as the drowning may feel, that to sink would be nothing beside the pain of struggling to keep up.

Selden rose, and she drew a deep breath, feeling that soon she could yield to the blessed waves.

"Mrs. Fisher's? You say she was dining there? There's music afterward; I believe I had a card from her." He glanced at the foolish pink-faced clock that was drumming out this hideous hour. "A quarter past ten? I might look in there now; the Fisher evenings are amusing. I haven't kept you up too late. Gerty? You look tired—I've rambled on and bored you." And in the unwonted overflow of his feelings, he left a cousinly kiss upon her cheek.

At Mrs. Fisher's, through the cigar-smoke of the studio, a dozen voices greeted Selden. A song was pending as he entered, and he dropped into a seat near his hostess, his eyes roaming in search of Miss Bart. But she was not there, and the discovery gave him a pang out of all proportion to its seriousness; since the note in his breast-pocket assured him that at four the next day they would meet. To his impatience it seemed immeasurably long to wait, and half-ashamed of the impulse, he leaned to Mrs. Fisher to ask, as the music ceased, if Miss Bart had not dined with her.

"Lily? She's just gone. She had to run off, I forget where. Wasn't she wonderful last night?"

"Who's that? Lily?" asked Jack Stepney, from the depths of a neighboring arm-chair. "Really, you know, I'm no prude, but when it comes to a girl standing there as if she was up at auction—I thought seriously of speaking to cousin Julia."

"You didn't know Jack had become our social censor?" Mrs. Fisher said to Selden with a laugh; and Stepney spluttered, amid the general derision: "But she's a cousin, hang it, and when a man's married—*Town Talk* was full of her this morning."

"Yes: lively reading that was," said Mr. Ned Van Alstyne, stroking his moustache to hide the smile behind it. "Buy the dirty sheet? No, of course not; some fellow showed it to me—but I'd heard the stories before. When a girl's as good-looking as that she'd better marry; then no questions are asked. In our imperfectly organized society there is no provision as yet for the young woman who claims the privileges of marriage without assuming its obligations."

"Well, I understand Lily is about to assume them in the shape of Mr. Rosedale," Mrs. Fisher said with a laugh.

"Rosedale—good heavens!" exclaimed Van Alstyne, dropping his eye-glass. "Stepney, that's your fault for foisting the brute on us."

"Oh, confound it, you know, we don't *marry* Rosedale in our family," Stepney languidly protested; but his wife, who sat in oppressive bridal finery at the other side of the room, quelled him with the judicial reflection: "In Lily's circumstances it's a mistake to have too high a standard."

"I hear even Rosedale has been scared by the talk lately," Mrs. Fisher rejoined; "but the sight of her last night sent him off his head. What do you think he said to me after her *tableau?* 'My God, Mrs. Fisher, if I could get Paul Morpeth to paint her like that, the picture'd appreciate a hundred per cent in ten years.'"

"By Jove,—but isn't she about somewhere?" exclaimed Van Alstyne, restoring his glass with an uneasy glance.

"No; she ran off while you were all mixing the punch down stairs. Where was she going, by the way? What's on tonight? I hadn't heard of anything."

"Oh, not a party, I think," said an inexperienced young Farish who had arrived late. "I put her in her cab as I was coming in, and she gave the driver the Trenors' address."

"The Trenors'?" exclaimed Mrs. Jack Stepney. "Why, the house is closed—Judy telephoned me from Bellomont this evening."

"Did she? That's queer. I'm sure I'm not mistaken. Well, come now, Trenor's there, anyhow—I—oh, well—the fact is, I've no head for numbers," he broke off, admonished by the nudge of an adjoining foot, and the smile that circled the room.

In its unpleasant light Selden had risen and was shaking hands with his hostess. The air of the place stifled him, and he wondered why he had stayed in it so long.

On the doorstep he stood still, remembering a phrase of Lily's: "It seems to me you spend a good deal of time in the element you disapprove of."

Well—what had brought him there but the quest of her? It was her element, not his. But he would lift her out of it, take her beyond! That *Beyond!* on her letter was like a cry for rescue. He knew that Perseus's* task is not done when he has loosed Andromeda's chains, for her limbs are numb with bondage, and she cannot rise and walk, but clings to him with dragging arms as he beats back to land with his burden. Well, he had strength for both—it was her weakness which had put the strength in him. It was not, alas, a clean rush of waves they had to win through, but a clogging morass of old associations and habits, and for the moment its vapours were in his throat. But he would see clearer, breathe freer in her presence: she was at once the dead weight at his breast and the spar which should float them to safety. He smiled at the whirl of metaphor with which he was trying to build up a defence against the influences of the last hour. It was pitiable that he, who knew the mixed motives on which social judgments depend, should still feel himself so swayed by them. How could he lift Lily to a freer vision of life, if his own view of her was to be coloured by any mind in which he saw her reflected?

The moral oppression had produced a physical craving for air, and he strode on, opening his lungs to the reverberating coldness of the night. At the corner of Fifth Avenue Van Alstyne hailed him with an offer of company.

"Walking? A good thing to blow the smoke out of one's head. Now that women have taken to tobacco we live in a bath of nicotine. It would be a curious thing to study the effect of cigarettes on the relation of the sexes. Smoke is almost as great a solvent as divorce: both tend to obscure the moral issue."

Nothing could have been less consonant with Selden's mood than Van Alstyne's after-dinner aphorisms, but as long as the latter confined himself to generalities his listener's nerves were in control. Happily Van Alstyne prided himself on his summing up of social aspects, and with Selden for audience was eager to show the sureness of his touch. Mrs. Fisher lived in an East side street near the Park, and as the two men walked down Fifth Avenue the new architectural developments of that versatile thoroughfare invited Van Alstyne's comment.

---

*The heroic son of Zeus and Danaë in Greek mythology slew the gorgon Medusa and later rescued Andromeda from a sea monster.

"That Greiner house, now—a typical rung in the social ladder! The man who built it came from a *milieu* where all the dishes are put on the table at once. His façade is a complete architectural meal; if he had omitted a style his friends might have thought the money had given out. Not a bad purchase for Rosedale, though: attracts attention, and awes the Western sight-seer. By and bye he'll get out of that phase, and want something that the crowd will pass and the few pause before. Especially if he marries my clever cousin——"

Selden dashed in with the query: "And the Wellington Brys'? Rather clever of its kind, don't you think?"

They were just beneath the wide white façade, with its rich restraint of line, which suggested the clever corseting of a redundant figure.

"That's the next stage: the desire to imply that one has been to Europe, and has a standard. I'm sure Mrs. Bry thinks her house a copy of the *Trianon;** in America every marble house with gilt furniture is thought to be a copy of the *Trianon*. What a clever chap that architect is, though—how he takes his client's measure! He has put the whole of Mrs. Bry in his use of the composite order. Now for the Trenors, you remember, he chose the Corinthian:† exuberant, but based on the best precedent. The Trenor house is one of his best things—doesn't look like a banqueting-hall turned inside out. I hear Mrs. Trenor wants to build out a new ball-room, and that divergence from Gus on that point keeps her at Bellomont. The dimensions of the Brys' ball-room must rankle: you may be sure she knows 'em as well as if she'd been there last night with a yard-measure. Who said she was in town, by the way? That Farish boy? She isn't, I know; Mrs. Stepney was right; the house is dark, you see: I suppose Gus lives in the back."

He had halted opposite the Trenors' corner, and Selden perforce stayed his steps also. The house loomed obscure and unin-

---

*The Grand Trianon, also known as the Marble Trianon, is a small seventeenth-century palace on the grounds of the huge royal palace of the French kings at Versailles.

†Elaborate style of classical Greek architecture.

habited; only an oblong gleam above the door spoke of provisional occupancy.

"They've bought the house at the back: it gives them a hundred and fifty feet in the side street. There's where the ballroom's to be, with a gallery connecting it: billiard-room and so on above. I suggested changing the entrance, and carrying the drawing-room across the whole Fifth Avenue front: you see the front door corresponds with the windows—"

The walking-stick which Van Alstyne swung in demonstration dropped to a startled "Hallo!" as the door opened and two figures were seen silhouetted against the hall-light. At the same moment a hansom halted at the curb-stone, and one of the figures floated down to it in a haze of evening draperies; while the other, black and bulky, remained persistently projected against the light.

For an immeasurable second the two spectators of the incident were silent; then the house-door closed, the hansom rolled off, and the whole scene slipped by as if with the turn of a stereopticon.

Van Alstyne dropped his eye-glass with a low whistle.

"A—hem—nothing of this, eh, Selden? As one of the family, I know I may count on you—appearances are deceptive—and Fifth Avenue is so imperfectly lighted——"

"Good night," said Selden, turning sharply down the side street without seeing the other's extended hand.

Alone with her cousin's kiss, Gerty stared upon her thoughts. He had kissed her before—but not with another woman on his lips. If he had spared her that she could have drowned quietly, welcoming the dark flood as it submerged her. But now the flood was shot through with glory, and it was harder to drown at sunrise than in darkness. Gerty hid her face from the light, but it pierced to the crannies of her soul. She had been so contented, life had seemed so simple and sufficient—why had he come to trouble her with new hopes? And Lily—Lily, her best friend! Woman-like, she accused the woman. Perhaps, had it not been for Lily, her fond imagining might have become truth. Selden had always liked her—had understood and sympathized with the modest independence of her life. He, who had the reputation of weighing all things in the nice balance of fastidious perceptions, had been uncritical and simple in his view of her: his cleverness had never overawed her because she had felt at home in his heart. And now she was thrust out, and the door barred against her by Lily's hand! Lily, for whose admission there she herself had pleaded! The situation was lighted up by a dreary flash of irony. She knew Selden—she saw how the force of her faith in Lily must have helped to dispel his hesitations. She remembered, too, how Lily had talked of him—she saw herself bringing the two together, making them known to each other. On Selden's part, no doubt, the wound inflicted was inconscient; he had never guessed her foolish secret; but Lily—Lily must have known! When, in such matters, are a woman's perceptions at fault? And if she knew, then she had deliberately despoiled her friend, and in mere wantonness of power, since, even to Gerty's suddenly flaming jealousy, it seemed incredible that Lily should wish to be Selden's wife. Lily might be incapable of marrying for money, but she was equally incapable of living without it, and Selden's eager investigations into the small economies of house-keeping made him appear to Gerty as tragically duped as herself.

She remained long in her sitting-room, where the embers were crumbling to cold grey, and the lamp paled under its gay shade. Just beneath it stood the photograph of Lily Bart, looking out imperially on the cheap gim-cracks, the cramped furniture of the little room. Could Selden picture her in such an interior? Gerty felt the poverty, the insignificance of her surroundings: she beheld her life as it must appear to Lily. And the cruelty of Lily's judgments smote upon her memory. She saw that she had dressed her idol with attributes of her own making. When had Lily ever really felt, or pitied, or understood? All she wanted was the taste of new experiences: she seemed like some cruel creature experimenting in a laboratory.

The pink-faced clock drummed out another hour, and Gerty rose with a start. She had an appointment early the next morning with a district visitor on the East Side.* She put out her lamp,

---

*Social worker on the Lower East Side of Manhattan, once home to many poor Jewish and Italian immigrants.

covered the fire, and went into her bedroom to undress. In the little glass above her dressing-table she saw her face reflected against the shadows of the room, and tears blotted the reflection. What right had she to dream the dreams of loveliness? A dull face invited a dull fate. She cried quietly as she undressed, laying aside her clothes with her habitual precision, setting everything in order for the next day, when the old life must be taken up as though there had been no break in its routine. Her servant did not come till eight o'clock, and she prepared her own tea-tray and placed it beside the bed. Then she locked the door of the flat, extinguished her light and lay down. But on her bed sleep would not come, and she lay face to face with the fact that she hated Lily Bart. It closed with her in the darkness like some formless evil to be blindly grappled with. Reason, judgment, renunciation, all the sane daylight forces, were beaten back in the sharp struggle for self-preservation. She wanted happiness—wanted it as fiercely and unscrupulously as Lily did, but without Lily's power of obtaining it. And in her conscious impotence she lay shivering, and hated her friend——

A ring at the door-bell caught her to her feet. She struck a light and stood startled, listening. For a moment her heart beat incoherently, then she felt the sobering touch of fact, and remembered that such calls were not unknown in her charitable work. She flung on her dressing-gown to answer the summons, and unlocking her door, confronted the shining vision of Lily Bart.

Gerty's first movement was one of revulsion. She shrank back as though Lily's presence flashed too sudden a light upon her misery. Then she heard her name in a cry, had a glimpse of her friend's face, and felt herself caught and clung to.

"Lily—what is it?" she exclaimed.

Miss Bart released her, and stood breathing brokenly, like one who has gained shelter after a long flight.

"I was so cold—I couldn't go home. Have you a fire?"

Gerty's compassionate instincts, responding to the swift call of habit, swept aside all her reluctances. Lily was simply some one who needed help—for what reason, there was no time to pause and conjecture: disciplined sympathy checked the wonder

on Gerty's lips, and made her draw her friend silently into the
sitting-room and seat her by the darkened hearth.

"There is kindling wood here: the fire will burn in a minute."

She knelt down, and the flame leapt under her rapid hands.
It flashed strangely through the tears which still blurred her
eyes, and smote on the white ruin of Lily's face. The girls looked
at each other in silence; then Lily repeated: "I couldn't go home."

"No—no—you came here, dear! You're cold and tired—sit
quiet, and I'll make you some tea."

Gerty had unconsciously adopted the soothing note of her
trade: all personal feeling was merged in the sense of ministry,
and experience had taught her that the bleeding must be stayed
before the wound is probed.

Lily sat quiet, leaning to the fire: the clatter of cups behind
her soothed her as familiar noises hush a child whom silence has
kept wakeful. But when Gerty stood at her side with the tea she
pushed it away, and turned an estranged eye on the familiar
room.

"I came here because I couldn't bear to be alone," she said.

Gerty set down the cup and knelt beside her.

"Lily! Something has happened—can't you tell me?"

"I couldn't bear to lie awake in my room till morning. I hate
my room at Aunt Julia's—so I came here———"

She stirred suddenly, broke from her apathy, and clung to
Gerty in a fresh burst of fear.

"Oh, Gerty, the furies . . . you know the noise of their
wings—alone, at night, in the dark? But you don't know—there
is nothing to make the dark dreadful to you———"

The words, flashing back on Gerty's last hours, struck from
her a faint derisive murmur; but Lily, in the blaze of her own
misery, was blinded to everything outside it.

"You'll let me stay? I shan't mind when daylight comes—Is it
late? Is the night nearly over? It must be awful to be sleepless—
everything stands by the bed and stares———"

Miss Farish caught her straying hands. "Lily, look at me!
Something has happened—an accident? You have been frightened—what has frightened you? Tell me if you can—a word or
two—so that I can help you."

Lily shook her head.

"I am not frightened: that's not the word. Can you imagine looking into your glass some morning and seeing a disfigurement—some hideous change that has come to you while you slept? Well, I seem to myself like that—I can't bear to see myself in my own thoughts—I hate ugliness, you know—I've always turned from it—but I can't explain to you—you wouldn't understand."

She lifted her head and her eyes fell on the clock.

"How long the night is! And I know I shan't sleep tomorrow. Some one told me my father used to lie sleepless and think of horrors. And he was not wicked, only unfortunate—and I see now how he must have suffered, lying alone with his thoughts! But I am bad—a bad girl—all my thoughts are bad—I have always had bad people about me. Is that any excuse? I thought I could manage my own life—I was proud—proud! but now I'm on their level——"

Sobs shook her, and she bowed to them like a tree in a dry storm.

Gerty knelt beside her, waiting, with the patience born of experience, till this gust of misery should loosen fresh speech. She had first imagined some physical shock, some peril of the crowded streets, since Lily was presumably on her way home from Carry Fisher's; but she now saw that other nerve-centres were smitten, and her mind trembled back from conjecture.

Lily's sobs ceased, and she lifted her head.

"There are bad girls in your slums. Tell me—do they ever pick themselves up? Ever forget, and feel as they did before?"

"Lily! you mustn't speak so—you're dreaming."

"Don't they always go from bad to worse? There's no turning back—your old self rejects you, and shuts you out."

She rose, stretching her arms as if in utter physical weariness. "Go to bed, dear! You work hard and get up early. I'll watch here by the fire, and you'll leave the light, and your door open. All I want is to feel that you are near me." She had both hands on Gerty's shoulders, with a smile that was like sunrise on a sea strewn with wreckage.

"I can't leave you, Lily. Come and lie on my bed. Your hands are frozen—you must undress and be made warm." Gerty paused with sudden compunction. "But Mrs. Peniston—it's past mid-night! What will she think?"

"She goes to bed. I have a latch-key. It doesn't matter—I can't go back there."

"There's no need to: you shall stay here. But you must tell me where you have been. Listen, Lily—it will help you to speak!" She regained Miss Bart's hands, and pressed them against her. "Try to tell me—it will clear your poor head. Listen—you were dining at Carry Fisher's." Gerty paused and added with a flash of heroism: "Lawrence Selden went from here to find you."

At the word, Lily's face melted from locked anguish to the open misery of a child. Her lips trembled and her gaze widened with tears.

"He went to find me? And I missed him! Oh, Gerty, he tried to help me. He told me—he warned me long ago—he foresaw that I should grow hateful to myself!"

The name, as Gerty saw with a clutch at the heart, had loosened the springs of self-pity in her friend's dry breast, and tear by tear Lily poured out the measure of her anguish. She had dropped sideways in Gerty's big arm-chair, her head buried where lately Selden's had leaned, in a beauty of abandonment that drove home to Gerty's aching senses the inevitablenees of her own defeat. Ah, it needed no deliberate purpose on Lily's part to rob her of her dream! To look on that prone loveliness was to see in it a natural force, to recognize that love and power belong to such as Lily, as renunciation and service are the lot of those they despoil. But if Selden's infatuation seemed a fatal necessity, the effect that his name produced shook Gerty's steadfastness with a last pang. Men pass through such superhuman loves and outlive them: they are the probation subduing the heart to human joys. How gladly Gerty would have welcomed the ministry of healing: how willingly have soothed the sufferer back to tolerance of life! But Lily's self-betrayal took this last hope from her. The mortal maid on the shore is helpless against the siren who loves her prey: such victims are floated back dead from their adventure.

Lily sprang up and caught her with strong hands. "Gerty, you know him—you understand him—tell me; if I went to him, if I told him everything—if I said: 'I am bad through and through—

I want admiration, I want excitement, I want money—' yes, *money!* That's my shame, Gerty—and it's known, it's said of me—it's what men think of me— If I said it all to him—told him the whole story—said plainly: 'I've sunk lower than the lowest, for I've taken what they take, and not paid as they pay'—oh, Gerty, you know him, you can speak for him: if I told him everything would he loathe me? Or would he pity me, and understand me, and save me from loathing myself?"

Gerty stood cold and passive. She knew the hour of her probation had come, and her poor heart beat wildly against its destiny. As a dark river sweeps by under a lightning flash, she saw her chance of happiness surge past under a flash of temptation. What prevented her from saying: "He is like other men"? She was not so sure of him, after all! But to do so would have been like blaspheming her love. She could not put him before herself in any light but the noblest: she must trust him to the height of her own passion.

"Yes: I know him; he will help you," she said; and in a moment Lily's passion was weeping itself out against her breast.

There was but one bed in the little flat, and the two girls lay down on it side by side when Gerty had unlaced Lily's dress and persuaded her to put her lips to the warm tea. The light extinguished, they lay still in the darkness, Gerty shrinking to the outer edge of the narrow couch to avoid contact with her bedfellow. Knowing that Lily disliked to be caressed, she had long ago learned to check her demonstrative impulses toward her friend. But tonight every fibre in her body shrank from Lily's nearness: it was torture to listen to her breathing, and feel the sheet stir with it. As Lily turned, and settled to completer rest, a strand of her hair swept Gerty's cheek with its fragrance. Everything about her was warm and soft and scented: even the stains of her grief became her as rain-drops do the beaten rose. But as Gerty lay with arms drawn down her side, in the motionless narrowness of an effigy, she felt a stir of sobs from the breathing warmth beside her, and Lily flung out her hand, groped for her friend's, and held it fast.

"Hold me, Gerty, hold me, or I shall think of things," she moaned; and Gerty silently slipped an arm under her, pillowing her head in its hollow as a mother makes a nest for a tossing child. In the warm hollow Lily lay still and her breathing grew low and regular. Her hand still clung to Gerty's as if to ward off evil dreams, but the hold of her fingers relaxed, her head sank deeper into its shelter, and Gerty felt that she slept.

15

WHEN LILY WOKE SHE had the bed to herself, and the winter light was in the room.

She sat up, bewildered by the strangeness of her surroundings; then memory returned, and she looked about her with a shiver. In the cold slant of light reflected from the back wall of a neighbouring building, she saw her evening dress and opera cloak lying in a tawdry heap on a chair. Finery laid off is as unappetizing as the remains of a feast, and it occurred to Lily that, at home, her maid's vigilance had always spared her the sight of such incongruities. Her body ached with fatigue, and with the constriction of her attitude in Gerty's bed. All through her troubled sleep she had been conscious of having no space to toss in, and the long effort to remain motionless made her feel as if she had spent her night in a train.

This sense of physical discomfort was the first to assert itself; then she perceived, beneath it, a corresponding mental prostration, a languor of horror more insufferable than the first rush of her disgust. The thought of having to wake every morning with this weight on her breast roused her tired mind to fresh effort. She must find some way out of the slough into which she had stumbled: it was not so much compunction as the dread of her morning thoughts that pressed on her the need of action. But she was unutterably tired; it was weariness to think connectedly. She lay back, looking about the poor slit of a room with a renewal of physical distaste. The outer air, penned between high buildings, brought no freshness through the window; steam-heat was beginning to sing in a coil of dingy pipes, and a smell of cooking penetrated the crack of the door.

The door opened, and Gerty, dressed and hatted, entered with a cup of tea. Her face looked sallow and swollen in the dreary light, and her dull hair shaded imperceptibly into the tones of her skin.

She glanced shyly at Lily, asking in an embarrassed tone how she felt; Lily answered with the same constraint, and raised herself up to drink the tea.

"I must have been over-tired last night; I think I had a nervous attack in the carriage," she said, as the drink brought clearness to her sluggish thoughts.

"You were not well; I am so glad you came here," Gerty returned.

"But how am I to get home? And Aunt Julia——?"

"She knows; I telephoned early, and your maid has brought your things. But won't you eat something? I scrambled the eggs myself."

Lily could not eat; but the tea strengthened her to rise and dress under her maid's searching gaze. It was a relief to her that Gerty was obliged to hasten away: the two kissed silently, but without a trace of the previous night's emotion.

Lily found Mrs. Peniston in a state of agitation. She had sent for Grace Stepney and was taking digitalis. Lily breasted the storm of enquiries as best she could, explaining that she had had an attack of faintness on her way back from Carry Fisher's; that, fearing she would not have strength to reach home, she had gone to Miss Farish's instead; but that a quiet night had restored her, and that she had no need of a doctor.

This was a relief to Mrs. Peniston, who could give herself up to her own symptoms, and Lily was advised to go and lie down, her aunt's panacea for all physical and moral disorders. In the solitude of her own room she was brought back to a sharp contemplation of facts. Her daylight view of them necessarily differed from the cloudy vision of the night. The winged furies were now prowling gossips who dropped in on each other for tea. But her fears seemed the uglier, thus shorn of their vagueness; and besides, she had to act, not rave. For the first time she forced herself to reckon up the exact amount of her debt to Trenor; and the result of this hateful computation was the discovery that she had, in all, received nine thousand dollars from him. The flimsy pretext on which it had been given and received shrivelled up in the blaze of her shame: she knew that not a penny of it was her own, and that to restore her self-respect she must at once repay the whole amount. The inability thus to solace her outraged feelings gave her a paralyzing sense of insignificance. She was realizing for the first time that a woman's dignity may cost more to keep up than her carriage; and that the maintenance of a moral attribute should be dependent on dollars and cents, made the world appear a more sordid place than she had conceived it.

After luncheon, when Grace Stepney's prying eyes had been removed, Lily asked for a word with her aunt. The two ladies went upstairs to the sitting-room, where Mrs. Peniston seated herself in her black satin arm-chair tufted with yellow buttons, beside a bead-work table bearing a bronze box with a miniature of Beatrice Cenci[2] in the lid. Lily felt for these objects the same distaste which the prisoner may entertain for the fittings of the court-room. It was here that her aunt received her rare confidences, and the pink-eyed smirk of the turbaned Beatrice was associated in her mind with the gradual fading of the smile from Mrs. Peniston's lips. That lady's dread of a scene gave her an inexorableness which the greatest strength of character could not have produced, since it was independent of all considerations of right or wrong; and knowing this, Lily seldom ventured to assail it. She had never felt less like making the attempt than on the present occasion; but she had sought in vain for any other means of escape from an intolerable situation.

Mrs. Peniston examined her critically. "You're a bad colour, Lily: this incessant rushing about is beginning to tell on you," she said.

Miss Bart saw an opening. "I don't think it's that, Aunt Julia; I've had worries," she replied.

"Ah," said Mrs. Peniston, shutting her lips with the snap of a purse closing against a beggar.

"I'm sorry to bother you with them," Lily continued, "but I really believe my faintness last night was brought on partly by anxious thoughts——"

"I should have said Carry Fisher's cook was enough to account for it. She has a woman who was with Maria Melson in

1891—the spring of the year we went to Aix*—and I remember dining there two days before we sailed, and feeling *sure* the coppers† hadn't been scoured."

"I don't think I ate much; I can't eat or sleep." Lily paused, and then said abruptly: "The fact is, Aunt Julia, I owe some money."

Mrs. Peniston's face clouded perceptibly, but did not express the astonishment her niece had expected. She was silent, and Lily was forced to continue: "I have been foolish——"

"No doubt you have: extremely foolish," Mrs. Peniston interposed. "I fail to see how any one with your income, and no expenses—not to mention the handsome presents I've always given you——"

"Oh, you've been most generous, Aunt Julia; I shall never forget your kindness. But perhaps you don't quite realize the expense a girl is put to nowadays——"

"I don't realize that *you* are put to any expense except for your clothes and your railway fares. I expect you to be handsomely dressed; but I paid Céleste's bill for you last October."

Lily hesitated: her aunt's implacable memory had never been more inconvenient. "You were as kind as possible; but I have had to get a few things since——"

"What kind of things? Clothes? How much have you spent? Let me see the bill—I daresay the woman is swindling you."

"Oh, no, I think not: clothes have grown so frightfully expensive; and one needs so many different kinds, with country visits, and golf and skating, and Aiken‡ and Tuxedo——"

"Let me see the bill," Mrs. Peniston repeated.

Lily hesitated again. In the first place, Mme. Céleste had not yet sent in her account, and secondly, the amount it represented was only a fraction of the sum that Lily needed.

"She hasn't sent in the bill for my winter things, but I *know*

---

*Aix-les-Bains, fashionable mountain spa in the Savoy region of France.
†Copper cooking pans.
‡Fashionable resort in South Carolina.

it's large; and there are one or two other things; I've been careless and imprudent—I'm frightened to think of what I owe——"

She raised the troubled loveliness of her face to Mrs. Peniston, vainly hoping that a sight so moving to the other sex might not be without effect upon her own. But the effect produced was that of making Mrs. Peniston shrink back apprehensively.

"Really, Lily, you are old enough to manage your own affairs, and after frightening me to death by your performance of last night you might at least choose a better time to worry me with such matters." Mrs. Peniston glanced at the clock, and swallowed a tablet of digtalis. "If you owe Céleste another thousand, she may send me her account," she added, as though to end the discussion at any cost.

"I am very sorry, Aunt Julia; I hate to trouble you at such a time; but I have really no choice—I ought to have spoken sooner—I owe a great deal more than a thousand dollars."

"A great deal more? Do you owe two? She must have robbed you!"

"I told you it was not only Céleste. I—there are other bills—more pressing—that must be settled."

"What on earth have you been buying? Jewelry? You must have gone off your head," said Mrs. Peniston with asperity. "But if you have run into debt, you must suffer the consequences, and put aside your monthly income till your bills are paid. If you stay quietly here until next spring, instead of racing about all over the country, you will have no expenses at all, and surely in four or five months you can settle the rest of your bills if I pay the dress-maker now."

Lily was again silent. She knew she could not hope to extract even a thousand dollars from Mrs. Peniston on the mere plea of paying Céleste's bill: Mrs. Peniston would expect to go over the dress-maker's account, and would make out the cheque to her and not to Lily. And yet the money must be obtained before the day was over!

"The debts I speak of are—different—not like tradesmen's bills," she began confusedly; but Mrs. Peniston's look made her almost afraid to continue. Could it be that her aunt suspected anything? The idea precipitated Lily's avowal.

"The fact is, I've played cards a good deal—bridge; the

women all do it; girls too—it's expected. Sometimes I've won—won a good deal—but lately I've been unlucky—and of course such debts can't be paid off gradually——"

She paused: Mrs. Peniston's face seemed to be petrifying as she listened.

"Cards—you've played cards for money? It's true, then: when I was told so I wouldn't believe it. I won't ask if the other horrors I was told were true too; I've heard enough for the state of my nerves. When I think of the example you've had in this house! But I suppose it's your foreign bringing-up—no one knew where your mother picked up her friends. And her Sundays were a scandal—that I know." Mrs. Peniston wheeled round suddenly. "You play cards on Sunday?"

Lily flushed with the recollection of certain rainy Sundays at Bellomont and with the Dorsets.

"You're hard on me, Aunt Julia: I have never really cared for cards, but a girl hates to be thought priggish and superior, and one drifts into doing what the others do. I've had a dreadful lesson, and if you'll help me out this time I promise you——"

Mrs. Peniston raised her hand warningly. "You needn't make a ny promises: it's unnecessary. When I offered you a home I didn't undertake to pay your gambling debts."

"Aunt Julia! You don't mean that you won't help me?"

"I shall certainly not do anything to give the impression that I countenance your behaviour. If you really owe your dressmaker, I will settle with her—beyond that I recognize no obligation to assume your debts."

Lily had risen, and stood pale and quivering before her aunt. Pride stormed in her, but humiliation forced the cry from her lips: "Aunt Julia, I shall be disgraced—I——" But she could go no farther. If her aunt turned such a stony ear to the fiction of the gambling debts, in what spirit would she receive the terrible avowal of the truth?

"I consider that you *are* disgraced, Lily: disgraced by your conduct far more than by its results. You say your friends have persuaded you to play cards with them; well, they may as well learn a lesson too. They can probably afford to lose a little money—and at any rate, I am not going to waste any of mine in paying them. And now I must ask you to leave me—this scene has been extremely painful, and I have my own health to consider. Draw down the blinds, please; and tell Jennings I will see no one this afternoon but Grace Stepney."

Lily went up to her own room and bolted the door. She was trembling with fear and anger—the rush of the furies' wings was in her ears. She walked up and down the room with blind irregular steps. The last door of escape was closed—she felt herself shut in with her dishonour——

Suddenly her wild pacing brought her before the clock on the chimney-piece. Its hands stood at half-past three, and she remembered that Selden was to come to her at four. She had meant to put him off with a word—but now her heart leaped at the thought of seeing him. Was there not a promise of rescue in his love? As she had lain at Gerty's side the night before, she had thought of his coming, and of the sweetness of weeping out her pain upon his breast. Of course she had meant to clear herself of its consequences before she met him—she had never really doubted that Mrs. Peniston would come to her aid. And she had felt, even in the full storm of her misery, that Selden's love could not be her ultimate refuge; only it would be so sweet to take a moment's shelter there, while she gathered fresh strength to go on.

But now his love was her only hope, and as she sat alone with her wretchedness the thought of confiding in him became as seductive as the river's flow to the suicide. The first plunge would be terrible—but afterward, what blessedness might come! She remembered Gerty's words: "I know him—he will help you"; and her mind clung to them as a sick person might cling to a healing relic. Oh, if he really understood—if he would help her to gather up her broken life, and put it together in some new semblance in which no trace of the past should remain! He had always made her feel that she was worthy of better things, and she had never been in greater need of such solace. Once and again she shrank at the thought of imperilling his love by her confession: for love was what she needed—it would take the glow of passion to weld together the shattered fragments of her self-esteem. But she recurred to Gerty's words and held fast to them. She was sure that Gerty knew Selden's feeling for her, and it had never dawned upon her blindness that Gerty's own judgment of him was coloured by emotions far more ardent than her own.

Four o'clock found her in the drawing-room: she was sure that Selden would be punctual. But the hour came and passed—it moved on feverishly, measured by her impatient heart-beats. She had time to take a fresh survey of her wretchedness, and to fluctuate anew between the impulse to confide in Selden and the dread of destroying his illusions. But as the minutes passed the need of throwing herself on his comprehension became more urgent: she could not bear the weight of her misery alone. There would be a perilous moment, perhaps: but could she not trust to her beauty to bridge it over, to land her safe in the shelter of his devotion?

But the hour sped on and Selden did not come. Doubtless he had been detained, or had misread her hurriedly scrawled note, taking the four for a five. The ringing of the door-bell a few minutes after five confirmed this supposition, and made Lily hastily resolve to write more legibly in future. The sound of steps in the hall, and of the butler's voice preceding them, poured fresh energy into her veins. She felt herself once more the alert and competent moulder of emergencies, and the remembrance of her power over Selden flushed her with sudden confidence. But when the drawing-room door opened it was Rosedale who came in.

The reaction caused her a sharp pang, but after a passing movement of irritation at the clumsiness of fate, and at her own carelessness in not denying the door to all but Selden, she controlled herself and greeted Rosedale amicably. It was annoying that Selden, when he came, should find that particular visitor in possession, but Lily was mistress of the art of ridding herself of superfluous company, and to her present mood Rosedale seemed distinctly negligible.

His own view of the situation forced itself upon her after a few moments' conversation. She had caught at the Brys' entertainment as an easy impersonal subject, likely to tide them over the interval till Selden appeared, but Mr. Rosedale, tenaciously planted beside the tea-table, his hands in his pockets, his legs a little too freely extended, at once gave the topic a personal turn.

"Pretty well done—well, yes, I suppose it was: Welly Bry's

got his back up and don't mean to let go till he's got the hang of the thing. Of course, there were things here and there—things Mrs. Fisher couldn't be expected to see to—the champagne wasn't cold, and the coats got mixed in the coat-room. I would have spent more money on the music. But that's my character: if I want a thing I'm willing to pay: I don't go up to the counter, and then wonder if the article's worth the price. I wouldn't be satisfied to entertain like the Welly Brys; I'd want something that would look more easy and natural, more as if I took it in my stride. And it takes just two things to do that, Miss Bart: money, and the right woman to spend it."

He paused, and examined her attentively while she affected to rearrange the tea-cups.

"I've got the money," he continued, clearing his throat, "and what I want is the woman—and I mean to have her too."

He leaned forward a little, resting his hands on the head of his walking-stick. He had seen men of Ned Van Alstyne's type bring their hats and sticks into a drawing-room, and he thought it added a touch of elegant familiarity to their appearance.

Lily was silent, smiling faintly, with her eyes absently resting on his face. She was in reality reflecting that a declaration would take some time to make, and that Selden must surely appear before the moment of refusal had been reached. Her brooding look, as of a mind withdrawn yet not averted, seemed to Mr. Rosedale full of a subtle encouragement. He would not have liked any evidence of eagerness.

"I mean to have her too," he repeated, with a laugh intended to strengthen his self-assurance. "I generally *have* got what I wanted in life, Miss Bart. I wanted money, and I've got more than I know how to invest; and now the money doesn't seem to be of any account unless I can spend it on the right woman. That's what I want to do with it: I want my wife to make all the other women feel small. I'd never grudge a dollar that was spent on that. But it isn't every woman can do it, no matter how much you spend on her. There was a girl in some history book who wanted gold shields, or something, and the fellows threw 'em at her, and she was crushed under 'em: they killed her.[3] Well, that's true enough: some women looked buried under their jewelry. What I want is a woman who'll hold her head higher the more diamonds I put on it. And when I looked at you the other night at the Brys', in that plain white dress, looking as if you had a crown on, I said to myself: 'By gad, if she had one she'd wear it as if it grew on her.'"

Still Lily did not speak, and he continued, warming with his theme: "Tell you what it is, though, that kind of woman costs more than all the rest of 'em put together. If a woman's going to ignore her pearls, they want to be better than anybody else's— and so it is with everything else. You know what I mean—you know it's only the showy things that are cheap. Well, I should want my wife to be able to take the earth for granted if she wanted to. I know there's one thing vulgar about money, and that's the thinking about it; and my wife would never have to demean herself in that way." He paused, and then added, with an unfortunate lapse to an earlier manner: "I guess you know the lady I've got in view, Miss Bart."

Lily raised her head, brightening a little under the challenge. Even through the dark tumult of her thoughts, the clink of Mr. Rosedale's millions had a faintly seductive note. Oh, for enough of them to cancel her one miserable debt. But the man behind them grew increasingly repugnant in the light of Selden's expected coming. The contrast was too grotesque: she could scarcely suppress the smile it provoked. She decided that directness would be best.

"If you mean me, Mr. Rosedale, I am very grateful—very much flattered; but I don't know what I have ever done to make you think——"

"Oh, if you mean you're not dead in love with me, I've got sense enough left to see that. And I ain't talking to you as if you were—I presume I know the kind of talk that's expected under those circumstances. I'm confoundedly gone on you—that's about the size of it—and I'm just giving you a plain business statement of the consequences. You're not very fond of me— *yet*—but you're fond of luxury, and style, and amusement, and of not having to worry about cash. You like to have a good time, and not to have to settle for it; and what I propose to do is to provide for the good time and do the settling."

He paused, and she returned with a chilling smile: "You are

mistaken in one point, Mr. Rosedale: whatever I enjoy I am prepared to settle for."

She spoke with the intention of making him see that, if his
words implied a tentative allusion to her private affairs, she was
prepared to meet and repudiate it. But if he recognized her
meaning it failed to abash him, and he went on in the same tone:
"I didn't mean to give offence; excuse me if I've spoken too
plainly. But why ain't you straight with me—why do you put up
that kind of bluff? You know there've been times when you were
bothered—damned bothered—and as a girl gets older, and
things keep moving along, why, before she knows it, the things
she wants are liable to move past her and not come back. I don't
say it's anywhere near that with you yet.; but you've had a taste
of bothers that a girl like yourself ought never to have known
about, and what I'm offering you is the chance to turn your back
on them once for all."

The colour burned in Lily's face as he ended; there was no
mistaking the point he meant to make, and to permit it to pass
unheeded was a fatal confession of weakness, while to resent it
too openly was to risk offending him at a perilous moment. Indignation quivered on her lip; but it was quelled by the secret
voice which warned her that she must not quarrel with him. He
knew too much about her, and even at the moment when it was
essential that he should show himself at his best, he did not
scruple to let her see how much he knew. How then would he
use his power when her expression of contempt had dispelled his
one motive for restraint? Her whole future might hinge on her
way of answering him: she had to stop and consider that, in the
stress of her other anxieties, as a breathless fugitive may have to
pause at the cross-roads and try to decide coolly which turn to
take.

"You are quite right, Mr. Rosedale. I *have* had bothers; and
I am grateful to you for wanting to relieve me of them. It is
not always easy to be quite independent and self-respecting
when one is poor and lives among rich people; I have been
careless about money, and have worried about my bills. But I
should be selfish and ungrateful if I made that a reason for accepting all you offer, with no better return to make than the
desire to be free from my anxieties. You must give me time—

time to think of your kindness—and of what I could give you in
return for it——"

She held out her hand with a charming gesture in which dismissal was shorn of its rigour. Its hint of future leniency made
Rosedale rise in obedience to it, a little flushed with his
unhoped-for success, and disciplined by the tradition of his blood
to accept what was conceded, without undue haste to press for
more. Something in his prompt acquiescence frightened her; she
felt behind it the stored force of a patience that might subdue the
strongest will. But at least they had parted amicably, and he was
out of the house without meeting Selden—Selden, whose continued absence now smote her with a new alarm. Rosedale had
remained over an hour, and she understood that it was now too
late to hope for Selden. He would write explaining his absence,
of course; there would be a note from him by the late post. But
her confession would have to be postponed; and the chill of the
delay settled heavily on her fagged spirit.

It lay heavier when the postman's last ring brought no note
for her, and she had to go upstairs to a lonely night—a night as
grim and sleepless as her tortured fancy had pictured it to Gerty.
She had never learned to live with her own thoughts, and to be
confronted with them through such hours of lucid misery made
the confused wretchedness of her previous vigil seem easily bear-
able.

Daylight disbanded the phantom crew, and made it clear to
her that she would hear from Selden before noon; but the day
passed without his writing or coming. Lily remained at home,
lunching and dining alone with her aunt, who complained of
flutterings of the heart, and talked icily on general topics. Mrs.
Peniston went to bed early, and when she had gone Lily sat
down and wrote a note to Selden. She was about to ring for a
messenger to despatch it when her eye fell on a paragraph in the
evening paper which lay at her elbow: "Mr. Lawrence Selden
was among the passengers sailing this afternoon for Havana*
and the West Indies on the Windward Liner Antilles."

---

*In the wake of the Spanish-American War in 1898, Cuba was an
American protectorate until 1902.

She laid down the paper and sat motionless, staring at her note. She understood now that he was never coming—that he had gone away because he was afraid that he might come. She rose, and walking across the floor stood gazing at herself for a long time in the brightly-lit mirror above the mantelpiece. The lines in her face came out terribly—she looked old; and when a girl looks old to herself, how does she look to other people? She moved away, and began to wander aimlessly about the room, fitting her steps with mechanical precision between the monstrous roses of Mrs. Peniston's Axminister.* Suddenly she noticed that the pen with which she had written to Selden still rested against the uncovered inkstand. She seated herself again, and taking out an envelope, addressed it rapidly to Rosedale. Then she laid out a sheet of paper, and sat over it with suspended pen. It had been easy enough to write the date, and "Dear Mr. Rosedale"—but after that her inspiration flagged. She meant to tell him to come to her, but the words refused to shape themselves. At length she began: "I have been thinking——" then she laid the pen down, and sat with her elbows on the table and her face hidden in her hands.

Suddenly she started up at the sound of the door-bell. It was not late—barely ten o'clock—and there might still be a note from Selden, or a message—or he might be there himself, on the other side of the door! The announcement of his sailing might have been a mistake—it might be another Lawrence Selden who had gone to Havana—all these possibilities had time to flash through her mind, and build up the conviction that she was after all to see or hear from him, before the drawing-room door opened to admit a servant carrying a telegram.

Lily tore it open with shaking hands, and read Bertha Dorset's name below the message: "Sailing unexpectedly to-morrow. Will you join us on a cruise in Mediterranean?"

---

*High-quality carpet from a town in southwestern England.

BOOK TWO

I

IT CAME VIVIDLY TO Selden on the Casino steps that Monte Carlo* had, more than any other place he knew, the gift of accommodating itself to each man's humour.

His own, at the moment, lent it a festive readiness of welcome that might well, in a disenchanted eye, have turned to paint and facility. So frank an appeal for participation—so outspoken a recognition of the holiday vein in human nature—struck refreshingly on a mind jaded by prolonged hard work in surroundings made for the discipline of the senses. As he surveyed the white square set in an exotic coquetry of architecture, the studied tropicality of the gardens, the groups loitering in the foreground against mauve mountains which suggested a sublime stage-setting forgotten in a hurried shifting of scenes—as he took in the whole outspread effect of light and leisure, he felt a movement of revulsion from the last few months of his life.

The New York winter had presented an interminable perspective of snow-burdened days, reaching toward a spring of raw sunshine and furious air, when the ugliness of things rasped the eye as the gritty wind ground into the skin. Selden, immersed in his work, had told himself that external conditions did not matter to a man in his state, and that cold and ugliness were a good tonic for relaxed sensibilities. When an urgent case summoned him abroad to confer with a client in Paris, he broke reluctantly with the routine of the office; and it was only now that, having despatched his business, and slipped away for a week in the south, he began to feel the renewed zest of spectatorship that is the solace of those who take an objective interest in life.

---

*The capital of Monaco, on the French Riviera, has long been famous for its casinos.

The multiplicity of its appeals—the perpetual surprise of its contrasts and resemblances! All these tricks and turns of the show were upon him with a spring as he descended the Casino steps and paused on the pavement at its doors. He had not been abroad for seven years—and what changes the renewed contact produced! If the central depths were untouched, hardly a pin-point of surface remained the same. And this was the very place to bring out the completeness of the renewal. The sublimities, the perpetuities, might have left him as he was: but this tent pitched for a day's revelry spread a roof of oblivion between himself and his fixed sky.

It was mid-April, and one felt that the revelry had reached its climax and that the desultory groups in the square and gardens would soon dissolve and re-form in other scenes. Meanwhile the last moments of the performance seemed to gain an added brightness from the hovering threat of the curtain. The quality of the air, the exuberance of the flowers, the blue intensity of sea and sky, produced the effect of a closing *tableau*, when all the lights are turned on at once. This impression was presently heightened by the way in which a consciously conspicuous group of people advanced to the middle front, and stood before Selden with the air of the chief performers gathered together by the exigencies of the final effect. Their appearance confirmed the impression that the show had been staged regardless of expense, and emphasized its resemblance to one of those "costume-plays" in which the protagonists walk through the passions without displacing a drapery. The ladies stood in unrelated attitudes calculated to isolate their effects, and the men hung about them as irrelevantly as stage heroes whose tailors are named in the programme. It was Selden himself who unwittingly fused the group by arresting the attention of one of its members.

"Why, Mr. Selden!" Mrs. Fisher exclaimed in surprise; and with a gesture toward Mrs. Jack Stepney and Mrs. Wellington Bry, she added plaintively: "We're starving to death because we can't decide where to lunch."

Welcomed into their group, and made the confidant of their difficulty, Selden learned with amusement that there were several places where one might miss something by not lunching, or forfeit something by lunching; so that eating actually became a minor consideration on the very spot consecrated to its rites.

"Of course one gets the best things at the *Terrasse**— but that looks as if one hadn't any other reason for being there: the Americans who don't know any one always rush for the best food. And the Duchess of Beltshire has taken up Bécassin's lately," Mrs. Bry earnestly summed up.

Mrs. Bry, to Mrs. Fisher's despair, had not progressed beyond the point of weighing her social alternatives in public. She could not acquire the air of doing things because she wanted to, and making her choice the final seal of their fitness.

Mr. Bry, a short pale man, with a business face and leisure clothes, met the dilemma hilariously.

"I guess the Duchess goes where it's cheapest, unless she can get her meal paid for. If you offered to blow her off at the *Terrasse* she'd turn up fast enough."

But Mrs. Jack Stepney interposed. "The Grand Dukes go to that little place at the Condamine.† Lord Hubert says it's the only restaurant in Europe where they can cook peas."

Lord Hubert Dacey, a slender shabby-looking man, with a charming worn smile, and the air of having spent his best years in piloting the wealthy to the right restaurant, assented with gentle emphasis: "It's quite that."

"Peas?" said Mr. Bry contemptuously. "Can they cook terrapin? It just shows," he continued, "what these European markets are, when a fellow can make a reputation cooking peas!"

Jack Stepney intervened with authority. "I don't know that I quite agree with Dacey: there's a little hole in Paris, off the Quai Voltaire—but in any case, I can't advise the Condamine *gargote;*‡ at least not with ladies."

Stepney, since his marriage, had thickened and grown prudish, as the Van Osburgh husbands were apt to do; but his wife, to his surprise and discomfiture, had developed an earth-shaking fastness of gait which left him trailing breathlessly in her wake.

---

*An expensive restaurant in the Casino at Monte Carlo.
†The port and commercial quarter in Monte Carlo.
‡Cheap restaurant (French).

"That's where we'll go then!" she declared, with a heavy toss of her plumage. "I'm so tired of the *Terrasse:* it's as dull as one of mother's dinners. And Lord Hubert has promised to tell us who all the awful people are at the other place—hasn't he, Carry? Now, Jack, don't look so solemn!"

"Well," said Mrs. Bry, "all I want to know is who their dress-makers are."

"No doubt Dacey can tell you that too," remarked Stepney, with an ironic intention which the other received with the light murmur, "I can at least *find out*, my dear fellow"; and Mrs. Bry having declared that she couldn't walk another step, the party hailed two or three of the light phaetons* which hover atten-tively on the confines of the gardens, and rattled off in proces-sion toward the Condamine.

Their destination was one of the little restaurants over-hanging the boulevard which dips steeply down from Monte Carlo to the low intermediate quarter along the quay. From the window in which they presently found themselves installed, they overlooked the intense blue curve of the harbour, set between the verdure of twin promontories: to the right, the cliff of Monaco, topped by the mediæval silhouette of its church and castle, to the left the terraces and pinnacles of the gambling-house. Between the two, the waters of the bay were furrowed by a light coming and going of pleasure-craft, through which, just at the culminating moment of luncheon, the majestic advance of a great steam-yacht drew the company's attention from the peas.

"By Jove, I believe that's the Dorsets back!" Stepney ex-claimed; and Lord Hubert, dropping his single eye-glass, cor-roborated: "It's the *Sabrina*[4]—yes."

"So soon? They were to spend a month in Sicily," Mrs. Fisher observed.

"I guess they feel as if they had: there's only one up-to-date hotel in the whole place," said Mr. Bry disparagingly.

"It was Ned Silverton's idea—but poor Dorset and Lily Bart must have been horribly bored." Mrs. Fisher added in an under-tone to Selden: "I do hope there hasn't been a row."

---

*Light, four-wheeled, two-seated open carriages.

"It's most awfully jolly having Miss Bart back," said Lord Hubert, in his mild deliberate voice; and Mrs. Bry added ingenuously: "I daresay the Duchess will dine with us, now that Lily's here."

"The Duchess admires her immensely: I'm sure she'd be charmed to have it arranged," Lord Hubert agreed, with the professional promptness of the man accustomed to draw his profit from facilitating social contacts: Selden was struck by the businesslike change in his manner.

"Lily has been a tremendous success here," Mrs. Fisher continued, still addressing herself confidentially to Selden. "She looks ten years younger—I never saw her so handsome. Lady Skiddaw took her everywhere in Cannes, and the Crown Princess of Macedonia had her to stop for a week at Cimiez.* People say that was one reason why Bertha whisked the yacht off to Sicily: the Crown Princess didn't take much notice of her, and she couldn't bear to look on at Lily's triumph."

Selden made no reply. He was vaguely aware that Miss Bart was cruising in the Mediterranean with the Dorsets, but it had not occurred to him that there was any chance of running across her on the Riviera, where the season was virtually at an end. As he leaned back, silently contemplating his filigree cup of Turkish coffee, he was trying to put some order in his thoughts, to tell himself how the news of her nearness was really affecting him. He had a personal detachment enabling him, even in moments of emotional high-pressure, to get a fairly clear view of his feelings, and he was sincerely surprised by the disturbance which the sight of the *Sabrina* had produced in him. He had reason to think that his three months of engrossing professional work, following on the sharp shock of his disillusionment, had cleared his mind of its sentimental vapours. The feeling he had nourished and given prominence to was one of thankfulness for his escape: he was like a traveller so grateful for rescue from a dangerous accident that at first he is hardly conscious of his bruises. Now he suddenly felt the latent ache, and realized that after all he had not come off unhurt.

---

*Fashionable hotel section of Nice.

An hour later, at Mrs. Fisher's side in the Casino gardens, he was trying to find fresh reasons for forgetting the injury received in the contemplation of the peril avoided. The party had dispersed with the loitering indecision characteristic of social movements at Monte Carlo, where the whole place, and the long gilded hours of the day, seem to offer an infinity of ways of being idle. Lord Hubert Dacey had finally gone off in quest of the Duchess of Beltshire, charged by Mrs. Bry with the delicate negotiation of securing that lady's presence at dinner, the Stepneys had left for Nice in their motor-car, and Mr. Bry had departed to take his place in the pigeon-shooting match which was at the moment engaging his highest faculties.

Mrs. Bry, who had a tendency to grow red and stertorous after luncheon, had been judiciously prevailed upon by Carry Fisher to withdraw to her hotel for an hour's repose; and Selden and his companion were thus left to a stroll propitious to confidences. The stroll soon resolved itself into a tranquil session on a bench overhung with laurel and Banksian roses,* from which they caught a dazzle of blue sea between marble balusters, and the fiery shafts of cactus-blossoms shooting meteor-like from the rock. The soft shade of their niche, and the adjacent glitter of the air, were conducive to an easy lounging mood, and to the smoking of many cigarettes; and Selden, yielding to these influences, suffered Mrs. Fisher to unfold to him the history of her recent experiences. She had come abroad with the Welly Brys at the moment when fashion flees the inclemency of the New York spring. The Brys, intoxicated by their first success, already thirsted for new kingdoms, and Mrs. Fisher, viewing the Riviera as an easy introduction to London society, had guided their course thither. She had affiliations of her own in every capital, and a facility for picking them up again after long absences; and the carefully disseminated rumour of the Brys' wealth had at once gathered about them a group of cosmopolitan pleasure-seekers.

"But things are not going as well as I expected," Mrs. Fisher

---

*First cultivated by the English botanist Sir Joseph Banks (1744–1820).

frankly admitted. "It's all very well to say that everybody with money can get into society; but it would be truer to say that *nearly* everybody can. And the London market is so glutted with new Americans that, to succeed there now, they must be either very clever or awfully queer. The Brys are neither. *He* would get on well enough if she'd let him alone; they like his slang and his brag and his blunders. But Louisa spoils it all by trying to repress him and put herself forward. If she'd be natural herself—fat and vulgar and bouncing—it would be all right; but as soon as she meets anybody smart she tries to be slender and queenly. She tried it with the Duchess of Beltshire and Lady Skiddaw, and they fled. I've done my best to make her see her mistake—I've said to her again and again: 'Just let yourself go, Louisa'; but she keeps up the humbug even with me—I believe she keeps on being queenly in her own room, with the door shut.

"The worst of it is," Mrs. Fisher went on, "that she thinks it's all *my* fault. When the Dorsets turned up here six weeks ago, and everybody began to make a fuss about Lily Bart, I could see Louisa thought that if she'd had Lily in tow instead of me she would have been hobnobbing with all the royalties by this time. She doesn't realize that it's Lily's beauty that does it: Lord Hubert tells me Lily is thought even handsomer than when he knew her at Aix ten years ago. It seems she was tremendously admired there. An Italian Prince, rich and the real thing, wanted to marry her; but just at the critical moment a good-looking step-son turned up, and Lily was silly enough to flirt with him while her marriage-settlements with the step-father were being drawn up. Some people said the young man did it on purpose. You can fancy the scandal: there was an awful row between the men, and people began to look at Lily so queerly that Mrs. Peniston had to pack up and finish her cure elsewhere. Not that *she* ever understood: to this day she thinks that Aix didn't suit her, and mentions her having been sent there as proof of the incompetence of French doctors. That's Lily all over, you know: she works like a slave preparing the ground and sowing her seed; but the day she ought to be reaping the harvest she oversleeps herself or goes off on a picnic."

Mrs. Fisher paused and looked reflectively at the deep shimmer of sea between the cactus-flowers. "Sometimes," she added,

"I think it's just flightiness—and sometimes I think it's because, at heart, she despises the things she's trying for. And it's the difficulty of deciding that makes her such an interesting study." She glanced tentatively at Selden's motionless profile, and resumed with a slight sigh: "Well, all I can say is, I wish she'd give *me* some of her discarded opportunities. I wish we could change places now, for instance. She could make a very good thing out of the Brys if she managed them properly, and I should know just how to look after George Dorset while Bertha is reading Verlaine* with Neddy Silverton."

She met Selden's sound of protest with a sharp derisive glance. "Well, what's the use of mincing matters? We all know that's what Bertha brought her abroad for. When Bertha wants to have a good time she has to provide occupation for George. At first I thought Lily was going to play her cards well *this* time, but there are rumours that Bertha is jealous of her success here and at Cannes, and I shouldn't be surprised if there were a break any day. Lily's only safeguard is that Bertha needs her badly— oh, very badly. The Silverton affair is in the acute stage: it's necessary that George's attention should be pretty continuously distracted. And I'm bound to say Lily *does* distract it: I believe he'd marry her tomorrow if he found out there was anything wrong with Bertha. But you know him—he's as blind as he's jealous; and of course Lily's present business is to keep him blind. A clever woman might know just the right moment to tear off the bandage: but Lily isn't clever in that way, and when George does open his eyes she'll probably contrive not to be in his line of vision."

Selden tossed away his cigarette. "By Jove—it's time for my train," he exclaimed, with a glance at his watch; adding, in reply to Mrs. Fisher's surprised comment—"Why, I thought of course you were at Monte!"—a murmured word to the effect that he was making Nice his head-quarters.

"The worst of it is, she snubs the Brys now," he heard irrelevantly flung after him.

---

*The French Symbolist poet Paul Verlaine (1844–1896) wrote some of the finest and most musical lyrics in the language.

Ten minutes later, in the high-perched bedroom of an hotel overlooking the Casino, he was tossing his effects into a couple of gaping portmanteaux,* while the porter waited outside to transport them to the cab at the door. It took but a brief plunge down the steep white road to the station to land him safely in the afternoon express for Nice; and not till he was installed in the corner of an empty carriage, did he exclaim to himself, with a reaction of self-contempt: "What the deuce am I running away from?"

The pertinence of the question checked Selden's fugitive impulse before the train had started. It was ridiculous to be flying like an emotional coward from an infatuation his reason had conquered. He had instructed his bankers to forward some important business letters to Nice, and at Nice he would quietly await them. He was already annoyed with himself for having left Monte Carlo, where he had intended to pass the week which remained to him before sailing; but it would now be difficult to return on his steps without an appearance of inconsistency from which his pride recoiled. In his inmost heart he was not sorry to put himself beyond the probability of meeting Miss Bart. Completely as he had detached himself from her, he could not yet regard her merely as a social instance; and viewed in a more personal way she was not likely to be a reassuring object of study. Chance encounters, or even the repeated mention of her name, would send his thoughts back into grooves from which he had resolutely detached them; whereas, if she could be entirely excluded from his life, the pressure of new and varied impressions, with which no thought of her was connected, would soon complete the work of separation. Mrs. Fisher's conversation had, indeed, operated to that end; but the treatment was too painful to be voluntarily chosen while milder remedies were untried; and Selden thought he could trust himself to return gradually to a reasonable view of Miss Bart, if only he did not see her.

Having reached the station early, he had arrived at this point in his reflections before the increasing throng on the platform warned him that he could not hope to preserve his privacy; the

---

*Large traveling bags.

next moment there was a hand on the door; and he turned to confront the very face he was fleeing.

Miss Bart, glowing with the haste of a precipitate descent upon the train, headed a group composed of the Dorsets, young Silverton and Lord Hubert Dacey, who had barely time to spring into the carriage, and envelop Selden in ejaculations of surprise and welcome, before the whistle of departure sounded. The party, it appeared, were hastening to Nice in response to a sudden summons to dine with the Duchess of Beltshire and to see the water-fête* in the bay; a plan evidently improvised—in spite of Lord Hubert's protesting "Oh, I say, you know,"—for the express purpose of defeating Mrs. Bry's endeavour to capture the Duchess.

During the laughing relation of this manœuvre, Selden had time for a rapid impression of Miss Bart, who had seated herself opposite to him in the golden afternoon light. Scarcely three months had elapsed since he had parted from her on the threshold of the Brys' conservatory; but a subtle change had passed over the quality of her beauty. Then it had had a transparency through which the fluctuations of the spirit were sometimes tragically visible; now its impenetrable surface suggested a process of crystallization which had fused her whole being into one hard brilliant substance. The change had struck Mrs. Fisher as a rejuvenation: to Selden it seemed like that moment of pause and arrest when the warm fluidity of youth is chilled into its final shape.

He felt it in the way she smiled on him, and in the readiness and competenee with which, flung unexpectedly into his presence, she took up the thread of their intercourse as though that thread had not been snapped with a violence from which he still reeled. Such facility sickened him—but he told himself that it was with the the pang which precedes recovery. Now he would really get well—would eject the last drop of poison from his blood. Already he felt himself calmer in her presence than he had learned to be in the thought of her. Her assumptions and elisions, her short-cuts and long *détours*, the skill with which she

---

*Festival on the water with rockets and illuminated boats.

contrived to meet him at a point from which no inconvenient
glimpses of the past were visible, suggested what opportunities
she had had for practising such arts since their last meeting. He
felt that she had at last arrived at an understanding with herself:
had made a pact with her rebellious impulses, and achieved a
uniform system of self-government, under which all vagrant
tendencies were either held captive or forced into the service of
the state.

And he saw other things too in her manner: saw how it had
adjusted itself to the hidden intricacies of a situation in which,
even after Mrs. Fisher's elucidating flashes, he still felt himself
agrope. Surely Mrs. Fisher could no longer charge Miss Bart
with neglecting her opportunities! To Selden's exasperated observation she was only too completely alive to them. She was
"perfect" to every one: subservient to Bertha's anxious predominance, good-naturedly watchful of Dorset's moods, brightly
companionable to Silverton and Dacey, the latter of whom met
her on an evident footing of old admiration, while young Silverton, portentously self-absorbed, seemed conscious of her only as
of something vaguely obstructive. And suddenly, as Selden
noted the fine shades of manner by which she harmonized herself with her surroundings, it flashed on him that, to need such
adroit handling, the situation must indeed be desperate. She was
on the edge of something—that was the impression left with
him. He seemed to see her poised on the brink of a chasm, with
one graceful foot advanced to assert her unconsciousness that
the ground was failing her.

On the Promenade des Anglais,* where Ned Silverton hung
on him for the half hour before dinner, he received a deeper impression of the general insecurity. Silverton was in a mood of Ti-
tanic pessimism. How any one could come to such a damned
hole as the Riviera—any one with a grain of imagination—with
the whole Mediterranean to choose from: but then, if one's estimate of a place depended on the way they broiled a spring

---

*Seafront promenade in Nice named for English visitors (des
Anglais), with fine views of the Mediterranean on one side and of
luxurious hotels on the other.

chicken! Gad! what a study might be made of the tyranny of the stomach—the way a sluggish liver or insufficient gastric juices might affect the whole course of the universe, overshadow everything in reach—chronic dyspepsia ought to be among the "statutory causes";* a woman's life might be ruined by a man's inability to digest fresh bread. Grotesque? Yes—and tragic—like most absurdities. There's nothing grimmer than the tragedy that wears a comic mask. . . . Where was he? Oh—the reason they chucked Sicily and rushed back? Well—partly, no doubt, Miss Bart's desire to get back to bridge and smartness. Dead as a stone to art and poetry—the light never *was* on sea or land for her! And of course she persuaded Dorset that the Italian food was bad for him. Oh, she could make him believe anything— *anything!* Mrs. Dorset was aware of it—oh, perfectly: nothing *she* didn't see! But she could hold her tongue—she'd had to, often enough. Miss Bart was an intimate friend—she wouldn't hear a word against her. Only it hurts a woman's pride—there are some things one doesn't get used to . . . All this in confidence, of course? Ah—and there were the ladies signalling from the balcony of the hotel. . . . He plunged across the Promenade, leaving Selden to a meditative cigar.

The conclusions it led him to were fortified, later in the evening, by some of those faint corroborative hints that generate a light of their own in the dusk of a doubting mind. Selden, stumbling on a chance acquaintance, had dined with him, and adjourned, still in his company, to the brightly lit Promenade, where a line of crowded stands commanded the glittering darkness of the waters. The night was soft and persuasive. Overhead hung a summer sky furrowed with the rush of rockets; and from the east a late moon, pushing up beyond the lofty bend of the coast, sent across the bay a shaft of brightness which paled to ashes in the red glitter of the illuminated boats. Down the lantern-hung Promenade, snatches of band-music floated above the hum of the crowd and the soft tossing of boughs in dusky gardens; and between these gardens and the backs of the stands

---

*Dorset jokes that his stomach troubles should be the basis of a lawsuit.

there flowed a stream of people in whom the vociferous carnival mood seemed tempered by the growing languor of the season.

Selden and his companion, unable to get seats on one of the stands facing the bay, had wandered for a while with the throng, and then found a point of vantage on a high garden-parapet above the Promenade. Thence they caught but a triangular glimpse of the water, and of the flashing play of boats across its surface; but the crowd in the street was under their immediate view, and seemed to Selden, on the whole, of more interest than the show itself. After a while, however, he wearied of his perch and, dropping alone to the pavement, pushed his way to the first corner and turned into the moonlit silence of a side street. Long garden-walls overhung by trees made a dark boundary to the pavement; an empty cab trailed along the deserted thoroughfare, and presently Selden saw two persons emerge from the opposite shadows, signal to the cab, and drive off in it toward the centre of the town. The moonlight touched them as they paused to enter the carriage, and he recognized Mrs. Dorset and young Silverton.

Beneath the nearest lamp-post he glanced at his watch and saw that the time was close on eleven. He took another cross street, and without breasting the throng on the Promenade, made his way to the fashionable club which overlooks that thoroughfare. Here, amid the blaze of crowded baccarat* tables, he caught sight of Lord Hubert Dacey, seated with his habitual worn smile behind a rapidly dwindling heap of gold. The heap being in due course wiped out, Lord Hubert rose with a shrug, and joining Selden, adjourned with him to the deserted terrace of the club. It was now past midnight, and the throng on the stands was dispersing, while the long trails of red-lit boats scattered and faded beneath a sky repossessed by the tranquil splendour of the moon.

Lord Hubert looked at his watch. "By Jove, I promised to join the Duchess for supper at the *London House;* but it's past twelve, and I suppose they've all scattered. The fact is, I lost

---

*French card game with a banker and two or more players who bet against him.

them in the crowd soon after dinner, and took refuge here, for my sins. They had seats on one of the stands, but of course they couldn't stop quiet: the Duchess never can. She and Miss Bart went off in quest of what they call adventures—gad, it ain't their fault if they don't have some queer ones!" He added tentatively, after pausing to grope for a cigarette: "Miss Bart's an old friend of yours, I believe? So she told me.—Ah, thanks—I don't seem to have one left." He lit Selden's proffered cigarette, and continued, in his high-pitched drawling tone: "None of my business, of course, but I didn't introduce her to the Duchess. Charming woman, the Duchess, you understand; and a very good friend of mine; but *rather* a liberal education."

Selden received this in silence, and after a few puffs Lord Hubert broke out again: "Sort of thing one can't communicate to the young lady—though young ladies nowadays are so competent to judge for themselves; but in this case—I'm an old friend too, you know . . . and there seemed no one else to speak to. The whole situation's a little mixed, as I see it—but there used to be an aunt somewhere, a diffuse and innocent person, who was great at bridging over chasms she didn't see . . . Ah, in New York, is she? Pity New York's such a long way off!"

2

MISS BART, EMERGING LATE the next morning from her cabin, found herself alone on the deck of the *Sabrina*.

The cushioned chairs, disposed expectantly under the wide awning, showed no signs of recent occupancy, and she presently learned from a steward that Mrs. Dorset had not yet appeared, and that the gentlemen—separately—had gone ashore as soon as they had breakfasted. Supplied with these facts, Lily leaned awhile over the side, giving herself up to a leisurely enjoyment of the spectacle before her. Unclouded sunlight enveloped sea and shore in a bath of purest radiancy. The purpling waters drew a sharp white line of foam at the base of the shore; against its irregular eminences, hotels and villas flashed from the greyish verdure of olive and eucalyptus; and the background of bare and finely-pencilled mountains quivered in a pale intensity of light.

How beautiful it was—and how she loved beauty! She had always felt that her sensibility in this direction made up for certain obtusenesses of feeling of which she was less proud; and during the last three months she had indulged it passionately. The Dorsets' invitation to go abroad with them had come as an almost miraculous release from crushing difficulties; and her faculty for renewing herself in new scenes, and casting off problems of conduct as easily as the surroundings in which they had arisen, made the mere change from one place to another seem, not merely a postponement, but a solution of her troubles. Moral complications existed for her only in the environment that had produced them; she did not mean to slight or ignore them, but they lost their reality when they changed their background. She could not have remained in New York without repaying the money she owed to Trenor; to acquit herself of that odious debt she might even have faced a marriage with Rosedale; but the accident of placing the Atlantic between herself and her obligations made them dwindle out of sight as if they had been milestones and she had travelled past them.

Her two months on the *Sabrina* had been especially calculated to aid this illusion of distance. She had been plunged into new scenes, and had found in them a renewal of old hopes and ambitions. The cruise itself charmed her as a romantic adventure. She was vaguely touched by the names and scenes amid which she moved, and had listened to Ned Silverton reading Theocritus* by moonlight, as the yacht rounded the Sicilian promontories, with a thrill of the nerves that confirmed her belief in her intellectual superiority. But the weeks at Cannes and Nice had really given her more pleasure. The gratification of being welcomed in high company, and of making her own ascendency felt there, so that she found herself figuring once more as the "beautiful Miss Bart" in the interesting journal devoted to recording the least movements of her cosmopolitan companions—all these experiences tended to throw into the extreme background of memory the prosaic and sordid difficulties from which she had escaped.

If she was faintly aware of fresh difficulties ahead, she was sure of her ability to meet them: it was characteristic of her to feel that the only problems she could not solve were those with which she was familiar. Meanwhile she could honestly be proud of the skill with which she had adapted herself to somewhat delicate conditions. She had reason to think that she had made herself equally necessary to her host and hostess; and if only she had seen any perfectly irreproachable means of drawing a financial profit from the situation, there would have been no cloud on her horizon. The truth was that her funds, as usual, were inconveniently low; and to neither Dorset nor his wife could this vulgar embarrassment be safely hinted. Still, the need was not a pressing one; she could worry along, as she had so often done before, with the hope of some happy change of fortune to sustain her; and meanwhile life was gay and beautiful and easy, and she was conscious of figuring not unworthily in such a setting.

She was engaged to breakfast that morning with the Duchess

---

*Greek pastoral poet (active c.310–250 B.C.), author of the *Idylls*.

of Beltshire, and at twelve o'clock she asked to be set ashore in
the gig. Before this she had sent her maid to enquire if she might
see Mrs. Dorset; but the reply came back that the latter was
tired, and trying to sleep. Lily thought she understood the reason of the rebuff. Her hostess had not been included in the
Duchess's invitation, though she herself had made the most loyal
efforts in that direction. But her grace* was impervious to hints,
and invited or omitted as she chose. It was not Lily's fault if Mrs.
Dorset's complicated attitudes did not fall in with the Duchess's
easy gait. The Duchess, who seldom explained herself, had not
formulated her objection beyond saying: "She's rather a bore, you
know. The only one of your friends I like is that little Mr. Bry—
he's funny—" but Lily knew enough not to press the point, and
was not altogether sorry to be thus distinguished at her friend's
expense. Bertha certainly *had* grown tiresome since she had
taken to poetry and Ned Silverton.

On the whole, it was a relief to break away now and then
from the Sabrina; and the Duchess's little breakfast, organized
by Lord Hubert with all his usual virtuosity, was the pleasanter
to Lily for not including her travelling-companions. Dorset, of
late, had grown more than usually morose and incalculable, and
Ned Silverton went about with an air that seemed to challenge
the universe. The freedom and lightness of the ducal intercourse
made an agreeable change from these complications, and Lily
was tempted, after luncheon, to adjourn in the wake of her companions to the hectic atmosphere of the Casino. She did not
mean to play; her diminished pocket-money offered small scope
for the adventure; but it amused her to sit on a divan, under the
doubtful protection of the Duchess's back, while the latter hung
above her stakes at a neighbouring table.

The rooms were packed with the gazing throng which, in the
afternoon hours, trickles heavily between the tables, like the
Sunday crowd in a lion-house. In the stagnant flow of the mass,
identities were hardly distinguishable; but Lily presently saw
Mrs. Bry cleaving her determined way through the doors, and,
in the broad wake she left, the light figure of Mrs. Fisher bob-

---

*That is, Her grace; the proper form of address for a duchess.

bing after her like a row-boat at the stern of a tug. Mrs. Bry pressed on, evidently animated by the resolve to reach a certain point in the rooms; but Mrs. Fisher, as she passed Lily, broke from her towing-line, and let herself float to the girl's side.

"Lose her?" she echoed the latter's query, with an indifferent glance at Mrs. Bry's retreating back. "I daresay—it doesn't matter: I *have* lost her already." And, as Lily exclaimed, she added: "We had an awful row this morning. You know, of course, that the Duchess chucked her at dinner last night, and she thinks it was my fault—my want of management. The worst of it is, the message—just a mere word by telephone—came so late that the dinner had to be paid for; and Bécassin *had* run it up—it had been so drummed into him that the Duchess was coming!" Mrs. Fisher indulged in a faint laugh at the remembrance. "Paying for what she doesn't get rankles so dreadfully with Louisa: I can't make her see that it's one of the preliminary steps to getting what you haven't paid for—and as I was the nearest thing to smash, she smashed me to atoms, poor dear!"

Lily murmured her commiseration. Impulses of sympathy came naturally to her, and it was instinctive to proffer her help to Mrs. Fisher.

"If there's anything I can do—if it's only a question of meeting the Duchess! I heard her say she thought Mr. Bry amusing——"

But Mrs. Fisher interposed with a decisive gesture. "My dear, I have my pride: the pride of my trade. *I* couldn't manage the Duchess, and I can't palm off your arts on Louisa Bry as mine. I've taken the final step: I go to Paris tonight with the Sam Gormers. *They're* still in the elementary stage; an Italian Prince is a great deal more than a Prince to them, and they're always on the brink of taking a courtier for one. To save them from that is my present mission." She laughed again at the picture. "But before I go I want to make my last will and testament—I want to leave you the Brys."

"Me?" Miss Bart joined in her amusement. "It's charming of you to remember me, dear; but really——"

"You're already so well provided for?" Mrs. Fisher flashed a sharp glance at her. "*Are* you, though, Lily—to the point of rejecting my offer?"

Miss Bart coloured slowly. "What I really meant was, that the Brys wouldn't in the least care to be so disposed of."

Mrs. Fisher continued to probe her embarrassment with an unflinching eye. "What you really meant was that you've snubbed the Brys horribly; and you know that they know it——"

"Carry!"

"Oh, on certain sides Louisa bristles with perceptions. If you'd even managed to have them asked once on the *Sabrina*— especially when royalties were coming! But it's not too late," she ended earnestly, "it's not too late for either of you."

Lily smiled. "Stay over, and I'll get the Duchess to dine with them."

"I shan't stay over—the Gormers have paid for my *salon-lit*,"* said Mrs. Fisher with simplicity. "But get the Duchess to dine with them all the same."

Lily's smile again flowed into a slight laugh: her friend's importunity was beginning to strike her as irrelevant. "I'm sorry I have been negligent about the Brys——" she began.

"Oh, as to the Brys—it's you I'm thinking of," said Mrs. Fisher abruptly. She paused, and then, bending forward, with a lowered voice: "You know we all went on to Nice last night when the Duchess chucked us. It was Louisa's idea—I told her what I thought of it."

Miss Bart assented. "Yes—I caught sight of you on the way back, at the station."

"Well, the man who was in the carriage with you and George Dorset—that horrid little Dabham who does 'Society Notes from the Riviera'—had been dining with us at Nice. And he's telling everybody that you and Dorset came back alone after midnight."

"Alone—? When he was with us?" Lily laughed, but her laugh faded into gravity under the prolonged implication of Mrs. Fisher's look. "We *did* come back alone—if that's so very dreadful! But whose fault was it? The Duchess was spending the night at Cimiez with the Crown Princess; Bertha got bored with

---

*Sleeping compartment on a train (French).

the show, and went off early, promising to meet us at the station. We turned up on time, but she didn't—she didn't turn up at all!"

Miss Bart made this announcement in the tone of one who presents, with careless assurance, a complete vindication; but Mrs. Fisher received it in a manner almost inconsequent. She seemed to have lost sight of her friend's part in the incident: her inward vision had taken another slant.

"Bertha never turned up at all? Then how on earth did she get back?"

"Oh, by the next train, I suppose; there were two extra ones for the *fête*. At any rate, I know she's safe on the yacht, though I haven't yet seen her; but you see it was not my fault," Lily summed up.

"Not your fault that Bertha didn't turn up? My poor child, if only you don't have to pay for it!" Mrs. Fisher rose—she had seen Mrs. Bry surging back in her direction. "There's Louisa, and I must be off—oh, we're on the best of terms externally; we're lunching together; but at heart it's *me* she's lunching on," she explained; and with a last hand-clasp and a last look, she added: "Remember, I leave her to you; she's hovering now, ready to take you in."

Lily carried the impression of Mrs. Fisher's leave-taking away with her from the Casino doors. She had accomplished, before leaving, the first step toward her reinstatement in Mrs. Bry's good graces. An affable advance—a vague murmur that they must see more of each other—an allusive glance to a near future that was felt to include the Duchess as well as the *Sabrina*—how easily it was all done, if one possessed the knack of doing it! She wondered at herself, as she had so often wondered, that, possessing the knack, she did not more consistently exercise it. But sometimes she was forgetful—and sometimes, could it be that she was proud? Today, at any rate, she had been vaguely conscious of a reason for sinking her pride, had in fact even sunk it to the point of suggesting to Lord Hubert Dacey, whom she ran across on the Casino steps, that he might really get the Duchess to dine with the Brys, if *she* undertook to have them asked on the *Sabrina*. Lord Hubert had promised his help, with the readiness on which she could always count: it was his only way of ever reminding her that he had once been ready to do so much more for her. Her path, in short, seemed to smooth itself before her as she advanced; yet the faint stir of uneasiness persisted. Had it been produced, she wondered, by her chance meeting with Selden? She thought not—time and change seemed so completely to have relegated him to his proper distance. The sudden and exquisite reaction from her anxieties had had the effect of throwing the recent past so far back that even Selden, as part of it, retained a certain air of unreality. And he had made it so clear that they were not to meet again; that he had merely dropped down to Nice for a day or two, and had almost his foot on the next steamer. No—that part of the past had merely surged up for a moment on the fleeing surface of events; and now that it was submerged again, the uncertainty, the apprehension persisted.

They grew to sudden acuteness as she caught sight of George Dorset descending the steps of the Hôtel de Paris and making for her across the square. She had meant to drive down to the quay and regain the yacht; but she now had the immediate impression that something more was to happen first.

"Which way are you going? Shall we walk a bit?" he began, putting the second question before the first was answered, and not waiting for a reply to either before he directed her silently toward the comparative seclusion of the lower gardens.

She detected in him at once all the signs of extreme nervous tension. The skin was puffed out under his sunken eyes, and its sallowness but paled to a leaden white against which his irregular eyebrows and long reddish moustache were relieved with a saturnine effect. His appearance, in short, presented an odd mixture of the bedraggled and the ferocious.

He walked beside her in silence, with quick precipitate steps, till they reached the embowered slopes to the east of the Casino; then, pulling up abruptly, he said: "Have you seen Bertha?"

"No—when I left the yacht she was not yet up."

He received this with a laugh like the whirring sound in a disabled clock. "Not yet up? Had she gone to bed? Do you know at what time she came on board? This morning at seven!" he exclaimed.

"At seven?" Lily started. "What happened—an accident to the train?"

He laughed again. "They missed the train—all the trains—they had to drive back."

"Well——?" She hesitated, feeling at once how little even this necessity accounted for the fatal lapse of hours.

"Well, they couldn't get a carriage at once—at that time of night, you know—" the explanatory note made it almost seem as though he were putting the case for his wife—"and when they finally did, it was only a one-horse cab, and the horse was lame!"

"How tiresome! I see," she affirmed, with the more earnestness because she was so nervously conscious that she did not; and after a pause she added: "I'm so sorry—but ought we to have waited?"

"Waited for the one-horse cab? It would scarcely have carried the four of us, do you think?"

She took this in what seemed the only possible way, with a laugh intended to sink the question itself in his humorous treatment of it. "Well, it would have been difficult; we should have had to walk by turns. But it would have been jolly to see the sunrise."

"Yes: the sunrise *was* jolly," he agreed.

"Was it? You saw it, then?"

"I saw it, yes; from the deck. I waited up for them."

"Naturally—I suppose you were worried. Why didn't you call on me to share your vigil?"

He stood still, dragging at his moustache with a lean weak hand. "I don't think you would have cared for its *dénouement*,"* he said with sudden grimness.

Again she was disconcerted by the abrupt change in his tone, and as in one flash she saw the peril of the moment, and the need of keeping her sense of it out of her eyes.

"*Dénouement*—isn't that too big a word for such a small incident? The worst of it, after all, is the fatigue which Bertha has probably slept off by this time."

She clung to the note bravely, though its futility was now plain to her in the glare of his miserable eyes.

"Don't—don't——!" he broke out, with the hurt cry of a

---

*Final outcome or resolution of a plot (French).

child; and while she tried to merge her sympathy, and her resolve to ignore any cause for it, in one ambiguous murmur of deprecation, he dropped down on the bench near which they had paused, and poured out the wretchedness of his soul.

It was a dreadful hour—an hour from which she emerged shrinking and seared, as though her lids had been scorched by its actual glare. It was not that she had never had premonitory glimpses of such an outbreak; but rather because, here and there throughout the three months, the surface of life had shown such ominous cracks and vapours that her fears had always been on the alert for an upheaval. There had been moments when the situation had presented itself under a homelier yet more vivid image—that of a shaky vehicle, dashed by unbroken steeds over a bumping road, while she cowered within, aware that the harness wanted mending, and wondering what would give way first. Well—everything had given way now; and the wonder was that the crazy outfit had held together so long. Her sense of being involved in the crash, instead of merely witnessing it from the road, was intensified by the way in which Dorset, through his furies of denunciation and wild reactions of self-contempt, made her feel the need he had of her, the place she had taken in his life. But for her, what ear would have been open to his cries? And what hand but hers could drag him up again to a footing of sanity and self-respect? All through the stress of the struggle with him, she had been conscious of something faintly maternal in her efforts to guide and uplift him. But for the present, if he clung to her, it was not in order to be dragged up, but to feel some one floundering in the depths with him: he wanted her to suffer with him, not to help him to suffer less.

Happily for both, there was little physical strength to sustain his frenzy. It left him, collapsed and breathing heavily, to an apathy so deep and prolonged that Lily almost feared the passers-by would think it the result of a seizure, and stop to offer their aid. But Monte Carlo is, of all places, the one where human bond is least close, and odd sights are the least arresting. If a glance or two lingered on the couple, no intrusive sympathy disturbed them; and it was Lily herself who broke the silence by rising from her seat. With the clearing of her vision the sweep of peril had extended, and she saw that the post of danger was no longer at Dorset's side.

"If you won't go back, I must—don't make me leave you!" she urged.

But he remained mutely resistant, and she added: "What are you going to do? You really can't sit here all night."

"I can go to an hotel. I can telegraph my lawyers." He sat up, roused by a new thought. "By Jove, Selden's at Nice—I'll send for Selden!"

Lily, at this, reseated herself with a cry of alarm. "No, no, *no!*" she protested.

He swung round on her distrustfully. "Why not Selden? He's a lawyer, isn't he? One will do as well as another in a case like this."

"As badly as another, you mean. I thought you relied on *me* to help you."

"You do—by being so sweet and patient with me. If it hadn't been for you I'd have ended the thing long ago. But now it's got to end." He rose suddenly, straightening himself with an effort. "You can't want to see me ridiculous."

She looked at him kindly. "That's just it." Then, after a moment's pondering, almost to her own surprise she broke out with a flash of inspiration: "Well, go over and see Mr. Selden. You'll have time to do it before dinner."

"Oh, *dinner——*" he mocked her; but she left him with the smiling rejoinder: "Dinner on board, remember; we'll put it off till nine if you like."

It was past four already; and when a cab had dropped her at the quay, and she stood waiting for the gig to out off for her, she began to wonder what had been happening on the yacht. Of Silverton's whereabouts there had been no mention. Had he returned to the *Sabrina*? Or could Bertha—the dread alternative sprang on her suddenly—could Bertha, left to herself, have gone ashore to rejoin him? Lily's heart stood still at the thought. All her concern had hitherto been for young Silverton, not only because, in such affairs, the woman's instinct is to side with the man, but because his case made a peculiar appeal to her sympathies. He was so desperately in earnest, poor youth, and his earnestness was of so different a quality from Bertha's, though hers too was desperate enough. The difference was that Bertha was in earnest only about herself, while he was in earnest about her. But now, at the actual crisis, this difference seemed to throw the weight of destitution on Bertha's side, since at least he had her to suffer for, and she had only herself. At any rate, viewed less ideally, all the disadvantages of such a situation were for the woman; and it was to Bertha that Lily's sympathies now went out. She was not fond of Bertha Dorset, but neither was she without a sense of obligation, the heavier for having so little personal liking to sustain it. Bertha had been kind to her, they had lived together, during the last months, on terms of easy friendship, and the sense of friction of which Lily had recently become aware seemed to make it the more urgent that she should work undividedly in her friend's interest.

It was in Bertha's interest, certainly, that she had despatched Dorset to consult with Lawrence Selden. Once the grotesqueness of the situation accepted, she had seen at a glance that it was the safest in which Dorset could find himself. Who but Selden could thus miraculously combine the skill to save Bertha with the obligation of doing so? The consciousness that much skill would be required made Lily rest thankfully in the greatness of the obligation. Since he would *have* to pull Bertha through she could trust him to find a way; and she put the fullness of her trust in the telegram she managed to send him on her way to the quay.

Thus far, then, Lily felt that she had done well; and the conviction strengthened her for the task that remained. She and Bertha had never been on confidential terms, but at such a crisis the barriers of reserve must surely fall: Dorset's wild allusions to the scene of the morning made Lily feel that they were down already, and that any attempt to rebuild them would be beyond Bertha's strength. She pictured the poor creature shivering behind her fallen defences and awaiting with suspense the moment when she could take refuge in the first shelter that offered. If only that shelter had not already offered itself elsewhere! As the gig traversed the short distance between the quay and the yacht, Lily grew more than ever alarmed at the possible consequences of her long absence. What if the wretched Bertha, finding in all the long hours no soul to turn to—but by

this time Lily's eager foot was on the side-ladder, and her first
step on the *Sabrina* showed the worst of her apprehensions to
be unfounded; for there, in the luxurious shade of the afterdeck,
the wretched Bertha, in full command of her usual attenuated
elegance, sat dispensing tea to the Duchess of Beltshire and
Lord Hubert.

The sight filled Lily with such surprise that she felt that
Bertha, at least, must read its meaning in her look, and she was
proportionately disconcerted by the blankness of the look returned. But in an instant she saw that Mrs. Dorset had, of necessity, to look blank before the others, and that, to mitigate the
effect of her own surprise, she must at once produce some simple reason for it. The long habit of rapid transitions made it easy
for her to exclaim to the Duchess: "Why, I thought you'd gone
back to the Princess!" and this sufficed for the lady she addressed, if it was hardly enough for Lord Hubert.

At least it opened the way to a lively explanation of how the
Duchess was, in fact, going back the next moment, but had first
rushed out to the yacht for a word with Mrs. Dorset on the subject of tomorrow's dinner—the dinner with the Brys, to which
Lord Hubert had finally insisted on dragging them.

"To save my neck, you know!" he explained, with a glance
that appealed to Lily for some recognition of his promptness;
and the Duchess added, with her noble candour: "Mr. Bry has
promised him a tip, and he says if we go he'll pass it on to us."

This led to some final pleasantries, in which, as it seemed to
Lily, Mrs. Dorset bore her part with astounding bravery, and at
the close of which Lord Hubert, from half way down the side-
ladder, called back, with an air of numbering heads: "And of
course we may count on Dorset too?"

"Oh, count on him," his wife assented gaily. She was keeping
up well to the last—but as she turned back from waving her
adieux over the side, Lily said to herself that the mask must drop
and the soul of fear look out.

Mrs. Dorset turned back slowly; perhaps she wanted time to
steady her muscles; at any rate, they were still under perfect control when, dropping once more into her seat behind the tea-
table, she remarked to Miss Bart with a faint touch of irony: "I
suppose I ought to say good morning."

If it was a cue, Lily was ready to take it, though with only the vaguest sense of what was expected of her in return. There was something unnerving in the contemplation of Mrs. Dorset's composure, and she had to force the light tone in which she answered: "I tried to see you this morning, but you were not yet up."

"No—I got to bed late. After we missed you at the station I thought we ought to wait for you till the last train." She spoke very gently, but with just the least tinge of reproach.

"You missed us? You waited for us at the station?" Now indeed Lily was too far adrift in bewilderment to measure the other's words or keep watch on her own. "But I thought you didn't get to the station till after the last train had left!"

Mrs. Dorset, examining her between lowered lids, met this with the immediate query: "Who told you that?"

"George—I saw him just now in the gardens."

"Ah, is that George's version? Poor George—he was in no state to remember what I told him. He had one of his worst attacks this morning, and I packed him off to see the doctor. Do you know if he found him?"

Lily, still lost in conjecture, made no reply, and Mrs. Dorset settled herself indolently in her seat. "He'll wait to see him; he was horribly frightened about himself. It's very bad for him to be worried, and whenever anything upsetting happens, it always brings on an attack."

This time Lily felt sure that a cue was being pressed on her; but it was put forth with such startling suddenness, and with so incredible an air of ignoring what it led up to, that she could only falter out doubtfully: "Anything upsetting?"

"Yes—such as having you so conspicuously on his hands in the small hours. You know, my dear, you're rather a big responsibility in such a scandalous place after midnight."

At that—at the complete unexpectedness and the inconceivable audacity of it—Lily could not restrain the tribute of an astonished laugh.

"Well, really—considering it was you who burdened him with the responsibility!"

Mrs. Dorset took this with an exquisite mildness. "By not having the superhuman cleverness to discover you in that frightful rush for the train? Or the imagination to believe that you'd take it without us—you and he all alone—instead of waiting quietly in the station till we *did* manage to meet you?"

Lily's colour rose: it was growing clear to her that Bertha was pursuing an object, following a line she had marked out for herself. Only, with such a doom impending, why waste time in these childish efforts to avert it? The puerility of the attempt disarmed Lily's indignation: did it not prove how horribly the poor creature was frightened?

"No; by our simply all keeping together at Nice," she returned.

"Keeping together? When it was you who seized the first opportunity to rush off with the Duchess and her friends? My dear Lily, you are not a child to be led by the hand!"

"No—nor to be lectured, Bertha, really; if that's what you are doing to me now."

Mrs. Dorset smiled on her reproachfully. "Lecture you—I? Heaven forbid! I was merely trying to give you a friendly hint. But it's usually the other way round, isn't it? I'm expected to take hints, not to give them: I've positively lived on them all these last months."

"Hints—from me to you?" Lily repeated.

"Oh, negative ones merely—what not to be and to do and to see. And I think I've taken them to admiration. Only, my dear, if you'll let me say so, I didn't understand that one of my negative duties was *not* to warn you when you carried your imprudence too far."

A chill of fear passed over Miss Bart: a sense of remembered treachery that was like the gleam of a knife in the dusk. But compassion, in a moment, got the better of her instinctive recoil. What was this outpouring of senseless bitterness but the tracked creature's attempt to cloud the medium through which it was fleeing? It was on Lily's lips to exclaim: "You poor soul, don't double and turn—come straight back to me, and we'll find a way out!" But the words died under the impenetrable insolence of Bertha's smile. Lily sat silent, taking the brunt of it quietly, letting it spend itself on her to the last drop of its accumulated falseness; then, without a word, she rose and went down to her cabin.

3

MISS BART'S TELEGRAM CAUGHT Lawrence Selden at the door of his hotel; and having read it, he turned back to wait for Dorset. The message necessarily left large gaps for conjecture; but all that he had recently heard and seen made these but too easy to fill in. On the whole he was surprised; for though he had perceived that the situation contained all the elements of an explosion, he had often enough, in the range of his personal experience, seen just such combinations subside into harmlessness. Still, Dorset's spasmodic temper, and his wife's reckless disregard of appearances, gave the situation a peculiar insecurity; and it was less from the sense of any special relation to the case than from a purely professional zeal, that Selden resolved to guide the pair to safety. Whether, in the present instance, safety for either lay in repairing so damaged a tie, it was no business of his to consider: he had only, on general principles, to think of averting a scandal, and his desire to avert it was increased by his fear of its involving Miss Bart. There was nothing specific in this apprehension; he merely wished to spare her the embarrassment of being ever so remotely connected with the public washing of the Dorset linen.

How exhaustive and unpleasant such a process would be, he saw even more vividly after his two hours' talk with poor Dorset. If anything came out at all, it would be such a vast unpacking of accumulated moral rags as left him, after his visitor had gone, with the feeling that he must fling open the windows and have his room swept out. But nothing should come out; and happily for his side of the case, the dirty rags, however pieced together, could not, without considerable difficulty, be turned into a homogeneous grievance. The torn edges did not always fit—there were missing bits, there were disparities of size and colour, all of which it was naturally Selden's business to make the most of in

putting them under his client's eye. But to a man in Dorset's
mood the completest demonstration could not carry conviction,
and Selden saw that for the moment all he could do was to
soothe and temporize, to offer sympathy and to counsel prudence. He let Dorset depart charged to the brim with the sense
that, till their next meeting, he must maintain a strictly non-
committal attitude; that, in short, his share in the game consisted for the present in looking on. Selden knew, however, that
he could not long keep such violences in equilibrium; and he
promised to meet Dorset, the next morning, at an hotel in
Monte Carlo. Meanwhile he counted not a little on the reaction
of weakness and self-distrust that, in such natures, follows on
every unwonted expenditure of moral force; and his telegraphic
reply to Miss Bart consisted simply in the injunction: "Assume
that everything is as usual."

On this assumption, in fact, the early part of the following
day was lived through. Dorset, as if in obedience to Lily's imperative bidding, had actually returned in time for a late dinner
on the yacht. The repast had been the most difficult moment of
the day. Dorset was sunk in one of the abysmal silences which so
commonly followed on what his wife called his "attacks" that it
was easy, before the servants, to refer it to this cause; but Bertha
herself seemed, perversely enough, little disposed to make use of
this obvious means of protection. She simply left the brunt of
the situation on her husband's hands, as if too absorbed in a
grievance of her own to suspect that she might be the object of
one herself. To Lily this attitude was the most ominous, because
the most perplexing, element in the situation. As she tried to fan
the weak flicker of talk, to build up, again and again, the crumbling structure of "appearances," her own attention was perpetually distracted by the question: "What on earth can she be
driving at?" There was something positively exasperating in
Bertha's attitude of isolated defiance. If only she would have
given her friend a hint they might still have worked together
successfully; but how could Lily be of use, while she was thus
obstinately shut out from participation? To be of use was what
she honestly wanted; and not for her own sake but for the
Dorsets'. She had not thought of her own situation at all: she
was simply engrossed in trying to put a little order in theirs. But

the close of the short dreary evening left her with a sense of effort hopelessly wasted. She had not tried to see Dorset alone: she had positively shrunk from a renewal of his confidences. It was Bertha whose confidence she sought, and who should as eagerly have invited her own; and Bertha, as if in the infatuation of self-destruction, was actually pushing away her rescuing hand.

Lily, going to bed early, had left the couple to themselves; and it seemed part of the general mystery in which she moved that more than an hour should elapse before she heard Bertha walk down the silent passage and regain her room. The morrow, rising on an apparent continuance of the same conditions, revealed nothing of what had occurred between the confronted pair. One fact alone outwardly proclaimed the change they were all conspiring to ignore; and that was the non-appearance of Ned Silverton. No one referred to it, and this tacit avoidance of the subject kept it in the immediate foreground of consciousness. But there was another change, perceptible only to Lily; and that was that Dorset now avoided her almost as pointedly as his wife. Perhaps he was repenting his rash outpourings of the previous day; perhaps only trying, in his clumsy way, to conform to Selden's counsel to behave "as usual." Such instructions no more make for easiness of attitude than the photographer's behest to "look natural"; and in a creature as unconscious as poor Dorset of the appearance he habitually presented, the struggle to maintain a pose was sure to result in queer contortions.

It resulted, at any rate, in throwing Lily strangely on her own resources. She had learned, on leaving her room, that Mrs. Dorset was still invisible, and that Dorset had left the yacht early; and feeling too restless to remain alone, she too had herself ferried ashore. Straying toward the Casino, she attached herself to a group of acquaintances from Nice, with whom she lunched, and in whose company she was returning to the rooms when she encountered Selden crossing the square. She could not, at the moment, separate herself definitely from her party, who had hospitably assumed that she would remain with them till they took their departure; but she found time for a momentary pause of enquiry, to which he promptly returned: "I've seen him again—he's just left me."

She waited before him anxiously. "Well? what has happened? What *will* happen?"

"Nothing as yet—and nothing in the future, I think."

"It's over, then? It's settled? You're sure?"

He smiled. "Give me time. I'm not sure—but I'm a good deal surer." And with that she had to content herself, and hasten on to the expectant group on the steps.

Selden had in fact given her the utmost measure of his sureness, had even stretched it a shade to meet the anxiety in her eyes. And now, as he turned away, strolling down the hill toward the station, that anxiety remained with him as the visible justification of his own. It was not, indeed, anything specific that he feared: there had been a literal truth in his declaration that he did not think anything would happen. What troubled him was that, though Dorset's attitude had perceptibly changed, the change was not clearly to be accounted for. It had certainly not been produced by Selden's arguments, or by the action of his own soberer reason. Five minutes' talk sufficed to show that some alien influence had been at work, and that it had not so much subdued his resentment as weakened his will, so that he moved under it in a state of apathy, like a dangerous lunatic who has been drugged. Temporarily, no doubt, however exerted, it worked for the general safety: the question was how long it would last, and by what kind of reaction it was likely to be followed. On these points Selden could gain no light; for he saw that one effect of the transformation had been to shut him off from free communion with Dorset. The latter, indeed, was still moved by the irresistible desire to discuss his wrong; but, though he revolved about it with the same forlorn tenacity, Selden was aware that something always restrained him from full expression. His state was one to produce first weariness and then impatience in his hearer; and when their talk was over, Selden began to feel that he had done his utmost, and might justifiably wash his hands of the sequel.

It was in this mind that he had been making his way back to the station when Miss Bart crossed his path; but though, after his brief word with her, he kept mechanically on his course, he was conscious of a gradual change in his purpose. The change had been produced by the look in her eyes; and in his eagerness to define the nature of that look, he dropped into a seat in the gardens, and sat brooding upon the question. It was natural enough, in all conscience, that she should appear anxious: a young woman placed, in the close intimacy of a yachting-cruise, between a couple on the verge of disaster, could hardly, aside from her concern for her friends, be insensible to the awkwardness of her own position. The worst of it was that, in interpreting Miss Bart's state of mind, so many alternative readings were possible; and one of them, in Selden's troubled mind, took the ugly form suggested by Mrs. Fisher. If the girl was afraid, was she afraid for herself or for her friends? And to what degree was her dread of a catastrophe intensified by the sense of being fatally involved in it? The burden of offence lying manifestly with Mrs. Dorset, this conjecture seemed on the face of it gratuitously unkind; but Selden knew that in the most one-sided matrimonial quarrel there are generally counter-charges to be brought, and that they are brought with the greater audacity where the original grievance is so emphatic. Mrs. Fisher had not hesitated to suggest the likelihood of Dorset's marrying Miss Bart if "anything happened"; and though Mrs. Fisher's conclusions were notoriously rash, she was shrewd enough in reading the signs from which they were drawn. Dorset had apparently shown marked interest in the girl, and this interest might be used to cruel advantage in his wife's struggle for rehabilitation. Selden knew that Bertha would fight to the last round of powder: the rashness of her conduct was illogically combined with a cold determination to escape its consequences. She could be as unscrupulous in fighting for herself as she was reckless in courting danger, and whatever came to her hand at such moments was likely to be used as a defensive missile. He did not, as yet, see clearly just what course she was likely to take, but his perplexity increased his apprehension, and with it the sense that, before leaving, he must speak again with Miss Bart. Whatever her share in the situation—and he had always honestly tried to resist judging her by her surroundings—however free she might be from any personal connection with it, she would be better out of the way of a possible crash; and since she had appealed to him for help, it was clearly his business to tell her so.

This decision at last brought him to his feet, and carried him

back to the gambling rooms, within whose doors he had seen
her disappearing; but a prolonged exploration of the crowd
failed to put him on her traces. He saw instead, to his surprise,
Ned Silverton loitering somewhat ostentatiously about the tables; and the discovery that this actor in the drama was not only
hovering in the wings, but actually inviting the exposure of the
foot-lights, though it might have seemed to imply that all peril
was over, served rather to deepen Selden's sense of foreboding.
Charged with this impression he returned to the square, hoping
to see Miss Bart move across it, as every one in Monte Carlo
seemed inevitably to do at least a dozen times a day; but here
again he waited vainly for a glimpse of her, and the conclusion
was slowly forced on him that she had gone back to the *Sabrina*.
It would be difficult to follow her there, and still more difficult,
should he do so, to contrive the opportunity for a private word;
and he had almost decided on the unsatisfactory alternative of
writing, when the ceaseless diorama of the square suddenly unrolled before him the figures of Lord Hubert and Mrs. Bry.

Hailing them at once with his question, he learned from
Lord Hubert that Miss Bart had just returned to the *Sabrina* in
Dorset's company; an announcement so evidently disconcerting
to him that Mrs. Bry, after a glance from her companion, which
seemed to act like the pressure on a spring, brought forth the
prompt proposal that he should come and meet his friends at
dinner that evening—"At Bécassin's—little dinner to the
Duchess," she flashed out before Lord Hubert had time to re-
move the pressure.

Selden's sense of the privilege of being included in such company brought him early in the evening to the door of the restaurant, where he paused to scan the ranks of diners approaching
down the brightly lit terrace. There, while the Brys hovered
within over the last agitating alternatives of the *menu*, he kept
watch for the guests from the *Sabrina*, who at length rose on the
horizon in company with the Duchess, Lord and Lady Skiddaw
and the Stepneys. From this group it was easy for him to detach
Miss Bart on the pretext of a moment's glance into one of the
brilliant shops along the terrace, and to say to her, while they lingered together in the white dazzle of a jeweller's window, "I
stopped over to see you—to beg of you to leave the yacht."

The eyes she turned on him showed a quick gleam of her former fear. "To leave—? What do you mean? What has happened?"

"Nothing. But if anything should, why be in the way of it?"

The glare from the jeweller's window, deepening the pallour of her face, gave to its delicate lines the sharpness of a tragic mask. "Nothing will, I am sure; but while there's even a doubt left, how can you think I would leave Bertha?"

The words rang out on a note of contempt—was it possibly of contempt for himself? Well, he was willing to risk its renewal to the extent of insisting, with an undeniable throb of added interest: "You have yourself to think of, you know—" to which, with a strange fall of sadness in her voice, she answered, meeting his eyes: "If you knew how little difference that makes!"

"Oh, well, nothing *will* happen," he said, more for his own reassurance than for hers; and "Nothing, nothing, of course!" she valiantly assented, as they turned to overtake their companions.

In the thronged restaurant, taking their places about Mrs. Bry's illuminated board, their confidence seemed to gain support from the familiarity of their surroundings. Here were Dorset and his wife once more presenting their customary faces to the world, she engrossed in establishing her relation with an intensely new gown, he shrinking with dyspeptic dread from the multiplied solicitations of the *menu*. The mere fact that they thus showed themselves together, with the utmost openness the place afforded, seemed to declare beyond a doubt that their differences were composed. How this end had been attained was still matter for wonder, but it was clear that for the moment Miss Bart rested confidently in the result; and Selden tried to achieve the same view by telling himself that her opportunities for observation had been ampler than his own.

Meanwhile, as the dinner advanced through a labyrinth of courses, in which it became clear that Mrs. Bry had occasionally broken away from Lord Hubert's restraining hand, Selden's general watchfulness began to lose itself in a particular study of Miss Bart. It was one of the days when she was so handsome that to be handsome was enough, and all the rest—her grace, her quickness, her social felicities—seemed the overflow of a bounteous nature. But what especially struck him was the way in which she detached herself, by a hundred undefinable shades, from the persons who most abounded in her own style. It was in just such company, the fine flower and complete expression of the state she aspired to, that the differences came out with special poignancy, her grace cheapening the other woman's smartness as her finely-discriminated silences made their chatter dull. The strain of the last hours had restored to her face the deeper eloquence which Selden had lately missed in it, and the bravery of her words to him still fluttered in her voice and eyes. Yes, she was matchless—it was the one word for her; and he could give his admiration the freer play because so little personal feeling remained in it. His real detachment from her had taken place, not at the lurid moment of disenchantment, but now, in the sober after-light of discrimination, where he saw her definitely divided from him by the crudeness of a choice which seemed to deny the very differences he felt in her. It was before him again in its completeness—the choice in which she was content to rest: in the stupid costliness of the food and the showy dulness of the talk, in the freedom of speech which never arrived at wit and the freedom of act which never made for romance. The strident setting of the restaurant, in which their table seemed set apart in a special glare of publicity, and the presence at it of little Dabham of the "Riviera Notes," emphasized the ideals of a world where conspicuousness passed for distinction, and the society column had become the roll of fame.

It was as the immortalizer of such occasions that little Dabham, wedged in modest watchfulness between two brilliant neighbours, suddenly became the centre of Selden's scrutiny. How much did he know of what was going on, and how much, for his purpose, was still worth finding out? His little eyes were like tentacles thrown out to catch the floating intimations with which, to Selden, the air at moments seemed thick; then again it cleared to its normal emptiness, and he could see nothing in it for the journalist but leisure to note the elegance of the ladies' gowns. Mrs. Dorset's, in particular, challenged all the wealth of Mr. Dabham's vocabulary: it had surprises and subtleties worthy of what he would have called "the literary style." At first, as Selden had noticed, it had been almost too preoccupying to its wearer; but now she was in full command of it, and was even producing her effects with unwonted freedom. Was she not, indeed, too free, too fluent, for perfect naturalness? And was not Dorset, to whom his glance had passed by a natural transition, too jerkily wavering between the same extremes? Dorset indeed was always jerky; but it seemed to Selden that tonight each vibration swung him farther from his centre.

The dinner, meanwhile, was moving to its triumphant close, to the evident satisfaction of Mrs. Bry, who, throned in apoplectic majesty between Lord Skiddaw and Lord Hubert, seemed in spirit to be calling on Mrs. Fisher to witness her achievement. Short of Mrs. Fisher her audience might have been called complete; for the restaurant was crowded with persons mainly gathered there for the purpose of spectatorship, and accurately posted as to the names and faces of the celebrities they had come to see. Mrs. Bry, conscious that all her feminine guests came under that heading, and that each one looked her part to admiration, shone on Lily with all the pent-up gratitude that Mrs. Fisher had failed to deserve. Selden, catching the glance, wondered what part Miss Bart had played in organizing the entertainment. She did, at least, a great deal to adorn it; and as he watched the bright security with which she bore herself, he smiled to think that he should have fancied her in need of help. Never had she appeared more serenely mistress of the situation than when, at the moment of dispersal, detaching herself a little from the group about the table, she turned with a smile and a graceful slant of the shoulders to receive her cloak from Dorset.

The dinner had been protracted over Mr. Bry's exceptional cigars and a bewildering array of liqueurs, and many of the other tables were empty; but a sufficient number of diners still lingered to give relief to the leave-taking of Mrs. Bry's distinguished guests. This ceremony was drawn out and complicated by the fact that it involved, on the part of the Duchess and Lady Skiddaw, definite farewells, and pledges of speedy reunion in Paris, where they were to pause and replenish their wardrobes on the way to England. The quality of Mrs. Bry's hospitality, and of the tips her husband had presumably imparted, lent to the manner of the English ladies a general effusiveness which shed the rosiest light over their hostess's future. In its glow Mrs. Dorset and the Stepneys were also visibly included, and the whole scene had touches of intimacy worth their weight in gold to the watchful pen of Mr. Dabham.

A glance at her watch caused the Duchess to exclaim to her sister that they had just time to dash for their train, and the flurry of this departure over, the Stepneys, who had their motor at the door, offered to convey the Dorsets and Miss Bart to the quay. The offer was accepted, and Mrs. Dorset moved away with her husband in attendance. Miss Bart had lingered for a last word with Lord Hubert, and Stepney, on whom Mr. Bry was pressing a final, and still more expensive, cigar, called out: "Come on, Lily, if you're going back to the yacht."

Lily turned to obey; but as she did so, Mrs. Dorset, who had paused on her way out, moved a few steps back toward the table.

"Miss Bart is not going back to the yacht," she said in a voice of singular distinctness.

A startled look ran from eye to eye; Mrs. Bry crimsoned to the verge of congestion, Mrs. Stepney slipped nervously behind her husband, and Selden, in the general turmoil of his sensations, was mainly conscious of a longing to grip Dabham by the collar and fling him out into the street.

Dorset, meanwhile, had stepped back to his wife's side. His face was white, and he looked about him with cowed angry eyes. "Bertha!—Miss Bart . . . this is some misunderstanding . . . some mistake . . ."

"Miss Bart remains here," his wife rejoined incisively. "And, I think, George, we had better not detain Mrs. Stepney any longer."

Miss Bart, during this brief exchange of words, remained in admirable erectness, slightly isolated from the embarrassed group about her. She had paled a little under the shock of the insult, but the discomposure of the surrounding faces was not reflected in her own. The faint disdain of her smile seemed to lift her high above her antagonist's reach, and it was not till she had given Mrs. Dorset the full measure of the distance between them that she turned and extended her hand to her hostess.

"I am joining the Duchess tomorrow," she explained, "and it seemed easier for me to remain on shore for the night."

She held firmly to Mrs. Bry's wavering eye while she gave this explanation, but when it was over Selden saw her send a tentative glance from one to another of the women's faces. She read their incredulity in their averted looks, and in the mute wretchedness of the men behind them, and for a miserable half-second he thought she quivered on the brink of failure. Then, turning to him with an easy gesture, and the pale bravery of her recovered smile—"Dear Mr. Selden," she said, "you promised to see me to my cab."

Outside, the sky was gusty and overcast, and as Lily and Selden moved toward the deserted gardens below the restaurant, spurts of warm rain blew fitfully against their faces. The fiction of the cab had been tacitly abandoned; they walked on in silence, her hand on his arm, till the deeper shade of the gardens received them, and pausing beside a bench, he said: "Sit down a moment."

She dropped to the seat without answering, but the electric lamp at the bend of the path shed a gleam on the struggling misery of her face. Selden sat down beside her, waiting for her to speak, fearful lest any word he chose should touch too roughly on her wound, and kept also from free utterance by the wretched doubt which had slowly renewed itself within him. What had brought her to this pass? What weakness had placed her so abominably at her enemy's mercy? And why should Bertha Dorset have turned into an enemy at the very moment when she so obviously needed the support of her sex? Even while his nerves raged at the subjection of husbands to their wives, and at the cruelty of women to their kind, reason obstinately harped on the proverbial relation between smoke and fire. The memory of Mrs. Fisher's hints, and the corroboration of his own impressions, while they deepened his pity also increased his constraint, since, whichever way he sought a free outlet for sympathy, it was blocked by the fear of committing a blunder.

Suddenly it struck him that his silence must seem almost as accusatory as that of the men he had despised for turning from her; but before he could find the fitting word she had cut him short with a question.

"Do you know of a quiet hotel? I can send for my maid in the morning."

"An hotel—*here*—that you can go to alone? It's not possible."

She met this with a pale gleam of her old playfulness. "What *is*, then? It's too wet to sleep in the gardens."

"But there must be some one——"

"Some one to whom I can go? Of course—any number—but at *this* hour? You see my change of plan was rather sudden——"

"Good God—if you'd listened to me!" he cried, venting his helplessness in a burst of anger.

She still held him off with the gentle mockery of her smile. "But haven't I?" she rejoined. "You advised me to leave the yacht, and I'm leaving it."

He saw then, with a pang of self-reproach, that she meant neither to explain nor to defend herself; that by his miserable silence he had forfeited all chance of helping her, and that the decisive hour was past.

She had risen, and stood before him in a kind of clouded majesty, like some deposed princess moving tranquilly to exile.

"Lily!" he exclaimed, with a note of despairing appeal; but— "Oh, not now," she gently admonished him; and then, in all the sweetness of her recovered composure: "Since I must find shelter somewhere, and since you're so kindly here to help me——"

He gathered himself up at the challenge. "You will do as I tell you? There's but one thing, then; you must go straight to your cousins, the Stepneys."

"Oh—" broke from her with a movement of instinctive resistance; but he insisted: "Come—it's late, and you must appear to have gone there directly."

He had drawn her hand into his arm, but she held him back with a last gesture of protest. "I can't—I can't—not that—you don't know Gwen: you mustn't ask me!"

"I *must* ask you—you must obey me," he persisted, though infected at heart by her own fear.

Her voice sank to a whisper: "And if she refuses?"—but, "Oh, trust me—trust me!" he could only insist in return; and yielding to his touch, she let him lead her back in silence to the edge of the square.

In the cab they continued to remain silent through the brief drive which carried them to the illuminated portals of the Stepneys' hotel. Here he left her outside, in the darkness of the raised hood, while his name was sent up to Stepney, and he paced the showy hall, awaiting the latter's descent. Then minutes later the two men passed out together between the gold-laced custodians of the threshold; but in the vestibule Stepney drew up with a last flare of reluctance.

"It's understood, then?" he stipulated nervously, with his hand on Selden's arm. "She leaves tomorrow by the early train—and my wife's asleep, and can't be disturbed."

4

THE BLINDS OF MRS. Peniston's drawing-room were drawn down against the oppressive June sun, and in the sultry twilight the faces of her assembled relatives took on a fitting shadow of bereavement.

They were all there? Van Alstynes, Stepneys and Meisons—even a stray Peniston or two, indicating, by a greater latitude in dress and manner, the fact of remoter relationship and more settled hopes. The Peniston side was, in fact, secure in the knowledge that the bulk of Mr. Peniston's property "went back"; while the direct connection hung suspended on the disposal of his widow's private fortune and on the uncertainty of its extent. Jack Stepney, in his new character as the richest nephew, tacitly took the lead, emphasizing his importance by the deeper gloss of his mourning and the subdued authority of his manner; while his wife's bored attitude and frivolous gown proclaimed the heiress's disregard of the insignificant interests at stake. Old Ned Van Aistyne, seated next to her in a coat that made affliction dapper, twirled his white moustache to conceal the eager twitch of his lips; and Grace Stepney, red-nosed and smelling of crape, whispered emotionally to Mrs. Herbert Melson: "I couldn't *bear* to see the Niagara anywhere else!"

A rustle of weeds and quick turning of heads hailed the opening of the door, and Lily Bart appeared, tall and noble in her black dress, with Gerty Farish at her side. The women's faces, as she paused interrogatively on the threshold, were a study in hesitation. One or two made faint motions of recognition, which might have been subdued either by the solemnity of the scene, or by the doubt as to how far the others meant to go; Mrs. Jack Stepney gave a careless nod, and Grace Stepney, with a sepulchral gesture, indicated a seat at her side. But Lily, ignoring the invitation, as well as Jack Stepney's official attempt to direct her, moved across the room with her smooth free gait, and seated herself in a chair which seemed to have been purposely placed apart from the others.

It was the first time that she had faced her family since her return from Europe, two weeks earlier; but if she perceived any uncertainty in their welcome, it served only to add a tinge of irony to the usual composure of her bearing. The shock of dismay with which, on the dock, she had heard from Gerty Farish of Mrs. Peniston's sudden death, had been mitigated, almost at once, by the irrepressible thought that now, at last, she would be able to pay her debts. She had looked forward with considerable uneasiness to her first encounter with her aunt. Mrs. Peniston had vehemently opposed her niece's departure with the Dorsets, and had marked her continued disapproval by not writing during Lily's absence. The certainty that she had heard of the rupture with the Dorsets made the prospect of the meeting more formidable; and how should Lily have repressed a quick sense of relief at the thought that, instead of undergoing the anticipated ordeal, she had only to enter gracefully on a long-assured inheritance? It had been, in the consecrated phrase, "always understood" that Mrs. Peniston was to provide handsomely for her niece; and in the latter's mind the understanding had long since crystallized into fact.

"She gets everything, of course—I don't see what we're here for," Mrs. Jack Stepney remarked with careless loudness to Ned Van Alstyne; and the latter's deprecating murmur—"Julia was always a just woman"—might have been interpreted as signifying either acquiescence or doubt.

"Well, it's only about four hundred thousand," Mrs. Stepney rejoined with a yawn; and Grace Stepney, in the silence produced by the lawyer's preliminary cough, was heard to sob out: "They won't find a towel missing—I went over them with her the very day——"

Lily, oppressed by the close atmosphere, and the stifling odour of fresh mourning, felt her attention straying as Mrs. Peniston's lawyer, solemnly erect behind the Buhl* table at the

---

*André-Charles Buhl, also known as Boulle or Boule (1642–1732), noted French cabinetmaker who often decorated furniture with inlays of metals and pearls.

end of the room, began to rattle through the preamble of the will.

"It's like being in church," she reflected, wondering vaguely where Gwen Stepney had got such an awful hat. Then she noticed how stout Jack had grown—he would soon be almost as plethoric as Herbert Melson, who sat a few feet off, breathing puffily as he leaned his black-gloved hands on his stick.

"I wonder why rich people always grow fat—I suppose it's because there's nothing to worry them. If I inherit, I shall have to be careful of my figure," she mused, while the lawyer droned on through a labyrinth of legacies. The servants came first, then a few charitable institutions, then several remoter Melsons and Stepneys, who stirred consciously as their names rang out, and then subsided into a state of impassiveness befitting the solemnity of the occasion. Ned Van Alstyne, Jack Stepney, and a cousin or two followed, each coupled with the mention of a few thousands: Lily wondered that Grace Stepney was not among them. Then she heard her own name—"to my niece Lily Bart ten thousand dollars—" and after that the lawyer again lost himself in a coil of unintelligible periods, from which the concluding phrase flashed out with startling distinctness: "and the residue of my estate to my dear cousin and name-sake, Grace Julia Stepney."

There was a subdued gasp of surprise, a rapid turning of heads, and a surging of sable figures toward the corner in which Miss Stepney wailed out her sense of unworthiness through the crumpled ball of a black-edged handkerchief.

Lily stood apart from the general movement, feeling herself for the first time utterly alone. No one looked at her, no one seemed aware of her presence; she was probing the very depths of insignificance. And under her sense of the collective indifference came the acuter pang of hopes deceived. Disinherited—she had been disinherited—and for Grace Stepney! She met Gerty's lamentable eyes, fixed on her in a despairing effort at consolation, and the look brought her to herself. There was something to be done before she left the house: to be done with all the nobility she knew how to put into such gestures. She advanced to the group about Miss Stepney, and holding out her hand said simply: "Dear Grace, I am so glad."

The other ladies had fallen back at her approach, and a space created itself about her. It widened as she turned to go, and no one advanced to fill it up. She paused a moment, glancing about her, calmly taking the measure of her situation. She heard some one ask a question about the date of the will; she caught a fragment of the lawyer's answer—something about a sudden summons, and an "earlier instrument." Then the tide of dispersal began to drift past her; Mrs. Jack Stepney and Mrs. Herbert Melson stood on the doorstep awaiting their motor; a sympathizing group escorted Grace Stepney to the cab it was felt to be fitting she should take, though she lived but a street or two away; and Miss Bart and Gerty found themselves almost alone in the purple drawing-room, which more than ever, in its stuffy dimness, resembled a well-kept family vault, in which the last corpse had just been decently deposited.

In Gerty Farish's sitting-room, whither a hansom had carried the two friends, Lily dropped into a chair with a faint sound of laughter: it struck her as a humorous coincidence that her aunt's legacy should so nearly represent the amount of her debt to Trenor. The need of discharging that debt had reasserted itself with increased urgency since her return to America, and she spoke her first thought in saying to the anxiously hovering Gerty: "I wonder when the legacies will be paid."

But Miss Farish could not pause over the legacies; she broke into a larger indignation. "Oh, Lily, it's unjust; it's cruel—Grace Stepney must *feel* she has no right to all that money!"

"Any one who knew how to please Aunt Julia has a right to her money," Miss Bart rejoined philosophically.

"But she was devoted to you—she led every one to think——" Gerty checked herself in evident embarrassment, and Miss Bart turned to her with a direct look. "Gerty, be honest: this will was made only six weeks ago. She had heard of my break with the Dorsets?"

"Every one heard, of course, that there had been some disagreement—some misunderstanding——"

"Did you hear that Bertha turned me off the yacht?"

"Lily!"

"That was what happened, you know. She said I was trying

to marry George Dorset. She did it to make him think she was jealous. Isn't that what she told Gwen Stepney?"

"I don't know—I don't listen to such horrors."

"I *must* listen to them—I must know where I stand." She paused, and again sounded a faint note of derision. "Did you notice the women? They were afraid to snub me while they thought I was going to get the money—afterward they scuttled off as if I had the plague." Gerty remained silent, and she continued: "I stayed on to see what would happen. They took their cue from Gwen Stepney and Lulu Melson—I saw them watching to see what Gwen would do.—Gerty, I must know just what is being said of me."

"I tell you I don't listen——"

"One hears such things without listening." She rose and laid her resolute hands on Miss Farish's shoulders. "Gerty, are people going to cut me?"

"Your *friends*, Lily—how can you think it?"

"Who are one's friends at such a time? Who, but you, you poor trustful darling? And heaven knows what *you* suspect me of!" She kissed Gerty with a whimsical murmur. "You'd never let it make any difference—but then you're fond of criminals, Gerty! How about the irreclaimable ones, though? For I'm absolutely impenitent, you know."

She drew herself up to the full height of her slender majesty, towering like some dark angel of defiance above the troubled Gerty, who could only falter out: "Lily, Lily—how can you laugh about such things?"

"So as not to weep, perhaps. But no—I'm not of the tearful order. I discovered early that crying makes my nose red, and the knowledge has helped me through several painful episodes." She took a restless turn about the room, and then, reseating herself, lifted the bright mockery of her eyes to Gerty's anxious countenance.

"I shouldn't have minded, you know, if I'd got the money—" and at Miss Farish's protesting "Oh!" she repeated calmly: "Not a straw, my dear; for, in the first place, they wouldn't have quite dared to ignore me; and if they had, it wouldn't have mattered, because I should have been independent of them. But now—!" The irony faded from her eyes, and she bent a clouded face upon her friend.

"How can you talk so, Lily? Of course the money ought to have been yours, but after all that makes no difference. The important thing——" Gerty paused, and then continued firmly: "The important thing is that you should clear yourself—should tell your friends the whole truth."

"The whole truth?" Miss Bart laughed. "What is truth? Where a woman is concerned, it's the story that's easiest to believe. In this case it's a great deal easier to believe Bertha Dorset's story than mine, because she has a big house and an opera box, and it's convenient to be on good terms with her."

Miss Farish still fixed her with an anxious gaze. "But what *is* your story, Lily? I don't believe any one knows it yet."

"My story?—I don't believe I know it myself. You see I never thought of preparing a version in advance as Bertha did—and if I had, I don't think I should take the trouble to use it now."

But Gerty continued with her quiet reasonableness: "I don't want a version prepared in advance—but I want you to tell me exactly what happened from the beginning."

"From the beginning?" Miss Bart gently mimicked her. "Dear Gerty, how little imagination you good people have! Why, the beginning was in my cradle, I suppose—in the way I was brought up, and the things I was taught to care for. Or no— I won't blame anybody for my faults: I'll say it was in my blood, that I got it from some wicked pleasure-loving ancestress, who reacted against the homely virtues of New Amsterdam, and wanted to be back at the court of the Charleses!"* And as Miss Farish continued to press her with troubled eyes, she went on impatiently: "You asked me just now for the truth—well, the truth about any girl is that once she's talked about she's done for; and the more she explains her case the worse it looks—My good Gerty, you don't happen to have a cigarette about you?"

In her stuffy room at the hotel to which she had gone on landing, Lily Bart that evening reviewed her situation. It was the last week in June, and none of her friends were in town. The few rel-

---

*The reference is to the courts of English kings Charles I and Charles II, who reigned before and after the Puritan Commonwealth.

atives who had stayed on, or returned, for the reading of Mrs.
Peniston's will, had taken flight again that afternoon to Newport
or Long Island; and not one of them had made any proffer of
hospitality to Lily. For the first time in her life she found herself
utterly alone except for Gerty Farish. Even at the actual moment
of her break with the Dorsets she had not had so keen a sense of
its consequences, for the Duchess of Beltshire, hearing of the catastrophe from Lord Hubert, had instantly offered her protection, and under her sheltering wing Lily had made an almost
triumphant progress to London. There she had been sorely
tempted to linger on in a society which asked of her only to
amuse and charm it, without enquiring too curiously how she
had acquired her gift for doing so; but Selden, before they
parted, had pressed on her the urgent need of returning at once
to her aunt, and Lord Hubert, when he presently reappeared in
London, abounded in the same counsel. Lily did not need to be
told that the Duchess's championship was not the best road to
social rehabilitation, and as she was besides aware that her noble
defender might at any moment drop her in favour of a new *pro-
tégée*, she reluctantly decided to return to America. But she had
not been ten minutes on her native shore before she realized that
she had delayed too long to regain it. The Dorsets, the Stepneys,
the Brys—all the actors and witnesses in the miserable drama—
had preceded her with their version of the case; and, even had
she seen the least chance of gaining a hearing for her own,
some obscure disdain and reluctance would have restrained
her. She knew it was not by explanations and counter-charges
that she could ever hope to recover her lost standing; but even
had she felt the least trust in their efficacy, she would still have
been held back by the feeling which had kept her from defend-
ing herself to Gerty Farish—a feeling that was half pride and half
humiliation. For though she knew she had been ruthlesssly sacrificed to Bertha Dorset's determination to win back her husband, and though her own relation to Dorset had been that of the
merest good-fellowship, yet she had been perfectly aware from
the outset that her part in the affair was, as Carry Fisher brutally
put it, to distract Dorset's attention from his wife. That was what
she was "there for": it was the price she had chosen to pay for
three months of luxury and freedom from care. Her habit of res-

olutely facing the facts, in her rare moments of introspection, did not now allow her to put any false gloss on the situation. She had suffered for the very faithfulness with which she had carried out her part of the tacit compact, but the part was not a handsome one at best, and she saw it now in all the ugliness of failure.

She saw, too, in the same uncompromising light, the train of consequences resulting from that failure; and these became clearer to her with every day of her weary lingering in town. She stayed on partly for the comfort of Gerty Farish's nearness, and partly for lack of knowing where to go. She understood well enough the nature of the task before her. She must set out to regain, little by little, the position she had lost; and the first step in the tedious task was to find out, as soon as possible, on how many of her friends she could count. Her hopes were mainly centred on Mrs. Trenor, who had treasures of easy-going tolerance for those who were amusing or useful to her, and in the noisy rush of whose existence the still small voice of detraction was slow to make itself heard. But Judy, though she must have been apprised of Miss Bart's return, had not even recognized it by the formal note of condolence which her friend's bereavement demanded. Any advance on Lily's side might have been perilous: there was nothing to do but to trust to the happy chance of an accidental meeting, and Lily knew that, even so late in the season, there was always a hope of running across her friends in their frequent passages through town.

To this end she assiduously showed herself at the restaurants they frequented, where, attended by the troubled Gerty, she lunched luxuriously, as she said, on her expectations.

"My dear Gerty, you wouldn't have me let the headwaiter see that I've nothing to live on but Aunt Julia's legacy? Think of Grace Stepney's satisfaction if she came in and found us lunching on cold mutton and tea! What sweet shall we have today, dear—*Coupe Jacques* or *Pêches à la Melba?*"*

---

*French desserts: *Coupe Jacques* consists of fruit soaked in liqueurs and served on strawberry or lemon ice; *Pêches à la Melba* are cooked peaches served with vanilla ice cream and raspberry sauce and are named after the Australian soprano Nellie Melba (1861–1931).

She dropped the *menu* abruptly, with a quick heightening of colour, and Gerty, following her glance, was aware of the advance, from an inner room, of a party headed by Mrs. Trenor and Carry Fisher. It was impossible for these ladies and their companions—among whom Lily had at once distinguished both Trenor and Rosedale—not to pass, in going out, the table at which the two girls were seated; and Gerty's sense of the fact betrayed itself in the helpless trepidation of her manner. Miss Bart, on the contrary, borne forward on the wave of her buoyant grace, and neither shrinking from her friends nor appearing to lie in wait for them, gave to the encounter the touch of naturalness which she could impart to the most strained situations. Such embarrassment as was shown was on Mrs. Trenor's side, and manifested itself in the mingling of exaggerated warmth with imperceptible reservations. Her loudly affirmed pleasure at seeing Miss Bart took the form of a nebulous generalization, which included neither enquiries as to her future nor the expression of a definite wish to see her again. Lily, well-versed in the language of these omissions, knew that they were equally intelligible to the other members of the party: even Rosedale, flushed as he was with the importance of keeping such company, at once took the temperature of Mrs. Trenor's cordiality, and reflected it in his off-hand greeting of Miss Bart. Trenor, red and uncomfortable, had cut short his salutations on the pretext of a word to say to the head-waiter; and the rest of the group soon melted away in Mrs. Trenor's wake.

It was over in a moment—the waiter, *menu* in hand, still hung on the result of the choice between *Coupe Jacques* and *Pêches à la Melba*—but Miss Bart, in the interval, had taken the measure of her fate. Where Judy Trenor led, all the world would follow; and Lily had the doomed sense of the castaway who has signalled in vain to fleeing sails.

In a flash she remembered Mrs. Trenor's complaints of Carry Fisher's rapacity, and saw that they denoted an unexpected acquaintance with her husband's private affairs. In the large tumultuous disorder of the life at Bellomont, where no one seemed to have time to observe any one else, and private aims and personal interests were swept along unheeded in the rush of collective activities, Lily had fancied herself sheltered from inconvenient scrutiny; but if Judy knew when Mrs. Fisher borrowed money of her husband, was she likely to ignore the same transaction on Lily's part? If she was careless of his affections she was plainly jealous of his pocket; and in that fact Lily read the explanation of her rebuff. The immediate result of these conclusions was the passionate resolve to pay back her debt to Trenor. That obligation discharged, she would have but a thousand dollars of Mrs. Peniston's legacy left, and nothing to live on but her own small income, which was considerably less than Gerty Farish's wretched pittance; but this consideration gave way to the imperative claim of her wounded pride. She must be quits with the Trenors first; after that she would take thought for the future.

In her ignorance of legal procrastinations she had supposed that her legacy would be paid over within a few days of the reading of her aunt's will; and after an interval of anxious suspense, she wrote to enquire the cause of the delay. There was another interval before Mrs. Peniston's lawyer, who was also one of the executors, replied to the effect that, some questions having arisen relative to the interpretation of the will, he and his associates might not be in a position to pay the legacies till the close of the twelvemonth legally allotted for their settlement. Bewildered and indignant, Lily resolved to try the effect of a personal appeal; but she returned from her expedition with a sense of the powerlessness of beauty and charm against the unfeeling processes of the law. It seemed intolerable to live on for another year under the weight of her debt; and in her extremity she decided to turn to Miss Stepney, who still lingered in town, immersed in the delectable duty of "going over" her benefactress's effects. It was bitter enough for Lily to ask a favour of Grace Stepney, but the alternative was bitterer still; and one morning she presented herself at Mrs. Peniston's, where Grace, for the facilitation of her pious task, had taken up a provisional abode.

The strangeness of entering as a suppliant the house where she had so long commanded, increased Lily's desire to shorten the ordeal; and when Miss Stepney entered the darkened drawing-room, rustling with the best quality of crape, her visitor went straight to the point: would she be willing to advance the amount of the expected legacy?

Grace, in reply, wept and wondered at the request, bemoaned

the inexorableness of the law, and was astonished that Lily had
not realized the exact similarity of their positions. Did she think
that only the payment of the legacies had been delayed? Why,
Miss Stepney herself had not received a penny of her inheritance, and was paying rent—yes, actually!—for the privilege of
living in a house that belonged to her. She was sure it was not
what poor dear cousin Julia would have wished—she had told
the executors so to their faces; but they were inaccessible to reason, and there was nothing to do but to wait. Let Lily take example by her, and be patient—let them both remember how
beautifully patient cousin Julia had always been.

Lily made a movement which showed her imperfect assimi-
lation of this example. "But you will have everything, Grace—it
would be easy for you to borrow ten times the amount I am asking for."

"Borrow—easy for me to borrow?" Grace Stepney rose up
before her, in sable wrath. "Do you imagine for a moment that I
would raise money on my expectations from cousin Julia, when
I know so well her unspeakable horror of every transaction of the
sort? Why, Lily, if you must know the truth, it was the idea of
your being in debt that brought on her illness—you remember
she had a slight attack before you sailed. Oh, I don't know the
particulars, of course—I don't *want* to know them—but there
were rumours about your affairs that made her most unhappy—
no one could be with her without seeing that. I can't help it if
you are offended by my telling you this now—if I can do anything to make you realize the folly of your course, and how
deeply *she* disapproved of it, I shall feel it is the truest way of
making up to you for her loss."

5

IT SEEMED TO LILY, as Mrs. Peniston's door closed on her, that she was taking a final leave of her old life. The future stretched before her dull and bare as the deserted length of Fifth Avenue, and opportunities showed as meagerly as the few cabs trailing in quest of fares that did not come. The completeness of the analogy was, however, disturbed as she reached the sidewalk by the rapid approach of a hansom which pulled up at sight of her.

From beneath its luggage-laden top, she caught the wave of a signalling hand; and the next moment Mrs. Fisher, springing to the street, had folded her in a demonstrative embrace.

"My dear, you don't mean to say you're still in town? When I saw you the other day at Sherry's I didn't have time to ask——" She broke off, and added with a burst of frankness: "The truth is I was *horrid*, Lily, and I've wanted to tell you so ever since."

"Oh——" Miss Bart protested, drawing back from her penitent clasp; but Mrs. Fisher went on with her usual directness: "Look here, Lily, don't let's beat about the bush: half the trouble in life is caused by pretending there isn't any. That's not my way, and I can only say I'm thoroughly ashamed of myself for following the other women's lead. But we'll talk of that by and bye— tell me now where you're staying and what your plans are. I don't suppose you're keeping house in there with Grace Stepney, eh?—and it struck me you might be rather at loose ends."

In Lily's present mood there was no resisting the honest friendliness of this appeal, and she said with a smile: "I *am* at loose ends for the moment, but Gerty Farish is still in town, and she's good enough to let me be with her whenever she can spare the time."

Mrs. Fisher made a slight grimace. "H'm—that's a temperate joy. Oh, I know—Gerty's a trump, and worth all the rest of us put together; but *à la longue** you're used to a little higher sea-soning, aren't you, dear? And besides, I suppose she'll be off her-self before long—the first of August, you say? Well, look here, you can't spend your summer in town; we'll talk of that later too. But meanwhile, what do you say to putting a few things in a trunk and coming down with me to the Sam Gormers' tonight?"

And as Lily stared at the breathless suddenness of the sug-gestion, she continued with her easy laugh: "You don't know them and they don't know you; but that don't make a rap of dif-ference. They've taken the Van Alstyne place at Roslyn,† and I've got *carte blanche* to bring my friends down there—the more the merrier. They do things awfully well, and there's to be rather a jolly party there this week——" she broke off, checked by an un-definable change in Miss Bart's expression. "Oh, I don't mean *your* particular set, you know: rather a different crowd, but very good fun. The fact is, the Gormers have struck out on a line of their own: what they want is to have a good time, and to have it in their own way. They gave the other thing a few months' trial, under my distinguished auspices, and they were really doing ex-tremely well—getting on a good deal faster than the Brys, just because they didn't care as much—but suddenly they decided that the whole business bored them, and that what they wanted was a crowd they could really feel at home with. Rather original of them, don't you think so? Mattie Gormer *has* got aspirations still; women always have; but she's awfully easy-going, and Sam won't be bothered, and they both like to be the most important people in sight, so they've started a sort of continuous perfor-mance of their own, a kind of social Coney Island,‡ where every-body is welcome who can make noise enough and doesn't put on airs. *I* think it's awfully good fun myself—some of the artistic set, you know, any pretty actress that's going, and so on. This week, for instance, they have Audrey Anstell, who made such a hit last spring in 'The Winning of Winny'; and Paul Morpeth—he's painting Mattie Gormer—and the Dick Bellingers, and

---

*In the long run (French).
†Town on the north shore of Long Island.
‡Amusement park, with a long boardwalk, in Brooklyn, New York.

Kate Corby—well, every one you can think of who's jolly and makes a row. Now don't stand there with your nose in the air, my dear—it will be a good deal better than a broiling Sunday in town, and you'll find clever people as well as noisy ones—Morpeth, who admires Mattie enormously, always brings one or two of his set."

Mrs. Fisher drew Lily toward the hansom with friendly authority. "Jump in now, there's a dear, and we'll drive round to your hotel and have your things packed, and then we'll have tea, and the two maids can meet us at the train."

It was a good deal better than a broiling Sunday in town—of that no doubt remained to Lily as, reclining in the shade of a leafy verandah, she looked seaward across a stretch of greensward picturesquely dotted with groups of ladies in lace raiment and men in tennis flannels. The huge Van Alstyne house and its rambling dependencies were packed to their fullest capacity with the Gormers' week-end guests, who now, in the radiance of the Sunday forenoon, were dispersing themselves over the grounds in quest of the various distractions the place afforded: distractions ranging from tennis-courts to shooting-galleries, from bridge and whiskey within doors to motors and steam-launches without. Lily had the odd sense of having been caught up into the crowd as carelessly as a passenger is gathered in by an express train. The blonde and genial Mrs. Gormer might, indeed, have figured the conductor, calmly assigning seats to the rush of travellers, while Carry Fisher represented the porter pushing their bags into place, giving them their numbers for the dining-car, and warning them when their station was at hand. The train, meanwhile, had scarcely slackened speed—life whizzed on with a deafening rattle and roar, in which one traveller at least found a welcome refuge from the sound of her own thoughts.

The Gormer *milieu* represented a social out-skirt which Lily had always fastidiously avoided; but it struck her, now that she was in it, as only a flamboyant copy of her own world, a caricature approximating the real thing as the "society play" approaches the manners of the drawing-room. The people about her were doing the same things as the Trenors, the Van Osburghs and the Dorsets: the difference lay in a hundred shades of aspect and manner, from the pattern of the men's waistcoats to the inflexion of the women's voices. Everything was pitched in a higher key, and there was more of each thing: more noise, more colour, more champagne, more familiarity—but also greater good-nature, less rivalry, and a fresher capacity for enjoyment.

Miss Bart's arrival had been welcomed with an uncritical friendliness that first irritated her pride and then brought her to a sharp sense of her own situation—of the place in life which, for the moment, she must accept and make the best of it. These people knew her story—of that her first long talk with Carry Fisher had left no doubt: she was publicly branded as the heroine of a "queer" episode—but instead of shrinking from her as her own friends had done, they received her without question into the easy promiscuity of their lives. They swallowed her past as easily as they did Miss Anstell's, and with no apparent sense of any difference in the size of the mouthful: all they asked was that she should—in her own way, for they recognized a diversity of gifts—contribute as much to the general amusement as that graceful actress, whose talents, when off the stage, were of the most varied order. Lily felt at once that any tendency to be "stuck-up," to mark a sense of differences and distinctions, would be fatal to her continuance in the Gormer set. To be taken in on such terms—and into such a world!—was hard enough to the lingering pride in her; but she realized, with a pang of self-contempt, that to be excluded from it would, after all, be harder still. For, almost at once, she had felt the insidious charm of slipping back into a life where every material difficulty was smoothed away. The sudden escape from a stifling hotel in a dusty deserted city to the space and luxury of a great country-house fanned by sea breezes, had produced a state of moral lassitude agreeable enough after the nervous tension and physical discomfort of the past weeks. For the moment she must yield to the refreshment her senses craved—after that she would reconsider her situation, and take counsel with her dignity. Her enjoyment of her surroundings was, indeed, tinged by the unpleasant consideration that she was accepting the hospitality and courting the approval of people she had disdained under other conditions. But she was growing less sensitive on such points: a hard glaze of indifference was fast forming over her delicacies and susceptibilities, and each concession to expediency hardened the surface a little more.

On the Monday, when the party disbanded with uproarious adieux, the return to town threw into stronger relief the charms of the life she was leaving. The other guests were dispersing to take up the same existence in a different setting: some at Newport, some at Bar Harbour,* some in the elaborate rusticity of an Adirondack camp. Even Gerty Farish, who welcomed Lily's return with tender solicitude, would soon be preparing to join the aunt with whom she spent her summers on Lake George:† only Lily herself remained without plan or purpose, stranded in a backwater of the great current of pleasure. But Carry Fisher, who had insisted on transporting her to her own house, where she herself was to perch for a day or two on the way to the Brys' camp, came to the rescue with a new suggestion.

"Look here, Lily—I'll tell you what it is: I want you to take my place with Mattie Gormer this summer. They're taking a party out to Alaska next month in their private car,‡ and Mattie, who is the laziest woman alive, wants me to go with them, and relieve her of the bother of arranging things; but the Brys want me too—oh, yes, we've made it up: didn't I tell you?—and, to put it frankly, though I like the Gormers best, there's more profit for me in the Brys. The fact is, they want to try Newport this summer, and if I can make it a success for them they—well, they'll make it a success for *me*." Mrs. Fisher clasped her hands enthusiastically. "Do you know, Lily, the more I think of my idea the better I like it—quite as much for you as for myself. The Gormers have both taken a tremendous fancy to you, and the trip to Alaska is—well—the very thing I should want for you just at present."

Miss Bart lifted her eyes with a keen glance. "To take me out of my friends' way, you mean?" she said quietly; and Mrs. Fisher

---

*Summer resort on the coast of Maine.

†Resort in upstate New York.

‡Private railway car.

responded with a deprecating kiss: "To keep you out of their sight till they realize how much they miss you."

Miss Bart went with the Gormers to Alaska; and the expedition, if it did not produce the effect anticipated by her friend, had at least the negative advantage of removing her from the fiery centre of criticism and discussion. Gerty Farish had opposed the plan with all the energy of her somewhat inarticulate nature. She had even offered to give up her visit to Lake George, and remain in town with Miss Bart, if the latter would renounce her journey; but Lily could disguise her real distaste for this plan under a sufficiently valid reason.

"You dear innocent, don't you see," she protested, "that Carry is quite right, and that I must take up my usual life, and go about among people as much as possible? If my old friends choose to believe lies about me I shall have to make new ones, that's all; and you know beggars mustn't be choosers. Not that I don't like Mattie Gormer—I *do* like her: she's kind and honest and unaffected; and don't you suppose I feel grateful to her for making me welcome at a time when, as you've yourself seen, my own family have unanimously washed their hands of me?"

Gerty shook her head, mutely unconvinced. She felt not only that Lily was cheapening herself by making use of an intimacy she would never have cultivated from choice, but that, in drifting back now to her former manner of life, she was forfeiting her last chance of ever escaping from it. Gerty had but an obscure conception of what Lily's actual experience had been: but its consequences had established a lasting hold on her pity since the memorable night when she had offered up her own secret hope to her friend's extremity. To characters like Gerty's such a sacrifice constitutes a moral claim on the part of the person in whose behalf it has been made. Having once helped Lily, she must continue to help her; and helping her, must believe in her, because faith is the main-spring of such natures. But even if Miss Bart, after her renewed taste of the amenities of life, could have returned to the barrenness of a New York August, mitigated only by poor Gerty's presence, her worldly wisdom would have counselled her against such an act of abnegation. She knew that Carry Fisher was right: that an opportune absence might be the first step toward rehabilitation, and that, at any rate, to linger on in town out of season was a fatal admission of defeat.

From the Gormers' tumultuous progress across their native continent, she returned with an altered view of her situation. The renewed habit of luxury—the daily waking to an assured absence of care and presence of material ease—gradually blunted her appreciation of these values, and left her more conscious of the void they could not fill. Mattie Gormer's undiscriminating good-nature, and the slap-dash sociability of her friends, who treated Lily precisely as they treated each other—all these characteristic notes of difference began to wear upon her endurance; and the more she saw to criticize in her companions, the less justification she found for making use of them. The longing to get back to her former surroundings hardened to a fixed idea; but with the strengthening of her purpose came the inevitable perception that, to attain it, she must exact fresh concessions from her pride. These, for the moment, took the unpleasant form of continuing to cling to her hosts after their return from Alaska. Little as she was in the key of their *milieu*, her immense social facility, her long habit of adapting herself to others without suffering her own outline to be blurred, the skilled manipulation of all the polished implements of her craft, had won for her an important place in the Gormer group. If their resonant hilarity could never be hers, she contributed a note of easy elegance more valuable to Mattie Gormer than the louder passages of the band. Sam Gormer and his special cronies stood indeed a little in awe of her; but Mattie's following, headed by Paul Morpeth, made her feel that they prized her for the very qualities they most conspicuously lacked. If Morpeth, whose social indolence was as great as his artistic activity, had abandoned himself to the easy current of the Gormer existence, where the minor exactions of politeness were unknown or ignored, and a man could either break his engagements, or keep them in a painting-jacket and slippers, he still preserved his sense of differences, and his appreciation of graces he had no time to cultivate. During the preparations for the Brys' *tableaux* he had been immensely struck by Lily's plastic possibilities—"not the face: too self-controlled for expression; but the rest of her—gad, what a model she'd make!"—and though his abhorrence of the world in which he had seen her was too great for him to think of seeking her there, he was fully alive to the privilege of having her to look at and listen to while he lounged in Mattie Gormer's dishevelled drawing-room.

Lily had thus formed, in the tumult of her surroundings, a little nucleus of friendly relations which mitigated the crudeness of her course in lingering with the Gormers after their return. Nor was she without pale glimpses of her own world, especially since the breaking-up of the Newport season had set the social current once more toward Long Island. Kate Corby, whose tastes made her as promiscuous as Carry Fisher was rendered by her necessities, occasionally descended on the Gormers, where, after a first stare of surprise, she took Lily's presence almost too much as a matter of course. Mrs. Fisher, too, appearing frequently in the neighbourhood, drove over to impart her experiences and give Lily what she called the latest report from the weather-bureau; and the latter, who had never directly invited her confidence, could yet talk with her more freely than with Gerty Farish, in whose presence it was impossible even to admit the existence of much that Mrs. Fisher conveniently took for granted.

Mrs. Fisher, moreover, had no embarrassing curiosity. She did not wish to probe the inwardness of Lily's situation, but simply to view it from the outside, and draw her conclusions accordingly; and these conclusions, at the end of a confidential talk, she summed up to her friend in the succinct remark: "You must marry as soon as you can."

Lily uttered a faint laugh—for once Mrs. Fisher lacked originality. "Do you mean, like Gerty Farish, to recommend the unfailing panacea of 'a great man's love'?"

"No—I don't think either of my candidates would answer to that description," said Mrs. Fisher after a pause of reflection.

"Either? Are there actually two?"

"Well, perhaps I ought to say one and a half—for the moment."

Miss Bart received this with increasing amusement. "Other things being equal, I think I should prefer a half-husband: who is he?"

"Don't fly out at me till you hear my reasons—George Dorset."

"Oh——" Lily murmured reproachfully; but Mrs. Fisher pressed on unrebuffed. "Well, why not? They had a few weeks' honeymoon when they first got back from Europe, but now things are going badly with them again. Bertha has been behaving more than ever like a madwoman, and George's powers of credulity are very nearly exhausted. They're at their place here, you know, and I spent last Sunday with them. It was a ghastly party—no one else but poor Neddy Silverton, who looks like a galley-slave (they used to talk of my making that poor boy unhappy!)—and after luncheon George carried me off on a long walk, and told me the end would have to come soon."

Miss Bart made an incredulous gesture. "As far as that goes, the end will never come—Bertha will always know how to get him back when she wants him."

Mrs. Fisher continued to observe her tentatively. "Not if he has any one else to turn to! Yes—that's just what it comes to: the poor creature can't stand alone. And I remember him such a good fellow, full of life and enthusiasm." She paused, and went on, dropping her glance from Lily's: "He wouldn't stay with her ten minutes if he *knew*——"

"Knew——?" Miss Bart repeated.

"What *you* must, for instance—with the opportunities you've had! If he had positive proof, I mean——"

Lily interrupted her with a deep blush of displeasure. "Please let us drop the subject, Carry: it's too odious to me." And to divert her companion's attention she added, with an attempt at lightness: "And your second candidate? We must not forget him."

Mrs. Fisher echoed her laugh. "I wonder if you'll cry out just as loud if I say—Sim Rosedale?"

Miss Bart did not cry out: she sat silent, gazing thoughtfully at her friend. The suggestion, in truth, gave expression to a possibility which, in the last weeks, had more than once returned to her; but after a moment she said carelessly: "Mr. Rosedale wants a wife who can establish him in the bosom of the Van Osburghs and Trenors."

Mrs. Fisher caught her up eagerly. "And so *you* could—with

his money! Don't you see how beautifully it would work out for you both?"

"I don't see any way of making him see it," Lily returned, with a laugh intended to dismiss the subject.

But in reality it lingered with her long after Mrs. Fisher had taken leave. She had seen very little of Rosedale since her annexation by the Gormers, for he was still steadily bent on penetrating to the inner Paradise from which she was now excluded; but once or twice, when nothing better offered, he had turned up for a Sunday, and on these occasions he had left her in no doubt as to his view of her situation. That he still admired her was, more than ever, offensively evident; for in the Gormer circle, where he expanded as in his native element, there were no puzzling conventions to check the full expression of his approval. But it was in the quality of his admiration that she read his shrewd estimate of her case. He enjoyed letting the Gormers see that he had known "Miss Lily"—she was "Miss Lily" to him now—before they had had the faintest social existence: enjoyed more especially impressing Paul Morpeth with the distance to which their intimacy dated back. But he let it be felt that that intimacy was a mere ripple on the surface of a rushing social current, the kind of relaxation which a man of large interests and manifold preoccupations permits himself in his hours of ease.

The necessity of accepting this view of their past relation, and of meeting it in the key of pleasantry prevalent among her new friends, was deeply humiliating to Lily. But she dared less than ever to quarrel with Rosedale. She suspected that her rejection rankled among the most unforgettable of his rebuffs, and the fact that he knew something of her wretched transaction with Trenor, and was sure to put the basest construction on it, seemed to place her hopelessly in his power. Yet at Carry Fisher's suggestion a new hope had stirred in her. Much as she disliked Rosedale, she no longer absolutely despised him. For he was gradually attaining his object in life, and that, to Lily, was always less despicable than to miss it. With the slow unalterable persistency which she had always felt in him, he was making his way through the dense mass of social antagonisms. Already his wealth, and the masterly use he had made of it, were giving him an enviable prominence in the world of affairs, and placing Wall Street under obligations which only Fifth Avenue could repay. In response to these claims, his name began to figure on municipal committees and charitable boards; he appeared at banquets to distinguished strangers, and his candidacy at one of the fashionable clubs was discussed with diminishing opposition. He had figured once or twice at the Trenor dinners, and had learned to speak with just the right note of disdain of the big Van Osburgh crushes; and all he now needed was a wife whose affiliations would shorten the last tedious steps of his ascent. It was with that object that, a year earlier, he had fixed his affections on Miss Bart; but in the interval he had mounted nearer to the goal, while she had lost the power to abbreviate the remaining steps of the way. All this she saw with the clearness of vision that came to her in moments of despondency. It was success that dazzled her—she could distinguish facts plainly enough in the twilight of failure. And the twilight, as she now sought to pierce it, was gradually lighted by a faint spark of reassurance. Under the utilitarian motive of Rosedale's wooing she had felt, clearly enough, the heat of personal inclination. She would not have detested him so heartily had she not known that he dared to admire her. What, then, if the passion persisted, though the other motive had ceased to sustain it? She had never even tried to please him—he had been drawn to her in spite of her manifest disdain. What if she now chose to exert the power which, even in its passive state, he had felt so strongly? What if she made him marry her for love, now that he had no other reason for marrying her?

6

As became persons of their rising consequence, the Gormers were engaged in building a country-house on Long Island; and it was a part of Miss Bart's duty to attend her hostess on frequent visits of inspection to the new estate. There, while Mrs. Gormer plunged into problems of lighting and sanitation, Lily had leisure to wander, in the bright autumn air, along the tree-fringed bay to which the land declined. Little as she was addicted to solitude, there had come to be moments when it seemed a welcome escape from the empty noises of her life. She was weary of being swept passively along a current of pleasure and business in which she had no share; weary of seeing other people pursue amusement and squander money, while she felt herself of no more account among them than an expensive toy in the hands of a spoiled child.

It was in this frame of mind that, striking back from the shore one morning into the windings of an unfamiliar lane, she came suddenly upon the figure of George Dorset. The Dorset place was in the immediate neighbourhood of the Gormers' newly-acquired estate, and in her motor-flights thither with Mrs. Gormer, Lily had caught one or two passing glimpses of the couple; but they moved in so different an orbit that she had not considered the possibility of a direct encounter.

Dorset, swinging along with bent head, in moody abstraction, did not see Miss Bart till he was close upon her; but the sight, instead of bringing him to a halt, as she had half-expected, sent him toward her with an eagerness which found expression in his opening words.

"Miss Bart!—You'll shake hands, won't you? I've been hoping to meet you—I should have written to you if I'd dared." His face, with its tossed red hair and straggling moustache, had a driven uneasy look, as though life had become an unceasing race between himself and the thoughts at his heels.

The look drew a word of compassionate greeting from Lily, and he pressed on, as if encouraged by her tone: "I wanted to apologize—to ask you to forgive me for the miserable part I played——"

She checked him with a quick gesture. "Don't let us speak of it: I was very sorry for you," she said, with a tinge of disdain which, as she instantly perceived, was not lost on him.

He flushed to his haggard eyes, flushed so cruelly that she repented the thrust. "You might well be; you don't know—you must let me explain. I was deceived: abominably deceived——"

"I am still more sorry for you, then," she interposed, without irony; "but you must see that I am not exactly the person with whom the subject can be discussed."

He met this with a look of genuine wonder. "Why not? Isn't it to you, of all people, that I owe an explanation——"

"No explanation is necessary: the situation was perfectly clear to me."

"Ah——" he murmured, his head drooping again, and his irresolute hand switching at the underbrush along the lane. But as Lily made a movement to pass on, he broke out with fresh vehemence: "Miss Bart, for God's sake don't turn from me! We used to be good friends—you were always kind to me—and you don't know how I need a friend now."

The lamentable weakness of the words roused a motion of pity in Lily's breast. She too needed friends—she had tasted the pang of loneliness; and her resentment of Bertha Dorset's cruelty softened her heart to the poor wretch who was after all the chief of Bertha's victims.

"I still wish to be kind; I feel no ill-will toward you," she said. "But you must understand that after what has happened we can't be friends again—we can't see each other."

"Ah, you *are* kind—you're merciful—you always were!" He fixed his miserable gaze on her. "But why why can't we be friends— why not, when I've repented in dust and ashes?* Isn't it hard that you should condemn me to suffer for the falseness, the treachery

---

*The reference is to the Bible, Job 42:6, "Wherefore I abhor myself, and repent in dust and ashes" (KJV).

of others? I was punished enough at the time—is there to be no respite for me?"

"I should have thought you had found complete respite in the reconciliation which was effected at my expense," Lily began, with renewed impatience; but he broke in imploringly: "Don't put it that way—when that's been the worst of my punishment. My God! what could I do—wasn't I powerless? You were singled out as a sacrifice: any word I might have said would have been turned against you——"

"I have told you I don't blame you; all I ask you to understand is that, after the use Bertha chose to make of me—after all that her behaviour has since implied—it's impossible that you and I should meet."

He continued to stand before her, in his dogged weakness. "Is it—need it be? Mightn't there be circumstances——?" he checked himself, slashing at the wayside weeds in a wider radius. Then he began again: "Miss Bart, listen—give me a minute. If we're not to meet again, at least let me have a hearing now. You say we can't be friends after—after what has happened. But can't I at least appeal to your pity? Can't I move you if I ask you to think of me as a prisoner—a prisoner you alone can set free?"

Lily's inward start betrayed itself in a quick blush: was it possible that this was really the sense of Carry Fisher's adumbrations?

"I can't see how I can possibly be of any help to you," she murmured, drawing back a little from the mounting excitement of his look.

Her tone seemed to sober him, as it had so often done in his stormiest moments. The stubborn lines of his face relaxed, and he said, with an abrupt drop to docility: "You *would* see, if you'd be as merciful as you used to be: and heaven knows I've never needed it more."

She paused a moment, moved in spite of herself by this reminder of her influence over him. Her fibres had been softened by suffering, and the sudden glimpse into his mocked and broken life disarmed her contempt for his weakness.

"I am very sorry for you—I would help you willingly; but you must have other friends, other advisers."

"I never had a friend like you," he answered simply. "And besides—can't you see?—you're the only person"—his voice dropped to a whisper—"the only person who knows."

Again she felt her colour change; again her heart rose in precipitate throbs to meet what she felt was coming.

He lifted his eyes to her entreatingly. "You do see, don't you? You understand? I'm desperate—I'm at the end of my tether. I want to be free, and you can free me. I know you can. You don't want to keep me bound fast in hell, do you? You can't want to take such a vengeance as that. You were always kind—your eyes are kind now. You say you're sorry for me. Well, it rests with you to show it; and heaven knows there's nothing to keep you back. You understand, of course—there wouldn't be a hint of publicity—not a sound or a syllable to connect you with the thing. It would never come to that, you know: all I need is to be able to say definitely: 'I know this—and this—and this'—and the fight would drop, and the way be cleared, and the whole abominable business swept out of sight in a second."

He spoke pantingly, like a tired runner, with breaks of exhaustion between his words; and through the breaks she caught, as through the shifting rents of a fog, great golden vistas of peace and safety. For there was no mistaking the definite intention behind his vague appeal; she could have filled up the blanks without the help of Mrs. Fisher's insinuations. Here was a man who turned to her in the extremity of his loneliness and his humiliation: if she came to him at such a moment he would be hers with all the force of his deluded faith. And the power to make him so lay in her hand—lay there in a completeness he could not even remotely conjecture. Revenge and rehabilitation might be hers at a stroke—there was something dazzling in the completeness of the opportunity.

She stood silent, gazing away from him down the autumnal stretch of the deserted lane. And suddenly fear possessed her— fear of herself, and of the terrible force of the temptation. All her past weaknesses were like so many eager accomplices drawing her toward the path their feet had already smoothed. She turned quickly, and held out her hand to Dorset.

"Goodbye—I'm sorry; there's nothing in the world that I can do."

"Nothing? Ah, don't say that," he cried; "say what's true: that you abandon me like the others. You, the only creature who could have saved me!"

"Goodbye—goodbye," she repeated hurriedly; and as she moved away she heard him cry out on a last note of entreaty: "At least you'll let me see you once more?"

Lily, on regaining the Gormer grounds, struck rapidly across the lawn toward the unfinished house, where she fancied that her hostess might be speculating, and too resignedly, on the cause of her delay; for, like many unpunctual persons, Mrs. Gormer disliked to be kept waiting.

As Miss Bart reached the avenue, however, she saw a smart phaeton with a high-stepping pair disappear behind the shrubbery in the direction of the gate; and on the doorstep stood Mrs. Gormer, with a glow of retrospective pleasure on her open countenance. At sight of Lily the glow deepened to an embarrassed red, and she said with a slight laugh: "Did you see my visitor? Oh, I thought you came back by the avenue. It was Mrs. George Dorset—she said she'd dropped in to make a neighbourly call."

Lily met the announcement with her usual composure, though her experience of Bertha's idiosyncrasies would not have led her to include the neighbourly instinct among them; and Mrs. Gormer, relieved to see that she gave no sign of surprise, went on with a deprecating laugh: "Of course what really brought her was curiosity—she made me take her all over the house. But no one could have been nicer—no airs, you know, and so good-natured: I can quite see why people think her so fascinating."

This surprising event, coinciding too completely with her meeting with Dorset to be regarded as contingent upon it, had yet immediately struck Lily with a vague sense of foreboding. It was not in Bertha's habits to be neighbourly, much less to make advances to any one outside the immediate circle of her affinities. She had always consistently ignored the world of outer aspirants, or had recognized its individual members only when prompted by motives of self-interest; and the very capriciousness of her condescensions had, as Lily was aware, given them special value in the eyes of the persons she distinguished. Lily saw this now in Mrs. Gormer's unconcealable complacency, and in the happy irrelevance with which, for the next day or two, she quoted Bertha's opinions and speculated on the origin of her gown. All the secret ambitions which Mrs. Gormer's native indolence, and the attitude of her companions, kept in habitual abeyance, were now germinating afresh in the glow of Bertha's advances; and whatever the cause of the latter, Lily saw that, if they were followed up, they were likely to have a disturbing effect upon her own future.

She had arranged to break the length of her stay with her new friends by one or two visits to other acquaintances as recent; and on her return from this somewhat depressing excursion she was immediately conscious that Mrs. Dorset's influence was still in the air. There had been another exchange of visits, a tea at a country-club, an encounter at a hunt ball; there was even a rumour of an approaching dinner, which Mattie Gormer, with an unnatural effort at discretion, tried to smuggle out of the conversation whenever Miss Bart took part in it.

The latter had already planned to return to town after a farewell Sunday with her friends; and, with Gerty Farish's aid, had discovered a small private hotel where she might establish herself for the winter. The hotel being on the edge of a fashionable neighbourhood, the price of the few square feet she was to occupy was considerably in excess of her means; but she found a justification for her dislike of poorer quarters in the argument that, at this particular juncture, it was of the utmost importance to keep up a show of prosperity. In reality, it was impossible for her, while she had the means to pay her way for a week ahead, to lapse into a form of existence like Gerty Farish's. She had never been so near the brink of insolvency; but she could at least manage to meet her weekly hotel bill, and having settled the heaviest of her previous debts out of the money she had received from Trenor, she had a still fair margin of credit to go upon. The situation, however, was not agreeable enough to lull her to complete unconsciousness of its insecurity. Her rooms, with their cramped outlook down a sallow vista of brick walls and fireescapes, her lonely meals in the dark restaurant with its surcharged ceiling and haunting smell of coffee—all these material discomforts, which were yet to be accounted as so many privileges soon to be withdrawn, kept constantly before her the disadvantages of her state, and her mind reverted the more insistently to Mrs. Fisher's counsels. Beat about the question as she would, she knew the outcome of it was that she must try to marry Rosedale; and in this conviction she was fortified by an unexpected visit from George Dorset.

She found him, on the first Sunday after her return to town, pacing her narrow sitting-room to the imminent peril of the few knick-knacks with which she had tried to disguise its plush exuberances; but the sight of her seemed to quiet him, and he said meekly that he hadn't come to bother her—that he asked only to be allowed to sit for half an hour and talk of anything she liked. In reality, as she knew, he had but one subject: himself and his wretchedness; and it was the need of her sympathy that had drawn him back. But he began with a pretence of questioning her about herself, and as she replied, she saw that, for the first time, a faint realization of her plight penetrated the dense surface of his self-absorption. Was it possible that her old beast of an aunt had actually cut her off? That she was living alone like this because there was no one else for her to go to, and that she really hadn't more than enough to keep alive on till the wretched little legacy was paid? The fibres of sympathy were nearly atrophied in him, but he was suffering so intensely that he had a faint glimpse of what other sufferings might mean—and, as she perceived, an almost simultaneous perception of the way in which her particular misfortunes might serve him.

When at length she dismissed him, on the pretext that she must dress for dinner, he lingered entreatingly on the threshold to blurt out: "It's been such a comfort—do say you'll let me see you again—" But to this direct appeal it was impossible to give an assent; and she said with friendly decisiveness: "I'm sorry—but you know why I can't."

He coloured to the eyes, pushed the door shut, and stood before her embarrassed but insistent. "I know how you might, if you would—if things were different—and it lies with you to make them so. It's just a word to say, and you put me out of my misery!"

Their eyes met, and for a second she trembled again with the nearness of the temptation. "You're mistaken; I know nothing; I saw nothing," she exclaimed, striving by sheer force of reiteration, to build a barrier between herself and her peril; and as he turned away, groaning out "You sacrifice us both," she continued to repeat, as if it were a charm: "I know nothing—absolutely nothing."

Lily had seen little of Rosedale since her illuminating talk with Mrs. Fisher, but on the two or three occasions when they had met she was conscious of having distinctly advanced in his favour. There could be no doubt that he admired her as much as ever, and she believed it rested with herself to raise his admiration to the point where it should bear down the lingering counsels of expediency. The task was not an easy one; but neither was it easy, in her long sleepless nights, to face the thought of what George Dorset was so clearly ready to offer. Baseness for baseness, she hated the other least: there were even moments when a marriage with Rosedale seemed the only honourable solution of her difficulties. She did not indeed let her imagination range beyond the day of plighting: after that everything faded into a haze of material well-being, in which the personality of her benefactor remained mercifully vague. She had learned, in her long vigils, that there were certain things not good to think of, certain midnight images that must at any cost be exorcised—and one of these was the image of herself as Rosedale's wife.

Carry Fisher, on the strength, as she frankly owned, of the Brys' Newport success, had taken for the autumn months a small house at Tuxedo; and thither Lily was bound on the Sunday after Dorset's visit. Though it was nearly dinner-time when she arrived, her hostess was still out, and the firelit quiet of the small silent house descended on her spirit with a sense of peace and familiarity. It may be doubted if such an emotion had ever before been evoked by Carry Fisher's surroundings; but, contrasted to the world in which Lily had lately lived, there was an air of repose and stability in the very placing of the furniture, and in the quiet competence of the parlour-maid who led her up to her room. Mrs. Fisher's unconventionality was, after all, a merely superficial divergence from an inherited social creed, while the manners of the Gormer circle represented their first attempt to formulate such a creed for themselves.

It was the first time since her return from Europe that Lily had found herself in a congenial atmosphere, and the stirring of familiar associations had almost prepared her, as she descended the stairs before dinner, to enter upon a group of her old acquaintances. But this expectation was instantly checked by the reflection that the friends who remained loyal were precisely those who would be least willing to expose her to such encounters; and it was hardly with surprise that she found, instead, Mr. Rosedale kneeling domestically on the drawing-room hearth before his hostess's little girl.

Rosedale in the paternal rôle was hardly a figure to soften Lily; yet she could not but notice a quality of homely goodness in his advances to the child. They were not, at any rate, the premeditated and perfunctory endearments of the guest under his hostess's eye, for he and the little girl had the room to themselves; and something in his attitude made him seem a simple and kindly being compared to the small critical creature who endured his homage. Yes, he would be kind—Lily, from the threshold, had time to feel—kind in his gross, unscrupulous, rapacious way, the way of the predatory creature with his mate. She had but a moment in which to consider whether this glimpse of the fireside man mitigated her repugnance, or gave it, rather, a more concrete and intimate form; for at sight of her he was immediately on his feet again, the florid and dominant Rosedale of Mattie Gormer's drawing-room.

It was no surprise to Lily to find that he had been selected as her only fellow-guest. Though she and her hostess had not met since the latter's tentative discussion of her future, Lily knew that the acuteness which enabled Mrs. Fisher to lay a safe and pleasant course through a world of antagonistic forces was not infrequently exercised for the benefit of her friends. It was, in fact, characteristic of Carry that, while she actively gleaned her own stores from the fields of affluence, her real sympathies were on the other side—with the unlucky, the unpopular, the unsuccessful, with all her hungry fellow-toilers in the shorn stubble of success.

Mrs. Fisher's experience guarded her against the mistake of exposing Lily, for the first evening, to the unmitigated impression of Rosedale's personality. Kate Corby and two or three men dropped in to dinner, and Lily, alive to every detail of her friend's method, saw that such opportunities as had been contrived for her were to be deferred till she had, as it were, gained courage to make effectual use of them. She had a sense of acquiescing in this plan with the passiveness of a sufferer resigned to the surgeon's touch, and this feeling of almost lethargic helplessness continued when, after the departure of the guests, Mrs. Fisher followed her upstairs.

"May I come in and smoke a cigarette over your fire? If we talk in my room we shall disturb the child." Mrs. Fisher looked about her with the eye of the solicitous hostess. "I hope you've managed to make yourself comfortable, dear? Isn't it a jolly little house? It's such a blessing to have a few quiet weeks with the baby."

Carry, in her rare moments of prosperity, became so expansively maternal that Miss Bart sometimes wondered whether, if she could ever get time and money enough, she would not end devoting them both to her daughter.

"It's a well-earned rest: I'll say that for myself," she continued, sinking down with a sigh of content on the pillowed lounge near the fire. "Louisa Bry is a stern task-master: I often used to wish myself back with the Gormers. Talk of love making people jealous and suspicious—it's nothing to social ambition! Louisa used to lie awake at night wondering whether the women who called on *me* called on *her* because I was with her, or on *her* because she was with me; and she was always laying traps to find out what I thought. Of course I had to disown my oldest friends, rather than let her suspect she owed me the chance of making a single acquaintance—when, all the while, that was what she had me there for, and what she wrote me a handsome cheque for when the season was over!"

Mrs. Fisher was not a woman who talked of herself without cause, and the practice of direct speech, far from precluding in her an occasional resort to circuitous methods, served rather, at crucial moments, the purpose of the juggler's chatter while he shifts the contents of his sleeves. Through the haze of her cigarette smoke she continued to gaze meditatively at Miss Bart, who, having dismissed her maid, sat before the toilet-table shaking out over her shoulders the loosened undulations of her hair.

"Your hair's wonderful, Lily. Thinner—? What does that

matter, when it's so light and alive? So many women's worries seem to go straight to their hair—but yours looks as if there had never been an anxious thought under it. I never saw you look better than you did this evening. Mattie Gormer told me that Morpeth wanted to paint you—why don't you let him?"

Miss Bart's immediate answer was to address a critical glance to the reflection of the countenance under discussion. Then she said, with a slight touch of irritation: "I don't care to accept a portrait from Paul Morpeth."

Mrs. Fisher mused. "N—no. And just now, especially—well, he can do you after you're married." She waited a moment, and then went on: "By the way, I had a visit from Mattie the other day. She turned up here last Sunday—and with Bertha Dorset, of all people in the world!"

She paused again to measure the effect of this announcement on her hearer, but the brush in Miss Bart's lifted hand maintained its unwavering stroke from brow to nape.

"I never was more astonished," Mrs. Fisher pursued. "I don't know two women less predestined to intimacy—from Bertha's standpoint, that is; for of course poor Mattie thinks it natural enough that she should be singled out—I've no doubt the rabbit always thinks it is fascinating the anaconda. Well, you know I've always told you that Mattie secretly longed to bore herself with the really fashionable; and now that the chance has come, I see that she's capable of sacrificing all her old friends to it."

Lily laid aside her brush and turned a penetrating glance upon her friend. "Including *me?*" she suggested.

"Ah, my dear," murmured Mrs. Fisher, rising to push back a log from the hearth.

"That's what Bertha means, isn't it?" Miss Bart went on steadily. "For of course she always means something; and before I left Long Island I saw that she was beginning to lay her toils for Mattie."

Mrs. Fisher sighed evasively. "She has her fast now, at any rate. To think of that loud independence of Mattie's being only a subtler form of snobbishness! Bertha can already make her believe anything she pleases—and I'm afraid she's begun, my poor child, by insinuating horrors about you."

Lily flushed under the shadow of her drooping hair. "The

world is too vile," she murmured, averting herself from Mrs. Fisher's anxious scrutiny.

"It's not a pretty place; and the only way to keep a footing in it is to fight it on its own terms—and above all, my dear, not alone!" Mrs. Fisher gathered up her floating implications in a resolute grasp. "You've told me so little that I can only guess what has been happening; but in the rush we all live in there's no time to keep on hating any one without a cause, and if Bertha is still nasty enough to want to injure you with other people it must be because she's still afraid of you. From her standpoint there's only one reason for being afraid of you; and my own idea is that, if you want to punish her, you hold the means in your hand. I believe you can marry George Dorset tomorrow; but if you don't care for that particular form of retaliation, the only thing to save you from Bertha is to marry somebody else."

THE LIGHT PROJECTED ON the situation by Mrs. Fisher had the cheerless distinctness of a winter dawn. It outlined the facts with a cold precision unmodified by shade or colour, and refracted, as it were, from the blank walls of the surrounding limitations: she had opened windows from which no sky was ever visible. But the idealist subdued to vulgar necessities must employ vulgar minds to draw the inferences to which he cannot stoop; and it was easier for Lily to let Mrs. Fisher formulate her case than to put it plainly to herself. Once confronted with it, however, she went the full length of its consequences; and these had never been more clearly present to her than when, the next afternoon, she set out for a walk with Rosedale.

It was one of those still November days when the air is haunted with the light of summer, and something in the lines of the landscape, and in the golden haze which bathed them, recalled to Miss Bart the September afternoon when she had climbed the slopes of Bellomont with Selden. The importunate memory was kept before her by its ironic contrast to her present situation, since her walk with Selden had represented an irresistible flight from just such a climax as the present excursion was designed to bring about. But other memories importuned her also; the recollection of similar situations, as skilfully led up to, but through some malice of fortune, or her own unsteadiness of purpose, always failing of the intended result. Well, her purpose was steady enough now. She saw that the whole weary work of rehabilitation must begin again, and against far greater odds, if Bertha Dorset should succeed in breaking up her friendship with the Gormers; and her longing for shelter and security was intensified by the passionate desire to triumph over Bertha, as only wealth and predominance could triumph over her. As the wife of Rosedale—the Rosedale she felt it in her power to cre-

ate—she would at least present an invulnerable front to her
enemy.

She had to draw upon this thought, as upon some fiery stimulant, to keep up her part in the scene toward which Rosedale
was too frankly tending. As she walked beside him, shrinking in
every nerve from the way in which his look and tone made free
of her, yet telling herself that this momentary endurance of his
mood was the price she must pay for her ultimate power over
him, she tried to calculate the exact point at which concession
must turn to resistance, and the price *he* would have to pay be
made equally clear to him. But his dapper self-confidence
seemed impenetrable to such hints, and she made a sense of
something hard and self-contained behind the superficial
warmth of his manner.

They had been seated for some time in the seclusion of a
rocky glen above the lake, when she suddenly cut short the culmination of an impassioned period by turning upon him the
grave loveliness of her gaze.

"I *do* believe what you say, Mr. Rosedale," she said quietly;
"and I am ready to marry you whenever you wish."

Rosedale, reddening to the roots of his glossy hair, received
this announcement with a recoil which carried him to his feet,
where he halted before her in an attitude of almost comic discomfiture.

"For I suppose that is what you do wish," she continued, in
the same quiet tone. "And, though I was unable to consent when
you spoke to me in this way before, I am ready, now that I know
you so much better, to trust my happiness to your hands."

She spoke with the noble directness which she could command on such occasions, and which was like a large steady light
thrown across the tortuous darkness of the situation. In its inconvenient brightness Rosedale seemed to waver a moment, as
though conscious that every avenue of escape was unpleasantly
illuminated.

Then he gave a short laugh, and drew out a gold cigarette-
case, in which, with plump jewelled fingers, he groped for a
gold-tipped cigarette. Selecting one, he paused to contemplate it
a moment before saying: "My dear Miss Lily, I'm sorry if there's
been any little misapprehension between us—but you made me

feel my suit was so hopeless that I had really no intention of renewing it."

Lily's blood tingled with the grossness of the rebuff; but she checked the first leap of her anger, and said in a tone of gentle dignity: "I have no one but myself to blame if I gave you the impression that my decision was final."

Her word-play was always too quick for him, and this reply held him in puzzled silence while she extended her hand and added, with the faintest inflection of sadness in her voice: "Before we bid each other goodbye, I want at least to thank you for having once thought of me as you did."

The touch of her hand, the moving softness of her look, thrilled a vulnerable fibre in Rosedale. It was her exquisite inaccessibleness, the sense of distance she could convey without a hint of disdain, that made it most difficult for him to give her up.

"Why do you talk of saying goodbye? Ain't we going to be good friends all the same?" he urged, without releasing her hand.

She drew it away quietly. "What is your idea of being good friends?" she returned with a slight smile. "Making love to me without asking me to marry you?"

Rosedale laughed with a recovered sense of ease. "Well, that's about the size of it, I suppose. I can't help making love to you— I don't see how any man could; but I don't mean to ask you to marry me as long as I can keep out of it."

She continued to smile. "I like your frankness; but I am afraid our friendship can hardly continue on those terms."

She turned away, as though to mark that its final term had in fact been reached, and he followed her for a few steps with a baffled sense of her having after all kept the game in her own hands.

"Miss Lily——" he began impulsively; but she walked on without seeming to hear him.

He overtook her in a few quick strides, and laid an entreating hand on her arm. "Miss Lily—don't hurry away like that. You're beastly hard on a fellow; but if you don't mind speaking the truth I don't see why you shouldn't allow me to do the same."

She had paused a moment with raised brows, drawing away

instinctively from his touch, though she made no effort to evade his words.

"I was under the impression," she rejoined, "that you had done so without waiting for my permission."

"Well—why shouldn't you hear my reasons for doing it, then? We're neither of us such new hands that a little plain speaking is going to hurt us. I'm all broken up on you: there's nothing new in that. I'm more in love with you than I was this time last year; but I've got to face the fact that the situation is changed."

She continued to confront him with the same air of ironic composure. "You mean to say that I'm not as desirable a match as you thought me?"

"Yes; that's what I do mean," he answered resolutely. "I won't go into what's happened. I don't believe the stories about you— I don't *want* to believe them. But they're there, and my not believing them ain't going to alter the situation."

She flushed to her temples, but the extremity of her need checked the retort on her lip and she continued to face him composedly. "If they are not true," she said, "doesn't *that* alter the situation?"

He met this with a steady gaze of his small stock-taking eyes, which made her feel herself no more than some superfine human merchandise. "I believe it does in novels; but I'm certain it don't in real life. You know that as well as I do: if we're speaking the truth, let's speak the whole truth. Last year I was wild to marry you, and you wouldn't look at me: this year—well, you appear to be willing. Now, what has changed in the interval? Your situation, that's all. Then you thought you could do better; now——"

"You think you can?" broke from her ironically.

"Why, yes, I do: in one way, that is." He stood before her, his hands in his pockets, his chest sturdily expanded under its vivid waistcoat. "It's this way, you see: I've had a pretty steady grind of it these last years, working up my social position. Think it's funny I should say that? Why should I mind saying I want to get into society? A man ain't ashamed to say he wants to own a racing stable or a picture gallery. Well, a taste for society's just another kind of hobby. Perhaps I want to get even with some of the people who cold-shouldered me last year—put it that way if it sounds better. Anyhow, I want to have the run of the best houses; and I'm getting it too, little by little. But I know the quickest way to queer yourself with the right people is to be seen with the wrong ones; and that's the reason I want to avoid mistakes."

Miss Bart continued to stand before him in a silence that might have expressed either mockery or a half-reluctant respect for his candour, and after a moment's pause he went on: "There it is, you see. I'm more in love with you than ever, but if I married you now I'd queer myself for good and all, and everything I've worked for all these years would be wasted."

She received this with a look from which all tinge of resentment had faded. After the tissue of social falsehoods in which she had so long moved it was refreshing to step into the open daylight of an avowed expediency.

"I understand you," she said. "A year ago I should have been of use to you, and now I should be an encumbrance; and I like you for telling me so quite honestly." She extended her hand with a smile.

Again the gesture had a disturbing effect upon Mr. Rosedale's self-command. "By George, you're a dead game sport, you are!" he exclaimed; and as she began once more to move away, he broke out suddenly—"Miss Lily—stop. You know I don't believe those stories—I believe they were all got up by a woman who didn't hesitate to sacrifice you to her own convenience——"

Lily drew away with a movement of quick disdain: it was easier to endure his insolence than his commiseration.

"You are very kind; but I don't think we need discuss the matter farther."

But Rosedale's natural imperviousness to hints made it easy for him to brush such resistance aside. "I don't want to discuss anything; I just want to put a plain case before you," he persisted.

She paused in spite of herself, held by the note of a new purpose in his look and tone; and he went on, keeping his eyes firmly upon her: "The wonder to me is that you've waited so long to get square with that woman, when you've had the power in your hands." She continued silent, under the rush of aston-

ishment that his words produced, and he moved a step closer to
ask with low-toned directness: "Why don't you use those letters
of hers you bought last year?"

Lily stood speechless under the shock of the interrogation. In
the words preceding it she had conjectured, at most, an allusion
to her supposed influence over George Dorset; nor did the astonishing indelicacy of the reference diminish the likelihood of
Rosedale's resorting to it. But now she saw how far short of the
mark she had fallen; and the surprise of learning that he had discovered the secret of the letters left her, for the moment, unconscious of the special use to which he was in the act of putting his
knowledge.

Her temporary loss of self-possession gave him time to press
his point; and he went on quickly, as though to secure completer
control of the situation: "You see I know where you stand—I
know how completely she's in your power. That sounds like
stage-talk, don't it?—but there's a lot of truth in some of those
old gags; and I don't suppose you bought those letters simply because you're collecting autographs."

She continued to look at him with a deepening bewilderment: her only clear impression resolved itself into a scared sense
of his power.

"You're wondering how I found out about 'em?" he went on,
answering her look with a note of conscious pride. "Perhaps
you've forgotten that I'm the owner of the Benedick—but never
mind about that now. Getting on to things is a mighty useful ac-
complishment in business, and I've simply extended it to my private affairs. For this *is* partly my affair, you see—at least, it
depends on you to make it so. Let's look the situation straight in
the eye. Mrs. Dorset, for reasons we needn't go into, did you a
beastly bad turn last spring. Everybody knows what Mrs. Dorset
is, and her best friends wouldn't believe her on oath where their
own interests were concerned; but as long as they're out of the
row it's much easier to follow her lead than to set themselves
against it, and you've simply been sacrificed to their laziness and
selfishness. Isn't that a pretty fair statement of the case?—Well,
some people say you've got the neatest kind of an answer in your
hands: that George Dorset would marry you tomorrow, if you'd
tell him all you know, and give him the chance to show the lady

the door. I daresay he would; but you don't seem to care for that
particular form of getting even, and, taking a purely business
view of the question, I think you're right. In a deal like that, nobody comes out with perfectly clean hands, and the only way for
you to start fresh is to get Bertha Dorset to back you up, instead
of trying to fight her."

He paused long enough to draw breath, but not to give her
time for the expression of her gathering resistance; and as he
pressed on, expounding and elucidating his idea with the directness of the man who has no doubts of his cause, she found the
indignation gradually freezing on her lip, found herself held fast
in the grasp of his argument by the mere cold strength of its
presentation. There was no time now to wonder how he had
heard of her obtaining the letters: all her world was dark outside
the monstrous glare of his scheme for using them. And it was
not, after the first moment, the horror of the idea that held her
spell-bound, subdued to his will; it was rather its subtle affinity
to her own inmost cravings. He would marry her to-morrow if
she could regain Bertha Dorset's friendship; and to induce the
open resumption of that friendship, and the tacit retractation of
all that had caused its withdrawal, she had only to put to the lady
the latent menace contained in the packet so miraculously delivered into her hands. Lily saw in a flash the advantage of this
course over that which poor Dorset had pressed upon her. The
other plan depended for its success on the infliction of an open
injury, while this reduced the transaction to a private understanding, of which no third person need have the remotest hint.
Put by Rosedale in terms of business-like give-and-take, this
understanding took on the harmless air of a mutual accommo-
dation, like a transfer of property or a revision of boundary lines.
It certainly simplified life to view it as a perpetual adjustment, a
play of party politics, in which every concession had its recognized equivalent: Lily's mind was fascinated by this escape from
fluctuating ethical into a region of concrete weights and measures.

Rosedale, as she listened, seemed to read in her silence not
only a gradual acquiescence in his plan, but a dangerously far-
reaching perception of the chances it offered; for as she continued to stand before him without speaking, he broke out, with a

quick return upon himself: "You see how simple it is, don't you? Well, don't be carried away by the idea that it's *too* simple. It isn't exactly as if you'd started in with a clean bill of health. Now we're talking let's call things by their right names, and clear the whole business up. You know well enough that Bertha Dorset couldn't have touched you if there hadn't been—well—questions asked before—little points of interrogation, eh? Bound to happen to a good-looking girl with stingy relatives, I suppose; anyhow, they *did* happen, and she found the ground prepared for her. Do you see where I'm coming out? You don't want these little questions cropping up again. It's one thing to get Bertha Dorset into line—but what you want is to keep her there. You can frighten her fast enough—but how are you going to keep her frightened? By showing her that you're as powerful as she is. All the letters in the world won't do that for you as you are now; but with a big backing behind you, you'll keep her just where you want her to be. That's *my* share in the business—that's what I'm offering you. You can't put the thing through without me—don't run away with any idea that you can. In six months you'd be back again among your old worries, or worse ones; and here I am, ready to lift you out of 'em tomorrow if you say so. *Do* you say so, Miss Lily?" he added, moving suddenly nearer.

The words, and the movement which accompanied them, combined to startle Lily out of the state of tranced subservience into which she had insensibly slipped. Light comes in devious ways to the groping consciousness, and it came to her now through the disgusted perception that her would-be accomplice assumed, as a matter of course, the likelihood of her distrusting him and perhaps trying to cheat him of his share of the spoils. This glimpse of his inner mind seemed to present the whole transaction in a new aspect, and she saw that the essential baseness of the act lay in its freedom from risk.

She drew back with a quick gesture of rejection, saying, in a voice that was a surprise to her own ears: "You are mistaken—quite mistaken—both in the facts and in what you infer from them."

Rosedale stared a moment, puzzled by her sudden dash in a direction so different from that toward which she had appeared to be letting him guide her.

"Now what on earth does that mean? I thought we understood each other!" he exclaimed; and to her murmur of "Ah, we do *now*," he retorted with a sudden burst of violence: "I suppose it's because the letters are to *him*, then? Well, I'll be damned if I see what thanks you've got from him!"

8

THE AUTUMN DAYS DECLINED to winter. Once more the leisure world was in transition between country and town, and Fifth Avenue, still deserted at the week-end, showed from Monday to Friday a broadening stream of carriages between house-fronts gradually restored to consciousness.

The Horse Show, some two weeks earlier, had produced a passing semblance of reanimation, filling the theatres and restaurants with a human display of the same costly and high-stepping kind as circled daily about its ring. In Miss Bart's world the Horse Show, and the public it attracted, had ostensibly come to be classed among the spectacles disdained of the elect; but, as the feudal lord might sally forth to join in the dance on his village green, so society, unofficially and incidentally, still condescended to look in upon the scene. Mrs. Gormer, among the rest, was not above seizing such an occasion for the display of herself and her horses; and Lily was given one or two opportunities of appearing at her friend's side in the most conspicuous box the house afforded. But this lingering semblance of intimacy made her only the more conscious of a change in the relation between Mattie and herself, of a dawning discrimination, a gradually formed social standard, emerging from Mrs. Gormer's chaotic view of life. It was inevitable that Lily herself should constitute the first sacrifice to this new ideal, and she knew that, once the Gormers were established in town, the whole drift of fashionable life would facilitate Mattie's detachment from her. She had, in short, failed to make herself indispensable; or rather, her attempt to do so had been thwarted by an influence stronger than any she could exert. That influence, in its last analysis, was simply the power of money: Bertha Dorset's social credit was based on an impregnable bank-account.

Lily knew that Rosedale had overstated neither the difficulty of her own position nor the completeness of the vindication he offered: once Bertha's match in material resources, her superior gifts would make it easy for her to dominate her adversary. An understanding of what such domination would mean, and of the disadvantages accruing from her rejection of it, was brought home to Lily with increasing clearness during the early weeks of the winter. Hitherto, she had kept up a semblance of movement outside the main flow of the social current; but with the return to town, and the concentrating of scattered activities, the mere fact of not slipping back naturally into her old habits of life marked her as being unmistakably excluded from them. If one were not a part of the season's fixed routine, one swung unsphered in a void of social non-existence. Lily, for all her dissatisfied dreaming, had never really conceived the possibility of revolving about a different centre: it was easy enough to despise the world, but decidedly difficult to find any other habitable region. Her sense of irony never quite deserted her, and she could still note, with self-directed derision, the abnormal value suddenly acquired by the most tiresome and insignificant details of her former life. Its very drudgeries had a charm now that she was involuntarily released from them: card-leaving, note-writing, enforced civilities to the dull and elderly, and the smiling endurance of tedious dinners—how pleasantly such obligations would have filled the emptiness of her days! She did indeed leave cards in plenty; she kept herself, with a smiling and valiant persistence, well in the eye of her world; nor did she suffer any of those gross rebuffs which sometimes produce a wholesome reaction of contempt in their victim. Society did not turn away from her, it simply drifted by, preoccupied and inattentive, letting her feel, to the full measure of her humbled pride, how completely she had been the creature of its favour.

She had rejected Rosedale's suggestion with a promptness of scorn almost surprising to herself: she had not lost her capacity for high flashes of indignation. But she could not breathe long on the heights; there had been nothing in her training to develop any continuity of moral strength: what she craved, and really felt herself entitled to, was a situation in which the noblest attitude should also be the easiest. Hitherto her intermittent impulses of resistance had sufficed to maintain her self-respect. If she slipped she recovered her footing, and it was only afterward that she was aware of having recovered it each time on a slightly lower level. She had rejected Rosedale's offer without conscious effort; her whole being had risen against it; and she did not yet perceive that, by the mere act of listening to him, she had learned to live with ideas which would once have been intolerable to her.

To Gerty Farish, keeping watch over her with a tenderer if less discerning eye than Mrs. Fisher's, the results of the struggle were already distinctly visible. She did not, indeed, know what hostages Lily had already given to expediency; but she saw her passionately and irretrievably pledged to the ruinous policy of "keeping up." Gerty could smile now at her own early dream of her friend's renovation through adversity: she understood clearly enough that Lily was not of those to whom privation teaches the unimportance of what they have lost. But this very fact, to Gerty, made her friend the more piteously in want of aid, the more exposed to the claims of a tenderness she was so little conscious of needing.

Lily, since her return to town, had not often climbed Miss Farish's stairs. There was something irritating to her in the mute interrogation of Gerty's sympathy: she felt the real difficulties of her situation to be incommunicable to any one whose theory of values was so different from her own, and the restrictions of Gerty's life, which had once had the charm of contrast, now reminded her too painfully of the limits to which her own existence was shrinking. When at length, one afternoon, she put into execution the belated resolve to visit her friend, this sense of shrunken opportunities possessed her with unusual intensity. The walk up Fifth Avenue, unfolding before her, in the brilliance of the hard winter sunlight, an interminable procession of fastidiously-equipped carriages—giving her, through the little squares of brougham*-windows, peeps of familiar profiles bent above visiting-lists, of hurried hands dispensing notes and cards to attendant footmen—this glimpse of the ever-revolving

*A light carriage, whose driver sits outside and in front.

wheels of the great social machine made Lily more than ever conscious of the steepness and narrowness of Gerty's stairs, and of the cramped blind-alley of life to which they led. Dull stairs destined to be mounted by dull people: how many thousands of insignificant figures were going up and down such stairs all over the world at that very moment—figures as shabby and uninteresting as that of the middle-aged lady in limp black who descended Gerty's flight as Lily climbed to it!

"That was poor Miss Jane Silverton—she came to talk things over with me: she and her sister want to do something to support themselves," Gerty explained, as Lily followed her into the sitting-room.

"To support themselves? Are they so hard up?" Miss Bart asked with a touch of irritation: she had not come to listen to the woes of other people.

"I'm afraid they have nothing left: Ned's debts have swallowed up everything. They had such hopes, you know, when he broke away from Carry Fisher; they thought Bertha Dorset would be such a good influence, because she doesn't care for cards, and—well, she talked quite beautifully to poor Miss Jane about feeling as if Ned were her younger brother, and wanting to carry him off on the yacht, so that he might have a chance to drop cards and racing, and take up his literary work again."

Miss Farish paused with a sigh which reflected the perplexity of her departing visitor. "But that isn't all; it isn't even the worst. It seems that Ned has quarrelled with the Dorsets; or at least Bertha won't allow him to see her, and he is so unhappy about it that he has taken to gambling again, and going about with all sorts of queer people. And cousin Grace Van Osburgh accuses him of having had a very bad influence on Bertie, who left Harvard last spring, and has been a great deal with Ned ever since. She sent for Miss Jane, and made a dreadful scene; and Jack Stepney and Herbert Melson, who were there too, told Miss Jane that Bertie was threatening to marry some dreadful woman to whom Ned had introduced him, and that they could do nothing with him because now he's of age he has his own money. You can fancy how poor Miss Jane felt—she came to me at once, and seemed to think that if I could get her something to do she could earn enough to pay Ned's debts and send him away—I'm afraid she has no idea how long it would take her to pay for one of his evenings at bridge. And he was horribly in debt when he came back from the cruise—I can't see why he should have spent so much more money under Bertha's influence than Carry's: can you?"

Lily met this query with an impatient gesture. "My dear Gerty, I always understand how people can spend much more money—never how they can spend any less!"

She loosened her furs and settled herself in Gerty's easy-chair, while her friend busied herself with the tea-cups.

"But what can they do—the Miss Silvertons? How do they mean to support themselves?" she asked, conscious that the note of irritation still persisted in her voice. It was the very last topic she had meant to discuss—it really did not interest her in the least—but she was seized by a sudden perverse curiosity to know how the two colourless shrinking victims of young Silverton's sentimental experiments meant to cope with the grim necessity which lurked so close to her own threshold.

"I don't know—I am trying to find something for them. Miss Jane reads aloud very nicely—but it's so hard to find any one who is willing to be read to. And Miss Annie paints a little——"

"Oh, I know—apple-blossoms on blotting paper; just the kind of thing I shall be doing myself before long!" exclaimed Lily, starting up with a vehemence of movement that threatened destruction to Miss Farish's fragile tea-table.

Lily bent over to steady the cups; then she sank back into her seat. "I'd forgotten there was no room to dash about in— how beautifully one does have to behave in a small flat! Oh, Gerty, I wasn't meant to be good," she sighed out incoherently.

Gerty lifted an apprehensive look to her pale face, in which the eyes shone with a peculiar sleepless lustre.

"You look horribly tired, Lily; take your tea, and let me give you this cushion to lean against."

Miss Bart accepted the cup of tea, but put back the cushion with an impatient hand.

"Don't give me that! I don't want to lean back—I shall go to sleep if I do."

"Well, why not, dear? I'll be as quiet as a mouse," Gerty urged affectionately.

"No—no; don't be quiet; talk to me—keep me awake! I don't sleep at night, and in the afternoon a dreadful drowsiness creeps over me."

"You don't sleep at night? Since when?"

"I don't know—I can't remember." She rose and put the empty cup on the tea-tray. "Another, and stronger, please; if I don't keep awake now I shall see horrors tonight—perfect horrors!"

"But they'll be worse if you drink too much tea."

"No, no—give it to me; and don't preach, please," Lily returned imperiously. Her voice had a dangerous edge, and Gerty noticed that her hand shook as she held it out to receive the second cup.

"But you look so tired: I'm sure you must be ill——"

Miss Bart set down her cup with a start. "Do I look ill? Does my face show it?" She rose and walked quickly toward the little mirror above the writing-table. "What a horrid looking-glass—it's all blotched and discoloured. Any one would look ghastly in it!" She turned back, fixing her plaintive eyes on Gerty. "You stupid dear, why do you say such odious things to me? It's enough to make one ill to be told one looks so! And looking ill means looking ugly." She caught Gerty's wrists, and drew her close to the window. "After all, I'd rather know the truth. Look me straight in the face, Gerty, and tell me: am I perfectly frightful?"

"You're perfectly beautiful now, Lily: your eyes are shining, and your cheeks have grown so pink all of a sudden——"

"Ah, they *were* pale, then—ghastly pale, when I came in? Why don't you tell me frankly that I'm a wreck? My eyes are bright now because I'm so nervous—but in the mornings they look like lead. And I can see the lines coming in my face—the lines of worry and disappointment and failure! Every sleepless night leaves a new one—and how can I sleep, when I have such dreadful things to think about?"

"Dreadful things—what things?" asked Gerty, gently detaching her wrists from her friend's feverish fingers.

"What things? Well, poverty, for one—and I don't know any that's more dreadful." Lily turned away and sank with sudden weariness into the easy-chair near the tea-table. "You asked me just now if I could understand why Ned Silverton spent so much money. Of course I understand—he spends it on living with the rich. You think we live *on* the rich, rather than with them: and so we do, in a sense—but it's a privilege we have to pay for! We eat their dinners, and drink their wine, and smoke their cigarettes, and use their carriages and their opera-boxes and their private cars—yes, but there's a tax to pay on every one of those luxuries. The man pays it by big tips to the servants, by playing cards beyond his means, by flowers and presents—and—and—lots of other things that cost; the girl pays it by tips and cards too—oh, yes, I've had to take up bridge again—and by going to the best dress-makers, and having just the right dress for every occasion, and always keeping herself fresh and exquisite and amusing!"

She leaned back for a moment, closing her eyes, and as she sat there, her pale lips slightly parted, and the lids dropped above her flagged brilliant gaze, Gerty had a startled perception of the change in her face—of the way in which an ashen daylight seemed suddenly to extinguish its artificial brightness. She looked up, and the vision vanished.

"It doesn't sound very amusing, does it? And it isn't—I'm sick to death of it! And yet the thought of giving it all up nearly kills me—it's what keeps me awake at night, and makes me so crazy for your strong tea. For I can't go on in this way much longer, you know—I'm nearly at the end of my tether. And then what can I do—how on earth am I to keep myself alive? I see myself reduced to the fate of that poor Silverton woman—slinking about to employment agencies, and trying to sell painted blotting-pads to Women's Exchanges!* And there are thousands and thousands of women trying to do the same thing already, and not one of the number who has less idea how to earn a dollar than I have!"

She rose again with a hurried glance at the clock. "It's late, and I must be off—I have an appointment with Carry Fisher. Don't look so worried, you dear thing—don't think too much about the nonsense I've been talking." She was before the mir-

---

*Shops selling food and handicrafts to provide income for gentlewomen facing poverty.

ror again, adjusting her hair with a light hand, drawing down her
veil, and giving a dexterous touch to her furs. "Of course, you
know, it hasn't come to the employment agencies and the
painted blotting-pads yet; but I'm rather hard-up just for the
moment, and if I could find something to do—notes to write
and visiting lists to make up, or that kind of thing—it would tide
me over till the legacy is paid. And Carry has promised to find
somebody who wants a kind of social secretary—you know she
makes a specialty of the helpless rich."

Miss Bart had not revealed to Gerty the full extent of her anxiety. She was in fact in urgent and immediate need of money:
money to meet the vulgar weekly claims which could neither be
deferred nor evaded. To give up her apartment, and shrink to the
obscurity of a boarding-house, or the provisional hospitality of a
bed in Gerty Farish's sitting-room, was an expedient which
could only postpone the problem confronting her; and it seemed
wiser as well as more agreeable to remain where she was and find
some means of earning her living. The possibility of having to
do this was one which she had never before seriously considered,
and the discovery that, as a bread-winner, she was likely to prove
as helpless and ineffectual as poor Miss Silverton, was a severe
shock to her self-confidence.

Having been accustomed to take herself at the popular valu-
ation, as a person of energy and resource, naturally fitted to
dominate any situation in which she found herself, she vaguely
imagined that such gifts would be of value to seekers after social
guidance; but there was unfortunately no specific head under
which the art of saying and doing the right thing could be offered in the market, and even Mrs. Fisher's resourcefulness failed
before the difficulty of discovering a workable vein in the vague
wealth of Lily's graces. Mrs. Fisher was full of indirect expedients for enabling her friends to earn a living, and could consci-
entiously assert that she had put several opportunities of this
kind before Lily; but more legitimate methods of bread-winning
were as much out of her line as they were beyond the capacity of
the sufferers she was generally called upon to assist. Lily's failure
to profit by the chances already afforded her might, moreover,
have justified the abandonment of farther effort on her behalf;

but Mrs. Fisher's inexhaustible good-nature made her an adept at creating artificial demands in response to an actual supply. In the pursuance of this end she at once started on a voyage of discovery in Miss Bart's behalf; and as the result of her explorations she now summoned the latter with the announcement that she had "found something."

Left to herself, Gerty mused distressfully upon her friend's plight, and her own inability to relieve it. It was clear to her that Lily, for the present, had no wish for the kind of help she could give. Miss Farish could see no hope for her friend but in a life completely reorganized and detached from its old associations; whereas all Lily's energies were centred in the determined effort to hold fast to those associations, to keep herself visibly identified with them, as long as the illusion could be maintained. Pitiable as such an attitude seemed to Gerty, she could not judge it as harshly as Selden, for instance, might have done. She had not forgotten the night of emotion when she and Lily had lain in each other's arms, and she had seemed to feel her very heart's blood passing into her friend. The sacrifice she had made had seemed unavailing enough; no trace remained in Lily of the subduing influences of that hour; but Gerty's tenderness, disciplined by long years of contact with obscure and inarticulate suffering, could wait on its object with a silent forbearance which took no account of time. She could not, however, deny herself the solace of taking anxious counsel with Lawrence Selden, with whom, since his return from Europe, she had renewed her old relation of cousinly confidence.

Selden himself had never been aware of any change in their relation. He found Gerty as he had left her, simple, undemanding and devoted, but with a quickened intelligence of the heart which he recognized without seeking to explain it. To Gerty herself it would once have seemed impossible that she should ever again talk freely with him of Lily Bart; but what had passed in the secrecy of her own breast seemed to resolve itself, when the mist of the struggle cleared, into a breaking down of the bounds of self, a deflecting of the wasted personal emotion into the general current of human understanding.

It was not till some two weeks after her visit from Lily that

Gerty had the opportunity of communicating her fears to
Selden. The latter, having presented himself on a Sunday afternoon, had lingered on through the dowdy animation of his
cousin's tea-hour, conscious of something in her voice and eye
which solicited a word apart; and as soon as the last visitor was
gone Gerty opened her case by asking how lately he had seen
Miss Bart.

Selden's perceptible pause gave her time for a slight stir of
surprise.

"I haven't seen her at all—I've perpetually missed seeing her
since she came back."

This unexpected admission made Gerty pause too; and she
was still hesitating on the brink of her subject when he relieved
her by adding: "I've wanted to see her—but she seems to have
been absorbed by the Gormer set since her return from Europe."

"That's all the more reason: she's been very unhappy."

"Unhappy at being with the Gormers?"

"Oh, I don't defend her intimacy with the Gormers; but that
too is at an end now, I think. You know people have been very
unkind since Bertha Dorset quarrelled with her."

"Ah——" Selden exclaimed, rising abruptly to walk to the
window, where he remained with his eyes on the darkening
street while his cousin continued to explain: "Judy Trenor and
her own family have deserted her too—and all because Bertha
Dorset has said such horrible things. And she is very poor—you
know Mrs. Peniston cut her off with a small legacy, after giving
her to understand that she was to have everything."

"Yes—I know," Selden assented curtly, turning back into the
room, but only to stir about with restless steps in the circum-
scribed space between door and window. "Yes—she's been
abominably treated; but it's unfortunately the precise thing that
a man who wants to show his sympathy can't say to her."

His words caused Gerty a slight chill of disappointment.
"There would be other ways of showing your sympathy," she
suggested.

Selden, with a slight laugh, sat down beside her on the little
sofa which projected from the hearth. "What are you thinking
of, you incorrigible missionary?" he asked.

Gerty's colour rose, and her blush was for a moment her only answer. Then she made it more explicit by saying: "I am thinking of the fact that you and she used to be great friends—that she used to care immensely for what you thought of her—and that, if she takes your staying away as a sign of what you think now, I can imagine its adding a great deal to her unhappiness."

"My dear child, don't add to it still more—at least to your conception of it—by attributing to her all sorts of susceptibilities of your own." Selden, for his life, could not keep a note of dryness out of his voice; but he met Gerty's look of perplexity by saying more mildly: "But, though you immensely exaggerate the importance of anything I could do for Miss Bart, you can't exaggerate my readiness to do it—if you ask me to." He laid his hand for a moment on hers, and there passed between them, on the current of the rare contact, one of those exchanges of meaning which fill the hidden reservoirs of affection. Gerty had the feeling that he measured the cost of her request as plainly as she read the significance of his reply; and the sense of all that was suddenly clear between them made her next words easier to find.

"I do ask you, then; I ask you because she once told me that you had been a help to her, and because she needs help now as she has never needed it before. You know how dependent she has always been on ease and luxury—how she has hated what was shabby and ugly and uncomfortable. She can't help it—she was brought up with those ideas, and has never been able to find her way out of them. But now all the things she cared for have been taken from her, and the people who taught her to care for them have abandoned her too; and it seems to me that if some one could reach out a hand and show her the other side—show her how much is left in life and in herself——" Gerty broke off, abashed at the sound of her own eloquence, and impeded by the difficulty of giving precise expression to her vague yearning for her friend's retrieval. "I can't help her myself: she's passed out of my reach," she continued. "I think she's afraid of being a burden to me. When she was last here, two weeks ago, she seemed dreadfully worried about her future: she said Carry Fisher was trying to find something for her to do. A few days later she wrote me that she had taken a position as private secretary, and that I was not to be anxious, for everything was all right, and she would come in and tell me about it when she had time; but she has never come, and I don't like to go to her, because I am afraid of forcing myself on her when I'm not wanted. Once, when we were children, and I had rushed up after a long separation, and thrown my arms about her, she said: 'Please don't kiss me unless I ask you to, Gerty'—and she *did* ask me, a minute later; but since then I've always waited to be asked."

Selden had listened in silence, with the concentrated look which his thin dark face could assume when he wished to guard it against any involuntary change of expression. When his cousin ended, he said with a slight smile: "Since you've learned the wisdom of waiting, I don't see why you urge me to rush in——" but the troubled appeal of her eyes made him add, as he rose to take leave: "Still, I'll do what you wish, and not hold you responsible for my failure."

Selden's avoidance of Miss Bart had not been as unintentional as he had allowed his cousin to think. At first, indeed, while the memory of their last hour at Monte Carlo still held the full heat of his indignation, he had anxiously watched for her return; but she had disappointed him by lingering in England, and when she finally reappeared it happened that business had called him to the West, whence he came back only to learn that she was starting for Alaska with the Gormers. The revelation of this suddenly-established intimacy effectually chilled his desire to see her. If, at a moment when her whole life seemed to be breaking up, she could cheerfully commit its reconstruction to the Gormers, there was no reason why such accidents should ever strike her as irreparable. Every step she took seemed in fact to carry her farther from the region where, once or twice, he and she had met for an illumined moment; and the recognition of this fact, when its first pang had been surmounted, produced in him a sense of negative relief. It was much simpler for him to judge Miss Bart by her habitual conduct than by the rare deviations from it which had thrown her so disturbingly in his way; and every act of hers which made the recurrence of such deviations more unlikely, confirmed the sense of relief with which he returned to the conventional view of her.

But Gerty Farish's words had sufficed to make him see how little this view was really his, and how impossible it was for him to live quietly with the thought of Lily Bart. To hear that she was in need of help—even such vague help as he could offer—was to be at once repossessed by that thought; and by the time he reached the street he had sufficiently convinced himself of the urgency of his cousin's appeal to turn his steps directly toward Lily's hotel.

There his zeal met a check in unforeseen news that Miss Bart had moved away; but, on his pressing his enquiries, the clerk remembered that she had left an address, for which he presently began to search through his books.

It was certainly strange that she should have taken this step without letting Gerty Farish know of her decision; and Selden waited with a vague sense of uneasiness while the address was sought for. The process lasted long enough for uneasiness to turn to apprehension; but when at length a slip of paper was handed him, and he read on it: "Care of Mrs. Norma Hatch, Emporium Hotel," his apprehension passed into an incredulous stare, and this into the gesture of disgust with which he tore the paper in two, and turned to walk quickly homeward.

9

WHEN LILY WOKE ON the morning after her translation to the Emporium Hotel, her first feeling was one of purely physical satisfaction. The force of contrast gave an added keenness to the luxury of lying once more in a soft-pillowed bed, and looking across a spacious sunlit room at a breakfast-table set invitingly near the fire. Analysis and introspection might come later; but for the moment she was not even troubled by the excesses of the upholstery or the restless convolutions of the furniture. The sense of being once more lapped and folded in ease, as in some dense mild medium impenetrable to discomfort, effectually stilled the faintest note of criticism.

When, the afternoon before, she had presented herself to the lady to whom Carry Fisher had directed her, she had been conscious of entering a new world. Carry's vague presentment of Mrs. Norma Hatch (whose reversion to her Christian name was explained as the result of her latest divorce), left her under the implication of coming "from the West," with the not unusual extenuation of having brought a great deal of money with her. She was, in short, rich, helpless, unplaced: the very subject for Lily's hand. Mrs. Fisher had not specified the line her friend was to take; she owned herself unacquainted with Mrs. Hatch, whom she "knew about" through Melville Stancy, a lawyer in his leisure moments, and the Falstaff* of a certain section of festive club life. Socially, Mr. Stancy might have been said to form a connecting link between the Gormer world and the more dimly-lit region on which Miss Bart now found herself entering. It was, however, only figuratively that the illumination of Mrs. Hatch's

---

*Fat, witty, hard-drinking character in Shakespeare's *Henry IV, Parts I and II*, and *The Merry Wives of Windsor*.

world could be described as dim: in actual fact, Lily found her seated in a blaze of electric light, impartially projected from various ornamental excrescences on a vast concavity of pink damask and gilding, from which she rose like Venus from her shell.* The analogy was justified by the appearance of the lady, whose large-eyed prettiness had the fixity of something impaled and shown under glass. This did not preclude the immediate discovery that she was some years younger than her visitor, and that under her showiness, her ease, the aggression of her dress and voice, there persisted that ineradicable innocence which, in ladies of her nationality, so curiously coexists with startling extremes of experience.

The environment in which Lily found herself was as strange to her as its inhabitants. She was unacquainted with the world of the fashionable New York hotel—a world over-heated, over-upholstered, and over-fitted with mechanical appliances for the gratification of fantastic requirements, while the comforts of a civilized life were as unattainable as in a desert. Through this atmosphere of torrid splendour moved wan beings as richly upholstered as the furniture, beings without definite pursuits or permanent relations, who drifted on a languid tide of curiosity from restaurant to concert-hall, from palm-garden to music-room, from "art exhibit" to dress-maker's opening. High-stepping horses or elaborately equipped motors waited to carry these ladies into vague metropolitan distances, whence they returned, still more wan from the weight of their sables, to be sucked back into the stifling inertia of the hotel routine. Somewhere behind them, in the background of their lives, there was doubtless a real past, peopled by real human activities: they themselves were probably the product of strong ambitions, persistent energies, diversified contacts with the wholesome roughness of life; yet they had no more real existence than the poet's shades in limbo.†

---

*Roman goddess of love, who sprang from the sea; she is depicted on a seashell in the painting *The Birth of Venus*, by Sandro Botticelli.
†The reference is to Dante's *Divine Comedy* (early fourteenth century), in which he describes how righteous classical poets who died before the coming of Christ live in a region between heaven and hell.

Lily had not been long in this pallid world without discovering that Mrs. Hatch was its most substantial figure. That lady, though still floating in the void, showed faint symptoms of developing an outline; and in this endeavour she was actively seconded by Mr. Melville Stancy. It was Mr. Stancy, a man of large resounding presence, suggestive of convivial occasions and of a chivalry finding expression in "first-night" boxes* and thousand dollar *bonbonnières*,† who had transplanted Mrs. Hatch from the scene of her first development to the higher stage of hotel life in the metropolis. It was he who had selected the horses with which she had taken the blue ribbon at the Show, had introduced her to the photographer whose portraits of her formed the recurring ornament of "Sunday Supplements," and had got together the group which constituted her social world. It was a small group still, with heterogeneous figures suspended in large unpeopled spaces; but Lily did not take long to learn that its regulation was no longer in Mr. Stancy's hands. As often happens, the pupil had outstripped the teacher, and Mrs. Hatch was already aware of heights of elegance as well as depths of luxury beyond the world of the Emporium. This discovery at once produced in her a craving for higher guidance, for the adroit feminine hand which should give the right turn to her correspondence, the right "look" to her hats, the right succession to the items of her *menus*. It was, in short, as the regulator of a germinating social life that Miss Bart's guidance was required; her ostensible duties as secretary being restricted by the fact that Mrs. Hatch, as yet, knew hardly any one to write to.

The daily details of Mrs. Hatch's existence were as strange to Lily as its general tenor. The lady's habits were marked by an Oriental indolence and disorder peculiarly trying to her companion. Mrs. Hatch and her friends seemed to float together outside the bounds of time and space. No definite hours were kept; no fixed obligations existed: night and day flowed into one another in a blur of confused and retarded engagements, so that one had the impression of lunching at the tea-hour, while din-

---

*Prestigious theater boxes for the opening night of operas and plays.
†Fancy dishes for candy (French).

ner was often merged in the noisy after-theatre supper which prolonged Mrs. Hatch's vigil till day-light.

Through this jumble of futile activities came and went a strange throng of hangers-on—manicures, beauty-doctors, hair-dressers, teachers of bridge, of French, of "physical development": figures sometimes indistinguishable, by their appearance, or by Mrs. Hatch's relation to them, from the visitors constituting her recognized society. But strangest of all to Lily was the encounter, in this latter group, of several of her acquaintances. She had supposed, and not without relief, that she was passing, for the moment, completely out of her own circle; but she found that Mr. Stancy, one side of whose sprawling existence over-lapped the edge of Mrs. Fisher's world, had drawn several of its brightest ornaments into the circle of the Emporium. To find Ned Silverton among the habitual frequenters of Mrs. Hatch's drawing-room was one of Lily's first astonishments; but she soon discovered that he was not Mr. Stancy's most important re-cruit. It was on little Freddy Van Osburgh, the small slim heir of the Van Osburgh millions, that the attention of Mrs. Hatch's group was centred. Freddy, barely out of college, had risen above the horizon since Lily's eclipse, and she now saw with surprise what an effulgence he shed on the outer twilight of Mrs. Hatch's existence. This, then, was one of the things that young men "went in" for when released from the official social routine; this was the kind of "previous engagement" that so frequently caused them to disappoint the hopes of anxious hostesses. Lily had an odd sense of being behind the social tapestry, on the side where the threads were knotted and the loose ends hung. For a moment she found a certain amusement in the show, and in her own share of it: the situation had an ease and unconventionality distinctly refreshing after her experience of the irony of conventions. But these flashes of amusement were but brief reactions from the long disgust of her days. Compared with the vast gilded void of Mrs. Hatch's existence, the life of Lily's former friends seemed packed with ordered activities. Even the most ir-responsible pretty woman of her acquaintance had her inherited obligations, her conventional benevolences, her share in the working of the great civic machine; and all hung together in the solidarity of these traditional functions. The performance of specific duties would have simplified Miss Bart's position; but the vague attendance on Mrs. Hatch was not without its perplexities.

It was not her employer who created these perplexities. Mrs. Hatch showed from the first an almost touching desire for Lily's approval. Far from asserting the superiority of wealth, her beautiful eyes seemed to urge the plea of inexperience: she wanted to do what was "nice," to be taught how to be "lovely." The difficulty was to find any point of contact between her ideals and Lily's.

Mrs. Hatch swam in a haze of indeterminate enthusiasms, of aspirations culled from the stage, the newspapers, the fashion-journals, and a gaudy world of sport still more completely beyond her companion's ken. To separate from these confused conceptions those most likely to advance the lady on her way, was Lily's obvious duty; but its performance was hampered by rapidly-growing doubts. Lily was in fact becoming more and more aware of a certain ambiguity in her situation. It was not that she had, in the conventional sense, any doubt of Mrs. Hatch's irreproachableness. The lady's offences were always against taste rather than conduct; her divorce record seemed due to geographical rather than ethical conditions; and her worst laxities were likely to proceed from a wandering and extravagant good-nature. But if Lily did not mind her detaining her manicure for luncheon, or offering the "Beauty Doctor" a seat in Freddy Van Osburgh's box at the play, she was not equally at ease in regard to some less apparent lapses from convention. Ned Silverton's relation to Stancy seemed, for instance, closer and less clear than any natural affinities would warrant; and both appeared united in the effort to cultivate Freddy Van Osburgh's growing taste for Mrs. Hatch. There was as yet nothing definable in the situation, which might well resolve itself into a huge joke on the part of the other two; but Lily had a vague sense that the subject of their experiment was too young, too rich and too credulous. Her embarrassment was increased by the fact that Freddy seemed to regard her as cooperating with himself in the social development of Mrs. Hatch: a view that suggested, on his part, a permanent interest in the lady's future. There were moments when Lily found an ironic amusement in this aspect of the case. The thought of launching such a missile as Mrs. Hatch at the perfidious bosom of society was not without its charm: Miss Bart had even beguiled her leisure with visions of the fair Norma introduced for the first time to a family banquet at the Van Osburghs'. But the thought of being personally connected with the transaction was less agreeable; and her momentary flashes of amusement were followed by increasing periods of doubt.

The sense of these doubts was uppermost when, late one afternoon, she was surprised by a visit from Lawrence Selden. He found her alone in the wilderness of pink damask, for in Mrs. Hatch's world the tea-hour was not dedicated to social rites, and the lady was in the hands of her masseuse.

Selden's entrance had caused Lily an inward start of embarrassment; but his air of constraint had the effect of restoring her self-possession, and she took at once the tone of surprise and pleasure, wondering frankly that he should have traced her to so unlikely a place, and asking what had inspired him to make the search.

Selden met this with an unusual seriousness: she had never seen him so little master of the situation, so plainly at the mercy of any obstructions she might put in his way. "I wanted to see you," he said; and she could not resist observing in reply that he had kept his wishes under remarkable control. She had in truth felt his long absence as one of the chief bitternesses of the last months: his desertion had wounded sensibilities far below the surface of her pride.

Selden met the challenge with directness. "Why should I have come, unless I thought I could be of use to you? It is my only excuse for imagining you could want me."

This struck her as a clumsy evasion, and the thought gave a flash of keenness to her answer. "Then you have come now because you think you can be of use to me?"

He hesitated again. "Yes: in the modest capacity of a person to talk things over with."

For a clever man it was certainly a stupid beginning; and the idea that his awkwardness was due to the fear of her attaching a personal significance to his visit, chilled her pleasure in seeing him. Even under the most adverse conditions, that pleasure always made itself felt: she might hate him, but she had never been able to wish him out of the room. She was very near hating him now; yet the sound of his voice, the way the light fell on his thin dark hair, the way he sat and moved and wore his clothes—she was conscious that even these trivial things were inwoven with her deepest life. In his presence a sudden stillness came upon her, and the turmoil of her spirit ceased; but an impulse of resistance to this stealing influence now prompted her to say: "It's very good of you to present yourself in that capacity; but what makes you think I have anything particular to talk about?"

Though she kept the even tone of light intercourse, the question was framed in a way to remind him that his good offices were unsought; and for a moment Selden was checked by it. The situation between them was one which could have been cleared up only by a sudden explosion of feeling; and their whole training and habit of mind were against the chances of such an explosion. Selden's calmness seemed rather to harden into resistance, and Miss Bart's into a surface of glittering irony, as they faced each other from the opposite corners of one of Mrs. Hatch's elephantine sofas. The sofa in question, and the apartment peopled by its monstrous mates, served at length to suggest the turn of Selden's reply.

"Gerty told me that you were acting as Mrs. Hatch's secretary; and I knew she was anxious to hear how you were getting on."

Miss Bart received this explanation without perceptible softening. "Why didn't she look me up herself, then?" she asked.

"Because, as you didn't send her your address, she was afraid of being importunate." Selden continued with a smile: "You see no such scruples restrained me; but then I haven't as much to risk if I incur your displeasure."

Lily answered his smile. "You haven't incurred it as yet; but I have an idea that you are going to."

"That rests with you, doesn't it? You see my initiative doesn't go beyond putting myself at your disposal."

"But in what capacity? What am I to do with you?" she asked in the same light tone.

Selden again glanced about Mrs. Hatch's drawing-room;

then he said, with a decision which he seemed to have gathered from this final inspection: "You are to let me take you away from here."

Lily flushed at the suddenness of the attack; then she stiffened under it and said coldly: "And may I ask where you mean me to go?"

"Back to Gerty in the first place, if you will; the essential thing is that it should be away from here."

The unusual harshness of his tone might have shown her how much the words cost him; but she was in no state to measure his feelings while her own were in a flame of revolt. To neglect her, perhaps even to avoid her, at a time when she had most need of her friends, and then suddenly and unwarrantably to break into her life with this strange assumption of authority, was to rouse in her every instinct of pride and self-defence.

"I am very much obliged to you," she said, "for taking such an interest in my plans; but I am quite contented where I am, and have no intention of leaving."

Selden had risen, and was standing before her in an attitude of uncontrollable expectancy.

"That simply means that you don't know where you are!" he exclaimed.

Lily rose also, with a quick flash of anger. "If you have come here to say disagreeable things about Mrs. Hatch——"

"It is only with your relation to Mrs. Hatch that I am concerned."

"My relation to Mrs. Hatch is one I have no reason to be ashamed of. She has helped me to earn a living when my old friends were quite resigned to seeing me starve."

"Nonsense! Starvation is not the only alternative. You know you can always find a home with Gerty till you are independent again."

"You show such an intimate acquaintance with my affairs that I suppose you mean—till my aunt's legacy is paid?"

"I do mean that; Gerty told me of it," Selden acknowledged without embarrassment. He was too much in earnest now to feel any false constraint in speaking his mind.

"But Gerty does not happen to know," Miss Bart rejoined, "that I owe every penny of that legacy."

"Good God!" Selden exclaimed, startled out of his composure by the abruptness of the statement.

"Every penny of it, and more too," Lily repeated; "and you now perhaps see why I prefer to remain with Mrs. Hatch rather than take advantage of Gerty's kindness. I have no money left, except my small income, and I must earn something more to keep myself alive."

Selden hesitated a moment; then he rejoined in a quieter tone: "But with your income and Gerty's—since you allow me to go so far into the details of the situation—you and she could surely contrive a life together which would put you beyond the need of having to support yourself. Gerty, I know, is eager to make such an arrangement, and would be quite happy in it——"

"But I should not," Miss Bart interposed. "There are many reasons why it would be neither kind to Gerty nor wise for myself." She paused a moment, and as he seemed to await a farther explanation, added with a quick lift of her head: "You will perhaps excuse me from giving you these reasons."

"I have no claim to know them," Selden answered, ignoring her tone; "no claim to offer any comment or suggestion beyond the one I have already made. And my right to make that is simply the universal right of a man to enlighten a woman when he sees her unconsciously placed in a false position."

Lily smiled. "I suppose," she rejoined, "that by a false position you mean one outside of what we call society; but you must remember that I had been excluded from those sacred precincts long before I met Mrs. Hatch. As far as I can see, there is very little real difference in being inside or out, and I remember your once telling me that it was only those inside who took the difference seriously."

She had not been without intention in making this allusion to their memorable talk at Bellomont, and she waited with an odd tremor of the nerves to see what response it would bring; but the result of the experiment was disappointing. Selden did not allow the allusion to deflect him from his point; he merely said with completer fulness of emphasis: "The question of being inside or out is, as you say, a small one, and it happens to have nothing to do with the case, except in so far as Mrs. Hatch's desire to be inside may put you in the position I call false."

In spite of the moderation of his tone, each word he spoke had the effect of confirming Lily's resistance. The very apprehensions he aroused hardened her against him: she had been on the alert for the note of personal sympathy, for any sign of recovered power over him; and his attitude of sober impartiality, the absence of all response to her appeal, turned her hurt pride to blind resentment of his interference. The conviction that he had been sent by Gerty, and that, whatever straits he conceived her to be in, he would never voluntarily have come to her aid, strengthened her resolve not to admit him a hair's breadth farther into her confidence. However doubtful she might feel her situation to be, she would rather persist in darkness than owe her enlightenment to Selden.

"I don't know," she said, when he had ceased to speak, "why you imagine me to be situated as you describe; but as you have always told me that the sole object of a bringing-up like mine was to teach a girl to get what she wants, why not assume that that is precisely what I am doing?"

The smile with which she summed up her case was like a clear barrier raised against farther confidences: its brightness held him at such a distance that he had a sense of being almost out of hearing as he rejoined: "I am not sure that I have ever called you a successful example of that kind of bringing-up."

Her colour rose a little at the implication, but she steeled herself with a light laugh.

"Ah, wait a little longer—give me a little more time before you decide!" And as he wavered before her, still watching for a break in the impenetrable front she presented: "Don't give me up; I may still do credit to my training!" she affirmed.

"LOOK AT THOSE SPANGLES, Miss Bart—every one of 'em sewed on crooked."

The tall forewoman, a pinched perpendicular figure, dropped the condemned structure of wire and net on the table at Lily's aide, and passed on to the next figure in the line.

There were twenty of them in the work-room, their fagged profiles, under exaggerated hair, bowed in the harsh north light above the utensils of their art; for it was something more than an industry, surely, this creation of ever-varied settings for the face of fortunate womanhood. Their own faces were sallow with the unwholesomeness of hot air and sedentary toil, rather than with any actual signs of want: they were employed in a fashionble millinery establishment, and were fairly well clothed and well paid; but the youngest among them was as dull and colourless as the middle-aged. In the whole work-room there was only one skin beneath which the blood still visibly played; and that now burned with vexation as Miss Bart, under the lash of the forewoman's comment, began to strip the hat-frame of its overlapping spangles.

To Gerty Farish's hopeful spirit a solution appeared to have been reached when she remembered how beautifully Lily could trim hats. Instances of young lady-milliners establishing themselves under fashionable patronage, and imparting to their "creations" that indefinable touch which the professional hand can never give, had flattered Gerty's visions of the future, and convinced even Lily that her separation from Mrs. Norma Hatch need not reduce her to dependence on her friends.

The parting had occurred a few weeks after Selden's visit, and would have taken place sooner had it not been for the resistance set up in Lily by his ill-starred offer of advice. The sense of being involved in a transaction she would not have cared to examine too closely had soon afterward defined itself in the light of a hint from Mr. Stancy that, if she "saw them through," she would have no reason to be sorry. The implication that such loyalty would meet with a direct reward had hastened her flight, and flung her back, ashamed and penitent, on the broad bosom of Gerty's sympathy. She did not, however, propose to lie there prone, and Gerty's inspiration about the hats at once revived her hopes of profitable activity. Here was, after all, something that her charming listless hands could really do; she had no doubt of their capacity for knotting a ribbon or placing a flower to advantage. And of course only these finishing touches would be expected of her: subordinate fingers, blunt, grey, needle-pricked fingers, would prepare the shapes and stitch the linings, while she presided over the charming little front shop—a shop all white panels, mirrors, and moss-green hangings—where her finished creations, hats, wreaths, aigrettes,* and the rest, perched on their stands like birds just poising for flight.

But at the very outset of Gerty's campaign this vision of the green-and-white shop had been dispelled. Other young ladies of fashion had been thus "set-up," selling their hats by the mere attraction of a name and the reputed knack of tying a bow; but these privileged beings could command a faith in their powers materially expressed by the readiness to pay their shop-rent and advance a handsome sum for current expenses. Where was Lily to find such support? And even could it have been found, how were the ladies on whose approval she depended to be induced to give her their patronage? Gerty learned that whatever sympathy her friend's case might have excited a few months since had been imperilled, if not lost, by her association with Mrs. Hatch. Once again, Lily had withdrawn from an ambiguous situation in time to save her self-respect, but too late for public vindication. Freddy Van Osburgh was not to marry Mrs. Hatch; he had been rescued at the eleventh hour—some said by the efforts of Gus Trenor and Rosedale—and despatched to Europe with old Ned Van Alstyne; but the risk he had run would always be ascribed to Miss Bart's connivance, and would somehow serve as a

---

*Plumes of feathers worn as head ornaments.

summing-up and corroboration of the vague general distrust of her. It was a relief to those who had hung back from her to find themselves thus justified, and they were inclined to insist a little on her connection with the Hatch case in order to show that they had been right.

Gerty's quest, at any rate, brought up against a solid wall of resistance; and even when Carry Fisher, momentarily penitent for her share in the Hatch affair, joined her efforts to Miss Farish's, they met with no better success. Gerty had tried to veil her failure in tender ambiguities; but Carry, always the soul of candour, put the case squarely to her friend.

"I went straight to Judy Trenor; she has fewer prejudices than the others, and besides she's always hated Bertha Dorset. But what *have* you done to her, Lily? At the very first word about giving you a start she flamed out about some money you'd got from Gus; I never knew her so hot before. You know she'll let him do anything but spend money on his friends: the only reason she's decent to me now is that she knows I'm not hard up.— He speculated for you, you say? Well, what's the harm? He had no business to lose. He *didn't* lose? Then what on earth—but I never *could* understand you, Lily!"

The end of it was that, after anxious enquiry and much deliberation, Mrs. Fisher and Gerty, for once oddly united in their effort to help their friend, decided on placing her in the workroom of Mme. Regina's renowned millinery establishment. Even this arrangement was not effected without considerable negotiation, for Mme. Regina had a strong prejudice against untrained assistance, and was induced to yield only by the fact that she owed the patronage of Mrs. Bry and Mrs. Gormer to Carry Fisher's influence. She had been willing from the first to employ Lily in the show-room: as a displayer of hats, a fashionable beauty might be a valuable asset. But to this suggestion Miss Bart opposed a negative which Gerty emphatically supported, while Mrs. Fisher, inwardly unconvinced, but resigned to this latest proof of Lily's unreason, agreed that perhaps in the end it would be more useful that she should learn the trade. To Regina's work-room Lily was therefore committed by her friends, and there Mrs. Fisher left her with a sigh of relief, while Gerty's watchfulness continued to hover over her at a distance.

Lily had taken up her work early in January: it was now two months later, and she was still being rebuked for her inability to sew spangles on a hat-frame. As she returned to her work she heard a titter pass down the tables. She knew she was an object of criticism and amusement to the other work-women. They were, of course, aware of her history—the exact situation of every girl in the room was known and freely discussed by all the others—but the knowledge did not produce in them any awkward sense of class distinction: it merely explained why her untutored fingers were still blundering over the rudiments of the trade. Lily had no desire that they should recognize any social difference in her; but she had hoped to be received as their equal, and perhaps before long to show herself their superior by a special deftness of touch, and it was humiliating to find that, after two months of drudgery, she still betrayed her lack of early training. Remote was the day when she might aspire to exercise the talents she felt confident of possessing; only experienced workers were entrusted with the delicate art of shaping and trimming the hat, and the forewoman still held her inexorably to the routine of preparatory work.

She began to rip the spangles from the frame, listening absently to the buzz of talk which rose and fell with the coming and going of Miss Haines's* active figure. The air was closer than usual, because Miss Haines, who had a cold, had not allowed a window to be opened even during the noon recess; and Lily's head was so heavy with the weight of a sleepless night that the chatter of her companions had the incoherence of a dream.

"I *told* her he'd never look at her again; and he didn't. I wouldn't have, either—I think she acted real mean to him. He took her to the Arion Hall, and had a hack for her both ways. . . . She's taken ten bottles, and her headaches don't seem no better—but she's written a testimonial to say the first bottle cured her, and she got five dollars and her picture in the paper. . . . Mrs. Trenor's hat? The one with the green Paradise? Here, Miss Haines—it'll be ready right off. . . . That was one of the Trenor girls here yesterday with Mrs. George Dorset. How'd

---

*In French, *haine* means "hatred."

I know? Why, Madam sent for me to alter the flower in that Virot* hat—the blue tulle: she's tall and slight, with her hair fuzzed out—a good deal like Mamie Leach, on'y thinner. . . ."

On and on it flowed, a current of meaningless sound, on which, startlingly enough, a familiar name now and then floated to the surface. It was the strangest part of Lily's strange experience, the hearing of these names, the seeing the fragmentary and distorted image of the world she had lived in reflected in the mirror of the working-girls' minds. She had never before suspected the mixture of insatiable curiosity and contemptuous freedom with which she and her kind were discussed in this underworld of toilers who lived on their vanity and self-indulgence. Every girl in Mme. Regina's work-room knew to whom the headgear in her hands was destined, and had her opinion of its future wearer, and a definite knowledge of the latter's place in the social system. That Lily was a star fallen from that sky did not, after the first stir of curiosity had subsided, materially add to their interest in her. She had fallen, she had "gone under," and true to the ideal of their race, they were awed only by success—by the gross tangible image of material achievement. The consciousness of her different point of view merely kept them at a little distance from her, as though she were a foreigner with whom it was an effort to talk.

"Miss Bart, if you can't sew those spangles on more regular I guess you'd better give the hat to Miss Kilroy."

Lily looked down ruefully at her handiwork. The forewoman was right: the sewing on of the spangles was inexcusably bad. What made her so much more clumsy than usual? Was it a growing distaste for her task, or actual physical disability? She felt tired and confused: it was an effort to put her thoughts together. She rose and handed the hat to Miss Kilroy, who took it with a suppressed smile.

"I'm sorry; I'm afraid I am not well," she said to the forewoman.

Miss Haines offered no comment. From the first she had augured ill of Mme. Regina's consenting to include a fashionable

---

*French clothing designer.

apprentice among her workers. In that temple of art no raw be-
ginners were wanted, and Miss Haines would have been more
than human had she not taken a certain pleasure in seeing her
forebodings confirmed.

"You'd better go back to binding edges," she said drily.

Lily slipped out last among the band of liberated work-
women. She did not care to be mingled in their noisy dispersal:
once in the street, she always felt an irresistible return to her old
standpoint, an instinctive shrinking from all that was unpolished
and promiscuous. In the days—how distant they now seemed!—
when she had visited the Girls' Club with Gerty Farish, she had
felt an enlightened interest in the working-classes; but that was
because she looked down on them from above, from the happy
altitude of her grace and her beneficence. Now that she was on
a level with them, the point of view was less interesting.

She felt a touch on her arm, and met the penitent eye of Miss
Kilroy.

"Miss Bart, I guess you can sew those spangles on as well as
I can when you're feeling right. Miss Haines didn't act fair to
you."

Lily's colour rose at the unexpected advance: it was a long
time since real kindness had looked at her from any eyes but
Gerty's.

"Oh, thank you: I'm not particularly well, but Miss Haines
was right. I *am* clumsy."

"Well, it's mean work for anybody with a headache." Miss
Kilroy paused irresolutely. "You ought to go right home and lay
down. Ever try orangeine?"*

"Thank you." Lily held out her hand. "It's very kind of you—
I mean to go home."

She looked gratefully at Miss Kilroy, but neither knew what
more to say. Lily was aware that the other was on the point of
offering to go home with her, but she wanted to be alone and
silent—even kindness, the sort of kindness that Miss Kilroy
could give, would have jarred on her just then.

"Thank you," she repeated as she turned away.

---

*Orange-flavored drink.

She struck westward through the dreary March twilight, toward the street where her boarding-house stood. She had resolutely refused Gerty's offer of hospitality. Something of her mother's fierce shrinking from observation and sympathy was beginning to develop in her, and the promiscuity of small quarters and close intimacy seemed, on the whole, less endurable than the solitude of a hall bedroom* in a house where she could come and go unremarked among other workers. For a while she had been sustained by this desire for privacy and independence; but now, perhaps from increasing physical weariness, the lassitude brought about by hours of unwonted confinement she was beginning to feel acutely the ugliness and discomfort of her surroundings. The day's task done, she dreaded to return to her narrow room, with its blotched wall-paper and shabby paint; and she hated every step of the walk thither, through the degradation of a New York street in the last stages of decline from fashion to commerce.

But what she dreaded most of all was having to pass the chemist's at the corner of Sixth Avenue. She had meant to take another street: she had usually done so of late. But today her steps were irresistibly drawn toward the flaring plate-glass corner; she tried to take the lower crossing, but a laden dray crowded her back, and she struck across the street obliquely, reaching the sidewalk just opposite the chemist's door.

Over the counter she caught the eye of the clerk who had waited on her before, and slipped the prescription into his hand. There could be no question about the prescription: it was a copy of one of Mrs. Hatch's, obligingly furnished by that lady's chemist. Lily was confident that the clerk would fill it without hesitation; yet the nervous dread of a refusal, or even of an expression of doubt, communicated itself to her restless hands as she affected to examine the bottles of perfume stacked on the glass case before her.

The clerk had read the prescription without comment; but in the act of handing out the bottle he paused.

---

*Smallest and cheapest room in a boarding house.

"You don't want to increase the dose, you know," he remarked.

Lily's heart contracted. What did he mean by looking at her in that way?

"Of course not," she murmured, holding out her hand.

"That's all right: it's a queer-acting drug. A drop or two more, and off you go—the doctors don't know why."

The dread lest he should question her, or keep the bottle back, choked the murmur of acquiescence in her throat; and when at length she emerged safely from the shop she was almost dizzy with the intensity of her relief. The mere touch of the packet thrilled her tired nerves with the delicious promise of a night of sleep, and in the reaction from her momentary fear she felt as if the first fumes of drowsiness were already stealing over her.

In her confusion she stumbled against a man who was hurrying down the last steps of the elevated station.* He drew back, and she heard her name uttered with surprise. It was Rosedale, fur-coated, glossy and prosperous—but why did she seem to see him so far off, and as if through a mist of splintered crystals? Before she could account for the phenomenon she found herself shaking hands with him. They had parted with scorn on her side and anger upon his, but all trace of these emotions seemed to vanish as their hands met, and she was only aware of a confused wish that she might continue to hold fast to him.

"Why, what's the matter, Miss Lily? You're not well!" he exclaimed; and she forced her lips into a pallid smile of reassurance.

"I'm a little tired—its nothing. Stay with me a moment, please," she faltered. That she should be asking this service of Rosedale!

He glanced at the dirty and unpropitious corner on which they stood, with the shriek of the "elevated" and the tumult of trains and waggons contending hideously in their ears.

"We can't stay here; but let me take you somewhere for a cup

---

*"Elevated" refers to the trains that then ran above Sixth Avenue and other New York City streets.

of tea. The *Longworth* is only a few yards off, and there'll be no one there at this hour."

A cup of tea in quiet, somewhere out of the noise and ugliness, seemed for the moment the one solace she could bear. A few steps brought them to the ladies' door of the hotel he had named, and a moment later he was seated opposite to her, and the waiter had placed the tea-tray between them.

"Not a drop of brandy or whiskey first? You look regularly done up, Miss Lily. Well, take your tea strong, then; and, waiter, get a cushion for the lady's back."

Lily smiled faintly at the injunction to take her tea strong. It was the temptation she was always struggling to resist. Her craving for the keen stimulant was forever conflicting with that other craving for sleep—the midnight craving which only the little phial in her hand could still. But today, at any rate, the tea could hardly be too strong: she counted on it to pour warmth and resolution into her empty veins.

As she leaned back before him, her lids drooping in utter lassitude, though the first warm draught already tinged her face with returning life, Rosedale was seized afresh by the poignant surprise of her beauty. The dark pencilling of fatigue under her eyes, the morbid blue-veined pallour of the temples, brought out the brightness of her hair and lips, as though all her ebbing vitality were centred there. Against the dull chocolate-coloured background of the restaurant, the purity of her head stood out, as it had never done in the most brightly-lit ball-room. He looked at her with a startled uncomfortable feeling, as though her beauty were a forgotten enemy that had lain in ambush and now sprang out on him unawares.

To clear the air he tried to take an easy tone with her. "Why, Miss Lily, I haven't seen you for an age. I didn't know what had become of you."

As he spoke, he was checked by an embarrassing sense of the complications to which this might lead. Though he had not seen her he had heard of her; he knew of her connection with Mrs. Hatch, and of the talk resulting from it. Mrs. Hatch's *milieu* was one which he had once assiduously frequented, and now as devoutly shunned.

Lily, to whom the tea had restored her usual clearness of

mind, saw what was in his thoughts and said with a slight smile: "You would not be likely to know about me. I have joined the working classes."

He stared in genuine wonder. "You don't mean—? Why, what on earth are you doing?"

"Learning to be a milliner—at least *trying* to learn," she hastily qualified the statement.

Rosedale suppressed a low whistle of surprise. "Come off— you ain't serious, are you?"

"Perfectly serious. I'm obliged to work for my living."

"But I understood—I thought you were with Norma Hatch."

"You heard I had gone to her as her secretary?"

"Something of the kind, I believe." He leaned forward to re- fill her cup.

Lily guessed the possibilities of embarrassment which the topic held for him, and raising her eyes to his, she said suddenly: "I left her two months ago."

Rosedale continued to fumble awkwardly with the tea-pot, and she felt sure that he had heard what had been said of her. But what was there that Rosedale did not hear?

"Wasn't it a soft berth?" he enquired, with an attempt at lightness.

"Too soft—one might have sunk in too deep." Lily rested one arm on the edge of the table, and sat looking at him more in- tently than she had ever looked before. An uncontrollable im- pulse was urging her to put her case to this man, from whose curiosity she had always so fiercely defended herself.

"You know Mrs. Hatch, I think? Well, perhaps you can un- derstand that she might make things too easy for one."

Rosedale looked faintly puzzled, and she remembered that allusiveness was lost on him.

"It was no place for you, anyhow," he agreed, so suffused and immersed in the light of her full gaze that he found himself being drawn into strange depths of intimacy. He who had had to subsist on mere fugitive glances, looks winged in flight and swiftly lost under covert, now found her eyes settling on him with a brooding intensity that fairly dazzled him.

"I left," Lily continued, "lest people should say I was helping Mrs. Hatch to marry Freddy Van Osburgh—who is not in the

least too good for her—and as they still continue to say it, I see
that I might as well have stayed where I was."

"Oh, Freddy——" Rosedale brushed aside the topic with an
air of its unimportance which gave a sense of the immense perspective he had acquired. "Freddy don't count—but I knew *you*
weren't mixed up in that. It ain't your style."

Lily coloured slightly: she could not conceal from herself that
the words gave her pleasure. She would have liked to sit there,
drinking more tea, and continuing to talk of herself to Rosedale.
But the old habit of observing the conventions reminded her
that it was time to bring their colloquy to an end, and she made
a faint motion to push back her chair.

Rosedale stopped her with a protesting gesture. "Wait a
minute—don't go yet; sit quiet and rest a little longer. You look
thoroughly played out. And you haven't told me——" He broke
off, conscious of going farther than he had meant. She saw the
struggle and understood it; understood also the nature of the
spell to which she yielded as, with his eyes on her face, he began
again abruptly: "What on earth did you mean by saying just now
that you were learning to be a milliner?"

"Just what I said. I am an apprentice at Regina's."

"Good Lord—*you?* But what for? I knew your aunt had
turned you down: Mrs. Fisher told me about it. But I understood you got a legacy from her—"

"I got ten thousand dollars; but the legacy is not to be paid
till next summer."

"Well, but—look here: you could borrow on it any time you
wanted."

She shook her head gravely. "No; for I owe it already."

"Owe it? The whole ten thousand?"

"Every penny." She paused, and then continued abruptly,
with her eyes on his face: "I think Gus Trenor spoke to you once
about having made some money for me in stocks."

She waited, and Rosedale, congested with embarrassment,
muttered that he remembered something of the kind.

"He made about nine thousand dollars," Lily pursued, in the
same tone of eager communicativeness. "At the time, I understood that he was speculating with my own money: it was incredibly stupid of me, but I knew nothing of business. Afterward

I found out that he had *not* used my money—that what he said he had made for me he had really given me. It was meant in kindness, of course; but it was not the sort of obligation one could remain under. Unfortunately I had spent the money before I discovered my mistake; and so my legacy will have to go to pay it back. That is the reason why I am trying to learn a trade."

She made the statement clearly, deliberately, with pauses between the sentences, so that each should have time to sink deeply into her hearer's mind. She had a passionate desire that some one should know the truth about this transaction, and also that the rumour of her intention to repay the money should reach Judy Trenor's ears. And it had suddenly occurred to her that Rosedale, who had surprised Trenor's confidence, was the fitting person to receive and transmit her version of the facts. She had even felt a momentary exhilaration at the thought of thus relieving herself of her detested secret; but the sensation gradually faded in the telling, and as she ended her pallour was suffused with a deep blush of misery.

Rosedale continued to stare at her in wonder; but the wonder took the turn she had least expected.

"But see here—if that's the case, it cleans you out altogether?"

He put it to her as if she had not grasped the consequences of her act; as if her incorrigible ignorance of business were about to precipitate her into a fresh act of folly.

"Altogether—yes," she calmly agreed.

He sat silent, his thick hands clasped on the table, his little puzzled eyes exploring the recesses of the deserted restaurant.

"See here—that's fine," he exclaimed abruptly.

Lily rose from her seat with a deprecating laugh. "Oh, no—it's merely a bore," she asserted, gathering together the ends of her feather scarf.

Rosedale remained seated, too intent on his thoughts to notice her movement. "Miss Lily, if you want any backing—I like pluck——" broke from him disconnectedly.

"Thank you." She held out her hand. "Your tea has given me a tremendous backing. I feel equal to anything now."

Her gesture seemed to show a definite intention of dismissal, but her companion had tossed a bill to the waiter, and was slipping his short arms into his expensive overcoat.

"Wait a minute—you've got to let me walk home with you," he said.

Lily uttered no protest, and when he had paused to make sure of his change they emerged from the hotel and crossed Sixth Avenue again. As she led the way westward past a long line of areas which, through the distortion of their paintless rails, revealed with increasing candour the *disjecta membra** of bygone dinners, Lily felt that Rosedale was taking contemptuous note of the neighbourhood; and before the doorstep at which she finally paused he looked up with an air of incredulous disgust.

"This isn't the place? Some one told me you were living with Miss Farish."

"No: I am boarding here. I have lived too long on my friends."

He continued to scan the blistered brown stone front, the windows draped with discoloured lace, and the Pompeian[†] decoration of the muddy vestibule; then he looked back at her face and said with a visible effort: "You'll let me come and see you some day?"

She smiled, recognizing the heroism of the offer to the point of being frankly touched by it. "Thank you—I shall be very glad," she made answer, in the first sincere words she had ever spoken to him.

That evening in her own room Miss Bart—who had fled early from the heavy fumes of the basement dinner-table—sat musing upon the impulse which had led her to unbosom herself to Rosedale. Beneath it she discovered an increasing sense of loneliness—a dread of returning to the solitude of her room, while she could be anywhere else, or in any company but her own. Cir-

---

*Scattered remains (Latin).

†The reference is to signs of disrepair, as one would find in Pompeii, an ancient Roman city on the Bay of Naples buried by an eruption of Mount Vesuvius in A.D. 79.

cumstances, of late, had combined to cut her off more and more from her few remaining friends. On Carry Fisher's part the withdrawal was perhaps not quite involuntary. Having made her final effort on Lily's behalf, and landed her safely in Mme. Regina's work-room, Mrs. Fisher seemed disposed to rest from her labours; and Lily, understanding the reason, could not condemn her. Carry had in fact come dangerously near to being involved in the episode of Mrs. Norma Hatch, and it had taken some verbal ingenuity to extricate herself. She frankly owned to having brought Lily and Mrs. Hatch together, but then she did not know Mrs. Hatch—she had expressly warned Lily that she did not know Mrs. Hatch—and besides, she was not Lily's keeper, and really the girl was old enough to take care of herself. Carry did not put her own case so brutally, but she allowed it to be thus put for her by her latest bosom friend, Mrs. Jack Stepney: Mrs. Stepney, trembling over the narrowness of her only brother's escape, but eager to vindicate Mrs. Fisher, at whose house she could count on the "jolly parties" which had become a necessity to her since marriage had emancipated her from the Van Osburgh point of view.

Lily understood the situation and could make allowances for it. Carry had been a good friend to her in difficult days, and perhaps only a friendship like Gerty's could be proof against such an increasing strain. Gerty's friendship did indeed hold fast; yet Lily was beginning to avoid her also. For she could not go to Gerty's without risk of meeting Selden; and to meet him now would be pure pain. It was pain enough even to think of him, whether she considered him in the distinctness of her waking thoughts, or felt the obsession of his presence through the blur of her tormented nights. That was one of the reasons why she had turned again to Mrs. Hatch's prescription. In the uneasy snatches of her natural dreams he came to her sometimes in the old guise of fellowship and tenderness; and she would rise from the sweet delusion mocked and emptied of her courage. But in the sleep which the phial procured she sank far below such half-waking visitations, sank into depths of dreamless annihilation from which she woke each morning with an obliterated past.

Gradually, to be sure, the stress of the old thoughts would return; but at least they did not importune her waking hour. The drug gave her a momentary illusion of complete renewal, from which she drew strength to take up her daily work. The strength was more and more needed as the perplexities of her future increased. She knew that to Gerty and Mrs. Fisher she was only passing through a temporary period of probation, since they believed that the apprenticeship she was serving at Mme. Regina's would enable her, when Mrs. Peniston's legacy was paid, to realize the vision of the green-and-white shop with the fuller competence acquired by her preliminary training. But to Lily herself, aware that the legacy could not be put to such a use, the preliminary training seemed a wasted effort. She understood clearly enough that, even if she could ever learn to compete with hands formed from childhood for their special work, the small pay she received would not be a sufficient addition to her income to compensate her for such drudgery. And the realization of this fact brought her recurringly face to face with the temptation to use the legacy in establishing her business. Once installed, and in command of her own work-women, she believed she had sufficient tact and ability to attract a fashionable *clientèle;* and if the business succeeded she could gradually lay aside money enough to discharge her debt to Trenor. But the task might take years to accomplish, even if she continued to stint herself to the utmost; and meanwhile her pride would be crushed under the weight of an intolerable obligation.

These were her superficial considerations; but under them lurked the secret dread that the obligation might not always remain intolerable. She knew she could not count on her continuity of purpose, and what really frightened her was the thought that she might gradually accommodate herself to remaining indefinitely in Trenor's debt, as she had accommodated herself to the part allotted her on the *Sabrina*, and as she had so nearly drifted into acquiescing with Stancy's scheme for the advancement of Mrs. Hatch. Her danger lay, as she knew, in her old incurable dread of discomfort and poverty; in the fear of that mounting tide of dinginess against which her mother had so passionately warned her. And now a new vista of peril opened before her. She understood that Rosedale was ready to lend her money; and the longing to take advantage of his offer began to haunt her insidiously. It was of course impossible to accept a loan from Rosedale; but proximate possibilities hovered temptingly before her. She was quite sure that he would come and see her again, and almost sure that, if he did, she could bring him to the point of offering to marry her on the terms she had previously rejected. Would she still reject them if they were offered? More and more, with every fresh mischance befalling her, did the pursuing furies seem to take the shape of Bertha Dorset; and close at hand, safely locked among her papers, lay the means of ending their pursuit. The temptation, which her scorn of Rosedale had once enabled her to reject, now insistently returned upon her; and how much strength was left her to oppose it?

What little there was must at any rate be husbanded to the utmost; she could not trust herself again to the perils of a sleepless night. Through the long hours of silence the dark spirit of fatigue and loneliness crouched upon her breast, leaving her so drained of bodily strength that her morning thoughts swam in a haze of weakness. The only hope of renewal lay in the little bottle at her bed-side; and how much longer that hope would last she dared not conjecture.

LILY, LINGERING FOR A moment on the corner, looked out on the afternoon spectacle of Fifth Avenue.

It was a day in late April, and the sweetness of spring was in the air. It mitigated the ugliness of the long crowded thoroughfare, blurred the gaunt roof-lines, threw a mauve veil over the discouraging perspective of the side streets, and gave a touch of poetry to the delicate haze of green that marked the entrance to the Park.

As Lily stood there, she recognized several familiar faces in the passing carriages. The season was over, and its ruling forces had disbanded; but a few still lingered, delaying their departure for Europe, or passing through town on their return from the South. Among them was Mrs. Van Osburgh, swaying majestically in her C-spring barouche,* with Mrs. Percy Gryce at her side, and the new heir to the Gryce millions enthroned before them on his nurse's knees. They were succeeded by Mrs. Hatch's electric victoria,† in which that lady reclined in the lonely splendour of a spring toilet obviously designed for company; and a moment or two later came Judy Trenor, accompanied by Lady Skiddaw, who had come over for her annual tarpon fishing and a dip into "the street."

This fleeting glimpse of her past served to emphasize the sense of aimlessness with which Lily at length turned toward home. She had nothing to do for the rest of the day, nor for the days to come; for the season was over in millinery as well as in society, and a week earlier Mme. Regina had notified her that her services were no longer required. Mme. Regina always re-

---

*Four-wheeled carriage with two double seats facing each other.
†Early automobile based on the design of a two-passenger carriage.

duced her staff on the first of May, and Miss Bart's attendance had of late been so irregular—she had so often been unwell, and had done so little work when she came—that it was only as a favour that her dismissal had hitherto been deferred.

Lily did not question the justice of the decision. She was conscious of having been forgetful, awkward and slow to learn. It was bitter to acknowledge her inferiority even to herself, but the fact had been brought home to her that as a bread-winner she could never compete with professional ability. Since she had been brought up to be ornamental, she could hardly blame herself for failing to serve any practical purpose; but the discovery put an end to her consoling sense of universal efficiency.

As she turned homeward her thoughts shrank in anticipation from the fact that there would be nothing to get up for the next morning. The luxury of lying late in bed was a pleasure belonging to the life of ease; it had no part in the utilitarian existence of the boarding-house. She liked to leave her room early, and to return to it as late as possible; and she was walking slowly now in order to postpone the detested approach to her doorstep.

But the doorstep, as she drew near it, acquired a sudden interest from the fact that it was occupied—and indeed filled—by the conspicuous figure of Mr. Rosedale, whose presence seemed to take on an added amplitude from the meanness of his surroundings.

The sight stirred Lily with an irresistible sense of triumph. Rosedale, a day or two after their chance meeting, had called to enquire if she had recovered from her indisposition; but since then she had not seen or heard from him, and his absence seemed to betoken a struggle to keep away, to let her pass once more out of his life. If this were the case, his return showed that the struggle had been unsuccessful, for Lily knew he was not the man to waste his time in an ineffectual sentimental dalliance. He was too busy, too practical, and above all too much preoccupied with his own advancement, to indulge in such unprofitable asides.

In the peacock-blue parlour, with its bunches of dried pampas grass, and discoloured steel engravings of sentimental episodes, he looked about him with unconcealed disgust, laying

his hat distrustfully on the dusty console adorned with a Rogers
statuette.*

Lily sat down on one of the plush and rosewood sofas, and
he deposited himself in a rocking-chair draped with a starched
antimacassar which scraped unpleasantly against the pink fold of
skin above his collar.

"My goodness—you can't go on living here!" he exclaimed.

Lily smiled at his tone. "I am not sure that I can; but I have
gone over my expenses very carefully, and I rather think I shall
be able to manage it."

"Be able to manage it? That's not what I mean—it's no place
for you!"

"It's what *I* mean; for I have been out of work for the last
week."

"Out of work—out of work! What a way for you to talk! The
idea of your having to work—it's preposterous." He brought out
his sentences in short violent jerks, as though they were forced
up from a deep inner crater of indignation. "It's a farce—a crazy
farce," he repeated, his eyes fixed on the long vista of the room
reflected in the blotched glass between the windows.

Lily continued to meet his expostulations with a smile. "I
don't know why I should regard myself as an exception——" she
began.

"Because you *are;* that's why; and your being in a place like
this is a damnable outrage. I can't talk of it calmly."

She had in truth never seen him so shaken out of his usual
glibness; and there was something almost moving to her in his
inarticulate struggle with his emotions.

He rose with a start which left the rocking-chair quivering
on its beam ends, and placed himself squarely, before her.

"Look here, Miss Lily, I'm going to Europe next week:
going over to Paris and London for a couple of months—and
I can't leave you like this. I can't do it. I know it's none of my
business—you've let me understand that often enough; but
things are worse with you now than they have been before, and

---

*Mass-produced sculpture by the once-popular American artist John
Rogers (1829–1904).

you must see that you've got to accept help from somebody. You spoke to me the other day about some debt to Trenor. I know what you mean—and I respect you for feeling as you do about it."

A blush of surprise rose to Lily's pale face, but before she could interrupt him he had continued eagerly: "Well, I'll lend you the money to pay Trenor; and I won't—I—see here, don't take me up till I've finished. What I mean is, it'll be a plain business arrangement, such as one man would make with another. Now, what have you got to say against that?"

Lily's blush deepened to a glow in which humiliation and gratitude were mingled; and both sentiments revealed themselves in the unexpected gentleness of her reply.

"Only this: that it is exactly what Gus Trenor proposed; and that I can never again be sure of understanding the plainest business arrangement." Then, realizing that this answer contained a germ of injustice, she added, even more kindly: "Not that I don't appreciate your kindness—that I'm not grateful for it. But a business arrangement between us would in any case be impossible, because I shall have no security to give when my debt to Gus Trenor has been paid."

Rosedale received this statement in silence: he seemed to feel the note of finality in her voice, yet to be unable to accept it as closing the question between them.

In the silence Lily had a clear perception of what was passing through his mind. Whatever perplexity he felt as to the inexorableness of her course—however little he penetrated its motive—she saw that it unmistakably tended to strengthen her hold over him. It was as though the sense in her of unexplained scruples and resistances had the same attraction as the delicacy of feature, the fastidiousness of manner, which gave her an external rarity, an air of being impossible to match. As he advanced in social experience this uniqueness had acquired a greater value for him, as though he were a collector who had learned to distinguish minor differences of design and quality in some long-coveted object.

Lily, perceiving all this, understood that he would marry her at once, on the sole condition of a reconciliation with Mrs. Dorset; and the temptation was the less easy to put aside because, little by little, circumstances were breaking down her dislike for Rosedale. The dislike, indeed, still subsisted; but it was penetrated here and there by the perception of mitigating qualities in him: of a certain gross kindliness, a rather helpless fidelity of sentiment, which seemed to be struggling through the hard surface of his material ambitions.

Reading his dismissal in her eyes, he held out his hand with a gesture which conveyed something of this inarticulate conflict.

"If you'd only let me, I'd set you up over them all—I'd put you where you could wipe your feet on 'em!" he declared; and it touched her oddly to see that his new passion had not altered his old standard of values.

Lily took no sleeping-drops that night. She lay awake viewing her situation in the crude light which Rosedale's visit had shed on it. In fending off the offer he was so plainly ready to renew, had she not sacrificed to one of those abstract notions of honour that might be called the conventionalities of the moral life? What debt did she owe to a social order which had condemned and banished her without trial? She had never been heard in her own defence; she was innocent of the charge on which she had been found guilty; and the irregularity of her conviction might seem to justify the use of methods as irregular in recovering her lost rights. Bertha Dorset, to save herself, had not scrupled to ruin her by an open falsehood; why should she hesitate to make private use of the facts that chance had put her way? After all, half the opprobrium of such an act lies in the name attached to it. Call it blackmail and it becomes unthinkable; but explain that it injures no one, and that the rights regained by it were unjustly forfeited, and he must be a formalist indeed who can find no plea in its defence.

The arguments pleading for it with Lily were the old unanswerable ones of the personal situation: the sense of injury, the sense of failure, the passionate craving for a fair chance against the selfish despotism of society. She had learned by experience that she had neither the aptitude nor the moral constancy to remake her life on new lines; to become a worker among workers, and let the world of luxury and pleasure sweep by her unregarded. She could not hold herself much to blame for this ineffectiveness, and she was perhaps less to blame than she believed. Inherited tendencies had combined with early training to make her the highly specialized product she was: an organism as helpless out of its narrow range as the sea-anemone torn from the rock. She had been fashioned to adorn and delight; to what other end does nature round the rose-leaf and paint the hummingbird's breast? And was it her fault that the purely decorative mission is less easily and harmoniously fulfilled among social beings than in the world of nature? That it is apt to be hampered by material necessities or complicated by moral scruples?

These last were the two antagonistic forces which fought out their battle in her breast during the long watches of the night;* and when she rose the next morning she hardly knew where the victory lay. She was exhausted by the reaction of a night without sleep, coming after many nights of rest artificially obtained; and in the distorting light of fatigue the future stretched out before her grey, interminable, and desolate.

She lay late in bed, refusing the coffee and fried eggs which the friendly Irish servant thrust through her door, and hating the intimate domestic noises of the house and the cries and rumblings of the street. Her week of idleness had brought home to her with exaggerated force these small aggravations of the boarding-house world, and she yearned for that other luxurious world, whose machinery is so carefully concealed that one scene flows into another without perceptible agency.

At length she rose and dressed. Since she had left Mme. Regina's she had spent her days in the streets, partly to escape from the uncongenial promiscuities of the boarding-house, and partly in the hope that physical fatigue would help her to sleep. But once out of the house, she could not decide where to go for she had avoided Gerty since her dismissal from the milliner's and she was not sure of a welcome anywhere else.

The morning was in harsh contrast to the previous day. A cold grey sky threatened rain, and a high wind drove the dust in

---

*A reference to Henry Wadsworth Longfellow's poem "The Cross of Snow" (1879): "In the long, sleepless watches of the night."

wild spirals up and down the street. Lily walked up Fifth Avenue toward the Park, hoping to find a sheltered nook, where she might sit; but the wind chilled her, and after an hour's wandering under the tossing boughs she yielded to her increasing weariness, and took refuge in a little restaurant in Fifty-ninth Street. She was not hungry, and had meant to go without luncheon; but she was too tired to return home, and the long perspective of white tables showed alluringly through the windows.

The room was full of women and girls, all too much engaged in the rapid absorption of tea and pie to remark her entrance. A hum of shrill voices reverberated against the low ceiling, leaving Lily shut out in a little circle of silence. She felt a sudden pang of profound loneliness. She had lost the sense of time, and it seemed to her as though she had not spoken to any one for days. Her eyes sought the faces about her, craving a responsive glance, some sign of an intuition of her trouble. But the sallow preoccupied women, with their bags and note-books and rolls of music, were all engrossed in their own affairs, and even those who sat by themselves were busy running over proof-sheets or devouring magazines between their hurried gulps of tea. Lily alone was stranded in a great waste of disoccupation.

She drank several cups of the tea which was served with her portion of stewed oysters, and her brain felt clearer and livelier when she emerged once more into the street. She realized now that, as she sat in the restaurant, she had unconsciously arrived at a final decision. The discovery gave her an immediate illusion of activity: it was exhilarating to think that she had actually a reason for hurrying home. To prolong her enjoyment of the sensation she decided to walk; but the distance was so great that she found herself glancing nervously at the clocks on the way. One of the surprises of her unoccupied state was the discovery that time, when it is left to itself and no definite demands are made on it, cannot be trusted to move at any recognized pace. Usually it loiters; but just when one has come to count upon its slowness, it may suddenly break into a wild irrational gallop.

She found, however, on reaching home, that the hour was still early enough for her to sit down and rest a few minutes before putting her plan into execution. The delay did not perceptibly weaken her resolve. She was frightened and yet stimulated

by the reserved force of resolution which she felt within herself:
she saw it was going to be easier, a great deal easier, than she had
imagined.

At five o'clock she rose, unlocked her trunk, and took out a
sealed packet which she slipped into the bosom of her dress.
Even the contact with the packet did not shake her nerves as she
had half-expected it would. She seemed encased in a strong ar-
mour of indifference, as though the vigorous exertion of her will
had finally benumbed her finer sensibilities.

She dressed herself once more for the street, locked her door
and went out. When she emerged on the pavement, the day was
still high, but a threat of rain darkened the sky and cold gusts
shook the signs projecting from the basement shops along the
street. She reached Fifth Avenue and began to walk slowly
northward. She was sufficiently familiar with Mrs. Dorset's
habits to know that she could always be found at home after five.
She might not, indeed, be accessible to visitors, especially to a
visitor so unwelcome, and against whom it was quite possible
that she had guarded herself by special orders; but Lily had written a note which she meant to send up with her name, and
which she thought would secure her admission.

She had allowed herself time to walk to Mrs. Dorset's, thinking that the quick movement through the cold evening air would
help to steady her nerves; but she really felt no need of being
tranquillized. Her survey of the situation remained calm and unwavering.

As she reached Fiftieth Street the clouds broke abruptly, and
a rush of cold rain slanted into her face. She had no umbrella
and the moisture quickly penetrated her thin spring dress. She
was still half a mile from her destination, and she decided to
walk across to Madison Avenue and take the electric car. As she
turned into the side street, a vague memory stirred in her. The
row of budding trees, the new brick and limestone house-fronts,
the Georgian flat-house with flower-boxes on its balconies, were
merged together into the setting of a familiar scene. It was down
this street that she had walked with Selden, that September day
two years ago; a few yards ahead was the doorway they had entered together. The recollection loosened a throng of benumbed
sensations—longings, regrets, imaginings, the throbbing brood

of the only spring her heart had ever known. It was strange to find herself passing his house on such an errand. She seemed suddenly to see her action as he would see it—and the fact of his own connection with it, the fact that, to attain her end, she must trade on his name, and profit by a secret of his past, chilled her blood with shame. What a long way she had travelled since the day of their first talk together. Even then her feet had been set in the path she was now following—even then she had resisted the hand he had held out.

All her resentment of his fancied coldness was swept away in this overwhelming rush of recollection. Twice he had been ready to help her—to help her by loving her, as he had said—and if, the third time, he had seemed to fail her, whom but herself could she accuse? . . . Well, that part of her life was over; she did not know why her thoughts still clung to it. But the sudden longing to see him remained; it grew to hunger as she paused on the pavement opposite his door. The street was dark and empty, swept by the rain. She had a vision of his quiet room, of the bookshelves, and the fire on the hearth. She looked up and saw a light in his window; then she crossed the street and entered the house.

THE LIBRARY LOOKED AS she had pictured it. The green-shaded lamps made tranquil circles of light in the gathering dusk, a little fire flickered on the hearth, and Selden's easy-chair, which stood near it, had been pushed aside when he rose to admit her.

He had checked his first movement of surprise, and stood silent, waiting for her to speak, while she paused a moment on the threshold, assailed by a rush of memories.

The scene was unchanged. She recognized the row of shelves from which he had taken down his *La Bruyère*, and the worn arm of the chair he had leaned against while she examined the precious volume. But then the wide September light had filled the room, making it seem a part of the outer world: now the shaded lamps and the warm hearth, detaching it from the gathering darkness of the street, gave it a sweeter touch of intimacy.

Becoming gradually aware of the surprise under Selden's silence, Lily turned to him and said simply: "I came to tell you that I was sorry for the way we parted—for what I said to you that day at Mrs. Hatch's."

The words rose to her lips spontaneously. Even on her way up the stairs, she had not thought of preparing a pretext for her visit, but she now felt an intense longing to dispel the cloud of misunderstanding that hung between them.

Selden returned her look with a smile. "I was sorry too that we should have parted in that way; but I am not sure I didn't bring it on myself. Luckily I had foreseen the risk I was taking——"

"So that you really didn't care——?" broke from her with a flash of her old irony.

"So that I was prepared for the consequences," he corrected good-humouredly. "But we'll talk of all this later. Do come and sit by the fire. I can recommend that arm-chair, if you'll let me put a cushion behind you."

While he spoke she had moved slowly to the middle of the room, and paused near his writing-table, where the lamp, striking upward, cast exaggerated shadows on the pallour of her delicately-hollowed face.

"You look tired—do sit down," he repeated gently.

She did not seem to hear the request. "I wanted you to know that I left Mrs. Hatch immediately, after I saw you," she said, as though continuing her confession.

"Yes—yes; I know," he assented, with a rising tinge of embarrassment.

"And that I did so because you told me to. Before you came I had already begun to see that it would be impossible to remain with her—for the reasons you gave me; but I wouldn't admit it—I wouldn't let you see that I understood what you meant."

"Ah, I might have trusted you to find your own way out—don't overwhelm me with the sense of my officiousness!"

His light tone, in which, had her nerves been steadier, she would have recognized the mere effort to bridge over an awkward moment, jarred on her passionate desire to be understood. In her strange state of extra-lucidity, which gave her the sense of being already at the heart of the situation, it seemed incredible that any one should think it necessary to linger in the conventional outskirts of word-play and evasion.

"It was not that—I was not ungrateful," she insisted. But the power of expression failed her suddenly; she felt a tremor in her throat, and two tears gathered and fell slowly from her eyes.

Selden moved forward and took her hand. "You are very tired. Why won't you sit down and let me make you comfortable?"

He drew her to the arm-chair near the fire, and placed a cushion behind her shoulders.

"And now you must let me make you some tea: you know I always have that amount of hospitality at my command."

She shook her head, and two more tears ran over. But she did not weep easily, and the long habit of self-control reasserted itself, though she was still too tremulous to speak.

"You know I can coax the water to boil in five minutes," Seldon continued, speaking as though she were a troubled child.

His words recalled the vision of that other afternoon when

they had sat together over his tea-table and talked jestingly of her future. There were moments when that day seemed more remote than any other event in her life; and yet she could always relive it in its minutest detail.

She made a gesture of refusal. "No: I drink too much tea. I would rather sit quiet—I must go in a moment," she added confusedly.

Selden continued to stand near her, leaning against the mantelpiece. The tinge of constraint was beginning to be more distinctly perceptible under the friendly ease of his manner. Her self-absorption had not allowed her to perceive it at first; but now that her consciousness was once more putting forth its eager feelers, she saw that her presence was becoming an embarrassment to him. Such a situation can be saved only by an immediate outrush of feeling; and on Selden's side the determining impulse was still lacking.

The discovery did not disturb Lily as it might once have done. She had passed beyond the phase of well-bred reciprocity, in which every demonstration must be scrupulously proportioned to the emotion it elicits, and generosity of feeling is the only ostentation condemned. But the sense of loneliness returned with redoubled force as she saw herself forever shut out from Selden's inmost self. She had come to him with no definite purpose; the mere longing to see him had directed her; but the secret hope she had carried with her suddenly revealed itself in its death-pang.

"I must go," she repeated, making a motion to rise from her chair. "But I may not see you again for a long time, and I wanted to tell you that I have never forgotten the things you said to me at Bellomont, and that sometimes—sometimes when I seemed farthest from remembering them—they have helped me, and kept me from mistakes; kept me from really becoming what many people have thought me."

Strive as she would to put some order in her thoughts, the words would not come more clearly; yet she felt that she could not leave him without trying to make him understand that she had saved herself whole from the seeming ruin of her life.

A change had come over Selden's face as she spoke. Its

guarded look had yielded to an expression still untinged by personal emotion, but full of a gentle understanding.

"I am glad to have you tell me that; but nothing I have said has really made the difference. The difference is in yourself—it will always be there. And since it *is* there, it can't really matter to you what people think: you are so sure that your friends will always understand you."

"Ah, don't say that—don't say that what you have told me has made no difference. It seems to shut me out—to leave me all alone with the other people." She had risen and stood before him, once more completely mastered by the inner urgency of the moment. The consciousness of his half-divined reluctance had vanished. Whether he wished it or not, he must see her wholly for once before they parted.

Her voice had gathered strength, and she looked him gravely in the eyes as she continued. "Once—twice—you gave me the chance to escape from my life, and I refused it: refused it because I was a coward. Afterward I saw my mistake—I saw I could never be happy with what had contented me before. But it was too late: you had judged me—I understood. It was too late for happiness—but not too late to be helped by the thought of what I had missed. That is all I have lived on—don't take it from me now! Even in my worst moments it has been like a little light in the darkness. Some women are strong enough to be good by themselves, but I needed the help of your belief in me. Perhaps I might have resisted a great temptation, but the little ones would have pulled me down. And then I remembered—I remembered your saying that such a life could never satisfy me; and I was ashamed to admit to myself that it could. That is what you did for me—that is what I wanted to thank you for. I wanted to tell you that I have always remembered; and that I have tried—tried hard . . ."

She broke off suddenly. Her tears had risen again, and in drawing out her handkerchief her fingers touched the packet in the folds of her dress. A wave of colour suffused her, and the words died on her lips. Then she lifted her eyes to his and went on in an altered voice.

"I have tried hard—but life is difficult, and I am a very useless person. I can hardly be said to have an independent existence. I was just a screw or a cog in the great machine I called life, and when I dropped out of it I found I was of no use anywhere else. What can one do when one finds that one only fits into one hole? One must get back to it or be thrown out into the rubbish heap—and you don't know what it's like in the rubbish heap!"

Her lips wavered into a smile—she had been distracted by the whimsical remembrance of the confidences she had made to him, two years earlier, in that very room. Then she had been planning to marry Percy Gryce—what was it she was planning now?

The blood had risen strongly under Selden's dark skin, but his emotion showed itself only in an added seriousness of manner.

"You have something to tell me—do you mean to marry?" he said abruptly.

Lily's eyes did not falter, but a look of wonder, of puzzled self-interrogation, formed itself slowly in their depths. In the light of his question, she had paused to ask herself if her decision had really been taken when she entered the room.

"You always told me I should have to come to it sooner or later!" she said with a faint smile.

"And you have come to it now?"

"I shall have to come to it—presently. But there is something else I must come to first." She paused again, trying to transmit to her voice the steadiness of her recovered smile. "There is some one I must say goodbye to. Oh, not *you*—we are sure to see each other again—but the Lily Bart you knew. I have kept her with me all this time, but now we are going to part, and I have brought her back to you—I am going to leave her here. When I go out presently she will not go with me. I shall like to think that she has stayed with you—and she'll be no trouble, she'll take up no room."

She went toward him, and put out her hand, still smiling. "Will you let her stay with you?" she asked.

He caught her hand, and she felt in his the vibration of feeling that had not yet risen to his lips. "Lily—can't I help you?" he exclaimed.

She looked at him gently. "Do you remember what you said

to me once? That you could help me only by loving me? Well—you did love me for a moment; and it helped me. It has always helped me. But the moment is gone—it was I who let it go. And one must go on living. Goodbye."

She laid her other hand on his, and they looked at each other with a kind of solemnity, as though they stood in the presence of death. Something in truth lay dead between them—the love she had killed in him and could no longer call to life. But something lived between them also, and leaped up in her like an imperishable flame: it was the love his love had kindled, the passion of her soul for his.

In its light everything else dwindled and fell away from her. She understood now that she could not go forth and leave her old self with him: that self must indeed live on in his presence, but it must still continue to be hers.

Selden had retained her hand, and continued to scrutinize her with a strange sense of foreboding. The external aspect of the situation had vanished for him as completely as for her: he felt it only as one of those rare moments which lift the veil from their faces as they pass.

"Lily," he said in a low voice, "you mustn't speak in this way. I can't let you go without knowing what you mean to do. Things may change—but they don't pass. You can never go out of my life."

She met his eyes with an illumined look. "No," she said. "I see that now. Let us always be friends. Then I shall feel safe, whatever happens."

"Whatever happens? What do you mean? What is going to happen?"

She turned away quietly and walked toward the hearth.

"Nothing at present—except that I am very cold, and that before I go you must make up the fire for me."

She knelt on the hearthrug, stretching her hands to the embers. Puzzled by the sudden change in her tone, he mechanically gathered a handful of wood from the basket and tossed it on the fire. As he did so, he noticed how thin her hands looked against the rising light of the flames. He saw too, under the loose lines of her dress, how the curves of her figure had shrunk to angularity; he remembered long afterward how the red play of the flame sharpened the depression of her nostrils, and intensified the blackness of the shadows which struck up from her cheekbones to her eyes. She knelt there for a few moments in silence; a silence which he dared not break. When she rose he fancied that he saw her draw something from her dress and drop it into the fire; but he hardly noticed the gesture at the time. His faculties seemed tranced, and he was still groping for the word to break the spell.

She went up to him and laid her hands on his shoulders. "Goodbye," she said, and as he bent over her she touched his forehead with her lips.

13

THE STREET-LAMPS WERE lit, but the rain had ceased, and there was a momentary revival of light in the upper sky.

Lily walked on unconscious of her surroundings. She was still treading the buoyant ether which emanates from the high moments of life. But gradually it shrank away from her and she felt the dull pavement beneath her feet. The sense of weariness returned with accumulated force, and for a moment she felt that she could walk no farther. She had reached the corner of Forty-first Street and Fifth Avenue, and she remembered that in Bryant Park there were seats where she might rest.

That melancholy pleasure-ground was almost deserted when she entered it, and she sank down on an empty bench in the glare of an electric street-lamp. The warmth of the fire had passed out of her veins, and she told herself that she must not sit long in the penetrating dampness which struck up from the wet asphalt. But her will-power seemed to have spent itself in a last great effort, and she was lost in the blank reaction which follows on an unwonted expenditure of energy. And besides, what was there to go home to? Nothing but the silence of her cheerless room—that silence of the night which may be more racking to tired nerves than the most discordant noises: that, and the bottle of chloral* by her bed. The thought of the chloral was the only spot of light in the dark prospect: she could feel its lulling influence stealing over her already. But she was troubled by the thought that it was losing its power—she dared not go back to it too soon. Of late the sleep it had brought her had been more broken and less profound; there had been nights when she was perpetually floating up through it to consciousness. What if the

---

*Chloral hydrate, a rapidly acting sedative for nervous insomnia.

effect of the drug should gradually fail, as all narcotics were said to fail? She remembered the chemist's warning against increasing the dose; and she had heard before of the capricious and incalculable action of the drug. Her dread of returning to a sleepless night was so great that she lingered on, hoping that excessive weariness would reinforce the waning power of the chloral.

Night had now closed in, and the roar of traffic in Forty-second Street was dying out. As complete darkness fell on the square the lingering occupants of the benches rose and dispersed; but now and then a stray figure, hurrying homeward, struck across the path where Lily sat, looming black for a moment in the white circle of electric light. One or two of these passers-by slackened their pace to glance curiously at her lonely figure; but she was hardly conscious of their scrutiny.

Suddenly, however, she became aware that one of the passing shadows remained stationary between her line of vision and the gleaming asphalt; and raising her eyes she saw a young woman bending over her.

"Excuse me—are you sick?—Why, it's Miss Bart!" a half-familiar voice exclaimed.

Lily looked up. The speaker was a poorly-dressed young woman with a bundle under her arm. Her face had the air of unwholesome refinement which ill-health and over-work may produce, but its common prettiness was redeemed by the strong and generous curve of the lips.

"You don't remember me," she continued, brightening with the pleasure of recognition, "but I'd know you anywhere, I've thought of you such a lot. I guess my folks all know your name by heart. I was one of the girls at Miss Farish's club—you helped me to go to the country that time I had lung-trouble. My name's Nettie Struther. It was Nettie Crane then—but I daresay you don't remember that either."

Yes: Lily was beginning to remember. The episode of Nettie Crane's timely rescue from disease had been one of the most satisfying incidents of her connection with Gerty's charitable work. She had furnished the girl with the means to go to a sanatorium in the mountains: it struck her now with a peculiar irony that the money she had used had been Gus Trenor's.

She tried to reply, to assure the speaker that she had not forgotten; but her voice failed in the effort, and she felt herself
sinking under a great wave of physical weakness. Nettie
Struther, with a startled exclamation, sat down and slipped a
shabbily-clad arm behind her back.

"Why, Miss Bart, you *are* sick. Just lean on me a little till you
feel better."

A faint glow of returning strength seemed to pass into Lily
from the pressure of the supporting arm.

"I'm only tired—it is nothing," she found voice to say in a
moment; and then, as she met the timid appeal of her companion's eyes, she added involuntarily: "I have been unhappy—in
great trouble."

"*You* in trouble? I've always thought of you as being so high
up, where everything was just grand. Sometimes, when I felt real
mean, and got to wondering why things were so queerly fixed in
the world, I used to remember that *you* were having a lovely
time, anyhow, and that seemed to show there was a kind of justice somewhere. But you mustn't sit here too long—it's fearfully
damp. Don't you feel strong enough to walk on a little way
now?" she broke off.

"Yes—yes; I must go home," Lily murmured, rising.

Her eyes rested wonderingly on the thin shabby figure at her
side. She had known Nettie Crane as one of the discouraged victims of over-work and anæmic parentage: one of the superfluous
fragments of life destined to be swept prematurely into that social refuse-heap of which Lily had so lately expressed her dread.
But Nettie Struther's frail envelope was now alive with hope and
energy: whatever fate the future reserved for her, she would not
be cast into the refuse-heap without a struggle.

"I am very glad to have seen you," Lily continued, summon-
ing a smile to her unsteady lips. "It will be my turn to think of
you as happy—and the world will seem a less unjust place to me
too."

"Oh, but I can't leave you like this—you're not fit to go home
alone. And I can't go with you either!" Nettie Struther wailed
with a start of recollection. "You see, it's my husband's night-
shift—he's a motor-man—and the friend I leave the baby with
has to step upstairs to get *her* husband's supper at seven. I didn't

tell you I had a baby, did I? She'll be four months old day after tomorrow, and to look at her you wouldn't think I'd ever had a sick day. I'd give anything to show you the baby, Miss Bart, and we live right down the street here—it's only three blocks off." She lifted her eyes tentatively to Lily's face, and then added with a burst of courage: "Why won't you get right into the cars and come home with me while I get baby's supper? It's real warm in our kitchen, and you can rest there, and I'll take *you* home as soon as ever she drops off to sleep."

It *was* warm in the kitchen, which, when Nettie Struther's match had made a flame leap from the gas-jet above the table, revealed itself to Lily as extraordinarily small and almost miraculously clean. A fire shone through the polished flanks of the iron stove, and near it stood a crib in which a baby was sitting upright, with incipient anxiety struggling for expression on a countenance still placid with sleep.

Having passionately celebrated her reunion with her offspring, and excused herself in cryptic language for the lateness of her return, Nettie restored the baby to the crib and shyly invited Miss Bart to the rocking-chair near the stove.

"We've got a parlour too," she explained with pardonable pride; "but I guess it's warmer in here, and I don't want to leave you alone while I'm getting baby's supper."

On receiving Lily's assurance that she much preferred the friendly proximity of the kitchen fire, Mrs. Struther proceeded to prepare a bottle of infantile food, which she tenderly applied to the baby's impatient lips; and while the ensuing degustation went on, she seated herself with a beaming countenance beside her visitor.

"You're sure you won't let me warm up a drop of coffee for you, Miss Bart? There's some of baby's fresh milk left over— well, maybe you'd rather just sit quiet and rest a little while. It's too lovely having you here. I've thought of it so often that I can't believe it's really come true. I've said to George again and again: 'I just wish Miss Bart could see me *now*—' and I used to watch for your name in the papers, and we'd talk over what you were doing, and read the descriptions of the dresses you wore. I haven't seen your name for a long time, though, and I began to be afraid you were sick, and it worried me so that George said

I'd get sick myself, fretting about it." Her lips broke into a reminiscent smile. "Well, I can't afford to be sick again, that's a fact: the last spell nearly finished me. When you sent me off that time I never thought I'd come back alive, and I didn't much care if I did. You see I didn't know about George and the baby then."

She paused to readjust the bottle to the child's bubbling mouth.

"You precious—don't you be in too much of a hurry! Was it mad with mommer for getting its supper so late? Marry Anto'nette—that's what we call her: after the French queen in that play at the Garden—I told George the actress reminded me of you, and that made me fancy the name ... I never thought I'd get married, you know, and I'd never have had the heart to go on working just for myself."

She broke off again, and meeting the encouragement in Lily's eyes, went on, with a flush rising under her anæmic skin: "You see I wasn't only just *sick* that time you sent me off—I was dreadfully unhappy too. I'd known a gentleman where I was employed—I don't know as you remember I did type-writing in a big importing firm—and—well—I thought we were to be married: he'd gone steady with me six months and given me his mother's wedding ring. But I presume he was too stylish for me—he travelled for the firm, and had seen a great deal of society. Work girls aren't looked after the way you are, and they don't always know how to look after themselves. I didn't ... and it pretty near killed me when he went away and left off writing ... It was then I came down sick—I thought it was the end of everything. I guess it would have been if you hadn't sent me off. But when I found I was getting well I began to take heart in spite of myself. And then, when I got back home, George came round and asked me to marry him. At first I thought I couldn't, because we'd been brought up together, and I knew he knew about me. But after a while I began to see that that made it easier. I never could have told another man, and I'd never have married without telling; but if George cared for me enough to have me as I was, I didn't see why I shouldn't begin over again—and I did."

The strength of the victory shone forth from her as she lifted her irradiated face from the child on her knees.

"But, mercy, I didn't mean to go on like this about myself, with you sitting there looking so fagged out. Only it's so lovely having you here, and letting you see just how you've helped me." The baby had sunk back blissfully replete, and Mrs. Struther softly rose to lay the bottle aside. Then she paused before Miss Bart.

"I only wish I could help *you*—but I suppose there's nothing on earth I could do," she murmured wistfully.

Lily, instead of answering, rose with a smile and held out her arms; and the mother, understanding the gesture, laid her child in them.

The baby, feeling herself detached from her habitual anchorage, made an instinctive motion of resistance; but the soothing influences of digestion prevailed, and Lily felt the soft weight sink trustfully against her breast. The child's confidence in its safety thrilled her with a sense of warmth and returning life, and she bent over, wondering at the rosy blur of the little face, the empty clearness of the eyes, the vague tendrilly motions of the folding and unfolding fingers. At first the burden in her arms seemed as light as a pink cloud or a heap of down, but as she continued to hold the weight increased, sinking deeper, and penetrating her with a strange sense of weakness, as though the child entered into her and became a part of herself.

She looked up, and saw Nettie's eyes resting on her with tenderness and exultation.

"Wouldn't it be too lovely for anything if she could grow up to be just like you? Of course I know she never *could*—but mothers are always dreaming the craziest things for their children."

Lily clasped the child close for a moment and laid her back in her mother's arms.

"Oh, she must not do that—I should be afraid to come and see her too often!" she said with a smile; and then, resisting Mrs. Struther's anxious offer of companionship, and reiterating the promise that of course she would come back soon, and make George's acquaintance, and see the baby in her bath, she passed out of the kitchen and went alone down the tenement stairs.

As she reached the street she realized that she felt stronger and happier: the little episode had done her good. It was the first time she had ever come across the results of her spasmodic benevolence, and the surprised sense of human fellowship took the mortal chill from her heart.

It was not till she entered her own door that she felt the reaction of a deeper loneliness. It was long after seven o'clock, and the light and odours proceeding from the basement made it manifest that the boarding-house dinner had begun. She hastened up to her room, lit the gas, and began to dress. She did not mean to pamper herself any longer, to go without food because her surroundings made it unpalatable. Since it was her fate to live in a boarding-house, she must learn to fall in with the conditions of the life. Nevertheless she was glad that, when she descended to the heat and glare of the dining-room, the repast was nearly over.

In her own room again, she was seized with a sudden fever of activity. For weeks past she had been too listless and indifferent to set her possessions in order, but now she began to examine systematically the contents of her drawers and cupboard. She had a few handsome dresses left—survivals of her last phase of splendour, on the *Sabrina* and in London—but when she had been obliged to part with her maid she had given the woman a generous share of her cast-off apparel. The remaining dresses, though they had lost their freshness, still kept the long unerring lines, the sweep and amplitude of the great artist's stroke, and as she spread them out on the bed the scenes in which they had been worn rose vividly before her. An association lurked in every fold: each fall of lace and gleam of embroidery was like a letter in the record of her past. She was startled to find how the atmosphere of her old life enveloped her. But, after all, it was the life she had been made for: every dawning tendency in her had been carefully directed toward it, all her interests and activities had been taught to centre around it. She was like some rare flower grown for exhibition, a flower from which every bud had been nipped except the crowning blossom of her beauty.

Last of all, she drew forth from the bottom of her trunk a heap of white drapery which fell shapelessly across her arm. It was the Reynolds dress she had worn in the Bry *tableaux*. It had been impossible for her to give it away, but she had never seen it

since that night, and the long flexible folds, as she shook them
out, gave forth an odour of violets which came to her like a
breath from the flower-edged fountain where she had stood
with Lawrence Selden and disowned her fate. She put back the
dresses one by one, laying away with each some gleam of light,
some note of laughter, some stray waft from the rosy shores of
pleasure. She was still in a state of highly-wrought impression-
ability, and every hint of the past sent a lingering tremor along
her nerves.

She had just closed her trunk on the white folds of the
Reynolds dress when she heard a tap at her door, and the red fist
of the Irish maid-servant thrust in a belated letter. Carrying it to
the light, Lily read with surprise the address stamped on the
upper corner of the envelope. It was a business communication
from the office of her aunt's executors, and she wondered what
unexpected development had caused them to break silence before the appointed time.

She opened the envelope and a cheque fluttered to the floor.
As she stooped to pick it up the blood rushed to her face. The
cheque represented the full amount of Mrs. Peniston's legacy,
and the letter accompanying it explained that the executors, having adjusted the business of the estate with less delay than they
had expected, had decided to anticipate the date fixed for the
payment of the bequests.

Lily sat down beside the desk at the foot of her bed, and
spreading out the cheque, read over and over the *ten thousand
dollars* written across it in a steely business hand. Ten months
earlier the amount it stood for had represented the depths of
penury; but her standard of values had changed in the interval,
and now visions of wealth lurked in every flourish of the pen. As
she continued to gaze at it, she felt the glitter of the visions
mounting to her brain, and after a while she lifted the lid of the
desk and slipped the magic formula out of sight. It was easier to
think without those five figures dancing before her eyes; and she
had a great deal of thinking to do before she slept.

She opened her cheque-book, and plunged into such anxious
calculations as had prolonged her vigil at Bellomont on the
night when she had decided to marry Percy Gryce. Poverty sim-
plifies book-keeping, and her financial situation was easier to as-

certain than it had been then; but she had not yet learned the
control of money, and during her transient phase of luxury at the
Emporium she had slipped back into habits of extravagance
which still impaired her slender balance. A careful examination
of her cheque-book, and of the unpaid bills in her desk, showed
that, when the latter had been settled, she would have barely
enough to live on for the next three or four months, and even
after that, if she were to continue her present way of living, without earning any additional money, all incidental expenses must
be reduced to the vanishing point. She hid her eyes with a shudder, beholding herself at the entrance of that ever-narrowing
perspective down which she had seen Miss Silverton's dowdy
figure take its despondent way.

It was no longer, however, from the vision of material poverty
that she turned with the greatest shrinking. She had a sense of
deeper empoverishment—of an inner destitution compared to
which outward conditions dwindled into insignificance. It was
indeed miserable to be poor—to look forward to a shabby, anxious middle-age, leading by dreary degrees of economy and self-
denial to gradual absorption in the dingy communal existence of
the boarding-house. But there was something more miserable
still—it was the clutch of solitude at her heart, the sense of being
swept like a stray uprooted growth down the heedless current of
the years. That was the feeling which possessed her now—the
feeling of being something rootless and ephemeral, mere spin-
drift of the whirling surface of existence, without anything to
which the poor little tentacles of self could cling before the awful
flood submerged them. And as she looked back she saw that
there had never been a time when she had had any real relation
to life. Her parents too had been rootless, blown hither and
thither on every wind of fashion, without any personal existence
to shelter them from its shifting gusts. She herself had grown up
without any one spot of earth being dearer to her than another:
there was no centre of early pieties, of grave endearing traditions, to which her heart could revert and from which it could
draw strength for itself and tenderness for others. In whatever
form a slowly-accumulated past lives in the blood—whether in
the concrete image of the old house stored with visual memories,
or in the conception of the house not built with hands, but made

up of inherited passions and loyalties—it has the same power of broadening and deepening the individual existence, of attaching it by mysterious links of kinship to all the mighty sum of human striving.

Such a vision of the solidarity of life had never before come to Lily. She had had a premonition of it in the blind motions of her mating-instinct; but they had been checked by the disintegrating influences of the life about her. All the men and women she knew were like atoms whirling away from each other in some wild centrifugal dance: her first glimpse of the continuity of life had come to her that evening in Nettie Struther's kitchen.

The poor little working-girl who had found strength to gather up the fragments of her life, and build herself a shelter with them, seemed to Lily to have reached the central truth of existence. It was a meagre enough life, on the grim edge of poverty, with scant margin for possibilities of sickness or mischance, but it had the frail audacious permanence of a bird's nest built on the edge of a cliff—a mere wisp of leaves and straw, yet so put together that the lives entrusted to it may hang safely over the abyss.

Yes—but it had taken two to build the nest; the man's faith as well as the woman's courage. Lily remembered Nettie's words: *I knew he knew about me.* Her husband's faith in her had made her renewal possible—it is so easy for a woman to become what the man she loves believes her to be! Well—Selden had twice been ready to stake his faith on Lily Bart; but the third trial had been too severe for his endurance. The very quality of his love had made it the more impossible to recall to life. If it had been a simple instinct of the blood, the power of her beauty might have revived it. But the fact that it struck deeper, that it was inextricably wound up with inherited habits of thought and feeling, made it as impossible to restore to growth as a deep-rooted plant torn from its bed. Selden had given her of his best; but he was as incapable as herself of an uncritical return to former states of feeling.

There remained to her, as she had told him, the uplifting memory of his faith in her; but she had not reached the age when a woman can live on her memories. As she held Nettie Struther's child in her arms the frozen currents of youth had loosed themselves and run warm in her veins: the old life-hunger possessed her, and all her being clamoured for its share of personal happiness. Yes—it was happiness she still wanted, and the glimpse she had caught of it made everything else of no account. One by one she had detached herself from the baser possibilities, and she saw that nothing now remained to her but the emptiness of renunciation.

It was growing late, and an immense weariness once more possessed her. It was not the stealing sense of sleep, but a vivid wakeful fatigue, a wan lucidity of mind against which all the possibilities of the future were shadowed forth gigantically. She was appalled by the intense clearness of the vision; she seemed to have broken through the merciful veil which intervenes between intention and action, and to see exactly what she would do in all the long days to come. There was the cheque in her desk, for instance—she meant to use it in paying her debt to Trenor; but she foresaw that when the morning came she would put off doing so, would slip into gradual tolerance of the debt. The thought terrified her—she dreaded to fall from the height of her last moment with Lawrence Selden. But how could she trust herself to keep her footing? She knew the strength of the opposing impulses—she could feel the countless hands of habit dragging her back into some fresh compromise with fate. She felt an intense longing to prolong, to perpetuate, the momentary exaltation of her spirit. If only life could end now—end on this tragic yet sweet vision of lost possibilities, which gave her a sense of kinship with all the loving and foregoing in the world!

She reached out suddenly and, drawing the cheque from her writing-desk, enclosed it in an envelope which she addressed to her bank. She then wrote out a cheque for Trenor, and placing it, without an accompanying word, in an envelope inscribed with his name, laid the two letters side by side on her desk After that she continued to sit at the table, sorting her papers and writing, till the intense silence of the house reminded her of the lateness of the hour. In the street the noise of wheels had ceased, and the rumble of the "elevated" came only at long intervals through the deep unnatural hush. In the mysterious nocturnal separation from all outward signs of life, she felt herself more strangely confronted with her fate. The sensation made her brain reel, and she tried to shut out consciousness by pressing her hands against her eyes. But the terrible silence and emptiness seemed to symbolize her future—she felt as though the house, the street, the world were all empty, and she alone left sentient in a lifeless universe.

But this was the verge of delirium . . . she had never hung so near the dizzy brink of the unreal. Sleep was what she wanted—she remembered that she had not closed her eyes for two nights. The little bottle was at her bedside, waiting to lay its spell upon her. She rose and undressed hastily, hungering now for the touch of her pillow. She felt so profoundly tired that she thought she must fall asleep at once; but as soon as she had lain down every nerve started once more into separate wakefulness. It was as though a great blaze of electric light had been turned on in her head, and her poor little anguished self shrank and cowered in it, without knowing where to take refuge.

She had not imagined that such a multiplication of wakefulness was possible: her whole past was reënacting itself at a hundred different points of consciousness. Where was the drug that could still this legion of insurgent nerves? The sense of exhaustion would have been sweet compared to this shrill beat of activities; but weariness had dropped from her as though some cruel stimulant had been forced into her veins.

She could bear it—yes, she could bear it; but what strength would be left her the next day? Perspective had disappeared—the next day pressed close upon her, and on its heels came the days that were to follow—they swarmed about her like a shrieking mob. She must shut them out for a few hours; she must take a brief bath of oblivion. She put out her hand, and measured the soothing drops into a glass; but as she did so, she knew they would be powerless against the supernatural lucidity of her brain. She had long since raised the dose to its highest limit, but tonight she felt she must increase it. She knew she took a slight risk in doing so—she remembered the chemist's warning. If sleep came at all, it might be a sleep without waking. But after all that was but one chance in a hundred: the action of the drug was incalculable, and the addition of a few drops to the regular dose would probably do no more than procure for her the rest she so desperately needed. . . .

She did not, in truth, consider the question very closely—the physical craving for sleep was her only sustained sensation. Her mind shrank from the glare of thought as instinctively as eyes contract in a blaze of light—darkness, darkness was what she must have at any cost. She raised herself in bed and swallowed the contents of the glass; then she blew out her candle and lay down.

She lay very still, waiting with a sensuous pleasure for the first effects of the soporific. She knew in advance what form they would take—the gradual cessation of the inner throb, the soft approach of passiveness, as though an invisible hand made magic passes over her in the darkness. The very slowness and hesitancy of the effect increased its fascination: it was delicious to lean over and look down into the dim abysses of unconsciousness. Tonight the drug seemed to work more slowly than usual: each passionate pulse had to be stilled in turn, and it was long before she felt them dropping into abeyance, like sentinels falling asleep at their posts. But gradually the sense of complete subjugation came over her, and she wondered languidly what had made her feel so uneasy and excited. She saw now that there was nothing to be excited about—she had returned to her normal view of life. Tomorrow would not be so difficult after all: she felt sure that she would have the strength to meet it. She did not quite remember what it was that she had been afraid to meet, but the uncertainty no longer troubled her. She had been unhappy, and now she was happy—she had felt herself alone, and now the sense of loneliness had vanished.

She stirred once, and turned on her side, and as she did so, she suddenly understood why she did not feel herself alone. It was odd—but Nettie Struther's child was lying on her arm: she felt the pressure of its little head against her shoulder. She did not know how it had come there, but she felt no great surprise at the fact, only a gentle penetrating thrill of warmth and pleasure. She settled herself into an easier position, hollowing her arm to pillow the round downy head, and holding her breath lest a sound should disturb the sleeping child.

As she lay there she said to herself that there was something she must tell Selden, some word she had found that should make life clear between them. She tried to repeat the word,

which lingered vague and luminous on the far edge of thought—
she was afraid of not remembering it when she woke; and if she
could only remember it and say it to him, she felt that everything
would be well.

Slowly the thought of the word faded, and sleep began to en-
fold her. She struggled faintly against it, feeling that she ought
to keep awake on account of the baby; but even this feeling was
gradually lost in an indistinct sense of drowsy peace, through
which, of a sudden, a dark flush of loneliness and terror tore its
way.

She started up again, cold and trembling with the shock: for
a moment she seemed to have lost her hold of the child. But
no—she was mistaken—the tender pressure of its body was still
close to hers: the recovered warmth flowed through her once
more, she yielded to it, sank into it, and slept.

14

THE NEXT MORNING ROSE mild and bright, with a promise of summer in the air. The sunlight slanted joyously down Lily's street, mellowed the blistered house-front, gilded the paintless railings of the door-step, and struck prismatic glories from the panes of her darkened window.

When such a day coincides with the inner mood there is intoxication in its breath; and Selden, hastening along the street through the squalor of its morning confidences, felt himself thrilling with a youthful sense of adventure. He had cut loose from the familiar shores of habit, and launched himself on uncharted seas of emotion; all the old tests and measures were left behind, and his course was to be shaped by new stars.

That course, for the moment, led merely to Miss Bart's boarding-house; but its shabby door-step had suddenly become the threshold of the untried. As he approached he looked up at the triple row of windows, wondering boyishly which one of them was hers. It was nine o'clock, and the house, being tenanted by workers, already showed an awakened front to the street. He remembered afterward having noticed that only one blind was down. He noticed too that there was a pot of pansies on one of the window sills, and at once concluded that the window must be hers: it was inevitable that he should connect her with the one touch of beauty in the dingy scene.

Nine o'clock was an early hour for a visit, but Selden had passed beyond all such conventional observances. He only knew that he must see Lily Bart at once—he had found the word he meant to say to her, and it could not wait another moment to be said. It was strange that it had not come to his lips sooner—that he had let her pass from him the evening before without being able to speak it. But what did that matter, now that a new day had come? It was not a word for twilight, but for the morning.

Selden ran eagerly up the steps and pulled the bell; and even in his state of self-absorption it came as a sharp surprise to him that the door should open so promptly. It was still more of a surprise to see, as he entered, that it had been opened by Gerty Farish—and that behind her, in an agitated blur, several other figures ominously loomed.

"Lawrence!" Gerty cried in a strange voice, "how could you get here so quickly?"—and the trembling hand she laid on him seemed instantly to close about his heart.

He noticed the other faces, vague with fear and conjecture—he saw the landlady's imposing bulk sway professionally toward him; but he shrank back, putting up his hand, while his eyes mechanically mounted the steep black walnut stairs, up which he was immediately aware that his cousin was about to lead him.

A voice in the background said that the doctor might be back at any minute—and that nothing, upstairs, was to be disturbed. Some one else exclaimed: "It was the greatest mercy—" then Selden felt that Gerty had taken him gently by the hand, and that they were to be suffered to go up alone.

In silence they mounted the three flights, and walked along the passage to a closed door. Gerty opened the door, and Selden went in after her. Though the blind was down, the irresistible sunlight poured a tempered golden flood into the room, and in its light Selden saw a narrow bed along the wall, and on the bed, with motionless hands and calm unrecognizing face, the semblance of Lily Bart.

That it was her real self, every pulse in him ardently denied. Her real self had lain warm on his heart but a few hours earlier—what had he to do with this estranged and tranquil face which, for the first time, neither paled nor brightened at his coming?

Gerty, strangely tranquil too, with the conscious self-control of one who has ministered to much pain, stood by the bed, speaking gently, as if transmitting a final message.

"The doctor found a bottle of chloral—she had been sleeping badly for a long time, and she must have taken an over-dose by mistake. . . . There is no doubt of that—no doubt—there will be no question—he has been very kind. I told him that you and I would like to be left alone with her—to go over her things be-

fore any one else comes. I know it is what she would have
wished."

Selden was hardly conscious of what she said. He stood looking down on the sleeping face which seemed to be like a delicate
impalpable mask over the living lineaments he had known. He
felt that the real Lily was still there, close to him, yet invisible
and inaccessible; and the tenuity of the barrier between them
mocked him with a sense of helplessness. There had never been
more than a little impalpable barrier between them—and yet he
had suffered it to keep them apart! And now, though it seemed
slighter and frailer than ever, it had suddenly hardened to
adamant, and he might beat his life out against it in vain.

He had dropped on his knees beside the bed, but a touch
from Gerty aroused him. He stood up, and as their eyes met he
was struck by the extraordinary light in his cousin's face.

"You understand what the doctor has gone for? He has
promised that there shall be no trouble—but of course the for-
malities must be gone through. And I asked him to give us time
to look through her things first—"

He nodded, and she glanced about the small bare room. "It
won't take long," she concluded.

"No—it won't take long," he agreed.

She held his hand in hers a moment longer, and then, with a
last look at the bed, moved silently toward the door. On the
threshold she paused to add: "You will find me downstairs if you
want me."

Selden roused himself to detain her. "But why are you going?
She would have wished——"

Gerty shook her head with a smile. "No: this is what she
would have wished——" and as she spoke a light broke through
Selden's stony misery, and he saw deep into the hidden things of
love.

The door closed on Gerty, and he stood alone with the motionless sleeper on the bed. His impulse was to return to her
side, to fall on his knees, and rest his throbbing head against the
peaceful cheek on the pillow. They had never been at peace together, they two; and now he felt himself drawn downward into
the strange mysterious depths of her tranquillity.

But he remembered Gerty's warning words—he knew that,

though time had ceased in this room, its feet were hastening relentlessly toward the door. Gerty had given him this supreme half-hour, and he must use it as she willed.

He turned and looked about him, sternly compelling himself to regain his consciousness of outward things. There was very little furniture in the room. The shabby chest of drawers was spread with a lace cover, and set out with a few gold-topped boxes and bottles, a rose-coloured pin-cushion, a glass tray strewn with tortoise-shell hairpins—he shrank from the poignant intimacy of these trifles, and from the blank surface of the toilet-mirror about them.

These were the only traces of luxury, of that clinging to the minute observance of personal seemliness, which showed what her other renunciations must have cost. There was no other token of her personality about the room, unless it showed itself in the scrupulous neatness of the scant articles of furniture: a washing-stand, two chairs, a small writing-desk, and the little table near the bed. On this table stood the empty bottle and glass, and from these also he averted his eyes.

The desk was closed, but on its slanting lid lay two letters which he took up. One bore the address of a bank, and as it was stamped and sealed, Selden, after a moment's hesitation, laid it aside. On the other letter he read Gus Trenor's name; and the flap of the envelope was still ungummed.

Temptation leapt on him like the stab of a knife. He staggered under it, steadying himself against the desk. Why had she been writing to Trenor—writing, presumably, just after their parting of the previous evening? The thought unhallowed the memory of that last hour, made a mock of the word he had come to speak, and defiled even the reconciling silence upon which it fell. He felt himself flung back on all the ugly uncertainties from which he thought he had cast loose forever. After all, what did he know of her life? Only as much as she had chosen to show him, and measured by the world's estimate, how little that was! By what right—the letter in his hand seemed to ask—by what right was it he who now passed into her confidence through the gate which death had left unbarred? His heart cried out that it was by right of their last hour together, the hour when she her-

self had placed the key in his hand. Yes—but what if the letter
to Trenor had been written afterward?

He put it from him with sudden loathing, and setting his
lips, addressed himself resolutely to what remained of his task.
After all, that task would be easier to perform, now that his personal stake in it was annulled.

He raised the lid of the desk, and saw within it a cheque-book
and a few packets of bills and letters, arranged with the orderly
precision which characterized all her personal habits. He looked
through the letters first, because it was the most difficult part of
the work. They proved to be few and unimportant, but among
them he found, with a strange commotion of the heart, the note
he had written her the day after the Brys' entertainment.

"When may I come to you?"—his words overwhelmed him
with a realization of the cowardice which had driven him from
her at the very moment of attainment. Yes—he had always
feared his fate, and he was too honest to disown his cowardice
now; for had not all his old doubts started to life again at the
mere sight of Trenor's name?

He laid the note in his card-case, folding it away carefully, as
something made precious by the fact that she had held it so;
then, growing once more aware of the lapse of time, he continued his examination of the papers.

To his surprise, he found that all the bills were receipted;
there was not an unpaid account among them. He opened the
cheque-book, and saw that, the very night before, a cheque of
ten thousand dollars from Mrs. Peniston's executors had been
entered in it. The legacy, then, had been paid sooner than Gerty
had led him to expect. But, turning another page or two, he discovered with astonishment that, in spite of this recent accession
of funds, the balance had already declined to a few dollars. A
rapid glance at the stubs of the last cheques, all of which bore the
date of the previous day, showed that between four or five hundred dollars of the legacy had been spent in the settlement of
bills, while the remaining thousands were comprehended in one
cheque, made out, at the same time, to Charles Augustus Trenor.

Selden laid the book aside, and sank into the chair beside the
desk. He leaned his elbows on it, and hid his face in his hands.
The bitter waters of life surged high about him, their sterile taste

was on his lips. Did the cheque to Trenor explain the mystery or deepen it? At first his mind refused to act—he felt only the taint of such a transaction between a man like Trenor and a girl like Lily Bart. Then, gradually, his troubled vision cleared, old hints and rumours came back to him, and out of the very insinuations he had feared to probe, he constructed an explanation of the mystery. It was true, then, that she had taken money from Trenor; but true also, as the contents of the little desk declared, that the obligation had been intolerable to her, and that at the first opportunity she had freed herself from it, though the act left her face to face with bare unmitigated poverty.

That was all he knew—all he could hope to unravel of the story. The mute lips on the pillow refused him more than this—unless indeed they had told him the rest in the kiss they had left upon his forehead. Yes, he could now read into that farewell all that his heart craved to find there; he could even draw from it courage not to accuse himself for having failed to reach the height of his opportunity.

He saw that all the conditions of life had conspired to keep them apart; since his very detachment from the external influences which swayed her had increased his spiritual fastidiousness, and made it more difficult for him to live and love uncritically. But at least he *had* loved her—had been willing to stake his future on his faith in her—and if the moment had been fated to pass from them before they could seize it, he saw now that, for both, it had been saved whole out of the ruin of their lives.

It was this moment of love, this fleeting victory over themselves, which had kept them from atrophy and extinction; which, in her, had reached out to him in every struggle against the influence of her surroundings, and in him, had kept alive the faith that now drew him penitent and reconciled to her side.

He knelt by the bed and bent over her, draining their last moment to its lees;* and in the silence there passed between them the word which made all clear.

---

*The phrase echoes a line from "Ode to a Nightingale" (1819) by John Keats: "emptied some dull opiate to the drains."

ENDNOTES

1. (p. 163) *a translation of the* Eumenides . . . *and snatches an hour's repose:* In Greek mythology, Orestes is the son of Agamemnon and Clytemnestra, and the brother of Iphigenia and Electra. In the *Eumenides*, the third part of the tragedy *Oresteia*, Aeschylus tells how the Furies pursue Orestes when he murders Clytemnestra. She had taken revenge on Agamemnon for sacrificing Iphigenia to secure favorable winds for the Greek army to sail to war against the Trojans. In the prologue of the play, Orestes finds the Furies asleep in the cave of the oracle. At the end, the goddess Athena saves Orestes from the Furies' vengeance.

2. (p. 187) *Beatrice Cenci:* The daughter of a Roman nobleman, Beatrice (1577–1599) was arrested and executed for plotting to murder a relative who had developed an incestuous passion for her. Guido Reni's portrait of Beatrice plays a crucial role in Nathaniel Hawthorne's novel *The Marble Faun* (1860).

3. (p. 193) *There was a girl . . . they killed her:* The story that Rosedale refers to is from Livy's *The Rise of Rome*. When the Romans were fighting the Sabines, Spurius Tarpeius was in command of the Roman citadel. Titus Tatius, king of the Sabines, "induced Spurius' virgin daughter by a bribe of gold to admit his armed men into the citadel. . . . Once admitted they crushed her under the weight of their weapons either so that the citadel might appear to have been captured by force or to set an example for the future that no one should ever keep faith with a traitor" (from the T. J. Luce translation, Oxford University Press, 1998).

4. (p. 204) Sabrina: The Dorset's boat is named after a mythological water nymph. Sabrina was goddess of the River Severn in England and patroness of chastity in John Milton's masque *Comus* (1637): "Sabrina fair / Listen where thou art sitting / Under the glassy, cool, translucent wave, / In twisted braids of lilies knitting / The loose train of thy amber-dropping hair."

INSPIRED BY THE HOUSE OF MIRTH

"You're such a wonderful spectacle."
—Lawrence Selden to Lily Bart, in
the film *The House of Mirth*

A lavish film version of *The House of Mirth*, adapted and directed by Terence Davies, was released in 2000, almost a century after the novel was published.

The idea of seeing Lily Bart and her milieu come to life on screen is certainly appealing, and Davies's choice of actors—many familiar from their leading roles on television—was daring, though largely unsuccessful. Gillian Anderson, best known for her role as an icy FBI agent on *The X-Files*, is an attractive Lily Bart, but she fails to see that Wharton's heroine is not an irreproachable goddess. Eric Stoltz, of *Chicago Hope* fame, is a not-so-dashing Lawrence Selden. Dan Aykroyd, whose name became almost a household word based on his work on *Saturday Night Live* and such films as *Ghost Busters*, is too good-natured a fellow to be convincing as the duplicitous Gus Trenor. Laura Linney, the nice girl of the *Tales of the City* television miniseries, is not nearly mean enough in her role as the conniving socialite Bertha Dorset. It's hard enough to accept the rigid social conventions that dictate the action of the novel, and harder still to believe that these icons of popular culture are denizens of a stagnant and unrelenting social stratum. One successful piece of casting is Eleanor Bron, who played neurotic ice queens in such 1960s hits as *Bedazzled, Alfie, Two for the Road*, and *Women in Love*; she is sufficiently dour and judgmental as Julia Peniston, the aunt who withdraws the legacy that could have saved Lily.

The darkly lit *The House of Mirth* is beautifully photographed by Remi Adefarasin, who received an Academy Award nomination for Best Cinematography for his work in *Elizabeth* (1998).

And it must be said that director Davies demonstrates a fine eye for the details, right down to the gloves, corsets, and parasols, surrounding New York City high society at the dawn of the twentieth century. Davies's cinematic style—often described as static, with his shots fixed and close, his pace slow—is in evidence in *The House of Mirth*, providing a strong contrast with the sweeping visual approach of another Wharton adaptation, Martin Scorsese's *The Age of Innocence*. Davies's pacing and his static presentation create a stagnant atmosphere that is a fitting background for Lily Bart's introspection and the immobility that can result from living within such an unforgiving social setting. Davies has a penchant for tragedy, too: His darkly lit production succeeds in poignantly dramatizing Lily's reversal of fortune.

Right up to the gruesome end, though, it's hard to accept Lily's plight. We want Lily to adhere to today's standards and be a gutsy gal, to march into those stuffy drawing rooms and slap a few faces and give those stiffs a piece of her mind—which may only go to show that Wharton's novel belongs so much to a particular age that it will never translate to celluloid.

COMMENTS & QUESTIONS

In this section, we aim to provide the reader with an array of perspectives on the text, as well as questions that challenge those perspectives. The commentary has been culled from sources as diverse as reviews contemporaneous with the work, letters written by the author, literary criticism of later generations, and appreciations written throughout history. Following the commentary, a series of questions seeks to filter Edith Wharton's The House of Mirth *through a variety of points of view and bring about a richer understanding of this enduring work.*

Comments

THE INDEPENDENT

Mrs. Wharton's new novel is a story of society life, its refined ferocities, its sensual extravagances, its delicate immoralities and, above all, the tragedies which underlie its outward appearance of mirth and prosperity. Society, indeed, is the coming field in fiction for the author who knows how to reap his literary wheat from the tares that are sowed there. And we ought not to complain: These books are missionary efforts of a sensational kind, made in behalf of what is the most corrupt class of people in the world, if we are to take seriously the representations of writers like Mrs. Wharton and Robert Grant.

But there is a curious thing about the dogma upon which these stories are founded. It is that old-fashioned one, "the soul that sinneth it shall die." Now ministers have been obliged to abandon the rigors of this doctrine in the pulpit, or, at least, to emphasize it less; but these novelists dramatize it with all the terrors of their imagination, and they demonstrate it by the life of every character in the story. Thus the men and women in this novel who go about showing their ghastly mirth give the impression of being "hair hung and breeze shaken," as the old preachers would say, over the ancient lake of fire and brimstone. This same class of writers find their ethics by what may be called the dredging process. Formerly we all got our morals and golden texts from the lives of saints and from the Holy Scriptures, whether we were writing or actually living them. But now it is the fashion to get them out of the cesspools of vice. The author who can portray the most sins in the best style is the most popular literary preacher now. . . .

Some writers have a permanent literary style, others have merely a fleeting fashion of expression, which is not founded upon art and which is meant to appeal to the passing fancy of the public mind. Now some years ago, when Mrs. Wharton's stories first began to attract attention, it was claimed that she had that rare thing, distinction in literary style. And she still has a fine manner, but it is like the fine gowns of her heroines, a fashion of the times for interpreting decadent symptoms in human nature. What she says will not last, because it is simply the fashionable drawing of ephemeral types and still more ephemeral sentiments.

—from a review of *The House of Mirth* (July 20, 1905)

THE NATION

At least two serious and authoritative writers have expressed a view of Mirth in memorable words. The Preacher, whose wisdom is enshrined in the Book of Ecclesiastes, was a man of moods; in a dreary moment he turned a gloomy eye on Mirth, and described her house as the house of fools. Milton, a less impetuous poet than the Preacher, and, we are inclined to think, a man of greater discernment, of more sedate habits, gazed genially at Mirth, hailing her as a "Goddess fair and free," begging her to "admit him of her crew." In great literature, therefore, the character of Mirth and of the habitués of her house remains undetermined, and (for most of us) to consider any subject that has been inconclusively discussed in great literature is to dwell forever in the shadow of doubt. Mrs. Wharton, who is a serious writer and is already hailed in some quarters as an authoritative one, appears to have escaped the blight of indecision. Perhaps, while meditating Mirth, she overlooked Milton, and could therefore the more easily, with a clear conscience and earnest conviction, range herself beside the Preacher. At all events she has written a long book in support of his dictum, a tale of American society, which assures us that the Preacher was a prophet, and that a bitter epigram may incorporate literal truth.

—November 30, 1905

HENRY DWIGHT SEDGWICK
The House of Mirth shows a marked advance in acceptance of responsibility to art, a far larger sense of the value of composition, and a great increase of power in putting that sense to use. It is [Wharton's] feeling for composition that causes her to disregard both literary determinism and realism; these she deliberately sacrifices for the sake of obtaining the desired emphasis upon the figure of central interest. All the minor characters in the novel are adjuncts and accessories, illustration and decoration, to display the commanding figure of Lily Bart; she stands conspicuous, and all the others derive their importance from their relations to her. What they do, say, and think, is done, said, and thought in order to explain and give a high relief to Lily Bart. This mastery of composition is the great artistic achievement of the book, and justifies its immense success.

—from the *Atlantic Monthly* (August 1906)

HENRY JAMES
There are two or three grounds on which the author of "Ethan Frome," "The Valley of Decision" and "The House of Mirth" . . . would point the moral of the treasure of amusement sitting in the lap of method with a felicity peculiarly her own. If one of these is that she too has clearly a saturation—which it would be ever so interesting to determine and appreciate—we have it from her not in the crude state but in the extract, the extract that makes all the difference for our sense of an artistic economy. If the extract, as would appear, is the result of an artistic economy, as the latter is its logical motive, so we find it associated in Mrs. Wharton with such appeals to our interest, for instance, as the

fact that, absolutely sole among our students of this form, she suffers, she even encourages, her expression to flower into some sharp image or figure of her thought when that will make the thought more finely touch us. Her step, without straying, encounters the living analogy, which she gathers, in passing, without awkwardness of pause, and which the page then carries on its breast as a trophy plucked by a happy adventurous dash, a token of spirit and temper as well as a proof of vision.

—from *Notes on Novelists* (1914)

Questions

1. Why would any contemporary reader care about the high-society machinations of Wharton's novel? Do Wharton's privileged characters seem American to you at all? Or is it the distance between their lives and those of ordinary people that make ordinary people want to read about them?

2. In spite of the great differences in time and milieu, can you see a young American woman of the twenty-first century, say the daughter of a dentist or a corporate executive, facing essentially the same problems, choices, and temptations as Lily Bart?

3. What causes Lily's fall? Puritanism, an excess of wealth and leisure, Lily's purely individual foolishness, a punishing deity, accident?

4. Social conventions crush Lily. Reading this novel, did you find it difficult to understand why Lily wouldn't speak out—tell Selden how she feels about him, challenge Bertha's mean betrayal, let it be known what Gus Trenor is up to? Do you find it believable in the context of the novel that Lily acts as passively she does, and are you sympathetic to her plight?

5. Wharton chose a tragic ending. How do you think the novel could have ended positively? In the context of the novel, do you think Selden might have rescued Lily? That Lily might

have adjusted to a life beneath her social station? That she might have eventually married Rosedale?

6. What are some striking instances of Wharton's use of the telling detail?

FOR FURTHER READING

Biographies

Auchindoss, Louis. *Edith Wharton: A Woman in Her Time.* New York: Viking Press, 1971. Biography, criticism, and many good photos by a novelist of manners in the Wharton tradition.

Bell, Millicent. *Edith Wharton and Henry James: A Story of Their Friendship.* New York: Braziller, 1965. Uses their correspondence to portray their relationship.

Benstock, Shari. *No Gift from Chance: A Biography of Edith Wharton.* New York: Scribner's, 1994. The latest but not the best biography.

Clark, Kenneth. *Another Part of the Wood: A Self-Portrait.* 1974. Reprint: New York: Ballantine, 1976, pp. 206–208. Section cited provides insightful analysis of Wharton's character by a major art historian.

Flanner, Janet. "Edith Wharton (1862–1937)." *Paris Was Yesterday, 1925–1939.* 1972. Reprint: New York: Popular Library, no date, pp.171–178. Shrewd but catty memoir by the *New Yorker* correspondent in Paris.

Henry James, and Edith Wharton. *Letters, 1900–1915.* Edited by Lyall Powers. New York: Scribner's, 1990. Guarded politeness between master and disciple who became friends but disapproved of each other's work.

Lewis, R. W. B. *Edith Wharton: A Biography.* New York: Harper and Row, 1975. First-rate life of Wharton.

Wharton, Edith. *A Backward Glance.* 1934. Reprint: New York: Scribner's, 1964, pp. 204–208. Unrevealing autobiography, but section cited throws some light on the origins of the novel.

——— *Letters.* Edited by R. W. B. Lewis and Nancy Lewis. New York: Scribner's, 1988. Provides some insight about the composition and reception of the novel.

Criticism

Ammons, Elizabeth. *Edith Wharton's Argument with America.* Athens: University of Georgia Press, 1980, pp. 25–42. Section cited emphasizes Wharton's role as woman writer and the economic basis of the novel.

Ammons, Elizabeth, ed. *The House of Mirth: Authoritative Text, Backgrounds, and Contexts Criticism.* New York: Norton, 1990. Helpful background essays, boring reviews of 1905, and modern criticism by Millicent Bell, Louis Auchincloss, Cynthia Wolff, R. W. B. Lewis, Elizabeth Ammons, and Elaine Showalter.

Brookner, Anita. Introduction to *The House of Mirth.* New York: Scribner's, 1987, pp. 7–14. Sensitive reading of novel as "an implacable account of how things go wrong, and what is worse, how nearly they could have gone right."

Fryer, Judith. "Reading *Mrs. Lloyd.*" In *Edith Wharton: New Critical Essays,* edited by Alfred Bendixen and Annette Zilversmit. New York: Garland, 1992, pp. 27–55. Excellent analysis of the role of Reynolds' portrait in the tableaux vivants.

Gordon, Mary. Introduction to *The House of Mirth.* New York: Vintage Books/Library of America, 1990, pp. xi–xviii. Valuable essay, by an important contemporary novelist, on the economic, social, and sexual contradictions in Lily's character.

Hardwick, Elizabeth. Introduction to *The House of Mirth.* New York: Modern Library, 1999, pp. xi–xx. Emphasizes the craftsmanship, characterization, and portrayal of the social history of New York.

Howard, Maureen. "*The House of Mirth*: The Bachelor and the Baby." In *The Cambridge Companion to Edith Wharton,* edited by Millicent Bell. New York: Cambridge University Press, 1995, pp. 137–156. Describes the themes of concealment and revelation, and what must be discovered by the characters.

Howe, Irving. "Introduction: The Achievement of Edith Wharton" and "A Reading of *The House of Mirth.*" In *Edith Wharton: A Collection of Critical Essays.* Englewood Cliffs, NJ: Prentice-Hall, 1962, pp. 1–18, 119–129. Valuable account, by a major critic, of the style, tone, and structure. This volume also includes excellent essays by Edmund Wilson, Louis Auchincloss, Percy Lubbock, E. K. Brown, Q. D. Leavis, Alfred Kazin, Diana Trilling, Blake Nevius, Lionel Trilling, Vernon Parrington, and Louis Coxe.

Knights, Pamela. Introduction to *The House of Mirth*. New York: Everyman, 1991, pp. ix–xxxiii. Interesting essay, by an English academic, on the background, characters, and voices.

Mansfield, Katherine. "*The Age of Innocence*." In *Novels and Novelists*. 1930. Reprint: Boston: Beacon, 1959, pp. 307–308. Reveals defects in Wharton's portrayal of character.

McDowell, Margaret. *Edith Wharton*. Revised edition. Boston: Twayne Publishers, 1991, pp. 1–29. Convincing close reading with emphasis on character and themes.

Nevius, Blake. *Edith Wharton: A Study of Her Fiction*. Berkeley: University of California Press, 1953, pp. 53–77. Section cited emphasizes conflict between individual freedom and social responsibility.

Poirier, Richard. "Edith Wharton's *The House of Mirth*." In *A World Elsewhere: The Place of Style in American Literature*. 1966. Reprint: Madison: University of Wisconsin Press, 1985, pp. 219–235. On style and portrayal of society; makes some interesting comparisons with George Eliot.

Rideout, Walter. "Edith Wharton's *The House of Mirth*." In *Twelve Original Essays on Great American Novels*, edited by Charles Shapiro. Detroit: Wayne State University Press, 1958, pp. 148–176. Illuminating discussion of how design and detail contribute to meaning.

Showalter, Elaine, "The Death of the Lady (Novelist): Wharton's *The House of Mirth*," *Representations*, 9 (Winter 1985), pp. 133–149. Reprinted in *Edith Wharton: New Critical Essays*, edited by Alfred Bendixen. New York: Garland, 1992, pp. 3–26. Suggests that Wharton achieved artistic liberation while portraying Lily's entrapment and defeat.

Singley, Carol, ed. *A Historical Guide to Edith Wharton*. New York: Oxford University Press, 2003. Provides historical contexts for the life and work.

Supple, Barry, "A Business Elite: German-Jewish Financiers in Nineteenth-Century New York," *Business History Review*, 31

(1957), pp. 143–178. Useful discussion of the origins and rise of Jewish financiers from peddlers and merchants to competitors with New England Yankees.

Trilling, Diana, "*The House of Mirth* Revisited," *Harper's Bazaar*, 81 (December 1947), pp. 126–127, 181–186. Reprinted in *Edith Wharton: A Collection of Critical Essays*, edited by Irving Howe (see above), pp. 103–118. Argues that Wharton concentrated the anger of a lifetime in her telling indictment of social privilege.

Wharton, Edith. "Introduction to *The House of Mirth*" (1936). In *Uncollected Critical Writings*, edited and with an introduction by Frederick Wegener. Princeton, NJ: Princeton University Press, 1996, pp. 264–269. On her choice of subject and hostile reception by her social circle.

Wilson, Edmund. "Justice to Edith Wharton." In *The Wound and the Bow: Seven Studies in Literature.* 1941. Reprint: New York: Oxford University Press, 1965, pp. 159–173. Brilliant pioneering essay defines her major phase as 1905–1920 and traces her later decline.

Wolff, Cynthia Griffin. *A Feast of Words: The Triumph of Edith Wharton.* New York: Oxford University Press, 1977, pp. 109–133. Section cited provides psychoanalytical biography and criticism.

Yeazell, Ruth Bernard. "The Conspicuous Wasting of Lily Bart." *English Literary History*, 59 (Fall 1992), pp. 713–734. Intelligently argues that consciousness in the novel "defines itself by negating the world of appearances."

Adventures of Huckleberry Finn	Mark Twain	1-59308-000-X	$4.95
The Adventures of Tom Sawyer	Mark Twain	1-59308-068-9	$4.95
Aesop's Fables	Aesop	1-59308-062-X	$5.95
The Age of Innocence	Edith Wharton	1-59308-074-3	$4.95
Alice's Adventures in Wonderland and Through the Looking Glass	Lewis Carroll	1-59308-015-8	$5.95
Anna Karenina	Leo Tolstoy	1-59308-027-1	$8.95
The Art of War	Sun Tzu	1-59308-017-4	$7.95
		1-59308-016-6	$3.95
The Awakening and Selected Short Fiction	Kate Chopin	1-59308-001-8	$4.95
The Call of the Wild and White Fang	Jack London	1-59308-002-6	$4.95
Candide	Voltaire	1-59308-028-X	$4.95
The Collected Poems of Emily Dickinson	Emily Dickinson	1-59308-050-6	$5.95
The Complete Sherlock Holmes, Volume I	Sir Arthur Conan Doyle	1-59308-034-4	$7.95
The Complete Sherlock Holmes, Volume II	Sir Arthur Conan Doyle	1-59308-040-9	$7.95
David Copperfield	Charles Dickens	1-59308-063-8	$7.95
The Death of Ivan Ilych and Other Stories	Leo Tolstoy	1-59308-069-7	$7.95
Dracula	Bram Stoker	1-59308-004-2	$4.95
Frankenstein	Mary Shelley	1-59308-005-0	$3.95
Great Expectations	Charles Dickens	1-59308-006-9	$4.95
Grimm's Fairy Tales	Jacob and Wilhelm Grimm	1-59308-056-5	$7.95
Gulliver's Travels	Jonathan Swift	1-59308-057-3	$3.95
Hard Times	Charles Dickens	1-59308-107-3	$4.95
Heart of Darkness and Selected Short Fiction	Joseph Conrad	1-59308-021-2	$4.95
The House of Mirth	Edith Wharton	1-59308-104-9	$4.95
Howards End	E. M. Forster	1-59308-022-0	$6.95
The Hunchback of Notre Dame	Victor Hugo	1-59308-047-6	$5.95
The Idiot	Fyodor Dostoevsky	1-59308-058-1	$7.95
The Importance of Being Earnest and Four Other Plays	Oscar Wilde	1-59308-059-X	$6.95
The Inferno	Dante Alighieri	1-59308-051-4	$6.95
Jane Eyre	Charlotte Brontë	1-59308-007-7	$4.95
Jude the Obscure	Thomas Hardy	1-59308-035-2	$6.95
The Jungle	Upton Sinclair	1-59308-008-5	$4.95
Kim	Rudyard Kipling	1-59308-192-8	$4.95
The Last of the Mohicans	James Fenimore Cooper	1-59308-065-4	$4.95

(continued)

Les Misérables (ABRIDGED)	Victor Hugo	1-59308-066-2	$9.95
Main Street	Sinclair Lewis	1-59308-036-0	$5.95
Man and Superman and Three Other Plays	George Bernard Shaw	1-59308-067-0	$7.95
The Metamorphosis and Other Stories	Franz Kafka	1-59308-029-8	$6.95
Middlemarch	George Eliot	1-59308-023-9	$8.95
My Ántonia	Willa Cather	1-59308-024-7	$4.95
Moby-Dick	Herman Melville	1-59308-018-2	$9.95
Narrative of the Life of Frederick Douglass, an American Slave	Frederick Douglass	1-59308-041-7	$4.95
Notes From Underground, The Double and Other Stories	Fyodor Dostoevsky	1-59308-037-9	$4.95
O Pioneers!	Willa Cather	1-59308-019-0	$4.95
The Odyssey	Homer	1-59308-009-3	$5.95
Oliver Twist	Charles Dickens	1-59308-030-1	$4.95
The Origin of Species	Charles Darwin	1-59308-077-8	$7.95
Persuasion	Jane Austen	1-59308-048-4	$4.95
The Picture of Dorian Gray	Oscar Wilde	1-59308-025-5	$4.95
The Portrait of a Lady	Henry James	1-59308-096-4	$7.95
Pride and Prejudice	Jane Austen	1-59308-020-4	$4.95
The Prince and Other Writings	Niccolò Machiavelli	1-59308-060-3	$5.95
The Red Badge of Courage and Selected Short Fiction	Stephen Crane	1-59308-010-7	$3.95
Robinson Crusoe	Daniel Defoe	1-59308-011-5	$4.95
The Scarlet Letter	Nathaniel Hawthorne	1-59308-012-3	$3.95
Selected Stories of O. Henry	O. Henry	1-59308-042-5	$5.95
Sense and Sensibility	Jane Austen	1-59308-049-2	$4.95
Six Plays by Henrik Ibsen	Henrik Ibsen	1-59308-061-0	$8.95
Sons and Lovers	D. H. Lawrence	1-59308-013-1	$7.95
The Souls of Black Folk	W. E. B. Du Bois	1-59308-014-X	$5.95
The Strange Case of Dr. Jekyll and Mr. Hyde and Other Stories	Robert Louis Stevenson	1-59308-054-9	$3.95
A Tale of Two Cities	Charles Dickens	1-59308-055-7	$4.95
The Time Machine and The Invisible Man	H. G. Wells	1-59308-032-8	$4.95
The Turn of the Screw, The Aspern Papers and Two Stories	Henry James	1-59308-043-3	$5.95
Uncle Tom's Cabin	Harriet Beecher Stowe	1-59308-038-7	$5.95
Vanity Fair	William Makepeace Thackeray	1-59308-071-9	$7.95
The Varieties of Religious Experience	William James	1-59308-072-7	$7.95
Walden and Civil Disobedience	Henry David Thoreau	1-59308-026-3	$4.95
Ward No. 6 and Other Stories	Anton Chekhov	1-59308-003-4	$7.95

☞

BARNES & NOBLE CLASSICS

If you are an educator and would like to receive an
Examination or Desk Copy of a Barnes & Noble Classic edition,
please refer to Academic Resources on our website at
WWW.BN.COM/CLASSICS
or contact us at
B&NCLASSICS@BN.COM.

All prices are subject to change.